The Betrayal of Ka

The Transprophetics
Book One

Shea R. Oliver

Colorado Sky Media, LLC
1067 S. Hover Street, Suite E-179
Longmont, CO 80501

www.ColoradoSkyMedia.com

ISBN 978-0-9968231-1-1

This is a work of fiction derived solely from the creative mind of Shea R. Oliver.

All names, characters, businesses, places, events and incidents are products of the author's overly active imagination. Any resemblance to actual persons, living or dead, or actual business, places, events or incidences is purely coincidental.

Editing by Nancy Pile
Cover design and artwork by Estefano Burmistrov

For Michael and Brandon

Contents

Chapter 1
One Moment • One Decision

Kadamba Vorhoor kicked his feet up on his desk in the back of the classroom. The smug look on his face seemed to spread to his entire being. In two days, the school year would be over. After that, he only had one more year of required schooling, and then he'd have full adult and citizen rights.

Here in Stujorkian City, the capital of Lamaratia, on the planet Koranth, he would have plenty of options. He came from a good family. Perhaps he'd go on to further education. It was expected of him. His academic performance had been above average, but right now, he didn't care so much about that. He only had one thing on his mind—Jundana Kohart.

She was stunning in every way. Her dark skin was radiant. Her hair was long and silky, always perfectly framing her high cheekbones and piercing, dark eyes. She had a sleek, athletic build from running track, and every movement she made was graceful, and somehow both delicate and strong at the same time. Kadamba, who usually went by the shortened version, Ka, wondered if there was ever a more beautiful creature on the entire planet of Koranth.

Only two hours before, Jundana had bumped into Kadamba in the cafeteria. The box containing her drink had flipped through the air, managing to somehow land perfectly upright on Kadamba's tray. Unfazed, he simply smiled in her direction.

"Nice shot," Kadamba said, trying to sound as charming as he could, "It seems we must've been destined to run into each other like this today . . ."

"Sorry, Ka, I didn't mean to bump into you. And seriously—you're not that smooth," she replied with a smile.

"No need to apologize," Kadamba responded, handing her drink back. "You ready for tomorrow's test in Lormate's class?"

“I’m about as ready as I’ll ever be. I think he just enjoys watching us suffer.”

“You got that right. No way he even begins to care about us. He just wants to drag us through his class and make sure we suffer.” Looking at her, Kadamba realized that the time was right. He’d always liked Jundana, but being so close to her was more intense than he’d expected. Trying to act as casual as he could, he shrugged. “He’s just a jackass, and we’re outta here in a few days.”

“Yeah, that’s the truth,” she agreed.

“So, you want to chill on Schmarlo’s Landing sometime?” He hoped that he hadn’t sounded too desperate. Every nerve in his body was fighting not to wince as a response began to form on her lips. He was certain that he was about to get rejected and squashed by this beautiful creature.

“I’d like that. You wanna go today after school?”

“That’s perfect. I gotta little business to deal with first, but I’ll meet you there.”

As Jundana walked away, Kadamba realized he wasn’t breathing. As the air came rushing back into his lungs, he almost shouted out loud, but under his breath, he spoke softly, so that only he could hear, “I’m gonna rock your world, girl.”

*****

“Mr. Vorhoor! Get your feet on the floor and walk them to the front of this classroom, now!” Mr. Lormate barked at Kadamba, shaking him out of the wonderful reliving of his fateful encounter with Jundana.

Kadamba rolled his eyes back in his head, relishing the thought that he would only have to deal with this jerk of a teacher for a couple more days. He let his feet slap hard on the shiny surface of the floor. He tilted his head, lifting his chin higher and rotating his neck. The vertebrae in his neck popped loudly, and he rotated his head the other way, sending out another series of cracks.

Mr. Lormate glared at Kadamba and swept his hand across the podium, tapping his fingers in a rehearsed pattern. From the dull, institutional-grey wall behind him, a three-dimensional image of a bargabuko, a toad-like creature that covered most of the tropical belt of Koranth, began to appear. The nasty, little, puss-dipping, foul-smelling creatures were the bane of every teenage science student across the planet. At least this one appeared to be visual-only, a holographic one.

The image of the bargabuko began to grow in size and move outward from the wall. Then the smell hit the students full-on. This one was more than just visual-only. A holographic lab table began to rise up from the floor next to the podium, where Mr. Lormate sat on a stool, like an emperor gazing over his subservient peasants. The bargabuko grew twenty times larger than a real one and landed with a splat on the table. It bellowed out a croak that seemed like a hundred times louder than the creature's true croak, followed by its annoying belching sound and a spray of blue-green puss that landed on the students in the front row.

Sorenha Woohurra screeched as the puss hit her in the chest. As always, she was dressed impeccably, in a tight-fitting, one-piece pink outfit, with frills ruffling out from her waist, a style in vogue with current music celebrities. Curhuck Lhahnid cussed under his breath as he wiped the sticky, blue-green puss from his cheek. No one in the class could stand Mr. Lormate, and having the bargabuko generated in a full holographic reality furthered every student's distaste for the teacher.

Mr. Lormate's teeth began to show in a crooked smile as he raised his gaze from Sorenha to Kadamba. "Well, Mr. Vorhoor, do you just plan to let this bargabuko decorate your classmates with its saliva, or will you get up here and dispatch it for us? You are so relaxed back there that I have every confidence that you can open the specimen and identify each part of its respiratory system for our illumination."

Kadamba rapidly tapped on his desk with his fingers, wanting to get this over as quickly as possible. A shape like a knife began rising from the desk. His hand went to the handle of the blade, with his forearm hiding the blade's size. He grasped the handle, keeping the large blade out of sight. The correct protocol was to generate a surgeon's blade, slice the animal's throat, and then dissect the creature. But not today.

Kadamba was tired of Mr. Lormate's nasty, arrogant, and superior attitude. The blade in his hand was more like a jumbo military knife. Kadamba's fingers felt comfortable in the form-fitted handle. The tip of the blade grazed near the elbow on the inside of Kadamba's forearm, as he strode towards the front of the classroom. Kadamba didn't care if what he was about to do would get him in trouble. He was on cloud nine. He had a date with Jundana in a few hours, and school break was only two days away. This would be worth it.

Two strides from the podium, he raised his hand above his head, revealing the deadly weapon. The expression on Mr. Lormate's face was beyond epic. The teacher's jaw dropped, slightly to the left, with his chin pulling back towards his neck. His eyes doubled in size. Kadamba could only hope that the putrid smell in the room was rising not only from that nasty bargabuko, but also from the mess that he hoped the teacher was making in his pants.

With his final stride to the table, Kadamba brought his arm down quickly and as strongly as he could. He tensed every muscle in his core, even pulling himself slightly into a squatting position to drive the point of the knife squarely through the center of the bargabuko's skull. The thud was deafening as the creature's chin slammed into the table, driven downward by the intensity of the stroke. The blade guard of the knife was partially crushed into the top of the bargabuko's head, and the blade of the knife had driven clean through the head of the animal with its tip sticking out from the bottom of the table.

Mr. Lormate's expression changed from shock to outrage almost instantaneously, but as he opened his mouth to scream at Kadamba, the classroom erupted in a chorus of cheers, shouts, and laughter. Slamming his hand onto the podium and pounding it a few times, with his face turning from a deep red to almost blue, Mr. Lormate glared at Kadamba. The bargabuko, its spattered blood and puss, the lab table, and even the horrid odor—disappeared. The classroom became silent as the teacher stood from his stool, his face hardening even more.

"Mr. Vorhoor." The words hissed through Mr. Lormate's clenched teeth. He looked down at the podium and tapped his fingers very delicately. The wall behind him shimmered as it changed from a dull grey to a semi-translucent surface. A door-sized opening appeared, and a bright red line began to glow on the floor leading away from the classroom. The teacher's gaze met Kadamba's, and Kadamba knew he had probably gone too far. "Goodbye, Mr. Vorhoor."

*****

The school's superintendent had gone easy on Kadamba. After all, only two days were left in the school year, and even the faculty and staff thought of Mr. Lormate as an ass. He would have to spend two extra days at school, helping clean up the campus and preparing it for the break. Not even really a serious punishment.

Kadamba walked out of the school and onto the wide, translucent pedestrian walkway some twenty stories above the ground. Living in the capital of Stujorkian City, a metropolis with more than 135 million residents, was all that Kadamba had ever known, and it was home. He loved the wide, towering buildings of the central city, many stretching nearly two hundred stories into the sky. Like all major cities, the free transportation system was efficient and vast. He could wander and explore for hours on end. The pedestrian walkway spanned most of the central city. Below the walkway was a system of suspended, high-speed shuttle trains. Once the shuttle trains left the city, they dropped to ground level and fanned out into the vast plains that made up the metropolis.

On almost every corner of every block in the central city stood lift platforms that dropped to ground level from the pedestrian walkway. Adjacent to every platform was a wide, open staircase, leading to Stujorkian City's sub-city. The sub-city, nearly as large as the central city itself, burrowed over forty stories below the ground. Warwon's Deli was Kadamba's destination. The deli sat thirty stories below ground in a vast shopping plaza of narrow streets. While much of the sub-city was well-lit and open, Warwon's Deli was at the end of a poorly-lit, narrow street, in a part of the sub-city that someone like Kadamba should honestly try to avoid.

Kadamba took a deep breath, tried to put on the coldest, most intense face that he could, and began walking towards the deli. It was just like many delis. There was an open display of meats, cheeses, and other foodstuff that a patron could buy and take home. There was also a large display behind the counter that listed names, pictures, and prices of sandwiches and meals that could be prepared for takeaway. If you squeezed past the other customers, maybe you could find a table in the back too. Kadamba didn't bother to order. Pushing his way through the cranky, ill-mannered customers, he headed to the table in the far back of the narrow shop.

Two men, dressed in black, loose-fitting garb, played a card game at that final table. One of them wore dark glasses, despite that fact that it was already dark in the back corner of the shop. Neither looked up or acknowledged Kadamba as he approached. Here in Stujorkian City, weapons were prohibited. Only Corporate military were allowed to own or use any weapon that fired deadly projectiles, lasers, or energy blasts. In that dark corner of the sub-city, laws appeared to matter less. Kadamba could see the handles of guns protruding from the shoulder holsters, under the black jackets of both men. Kadamba stood silently at the table, hoping this would go well.

"Looks like a little bargabuko found its way into the sewer," one of the men remarked to the other, without looking up from his cards.

"And it's a damn pretty one too," responded the other.

"Oh, yeah, the Doctor, he likes them young and pristine. Sells better. Seems better. Thinks it's lower risk."

The man without glasses cocked his head towards Ka, looking him up and down.

"I'm here to see Doctor Z." The words seemed to fall flat, sounding weak coming out of Kadamba's mouth. Both men chuckled.

"If you ain't here to see Doc Z, standing there in your pretty schoolboy clothes, carrying a schoolboy backpack, then you'd be in for an experience that you don't even know exists." As the words oozed out of his mouth, the other man turned in his chair towards Kadamba. He slowly removed the glasses from his face and stared directly into Kadamba's eyes. Inside, the teenager was terrified. He wanted to turn and run, but didn't dare. With every bit of courage he could muster, Kadamba maintained the man's gaze, repeating, "I'm here to see Doctor Z."

The wall behind the table began to shimmer and turned semi-translucent. Kadamba could see that the room behind the wall looked like a spacious family room, with large sofas, a few chairs, and a table in the back. Kadamba could make out the shapes of three men standing on the back wall, looking as ominous as the two brutes sitting at the table. As an opening appeared in the wall, Kadamba knew that the man sitting comfortably on one of the large sofas was Doctor Z.

"Glad to see you found my office," proclaimed Doctor Z, as he stood up and walked to the opening. "Please, come on in, and let's do a little business."

Kadamba stepped through the opening, and it vanished. When he looked back, the wall had transformed into a beautiful scene of a lake in the mountains.

"You seem so nervous. Please have a seat, my young friend," said Doctor Z, his words as smooth as silk. His smile seemed to simply ooze a sense of ease and comfort, but at the same time seemed to hide something menacing.

“Thanks,” replied Kadamba as he sat down tensely on one of the couches.

“I’m glad you found my office. We’re very comfortable and completely safe here, Ka. Do you mind if I call you ‘Ka’?” asked Doctor Z.

“Okay,” replied Kadamba.

“Good. Now that we’ve dispensed with the formalities—how’s your business?” Doctor Z inquired softly, but it felt more like a demand. All of the pleasantries and courtesy seemed to evaporate for a moment as Kadamba looked into the dark, piercing eyes of his host.

This was Kadamba’s first time actually meeting Doctor Z. Only a few months before, Kadamba had been on one of his many solo trips exploring the sub-city, looking for choice, out-of-the-way places to knock back, without so many adult prying eyes. Schmarlo’s Landing was an awesome and popular place to hang out, but it was 118 stories up, and he always seemed to run into someone’s mom or dad or family friend. On top of that, once in a while, it was fun to go underground.

A man who called himself Fuentes had walked up and sat down at the table where Kadamba was eating alone, in a vast open food court. At first, Kadamba was startled. A strange man in a strange place should set off warning bells galore, but Fuentes was smooth, smoother than anyone Kadamba had ever met. They chatted for a while, and Kadamba revealed more about himself than he ever should, but he didn’t even realize what he had done. By the end of the conversation, Kadamba had a small box in his hands.

Inside the box were six small packages that could be peeled open to reveal a rectangular adhesive strip with a large bump in the middle. Kadamba had heard of these—project Rs, the rummbie dummbies, sweetum’s ride, and a host of other street names. It was rath, a relative newcomer to the underworld drug market. Stujorkian City, like everyplace else, had a thriving illegal drug scene. It was the same everywhere on Koranth: Some drugs were illegal, and some were legal and regulated.

The box and its contents were a gift from Fuentes to Kadamba. He could simply enjoy them alone or with his friends. He could even sell them if he liked. There were no strings attached. They were just a gift. If he wanted more, he would have to buy them. Before he left, Fuentes told Kadamba where he could be found next week if he wanted more, but he would need to bring money. Each ride with sweetum would cost twelve Konnary.

Kadamba began meeting regularly with Fuentes, always someplace different, but always in some out-of-the-way, very sketchy place in the sub-city.

Almost like a bolt of lightning, Kadamba had gone from being just another face in the crowd at his school, to being a popular kid. He even made some new friends at other schools. He loved the popularity and relished the attention that those little adhesive strips were showering upon him.

Only a week before, Fuentes instructed Kadamba to meet him in a very different location. The smell of seafood outside of the packaging plant was almost overwhelming, and that was before Fuentes had opened the nondescript, metal door. Struggling not to gag on the pungent odor in the air, Kadamba had followed Fuentes through a huge room, passing by long tables piled high with fish and other creatures that Kadamba couldn't identify. The workers, dressed in blood-spattered white smocks, barely even seemed to notice the pair as they passed by, on their way to the offices, situated in the middle of the building.

As they left the packaging plant and began to breathe the more palatable air, Fuentes praised Kadamba for how well he had handled this meeting. Although Kadamba didn't completely understand, the man that they had just meet with, Vratar, saw potential in the young teen and set up this meeting with a man named Doctor Z.

Kadamba cleared his throat. "Business is good, sir. It's really good."

The smile on Doctor Z's face spread even wider. He loved hearing that from any of the many teenagers that this branch of his organization had recruited. These kids were so easy to manipulate and use.

"I need twenty more," Kadamba declared, pulling a stack of Konnary from his backpack.

"My dear young friend!" exclaimed Doctor Z. "You must be one very intelligent, smart, resourceful businessman. I am impressed."

"Thanks."

Doctor Z, having taken the stack of bills from Ka, thumbed through them quickly. When he was done, he smiled and held the bills up. One of the brutes from the back of the room came forward, took the stack, and returned to the back of the room. He waved his hand across the wall, and an opening appeared in it, revealing what looked like a bookshelf covered in large stacks of Konnary. He placed

Kadamba's payment on a stack, waved his hand, and the opening disappeared.

"Yes, yes, my young friend. Business is good." Doctor Z stared at Kadamba for a few moments and began rubbing his chin. A faint smile started and then spread across his face, as if he suddenly had a wonderfully insightful idea. "I see so much see potential in you and in our new relationship, Ka."

"Thank you, sir. I hope we can both keep making good money," Kadamba answered, not knowing exactly what to say.

"Oh, I know we will." Doctor Z gestured again, and one of the other men in the back of the room walked forward with a box. He placed the box in Kadamba's hands with a smile.

"Thank you," Kadamba told him, "I'll let Fuentes know when I need more."

"Please. You need to open the box before you leave," instructed Doctor Z. "You and I are at the beginning of new partnership."

Kadamba, looking at the box in his hands, sat back down. Opening the box, he looked inside. It was filled with rath, but it was obvious that it was more than twenty packets.

"You're looking at two hundred packages of rath," explained the Doctor, smiling.

"I only gave you one hundred and forty Konnary. I can't buy this much."

"It's alright, Ka. I'm extending a line of credit to you."

Kadamba was stunned. He'd never seen this many rath in one place, and it was in his hands. Doctor Z smiled and continued, "You need to be back here in two weeks. Your line of credit is due then, Ka, and we'll see where we are on continuing to expand our relationship."

Kadamba placed the box in his backpack and walked towards the wall with the mountain lake. The wall began to shimmer, turned semi-translucent, and the opening reappeared. Kadamba stepped through, and it reformed into a wall behind him. Once again, he was standing at the table with the two menacing-looking brutes. Kadamba, looking down at them, realized they both were grinning.

"Seems the Doc likes you, boy. He's a nice guy. Wouldn't you say so?" asked one of the thugs.

"Yes. He sure is," replied Kadamba. He could feel his heart beginning to beat faster.

"You understand the Doctor is almost always nice to everyone," said the thug who continued to wear the dark glasses. Kadamba realized the brute was looking across the table at his grimacing partner. Then Kadamba realized why the two were so smug. The man without the glasses had drawn his laser gun, which was mostly hidden under the table, but Kadamba could see that it was pointed directly at him.

The man began to remove his glasses once again. "See. Here's how it works. In case you don't quite get it. Doc gets to be nice, and if things don't go his way, we make them go his way. Doctor Z always gets his. Do you get it now?"

Kadamba nodded his head affirmatively, walking around the table quickly, trying as hard as he could not trip and end up sprawled out on the floor. He was trembling on the inside but didn't dare show it. He simply walked out of Warwon's Deli, more than eager to get out of the sub-city. He quickly made his way to ground level and took a shuttle train to the stop for the gigantic building known as Schmarlo Tower.

The lobby of the building was enormous, stretching from the eighteenth to the twenty-fourth floor. Kadamba made his way to the bank of lifts and entered a large, crowded lift that zoomed directly to Schmarlo's Landing.

All the lift's four walls and its door were transparent. "Oh my, oh my" exclaimed the woman next to Kadamba, as the lift reached its destination, emerging in the middle of Schmarlo's Landing. They were surrounded by a grassy park, with children playing and people adorning the various benches in the park. The Landing covered half the surface area of the building, had three parks, a huge playground, and on both ends were numerous food vendors, along with a huge scattering of tables and chairs. The entire landing was contained by a nearly invisible force-field cover that protected visitors from the elements. The other half of the building continued to rise another fifty-eight stories into the wispy clouds that had formed on what was otherwise a beautiful day.

"Hey, Ka, my man!" a nearby voice called.

"What's up on this fine day, my man Stelky?" Kadamba replied, still trying to shake off the fear of being entangled with Doctor Z and his brutes.

"I got someone that wants to meet you. You know, a new potential friend."

"Stelky, my man, let us meet this person."

A serious look swept across Stelky's face. "Ka, listen, I'm just making the introduction. Dude wouldn't leave me alone until I brought him to you."

"Alright, we'll just see how this goes down," Kadamba assured him.

Kadamba had only met Stelky a few weeks before. He went to another school, but "business" had made them "friends." Stelky might not have been real smart, but he knew lots of people, and most kids knew Stelky could be trusted to be discrete. He wasn't interested in handling any of the rath himself. He just wanted a little finder's fee for each transaction that Kadamba made with his introductions.

A young boy, about 10 years old, walked up to the two of them, obviously trying to act older than he really was. "Little dude! What the hell? Get back to the playground and ride the slide or something!" barked Kadamba when he saw the boy.

"My money is as good as anyone's," the boy asserted.

"It ain't about money, kid. You're just too damn young to be messing around with rath," Kadamba explained firmly.

"Am not! You want my money or not?"

For a few moments, Kadamba thought about the "credit" that Doctor Z had just extended. He had never had so much rath, and he HAD to sell it. But this kid was just way too young to be messing with the stuff. Wasn't he? Rath was pretty tame compared to many of the drugs out there, or at least Ka thought so. It just mellowed you out, made you happy, and made lots of things seem really funny.

"No way, dude. It ain't happening," proclaimed Kadamba.

"I'll pay thirty Konnary each for three of them," stated the boy defiantly.

"Ain't no way you're walking around with almost a hundred in your little pockets."

The boy looked around. No one was nearby. He reached his hand into his pocket and pulled out a stack of bills. Kadamba looked at the bills, obviously struggling with what to do. He usually sold each packet for twenty, maybe even eighteen, to consistent customers.

Kadamba took a deep breath. "Alright, you win, but, little dude, you gotta be careful."

Chapter 2
A Hidden Transprophetic

Fifty-eight stories above Schmarlo's Landing, Tomar Donovackia kicked his feet onto his desk. No one would question anything he did. In any event, he was alone in his palatial office. He'd sent one of his assistants down to the Landing to get him a Greolsch pastry. He liked those meat-filled, sweet pastries but had little use for mingling with the people on the Landing. He had servants and assistants to meet his needs. After all, he was the Chairman of the newly renamed Donovackia Corporation. He'd led the shareholder revolt, ousted the previous Chairman, and now had begun a campaign of becoming the biggest Corporation on the twin planets of Koranth and Zoranth.

The two planets were in perfectly synchronized orbits, on absolutely opposite sides of their shared sun. In many respects, Koranth and Zoranth were very similar. Both had over a hundred separate countries, with a multitude of governments, and each had three dominate super-power countries that balanced each other and kept the entire planets from sinking into regional or global conflict. Despite all the differences in languages and skin colors and belief systems and so on, they were all pretty much the same. They were all human. In Tomar's mind, there were simply billions and billions of customers waiting.

He looked at the glass on his desk and began to stare intently at it. His focus became more and more concentrated. The glass began to vibrate, just barely perceptible. Tomar raised his hand, and the glass began to move upward. It hovered a few inches above the desk and then began to move across the room. Tomar focused, pushed his hand away from his body and then lowered it, gently setting the glass on the table across the room, using nothing but his mind. A smile spread across his face. He'd never let anyone see that he was a Transprophetic and doubted he ever would. In his mind, only charlatans and religious nut jobs ever revealed such a thing. It was nothing but a parlor trick, but it validated for him that he was more evolved and intelligent than those around him.

Ironically, it was one of his ancestors that had validated the existence of what had been previously believed to be impossible. Over a thousand years ago, Koranth thought itself alone in the universe. The appearance of a young girl, unlike any other, changed everything. Tomar's ancestor was a brilliant medical doctor with a passion for physics. The girl was brought to him for examination. She could move objects with nothing but the power of her will. The doctor validated that she truly could do this, but how? The next fifty years of Koranth's development were beyond radical. Nearly every notion, theory, and "accepted fact" in physics, physiology, psychology, chemistry, and every other scientific discipline was upended.

What had been discovered in this girl was not some superpower or god-like blessing; rather, it was a step in the evolution of the human species. For a very, very few, their minds could grasp concepts and gain experience from the world around them like no others. They simply learned to use the molecules, atoms, subatomic particles, and even sound and light waves around them. It appeared like magic but was no more than the mind and body doing things previously thought to be impossible.

Within a few years of the discovery of that little girl, a second evolutionary capability of the human mind was discovered, when a mastermind of a thief was shot while he was stealing a priceless piece of art in a national museum. The security was beyond impenetrable, but he managed to get in somehow. As he was dying, he told a story few would believe. He could move from one place to another in the blink of an eye, including through the smallest of holes, such as a keyhole.

Within a decade, another person was found to have the same capabilities. Much like flexing a muscle, she had learned to flex her molecular structure. It was like turning herself into a gaseous state and directing herself to another location to reappear.

Within a hundred years, a handful of corporations had arisen based on the new technologies that had been discovered. The two most significant inventions that came out of the advances and new scientific understandings were space travel and the portals. A twin planet on the exact opposite side of the sun was discovered, and, like separated human twins, Zoranth was experiencing the same changes as Koranth.

A pop-psychology historian had coined the phrase "trans-prophetics," and the name stuck. On both Koranth and Zoranth, the scientific validation of a next, even if rare, level of human evolution ushered in a new wave of human technology.

A knock on the office door shook Tomar from his thoughts, and he placed his feet back on the floor, sitting up straight at his desk.

"Mr. Donovackia, the board meeting will commence shortly," disclosed the short, stout man wearing business attire. By the look and the nod that Tomar gave the man, it was apparent that he was simply one of Tomar's small army of underlings.

"Make sure all the board members are comfortably seated in the boardroom, and tell them I will be there shortly," instructed Tomar.

"Yes, sir."

"Wait, tell them I have been detained by the Chief Executive Minster for Interplanetary Corporate Relations. Have them wait in the boardroom, and have lunch served."

Tomar smiled as the man nodded his head affirmatively and closed the door. "Let them sweat a little bit waiting for me," thought Tomar. After all, he had just upended the previous board of directors, renamed the company, and personally held the controlling interest in the organization. He was now firmly in charge of the third largest corporation on Koranth and intended to make it the largest, regardless of who stood in his way.

Chapter 3
A Life Goes Dark

Kadamba pocketed the cash from the little boy, looking around to make sure no one had seen the transaction. Stelky looked at Kadamba for a few moments. Kadamba reached into his pocket and counted out Stelky's cut.

"Here's yours, man. But seriously, I can't do that again. That kid was way too young," Kadamba muttered.

"I hear you, Ka. I figured you'd send him off with empty hands. But it's all cool," replied Stelky.

"Stelky, I gotta move more product than before. Find me some more customers, but, dude, stay out of the daycare centers! They gotta be a lot older than that."

The two of them started walking towards one of the corners of the Landing. Unofficially, it was where the older teenagers hung out. It was one area of Schmarlo's Landing that had the worst view, if such a thing could be said about a building on the edge of the central city, with stunning views of the suburbs, farmlands, and mountains, far off in the distance. Of course, Kadamba wasn't 118 stories up to look at the landscape.

She was sitting on the edge of a table, chatting full speed with a few of her friends when Kadamba walked up. She looked at him, and there was a little giggle from the other girls around the table.

"Jundana, girl, we'll be seeing you later!" one of the girl announced in a sassy tone. "Hope you got a good story to tell us tonight!"

Kadamba smiled, as his eyes met hers. "You wanna grab a pastry or drink or something?"

"Sure," Jundana replied softly.

The two of them headed further into the tangle of teenagers that were milling about, meandering to a vendor selling sweet frozen concoctions called Freezies. The line was long, but neither Kadamba nor Jundana cared. They were just enjoying their first real opportunity to be together. As they began to chat, Kadamba realized that they had been followed.

"Stelky, why are you standing behind us here in line?" Kadamba inquired in a slightly irritated voice.

"Yo, seriously, Ka, I love these Freezies," Stelky answered, defensively.

Jundana gently placed her hand on Kadamba's shoulder before he could reply. "It's alright, Ka. Stelky's cool."

Her touch was amazing. He felt the annoyance vaporize inside of him, and he couldn't believe the effect she was having on him. Just standing near her was so incredible. He was relaxed as if he was floating on a double dose of rath, but as excited as a little kid getting a giant stick of candy. He'd had a few girlfriends, and he'd thought he'd been in love before, but this was different. This was so much more intense.

A screeching scream ripped Kadamba's and everyone else's eardrums. "JUNDANA! JUNDANA! JUNDANA!" Her voice was in a panic. It was Sorenha Woohurra, still outfitted like she was going on stage at a big music concert.

"MAN! That chick has got some serious pipes!" Stelky exclaimed while poking his finger into his ear.

She came running up to Jundana and Kadamba, mouthing something that neither could understand. After a deep breath, she looked at Jundana and hastily explained, "Something's happening to Alorus. You gotta get over there." Her finger pointed to the playground where many people seemed to be watching something on the ground.

Jundana broke into a full sprint before Kadamba and Stelky even made a move in the playground's direction. When they ran up, Jundana was on the ground, kneeling over a child's body. A woman nearby, trying to calm her, was telling her that medics were on the way.

"Alorus! Alorus! Stay with me!" Jundana was pleading with the child, as tears were falling from her face. "Alorus! Alorus! You have to breathe! Listen to me, NOW! Look at me! Alorus, breathe!"

The child was beginning to shake violently, as if he was having a major seizure. Foam was beginning to pour out of his mouth, as his eyes rolled back in his head. The foam began to appear to have a red tint to it, as a medic came running up, carrying a large bag. Two more medics appeared almost immediately with a medical transportation board floating between them.

"Does the boy suffer from jakjaksonia episodes?" the paramedic quickly asked Jundana, as he quickly knelt beside the boy, opening his bag.

"No. He's totally healthy! What's wrong with him?" Jundana frantically demanded.

Stelky was bumped aside as a justice enforcement officer pushed his way through the growing crowd. When Stelky looked down at the kid, his eyes grew big, and he blurted out, "Ka, ain't that the kid you just hooked up with some …" His words trailed off as he realized that everyone was looking at him, and then everyone looked at Kadamba.

The paramedic spoke quickly and directly, "Son, what did you give this boy?"

"I didn't give him anything," Kadamba replied, as the knot in his stomach began to rapidly expand and twist.

The justice enforcement officer drew his gun from his holster at an astonishing speed. He pointed the weapon directly at Kadamba's chest.

"Ka, please!" Jundana's panic-stricken voice broke the tension-filled silence. "What happened?"

"I . . . I . . . I sold him three packs of rath about thirty minutes ago."

Tears burst from Jundana's eyes, as they glazed over with a layer of hatred. Kadamba wanted more than anything to have the world end right there. He'd never fallen from a state of such euphoria to absolute regret and panic.

He heard the electric-sounding buzz as the bolt of energy burst from the tip of the justice enforcement officer's gun. For a split second the entire world froze. He could see Jundana with her face in her hands. He could see the boy, lying on the ground. He could see the faces in the crowd either looking down sympathetically at the child, or looking at him with a terrible malice in their eyes. Then he felt the energy bolt hit him, and the world went black.

Chapter 4
Vegetables

"Sesame chicken and happy family!" cried out the short, plump, elderly Asian woman in the stained, white apron. Her hair was in bun, as it always was. She placed the brown paper bag on the counter, and looked softly at Dylan as he walked up to the counter. "You a good boy to come and get good Chinese takeout for your family," she told him in her thick Chinese accent while Dylan fumbled in his pocket for the money.

She smiled at him, as she always had. The wrinkles on her face made her seem kinder, and perhaps even wiser, than she really was. Dylan had been coming here for a while to get dinner for himself and his little brother. It was one of the many local take-out joints that he favored whenever his mother had to work late, which was more often than not. Both brothers could eat the sesame chicken until they were stuffed, but Dylan knew that he needed to order something like happy family. It had vegetables.

Putting his change on the counter, she told him to "have a nice evening and we see you soon!" She smiled again with that customer service smile designed to make the restaurant's customers feel as if they were truly loved by the family who owned The Wonderful Dragon.

Dylan knew better. He had always known better, but he looked into her eyes and in a polite voice told her, "Thank you, Ms. Faung. I'll see you again soon." She widened her smile and scurried back to work.

Dylan walked out the door and into the brisk autumn air. At 15, he couldn't drive, but it didn't matter. The walk was only two blocks. His home sat in the middle of what he thought of as a dull, average city block in Denver. It was a couple of blocks from a main street, and only a few blocks from each of the schools he and his brother attended. The streetlights were beginning to come on as he stepped onto the porch and opened the front door to his home.

"I'm gonna destroy every one of you motherfuckers!" yelled a young boy, as Dylan stepped into the living room. The young voice continued its bravado, "Leveling up after this round, you bunch of dumbasses can't keep up!"

Dylan stared at the boy, sitting on the floor, wearing headphones with a microphone that was tethered to a game console in the television stand. The boy was almost exactly four years younger than Dylan, but the difference in their size and stature seemed more than four years. Dylan had always been an above-average sized kid, and puberty had treated him right. The wisps of dark hair on his face had begun to thicken. His voice occasionally cracked but was deepening and sounding more and more masculine every day. He knew he was attractive. The girls at school knew it too, and he was very aware of how they felt about him.

Dylan's little brother was much smaller. He was one of the smaller kids in his class. His moppish, unkempt blond hair seemed to do little to hide his rounded face, which refused to stop looking like a little boy's face. No matter what he did, he just couldn't be as mature-looking as his older brother. And it wasn't for lack of trying. He once heard that eating too much chocolate would give you acne, and in the little boy's mind, acne made you look older. He managed to sneak to the corner store and buy three big bags of Hersey's Kisses and two king-sized dark chocolate candy bars. Every single bit of chocolate was consumed by the time he walked the four blocks home. As his stomach began to tie into knots, he just knew the discomfort would be worth it. The next day was an utter disappointment. Not only did his stomach still ache, but his face looked exactly the same. Not a single zit graced his cherub-like face.

The challenge to be like his older brother went beyond just looks. He was never interested in the toys that his friends played with. He wanted the same amusements as his brother. When Dylan stopped playing with action figures, so did he. When Dylan finally got the latest gaming system, he insisted on equal time, pushing himself to try to keep up with the records and achievements in each game that Dylan played.

"Seriously, Bjorn?" chided Dylan in a loud, nearly parental-sounding voice. "Do you have to cuss like an ill-tempered sailor every time you play that game?"

"Oh shit! My brother's home! I mean, whoops, sorry—oh dang! I gotta go!" Bjorn barked as he pulled the headphones away and turned to his older brother.

Despite sounding angry and stern, Dylan was far from it. From the day Bjorn was born, Dylan knew his little brother worshiped and looked up to him like no other. It was hard to be angry at the little guy who wanted more than anything to be respected, and be just like his cool, big brother.

"Let's have some dinner, little dude."

Bjorn, popping up from the floor, replied, "Cool! I'm starving man. Whadda we having?"

Dylan narrowed his eyes, and in his best, evil, bad-guy Chinese accent hissed, "I have visited the dragon lady and now bring us treasures of amazing flavor, deep from the Orient!"

Bjorn tilted his head and nodded in appreciation. Attempting to mimic his brother's Chinese accent, the boy stated emphatically, "You have done well. But have you reached a level of enlightenment that brings with it the wisdom to serve two orders of sesame chicken?"

Maintaining character, Dylan snapped his head towards his little brother, declaring, "Young student, you need your vegetables!"

Bjorn gave a huge sigh. He knew his brother was right, but he'd rather have more sesame chicken than snow peas and celery. The boys went into the kitchen, and Dylan removed the food from the paper bag, as Bjorn opened the cabinet and got out some plates.

Chapter 5

Lead, Follow, or Die

Tomar Donovackia burst into the corporate boardroom a few minutes after lunch had been served. About a dozen well-dressed individuals sat around the long, elegant table. Half of the board members had food in their mouths, as Tomar began to speak. He had timed this quite purposefully. The board's approval was technically required for major undertakings, and he intended for them to rubber stamp whatever plans he had. He wanted them enjoying a meal and focused on listening, and not asking too many questions.

"Ladies and gentlemen of the board, thank you for gathering together today for this meeting. I appreciate that it was on short notice and also appreciate that you all are in attendance today. Please continue to enjoy lunch. I have a number of items to cover today, and I will be conscientious of your time."

Tomar moved to the head of the table. He waved his hand across the table, and a small podium materialized in front of him. The other board members remained seated, with most continuing to eat, while Tomar stood over them and began his presentation. He tapped a few distinct places on the podium, and a three-dimensional representation of the galaxy rose up from the table's center.

"My esteemed board members, we are fortunate to be part of one of the Eleven Corporations that hold interplanetary licenses to conduct space travel, exploration, and economic development. We all, of course, agree that this system is wise, and none of us would want to revert to the days of the Exorthium Colonial Wars."

All of the board members nodded in agreement. They all knew their history. Shortly after space travel and the ability to build portals were discovered, Koranth and Zoranth became connected by a few such portals. The expense was astronomical. Portals were built in a matched set on one planet. One of the portals would then be sent by spaceship to its destination on the other planet. The pair of portals would enable a person or objects to go into one portal and be immediately transported through to its other corresponding portal.

Initially, it was a social and economic boom for countries on both planets, and a few corporations profited handsomely for the massive investment required to build and operate the portals. However, a discovery of a third life-sustaining planet, Exorthium, within their solar system changed had everything. Exorthium had limited life forms, as its conditions were extremely unfriendly. While humans could survive on the planet, the toxic environment would eventually kill anyone who stayed too long, but Exorthium had an abundance of mineral resources.

Even though a portal opening was only circular and four feet in diameter, it required enormous amounts of energy to operate, and corporations from both Koranth and Zoranth staked out claims on Exorthium. Massive resources were poured into transporting portals, power stations, and mining equipment to the new planet. As is human nature, conflicts eventually arose, and wars began. This period of colonization had been devastating to both Koranth and Zoranth.

After nearly a hundred years, Exorthium was divided, and a peace treaty was signed. As part of the treaty, the Ministry of Interplanetary Corporate Relations, known by most as "The Ministry," was formed to create a framework for space exploration and development. The solution ultimately resulted in Eleven Corporations that held exclusive rights to "develop" any planet that they discovered, without interference from any other corporations or governments. Fifty-two planets, beyond the solar system of Koranth and Zoranth, were identified as containing life, and, amazingly, each of the planets contained humans at some stage of evolution and development.

Over the next few centuries, technology continued to progress, and the twin planets reveled in the ongoing affirmation that they were the most advanced civilizations in the galaxy. Each of the Eleven Corporations managed to get one portal in place on another planet.

In those early days, many lessons were learned and had now become standard practice. Space travel remained astronomically expensive. While Exorthium had been exploited with power stations and equipment shipped by spaceship, it was practically impossible to transport a portal, all of its equipment, and sufficient power stations outside the solar system of Koranth and Zoranth. While perhaps that model might have eventually generated a profit, there were far, far more profitable models.

By far, the best way to harvest the grandest profits from a planet was to wait for the indigenous populations to advance to a point of having a significant global infrastructure in place on their own. If a planet were allowed to develop its own global trade, then everything—power, logistics, transportation, mining, agriculture, and qualified, low-cost labor—would be in place for planetary "development" to begin. The more advanced a planet, the quicker the profits would begin to flow. All that was needed was to wait for the right timing to install a portal on the planet and connect it to a reliable power source.

Once a portal was in place and operational, the first wave to pass through would be Corporate military. These military organizations were magnificently efficient at moving troops and gear though the small openings. Offensive and defensive weapons systems had been especially designed to be moved through the small portal openings. Within a day of a portal's activation, the military could establish a sizable contingent on the targeted planet, with a nearly absolute capability of defending the portal from any military or weapons that had been developed on that foreign planet by its own people. Within two weeks, a force would be assembled planet-side that would be ready to invade and dominate any location on the planet that it so desired.

After an initial show of force, it was always amazing how quickly entire planets would simply begin shipping whatever the Corporation wanted to the portal. Moving product through quickly and the occasional show of force were often all that was required to reap enormous profits.

One of the biggest challenges was getting the timing right. If a Corporation invaded too early, then a planet's power generating facilities, global logistics infrastructure, and its manufacturing, mining, and agricultural capabilities might be too limited to support the demands of the Corporation. Reasonable profits might be impossible, or at best, highly difficult to generate. If a Corporation invaded too late, an indigenous population might have developed their own advanced technologies, including weaponry and monitoring systems. This was thought to be very probable if the scientists on a foreign planet had discovered the scientific principles underlying the abilities of any Transprophetic. Given the changes that had occurred on Koranth and Zoranth when the science behind the Transprophetics was understood, no Corporation was willing to risk a planet discovering what was scientifically possible, until the Corporation was firmly in control of the planet and its resources. As populations were watched, this hypothesis had become accepted fact: Transprophetics would transform a planet, giving it the capability to resist development by a Corporation. Over the centuries, the standard operating procedure for planetary development had become to monitor a planet's infrastructure and trade development, while at the same time, watching for Transprophetics.

However, one of the massive challenges was simply watching a planet. Space travel to a planet consumed massive resources. The space travel took well over a year, or more, and was generally a one-way affair. While the explorers of Koranth and Zoranth had figured out how to move physically across the galaxy faster than the speed of light, a method of communicating beyond the speed of light had remained impossible.

All things considered, a corporation would launch an exploratory mission to a planet about once every 20 to 40 years, sending crews with more frequency as a planet neared its optimum point of profitability. The spaceships that carried those crews to the distant planets also contained a much smaller, faster unmanned return vessel that would send back artifacts, media, products, and crew reports. The most important item contained within these reports was the assessment of whether or not a planet was primed for invasion and development.

Tomar paused for a moment, looking around the room, as the board members nodded in agreement. A few shoved more food into their mouths or sipped their drinks as he continued his presentation.

"As would be expected of someone of my status and capabilities, I did not just take over this corporation to milk the existing profits of our two open portals. I am here to lead this Corporation to a bigger and brighter future, with an absolute dedication to the creation of ever bigger and brighter profits."

A few of the board members immediately raised their glasses to chorus a healthy, "Here! Here! To Tomar!" A smile crept across Tomar's face, as he gestured appreciatively to those members who had first raised their glasses.

He continued, "We face a serious challenge right now, as the four remaining planets to which we hold a license are not ready for portalization and development. One of these planets has a population barely capable of using metals. One seems to be suffering from a nearly global viral plague. And the final two remain mired in their own industrial revolutions. We must begin to seek out other options if we are to significantly improve the profits of this corporation.

"Since the formation of the Ministry of Interplanetary Corporate Relations, many assumptions have appeared to become fact in the minds of the people of Koranth and Zoranth. However, we are now mired with a system that is completely antiquated and does not serve the purposes of those leaders who would seek to maximize the opportunities that our advanced civilization should be reaping."

One of the board members who, was paying close attention interjected, "My esteemed Chairman, you certainly cannot be considering the folly of using a portal to transport an additional portal—can you?" Immediately, a grumble arose among the board members.

"Please, please, I am absolutely not trying to suggest something as dangerous, illegal, and as radical as that," replied Tomar.

"Well, we simply cannot go about trying to portalize a planet too early. The investment is absolutely ridiculous to bring a bunch of natives up to the level to which we can reasonably profit!" another member added.

"Please, my dear board members," Tomar stated firmly, regaining the board's attention, "we all are very aware of what has been tried—and the disastrous results. I do not intend to head down either of those paths."

On two separate occasions, Corporations believed that they had solved the challenges of bringing one portal through to another portal. The effort had resulted in an explosion of gigantic proportions. Hundreds of thousands had been killed by the blasts. The Ministry had expressly forbidden any Corporation from even beginning experimentation projects designed to attempt to use a portal to transport another portal. More than once, a planet had been portalized too soon and had nearly bankrupted those Corporations that had been overly eager to "develop" it.

Tomar paused again for a few moments to let the board's attention resettle on him.

"I am suggesting something altogether different. For the last few hundred years, we have all lived in a world of regulations, assumptions, and, frankly—a world of lazy arrogance! We have long thought of the Ministry of Interplanetary Corporate Relations as an organization that brings chaos under control and helps maintain our profits. I challenge that this is no longer true!

"A few hundred years after the Exorthium Colonial Wars, the Ministry granted the Eleven Corporations the licenses to explore space and control the portals. The number eleven has no significance in any religion, business text, or any other place other than we have always had eleven Corporations. We've blindly assumed that eleven is the perfect number—that some balance of power or some control exists in eleven. The Ministry has even bailed out Corporations when they have absolutely failed. The assumption of "eleven" has led to stagnation, lack of innovation, and most importantly—an absolute stranglehold on profitability. The time has come to leave those false assumptions behind."

Tomar stopped speaking and let his gaze wonder around the room. As he expected, some of the board members, especially those whom he had been unable to replace, had either a look of indignation or of shock. Society long ago seemed content with the concept of The Ministry of Interplanetary Corporate Relations and the Eleven Corporations. The Ministry was a five-member committee made up of two members from Koranth and two from Zoranth. They were elected on an eight-year, rotating basis. A fifth member, the Chief Executive of the Ministry, was elected every eleven years, and could come from either Koranth or Zoranth.

The Ministry was actually something of a point of pride among the people of the two planets. It was the only place that the two planets truly had worked in harmony with one another. On each planet, governments continued to quarrel, with occasional wars, trade disputes, and the like, but the Ministry remained strong.

The boardroom stayed quiet for a few moments. One of the members, whose face had shown a bit of shock, rose to his feet. He was an older gentleman, with a few extra pounds on his body. A sense of relief swept across the faces of those members who had been shocked and concerned by Tomar's statement. All eyes in the room turned to Greylorent Lamrainkia, as he spread his arms in a grandfatherly fashion. "My friends and colleagues, we are part of a wonderfully profitable system that has handsomely lined the pockets of our family and friends. Our new Chairman, young as he may be, means no disrespect to the system we have in place."

Tomar looked at the man with the respect that was expected. Greylorent Lamrainkia was a man of high standing and had been on the board longer than any other member. His position was nearly unassailable, and the members of the board whom Tomar had not replaced, looked to him for leadership. He had attempted to stop Tomar Donovackia's takeover, and some members of the board expected that he would maneuver a change soon that would oust Mr. Donovackia.

Everyone's eyes shifted back to Tomar, who acknowledged Greylorent with a nod of his head. It appeared as if Tomar was encouraging him to continue. The gesture had further emboldened Greylorent, so he proceeded. "Our Chairman is young and has much to learn about leading one of the Eleven. I am of certainty, that with our wise guidance, this young gentleman will be successful."

Tomar's face continued to show what appeared to be respect, but inside he was almost giddy with excitement. He was watching this pompous, arrogant buffoon swell himself up even further than expected. Tomar almost wanted to dance.

"As we all know," said Greylorent, "our Chairman has adeptly positioned himself to run this fine Corporation, with the support of its board. WE, the board, have the final say on the overall strategy and direction of the Corporation. Our joint decision-making power is what heads this company. The Chairman simply sits in the seat at the head of the table and recommends directions that we might potentially consider."

The tension level in the room suddenly rose as Greylorent finished his statement. He had made it clear that he believed himself powerful enough to oppose Tomar and that he believed Tomar's control of the Corporation was not as strong as Tomar wanted to believe. He lowered his arms, leaning over and placing his hands on the table. He gazed about the room and in a slow, deep, commanding voice stated, "These are the facts."

Tomar remained very calm and nearly unmoving, as the eyes in the room moved from intently regarding Greylorent to apprehensively staring at Tomar. He met each person's eyes, moving from board member to board member, but skipping Greylorent. The tension continued to soar in the room, as all members had expected a clash between the two men, but no one had expected it to escalate as quickly as it had.

"I may be young, but I am not as foolish as you," Tomar stated, as if it were an apparent fact. He tapped a few more buttons on his podium, trying not to snicker, for this was going so much better than he could ever have imagined. Over the next few minutes, Tomar brought up images of other companies, products, contracts, and people. He painted a picture of vastly overpriced, no-bid contracts going to companies that Greylorent secretly owned, of money and bribes flowing into the pockets of relatives of Greylorent, and other abuses of the man's position on the board. His presentation had been well researched and rehearsed. A few board members were visibly trying not to squirm in their seats.

During the rapid-fire presentation, Greylorent's face had vacillated between a crimson outrage and a white shade of fear. Of course, he had done all these things, as had many of the members of the board, who had not been replaced. While it may have been ethically questionable to some, it certainly wasn't completely illegal. As Tomar finished, Greylorent, very calmly, glared at the young Chairman.

"Well, you have certainly done your homework, young man," Greylorent let the word "young" get drawn out as if to emphasize the immaturity of youth. "You are beginning to understand the more complex workings of the Corporate world. I am glad you are learning, and it is certain that my example will help you as you attempt to become a leader. Although, you are starting at a very low point."

Tomar could contain himself no longer, and, as a grin spread across his face, he let out a small chuckle. He made a gesture, and a door materialized across the table from Greylorent. A member of the Donovockia Corporate military stepped through the door. He was completely decked out in battle gear. His body was covered with a dark armor that shimmered and reflected light in multiple directions. His battle helmet completely covered his head and face. He stepped into the room, and everyone drew back in shock.

"WHAT IS THIS OUTRAGE?" demanded Greylorent, in a booming, furious voice.

Tomar snickered again. It almost sounded evil this time, and he choked it off before it did. Looking at Greylorent, he began speaking in a constrained voice. "Your abuses of power and your pompous, arrogant attitude are of minimal concern. While you probably broke many laws in what you did, I doubt that we could prove it. However, a few—other things—*are* provable."

Tomar tapped again on the podium, and, in the middle of the table, a very disturbing three-dimensional scene appeared. It was of Greylorent, naked on top of a small female and obviously engaged in intercourse. Of the two, Greylorent was easily three times the size of the young woman. With each thrust, the woman let out a shriek that certainly sounded like agony.

Greylorent turned an ashen shade of white, as Tomar began to speak over the tortuous injury being inflicted in the scene on the table.

"One of your many enterprises includes an illegal house of prostitution, well-hidden underground here in the capital. Did you honestly think I would not find it? You are quite a vile and cruel man. Like so many men of power, you believe yourself above everyone else and—untouchable."

Gesturing towards the scene, Tomar continued, "You like to try every one of your new girls for yourself first, even if they resist. How many of your so-called employees truly understood what they were getting into? How many girls did you trick into lives of prostitution? How did you feel when this poor girl died beneath you? Was it remorse that guided you and the madam to dispose of the body?"

Tomar saw Greylorent's movement. Everything was falling into place. Tomar had humiliated his overbearing, self-righteous opponent, and Tomar's plan was playing out even more finely than he had hoped. One of Tomar's agents had secretly managed to slip a heart-weakening drug to each of the last three girls that had been recruited by Greylorent's madam. The drug failed to produce results in the first two girls, but when Greylorent went to sample the wares of the third girl, she resisted. Greylorent then became aggressive and violent, forcing himself on her. Due to her struggle, in combination with the drug, the girl's heart failed, and everything was secretly recorded for this moment. It was now playing out for the board members to witness.

Over the next few moments, the finale was going to play out perfectly. Tomar had recently modified the security protocol to enable board members to come and go in the building without any security checks of their belongings or person. He had discovered that Greylorent flaunted weapons laws and carried a concealed energy blaster whenever he could. It was apparent that he was reaching for it now.

As the gun broke free of where it had been concealed under Greylorent's cloak, the blast from the soldier's weapon hit Greylorent full force in the upper chest and neck. He slammed into his chair, rolled backwards, and smashed into the wall behind him. For a brief moment, he looked stunned. Then, his head slumped forward, pulling his body to the floor.

"This meeting is now adjourned. We will continue tomorrow morning," concluded Tomar, and, turning, he walked through a door that had appeared in the wall behind him.

*****

The stunningly beautiful woman was sitting in his chair when Tomar returned to his office. He looked at her and then gestured for the door to close. It vanished, leaving nothing but a wall behind him. She looked directly at him and, seductively running her tongue across her lips, began to laugh. A translucent monitor floated in the air above the desk. It was a live video of the boardroom, where the body of Greylorent Lamrainkia's body was being covered and hoisted onto a floating board to be taken to a morgue.

"Your script and performance today should win you an award. It was truly magnificent," she seductively stated, smiling at Tomar.

He walked over to the table where the glass, which he had moved, using nothing more than the power of his mind, rested. He stared at it for a few moments. Perhaps, he should think it back to the desk. She might be very impressed to discover that he was not only a ruthless, up-and-coming Corporate titan, but also a Transprophetic, but he changed his mind. Perhaps, some other day when it better suited his purpose. He was feeling intensely energized. He didn't need any tricks to get what he wanted. He was a powerful man on the rise and had just solidified his absolute control of the Corporation. He would get whatever he wanted.

Picking up the glass with his hand, he walked to his desk, placing it where a few hours previous it had sat. He walked to where she sat in his chair and dropped his hands to the armrests, holding each of them tightly. He looked deeply into her eyes. She wasn't young, but she wasn't old either. In many ways, age seemed unable to get a firm grasp on her. She had a confidence about her that few people ever were able to maintain for longer than a fleeting moment. Her long, black hair hung loosely and appeared to always be exactly how she wanted it. Every feature about her face was both soft and hard at the same time. She defied easy explanation. How a woman could dress in business attire and yet radiate the sensuality and sexuality as she did intrigued and mesmerized him.

"You may be the Chief Executive Minister of the Ministry for Interplanetary Corporate Relations, but you, my dear lady, are sitting in MY chair," Tomar told her.

She made no effort to get up; rather, she simply looked back into his eyes, as intently has he stared into hers. She gently placed her hand on his and began slowly running her hand up his arm, across his shoulder. Then spreading her fingers, she slid her hand to the back of his head. She closed her hand into a fist, balling up a mass of his hair, and pulled his head towards hers. Their lips locked in a violent embrace. The kiss was passionate, almost desperate, as if each were fighting for power and at the same time to be overtaken by the other.

As suddenly and as violently as she had pulled him to her, she pushed him away. He stood back up and smiled back down at her. Biting her lower lip, she grabbed his belt, pulling him close again. She slowly undid the latch, unbuttoned his pants, and then grabbed a handful of fabric by each of his hips. She threw the pants down his legs, and they clattered on the floor. He breathed out heavily as he stood there completely exposed. She put a hand on each of his hips and pushed him away, so that he stumbled backwards, with his feet tangled in his pants. His bare bottom barely caught the edge of his desk, leaving him sitting precariously. She rolled the chair quickly to him, landing each hand flat on each of his knees. She pushed her hands upward until only the tips of her fingernails were touching him, and began to run them up his legs, past his thighs and waist, under his shirt, continuing until her hands were up to his chest.

The air exploded from Tomar's lungs in a violent gasp. She was beyond anything that he had ever known. He looked down into her eyes, which were staring back into his, gleaming with a heinous tint. Her smile widened and she opened her mouth, bending towards him to take him where every man openly, or secretly, wants to go.

Chapter 6
Effective and Efficient

A few miles away, and a few stories underground, Kadamba began to regain consciousness. His head throbbed and his chest ached from the justice enforcement officer's energy blast. As he sat up and looked around, he realized that he was in a very small chamber. Actually, it was more of a box. It was about four feet tall and four feet wide by ten feet deep. The far end wall of the chamber was transparent, as were about two feet of the ceiling, the floor, and both side walls extending from that transparent end. Kadamba, sliding to the transparent section of this cage, realized there were hundreds of the chambers stacked at least three dozen high. The row of chambers that he was in faced another row of the little prison boxes.

As he scanned the chambers across from his, he could see men and women. Some were lying; some were sitting. Some wore normal clothing while others wore what looked like a bright orange one-piece, tight-fitting suit of some type. In one of the chambers, he could have sworn the man was naked, and in another it appeared to have water or something spraying on the inside. He looked down to see that the woman below him was curled up in a ball, with her head between her legs. As he looked to the left, he gave a little jump. The man in the next box was wide-eyed and flashing a toothy, hungry grin at him. Kadamba felt like a piece of meat that a starving man was about to devour. He looked away quickly, hoping the man would leave. On the right, the part of the box that he could see was empty.

Then he looked up. The top of the box was barely a foot from his face, and he was looking directly at another man's anus and testicles. The man was sitting naked looking down at Kadamba between his own legs, tittering. Kadamba, scooting away from the clear end of the box, closed his eyes. Tears began to flow as he starting remembering what had happened before the energy blast slammed into his chest, rendering him unconscious.

A screen abruptly appeared on the wall opposite the transparent wall. A woman's smiling face appeared and starting speaking, "Welcome to the Purostinov Justice Processing Center," the perky face announced with a smile featuring overly whitened teeth, high cheekbones, and unbelievably perfect dimples.

It appeared to be a recording and was incredibly annoying. Kadamba asked himself aloud, "Who the hell designs this crap?"

"We are a wholly-owned subsidiary of the Purostinov Government Services Company. We proudly serve the citizens of Stujorkian City, providing the most cost-effective and efficient justice processing in the nation. As a client of Purostinov, you will find your case handled quickly and professionally."

The recorded, smiling face continued to drone on for a few more minutes, but Kadamba was lost in his own thoughts. He was scared. Deep inside, he knew he had screwed up in a major way. He should have never sold rath to that kid. It was stupid, and he wished he could have those few moments back. He wanted to send the kid on his way, with his money back in his own little pocket and none of the drug. But it was too late.

He looked at the screen again, and the woman repeated what she had just stated, "Kadamba Vorhoor, your processing will begin in a few moments." The face appeared frozen for a few moments, and then cheerfully began again. "As a first-time client of the Purostinov Justice Processing Center, I will be glad to walk you through the initial steps of your first processing."

"Are you a recording or a real person?" Kadamba asked the screen. The woman appeared to look at Kadamba, almost seeming to lose her cheerful demeanor, but immediately began speaking again as a box appeared below the screen, materializing out of the wall.

"Please remove your clothes and place them in the bin," declared the perky woman on the screen with another fake smile.

With a laugh Kadamba responded, "I don't think so, lady. My clothes stay on me."

He stared intently at the image of the woman, still completely unable to tell if she was real or not. Once again she began to speak. "You have two minutes to remove all of your clothing and place them in the bin."

"Well, I just don't think it will work. I just can't strip with you staring at me," Kadamba maintained, watching the screen, hoping to see the now-still face either turn away or begin to speak again. He realized that in the corner of the screen a countdown timer had appeared. He watched it for a few moments. As it approached 1:00, he realized a current of some type was flowing through the floor. It began to hurt. He realized he couldn't move and felt the muscles throughout his body contracting more and more tightly.

"You now have one minute to place all of your clothing in the bin, or full electro-simulative shock will be applied," the perky voice informed him.

When the current ended, Kadamba quickly began removing his clothes throwing them into the bin. His underwear, which was the last thing he had removed, landed in the bin with nine seconds remaining. The bin began to draw into the wall, disappearing completely, leaving him sitting naked. As he began to shake, he realized he was even more scared than before. Without his clothes, he felt completely vulnerable. Covering his genitals, he looked back at the screen. The woman on the screen now seemed to have a malicious smile, even though she appeared perky and happy.

"Thank you for complying. You now have five minutes to complete any personal toilet needs. From the wall beside him, a bump began to emerge in the form of a very low toilet. This was humiliating, but he was actually slightly relieved. He realized that he really did need to go. He sat on the toilet and buried his face in his hands, not wanting to look at that horrible, cheerful face on the screen.

"Uh, is there . . . uh . . . any paper anywhere?" he asked when he was done.

"You now have one minute to complete your personal needs," the annoying face on the screen relayed with a smile.

"Seriously, can I please have some . . ." Before Kadamba could finish his request, a blast of water hit him squarely where he needed to be cleaned. "Thanks. I guess. I didn't realize it would do that."

Kadamba slid to the floor as the toilet dematerialized back into the wall. He curled up in a ball. This was the most terrible thing that had ever happened to him, and it all had happened so fast. As he began to think of what had transpired that day, he realized that he didn't know if it was still the same day. Was it day or night? Or had he been out for days, weeks, or months? He began to sob as he curled himself up tighter and tighter.

The woman on the screen smiled again. "You will now be sanitized for your initial conference with your Purostinov Justice Processing Center Representative. Please lie face down on the floor with your hands spread above your head and your legs spread wide."

Kadamba could barely hear the perky-sounding voice. He wanted it to go away. He wanted everything to go away. He closed his eyes as tightly as he could and demanded of himself that he wake up. This had to be a nightmare. It couldn't really be happening. He felt the current hit him again, and his muscles contracted even more tightly than before; his back and legs began to quake from the contraction. Then it was gone.

"Please lie face down on the floor with your hands spread above your head and your legs spread wide," the voice demanded.

Kadamba rolled himself out, complying with the overly pleasant voice's order. He suddenly felt bands wrap around his wrists and ankles, lifting him into the air. He opened his eyes in pain, only to realize that the wide-eyed weirdo in the box next to his was staring right at him. With utter disgust, he realized that the man was also naked, sitting cross-legged, and masturbating as he gleefully watched what was happening to Kadamba.

A humming noise began to grow louder as the air pressure in the room seemed to change. Kadamba slammed his eyes shut as the liquid began to hit him from every direction. It felt like a million tiny high-pressure streams coming at him from every direction and moving in random patterns. It shot into his ears and nose, causing him to cough, which, in turn, allowed the astringent-tasting liquid to spray into his mouth. One at a time, the bands would disappear, dropping him to hang by three limbs, rather than all four. The liquid stung every place it touched, not just from the pressure, but also from whatever it was. Even his mouth, throat, and lungs burned. Every inch of his body felt like it was on fire when the torture stopped.

The humming noise began ramping up again. He closed his eyes, as the spray hit him again. This time it was only water. It stung, but it was washing the burning sensation away. He breathed in and even tried swallowing some of the mist in the room. As the water stopped, he realized that he felt warm. He realized that it could have been worse; at least, it hadn't been cold water. The air began to move swiftly around him, and he guessed that he was now being dried. He wished he hadn't, but he looked over at the weirdo again, just in time to see the man paint his own ankles while wearing a sickeningly satisfied look on his face.

When the bands vaporized, Kadamba crashed into the floor.

The perky, smiling face began speaking again, "You should now feel sanitized and refreshed for your initial conference."

A surge of anger exploded into Kadamba's gut. "Fuck YOU!" he shouted at the screen, but the woman maintained her smile.

"Please note that your personalized uniform is now ready and waiting," she informed him.

Kadamba looked around and saw that a neatly folded, orange article of clothing was sitting a few inches away. Grabbing it, he saw that it was a large one-piece uniform that would cover him from his ankles to his wrists. He quickly shoved his feet into the opening in the back of the uniform and pulled it on as quickly as he could. It was a huge relief to no longer be naked with that pervert scanning every inch of his body. He looked over again, but the man was gone. Despite his being flexible and able to feel every inch of its opening, Kadamba couldn't figure out how to close the back opening of the uniform. He sat down cross-legged to try and solve this, when the back suddenly closed on its own, and the uniform seemed to shrink to become absolutely skintight.

Kadamba realized how out of his control that his life had become and that it had happened so fast. It couldn't have been that long ago, perhaps hours, that he had landed a date with Jundana and driven a knife through the skull of that bargabuko. He had been on top of the universe. Everything in his life had been going so well. Kadamba had the world in his hands and a lifetime of opportunity ahead of him. Now he sat in a small cage, which didn't even seem to have a door, dressed in a uniform that he didn't choose and didn't even know if he could remove.

The smiling face on the screen began again, "The Purostinov Justice Processing Center thanks you for your compliance, on this, your first time, being processed. Your compliance has earned you a five-minute opportunity to interact with your visitors."

The woman on the screen disappeared, and the countdown timer appeared again. The image changed to one of a stark room with two rows of benches. In the back of the room, a justice enforcement officer, in full battle armor, stood silently. On one of the benches, Kadamba's mom and dad sat quietly. His dad was holding his mom's hands, stroking them, very obviously trying to comfort her, even as tears showed in his own eyes.

Kadamba scooted himself closer to the screen to see them better, but the tears welling up in his eyes blurred his vision. "Mom. Dad. I'm here."

Almost in unison, his parents began spinning their heads around, calling his name and looking for a screen. His father stood and begged the guard, "Isn't there anyway we can see our son? Where is the screen? Please, please help." The enforcement officer remained motionless, with his helmet and visor hiding any hint of compassion or concern.

"Son, son, we can hear you, but we can't see you. Are you alright?"

Kadamba choked back, as hard as he could, on the tears. He tried to sound strong, but through his sobs, all he could say was, "Yes, I'm okay," and then, he didn't mean to, but it just came out, "Dad, I'm scared."

"It's going to be okay, son. I promise. We're doing everything we can," assured his dad, trying as hard as he could to sound confident. His heart was pounding in his chest, and all he wanted to do was pull his son close, wrap his arms around him, and protect him.

"Mom, I'm sorry. I'm so sorry. I didn't mean to make all this happen. I screwed up so bad."

"Kadamba, it's going to okay," she comforted him, barely able to get the words out through the sobs and tears. Her little baby was hurting, and she could do nothing. She couldn't even see him. She felt as if the world was being ripped apart, and she couldn't even pull her little boy close. He was her youngest, and the pain and agony in his voice tore into her heart, worse than anything she could imagine.

"Son," his father began again, as he regained some composure, "I don't want you to worry. I've already called Mr. Thomathius. If anyone can find a way to get this straightened out, he'll do it and do it quickly."

That terrible, perky, fake voice let Kadamba know that he had 30 seconds left. His father exploded in anger, not understanding why they couldn't talk longer. His mother, having turned an ashen shade, appeared to have trouble breathing. As her husband turned in panic towards her, Kadamba just kept repeating, "I love you. I'm sorry. I love you. I'm so sorry." And the screen went blank.

Kadamba completely collapsed on the floor. He continued to sob. He had done more than screw up his own life. He had utterly disappointed his parents, the two people whose love and care he had never questioned. He had crushed them too. He thought of his two older sisters, who had argued over who would care for their adorable, cute little brother. They would be devastated. He wondered how, and even if, he could ever face his own family again.

Once again, that terrible, happy voice irritatingly began to speak, "We are pleased to inform you that your initial conference with your Purostinov Justice Processing Center Representative will be held shortly. Your assigned representative is Ms. Ocampo Rasmussen. Your representative will process you in a timely and efficient manner. The Purostinov Justice Processing Center prides itself on having reduced spending on justice processing by an average of 3.8% for each of the last four years. Our goal of quick and effective justice processing is second to none."

Kadamba pulled himself into a seated position and began staring at the end wall. The screen had disappeared, but he was sure that it would be back with this representative of his. Suddenly, the cell began to move, as if a giant hand had plucked it out of the stack, without disturbing any other cells. As suddenly as it had started, the cell stopped moving, slamming Kadamba into the end wall of his cell.

Kadamba attempted to sit back up, as the wall dematerialized, and he found himself looking up at two justice enforcement officers in full battle gear. One was pointing an energy blaster at him, and the other had a long stick in his hand, with a gun-like handle that the guard gripped.

Kadamba moved onto all fours, intending to stand, when the guard placed the end of the stick on his back, right below his neck. The end of the stick locked to his uniform, sending a jolt of current through Kadamba's body. He felt like a pet on a leash, helpless to do anything, unless his master commanded it. The guard tugged on the handle, forcing Kadamba to stand. Kadamba, looking around, realized that he was in some type of interrogation room. There was a table with two chairs on its opposite sides. The guard led Kadamba to one of the chairs and forced him in it.

Another stream of electrical current surged through Kadamba, as one of the guards finally spoke. "Please comply" was all that he said while pointing at the table. On the table were the outlines of two arms. Apparently, he was supposed to put his hands and forearms flat on the table. Kadamba complied, and the moment his arms hit the table, straps rapidly emerged from beside his elbows and wrists, wrapping over the tops of his arms to clamp him tightly to the table. He felt a small surge as the guard's stick released his uniform, and the guards exited the room.

Within a few moments, a rather short, overweight woman came into the room, carrying a glass. She had an unhappy and annoyed look about her, like she really didn't want to be there. She sat down in the chair on the opposite side of the table and waved her hands across the table, tapping it in a few places. A monitor appeared above one side the table, facing so that both of them could see it. She glared at him, let out a heavy sigh, and drank the entire contents of the glass.

"Mr. Vorhoor," she began, with a terribly raspy-sounding voice, "I am Ocampo Rasmussen, your Purostinov Justice Processing Center Representative."

"Where are my parents?" Kadamba asked, feeling the knot in his stomach growing tighter and tighter.

She tapped on the table again, and his photo appeared on the monitor, filling half the screen. The other half was packed with text. She glanced at it for a moment and then released another exasperated sigh. "You have already had your allotted time with your family and visitors. We are going to process you now. Considering the facts of this case, it will NOT take long."

"I want to talk to my parents. Please."

"Mr. Vorhoor," she continued very sternly, as she tapped on a keyboard that had materialized on the table in front of her, "you are to be processed immediately. Your crimes have shifted you to adult processing. You will have no more visitors. Your processing will be done in an effective and efficient manner."

Kadamba regarded her with an obvious look of shock on his face. She let out another annoyed, heavy sigh, and pressed a few more keys. She then pointed to the monitor.

It was a scene of the playground at Schmarlo's Landing. He watched as the young boy to whom he had sold the rath came stumbling into the scene and collapsed. Panic ensued, and within a minute, Jundana was kneeling over the boy. He watched as the justice enforcement officer fired his weapon, knocking him unconscious. The medic, frantically digging in his bag, pulled out a syringe, shaped like a gun, and delivered something directly into the boy's neck. The boy seemed to calm, and the foaming from his mouth began to slow. The medic said something to Jundana. In response, she looked down at the boy and then collapsed on the boy's chest, obviously weeping and sobbing.

The screen went blank. Tears were running down Kadamba's face. "What happened?"

Ocampo looked at Kadamba with a disgusted look on her face. "The boy had a reaction to the rath. The medic administered a sedative and pain killer to ease the boy's passing. One in about a hundred people has a violent reaction to rath. Not one of them has survived."

A sudden wave of nausea hit Kadamba. The woman quickly tapped the keyboard, and a hole with a basin appeared in the table between Kadamba's strapped-down arms. A strap shot out of the table, wrapping itself around Kadamba's neck, and pulled his face towards the opening. The woman sat glaring at Kadamba as he heaved and vomited what little food was in his stomach into the opening.

He tried to look up, but the strap held him down. He could see the revulsion on her face as she hit another key. Multiple streams of the burning astringent liquid hit his face, followed again by warm water. The strap released its hold, and the hole disappeared.

Kadamba sat up. Time seemed to be suspended. He couldn't place what he was feeling. Everything was surreal. It was as if he were trapped in a nightmare but couldn't force himself to wake up. He sat there staring at the representative, not knowing what to do or say.

She let out a heavy, exasperated sigh. "Well, now that you've got that out of your system, let's finish this up. The Crime Review Committee has offered you three options. Option number one is to face an LD trial. Option number two is a ten-year assignment with the Exorthium Extraction Company. And your final option is a twenty-five year incarceration with the Morphinia Containment Company."

"Please. I don't understand," replied Kadamba.

"What's to understand, Mr. Vorhoor? You were carrying enough rath to get everyone on Schmarlo's Landing completely strung out for a month. You sold some to a child. He died. You are a drug dealer and a murderer. These are the facts—and those are your options." Her eyes seemed completely devoid of any pity, and Kadamba could feel her hatred of him beginning to grow.

Kadamba closed his eyes, letting the reality of this come slamming into him. Alorus, the little boy, was dead. Was he Jundana's little brother, cousin, or what? He completely had forgotten that he was carrying such an enormous amount of rath. That didn't really matter.

What mattered was that he had sold rath to the boy, and he knew he shouldn't have. Now, the boy was dead.

"I want to talk to my parents," begged Kadamba.

"Mr. Vorhoor, let me make this process very clear to you. We are very effective and efficient at processing justice cases. We do it quickly, neatly, and don't waste any unnecessary funds. Your case has already been reviewed by the Crime Review Committee, and you have been given three options. Should you fail to make a selection by the end of this meeting, the Committee will make the selection for you."

Ocampo Rasmussen, his "Purostinov Justice Processing Center Representative," let a small, cruel smile form at the corners of her mouth. She looked at him with disdain, but it appeared that she was enjoying watching him struggle. Perhaps it was natural. He was a drug dealer. He was now a murderer too. She got to administer the hand of justice, and it was being brought down quickly and with finality.

Kadamba began to gather his composure. It felt impossible, but he was trapped. He felt out of control, and his mind was swirling with too many thoughts and emotions. Was this a nightmare? He felt his heart began to race. His breathing began to get shallow and rapid. He looked at Ocampo, hoping to see some compassion. Weren't adults supposed to help children? She continued to stare coldly at him with nothing but disdain in her eyes. He closed his eyes tightly. Like every teenager, he wanted to be treated like an adult, and now—he was.

Closing his eyes, he forced himself to focus. He realized he hadn't even really understood the options she had presented. He took a few more deep breaths, telling himself to push the panic aside and not to scream. "What are my choices? I mean, can you please explain my options again?"

"Your first option is a LD trial, that is, a 'life-or-death trial.' Given your circumstances, the trial would be tomorrow, and your execution would be carried out within two days. As your representative, I can tell you that you would have no chance at getting returned to your life.

"Your second option is a ten-year assignment with the Exorthium Extraction Company. You would be immediately placed on a mining crew, transferred to the surface of Exorthium, and spend the next ten years working the mines there.

"Your final option is a twenty-five year incarceration with the Morphinia Containment Company. This option would have you placed in a containment facility of their choice for the next twenty-five years, after which, you would be free to return to society."

The knot began to tighten even further in Kadamba's stomach. Less than a day ago, the whole universe was his. Now he had to decide among three horrible fates. He could be executed in a few days. He could become a slave on a planet where, under good circumstances, people died from the conditions within seven years. Or, he could go to prison, where he had heard that unspeakable things happen.

"Can I please talk to my mom and dad?" begged Kadamba.

"Mr. Vorhoor, this meeting will be over in eight minutes. If you have not made a selection on your own, the Committee will assign a selection to you. As our company would have to bear the cost, I doubt you would have a LD trail. More than likely, you would be sent to the Exorthium Extraction Company, as they are offering a healthy bonus for each new 'employee' we provide for their operations."

In the flash of a moment, the world can change. A simple act that seems so innocent at first can set off a chain reaction that redefines an entire lifetime. Kadamba felt as if he were falling, spinning uncontrollably through the air, accelerating faster and faster towards the ground. A certain death. The image of it sat in Kadamba's head. Death. In three days this could all be over. The humiliation of the last few hours could be washed away. Fear would be over. As if he spread his arms while falling, the spinning stopped, and he saw the ground racing towards him. No, he didn't want to die, but even more than that, he didn't want to feel what was exploding inside of him, beginning to strangle his very thoughts. From the moment he saw Jundana's head drop to Alorus' chest, he felt it taking him over. Guilt. Remorse. Regret. Whatever words rushed through his mind, the feeling was the same, and what he had done could never be undone.

Ocampo Rasmussen snorted as Kadamba told her which option he wanted. She pressed a few buttons, stood up, and walked to the wall, as a door appeared. She looked back over her shoulder, a vicious smile spreading across her face. "You're going to get what you deserve."

Chapter 7

Ascension of the Protégé

Celestina Wiroviana's private shuttle would be leaving Stujorkian City shortly. She had received the message from her pilot that they were en route to the building's shuttle pad and would be arriving in twenty minutes. She rolled over and looked into Tomar's eyes.

"I suppose you are leaving soon?" he inquired.

"Only because the universe needs us to save it," she disclosed, with a coy look in her eyes.

Chuckling, they embraced in another passionate kiss. Their relationship was one of extreme passion and intensity, but also of distance and selfishness. He was now the Chairman of one of the Eleven. He commanded one of the most powerful organizations in the known universe. Only six Corporations were larger, but he knew that would soon change. She was the Chief Executive Minister of the Ministry for Interplanetary Corporate Relations. It was an elected position that arguably was the most powerful government position on the two planets, and more importantly, it regulated those powerful Eleven Corporations.

That their relationship should be a secret was more than an understatement. It was expressly forbidden by the bylaws of the Donovackia Corporation and the rules that governed the Ministry. For a Minister, especially the Chief Executive Minister, to be involved in an intimate relationship with any board member or employee of one of the Eleven, especially a Chairman of one, was simply unethical, and potentially very dangerous. But neither gave a damn. Power breeds arrogance, and often an arrogance that believes that rules only apply to others.

"In any event, my dear Tomar, you have a board meeting in a few hours. I wish I could be there to see their faces. After watching Greylorent blasted into that wall and slumping to the floor yesterday, I can only imagine how compliant and agreeable they will be to any of your ideas and suggestions."

He continued to study her as she dressed, knowing in a few moments she would slip into the secret elevator that connected his apartments with her official residence in Stujorkian City.

"You look radiant as always, my love," he declared, as she began to walk towards the door. She returned to the bed and kissed him one last time before she left.

"Behave while I am gone," she remarked, trying to sound serious.

"Perhaps, I will. Perhaps—I won't," he replied.

"Tomar," she warned seductively, "you never behave, and I promise to punish you the next time we are together."

She looked at the silk straps, which were tied to the bed posts, and both of them laughed. This relationship had what both of them craved in so many ways. With each other, they could express their secret desires, not just those that are played out in the bedroom, but also the lust for power that consumed each of them. They were soul mates. It was a cruel fate that had brought them together, when the rules forbade their love. Breaking those rules only fanned the flames of their desire and added intensity to each of their personal ambitions. Eventually, their relationship would be public, but only after they reshaped the universe to their vision.

*****

"My lady, welcome aboard," said one of her secretaries as she boarded her shuttle. As always, Celestina looked impeccable. She had long ago known that she was destined for great things, so she looked and dressed the part. With the shuttle was abuzz with activity, she headed towards her private office. While she had multiple "official residences," an "official office" in Stujorkian City, and another on Zoranth, in the beautiful city of Zanthantium, this shuttle and another nearly identical one on Zoranth were her real offices.

The morning was filled with the official business required of her position, and she executed her job with amazing precision. No Chief Executive of the Ministry had ever been so effective, efficient, or as ruthlessly focused and driven. She had gathered power to herself at an astounding rate. Those close to her in the Ministry knew that she was becoming an unstoppable force, but to the public on both Koranth and

Zoranth, she was loved and adored. She was heading to the Moran-Kathor Portal, which would transport her to Zoranth. Because her official duties would keep her there for some time, she decided a small detour was needed.

The shuttle, changing course, headed towards Fraterian City, in her home country of Beliasium. She would surprise her uncle at his country residence. Her parents had been killed in an accident when she was very young. Her father's older brother, Hareold Wiroviana, had taken her in and raised her as his own. He was driven man—a politician to his very core, but he loved her with all his heart.

When Celestina came under his care, he was already rising in the Beliasium Parliament. Her teen years were spent in the Prime Minister's palace, where he was reelected for multiple terms. She loved every bit of the pomp and circumstance of political life, and he preened as any proud father would when she followed him into politics. In many ways, it had emboldened him, and he accomplished the impossible. He became the first Interplanetary Corporate Relations Minister elected from a country that wasn't a superpower. Not even one of the Eleven Corporations was based in Beliasium.

As he had done when he was Prime Minister, he retained his position as one of the five elected Ministers and reaped the personal, professional, and financial rewards of such an office. However, his greatest achievement wasn't his own. It was guiding his niece, Celestina, through a meteoric rise of her own career. She followed in her uncle's path at a dizzying pace, trumping every achievement and milestone that he had set. Her election to Chief Executive Minister of the Ministry of Interplanetary Corporate Relations validated everything that he had ever done, every sacrifice that he had ever made. He may have been her uncle, but he had created her, and now he would follow his own pupil as if she were the master.

"Uncle!" she cried out as she walked to the small, open pagoda on the edge of a cliff, overlooking the ocean. The old man sat comfortably in a chair, the sea breeze blowing through his thin, white hair. He could not hear her as she approached due to the waves crashing on the rocks below. This was a private place, a place where he went to meditate, which was becoming more and more of the time. He found that he was at a point in his life where he longed for peaceful moments to drink in the beauty of the ocean. He was no fool. He knew his time was short and looked forward to finally resting.

"Uncle Hareold," she spoke gently as she approached him, so as not to startle him. He turned to her with a surprised, yet joyous look, a smile spreading widely across his entire face.

"My dearest Celestina! What a wonderful and excellent surprise. I had not expected to see you until the next meeting of the Ministry," he voiced warmly to his niece.

"I don't have long, Uncle, but I wanted to spend a little time with you before I headed over to Zoranth. There is so much to do, but we've accomplished so much. I just wanted to personally thank you."

"Celestina, you give me too much credit. You set everything up. All I did was meet with them and follow the plan that you laid out. You, my young lady, have architected more in the last two years than any Chief Executive Minister of the Ministry has since the Colonial Wars. You are to be commended," he delivered with sincerity and pride.

She attempted to interrupt him, but he silenced her with a determined look and a gesture. They were both Minsters and she the Chief Executive, but he was still her uncle, and she would always respect that.

"Only two years ago, the Ministry only dealt with issues concerning the Eleven Corporations. When you took office, you understood the historical significance of the Ministry. You quickly returned it to some of its very esteemed roots. You sent me to the meeting of the three factions of Greater Morlovia. Based on your plan, your insights, and your strategy, we avoided what would have been a devastating civil war. This comes on the heels of your guiding the Ministry to intervene and stop four major territorial disputes, including one that could have plummeted the entire planet of Zoranth into a global conflict.

"My beautiful niece, it is I that should be thanking you. You have made me prouder than I ever dreamed I could be. I wish your parents were here to tell you the same. You are truly a gifted and talented politician, and you are re-crafting the Ministry and our two planets with a vision that has long been neglected."

She was flattered by the old man's words. While he was simply another pawn in her game, he was an important one, and she wanted to play him out with the respect he deserved. She again tried to speak, and again, he demanded that she listen.

"You are sweet to come here to thank me in person, but I taught you all that I know, and therefore, I know why you are really here. You have sent me two proposals that you intend to present to the Ministry at our next official meeting in two months. These are radical and, to some, almost heretical ideas. You want to reduce the Ministry to three seats and allow the Donovackia Corporation to acquire Stameyerson Corporation and mount a hostile takeover of the Kathor Corporation."

Her mouth started to become a bit dry, as she tried to search his face for more emotion than he was revealing. If she could not convince him to support her proposals, then they would almost certainly fail. A smile moved across his face.

"Celestina, for generations we have had five Ministers and the Eleven Corporations. It has worked, but it has become stagnant. In your short time as Chief Executive Minster, you have achieved so much. I am not long for this life, but I know that in what time I have left, I will get to see you achieve many more amazing things. From this day forward, you have my unquestionable support for whatever proposal, plan, or idea you put forth."

She tried to maintain her composure but was simply too overjoyed. She had expected that she would have to debate with the old man about the proposals. They had played these games her whole life. Even if he supported her, he would make her vigorously defend her positions. He watched with a happy soul as he graduated his protégé to the next level. She reached out to wrap her arms around him.

"Now go, tend to the Ministry's business on Zoranth," he bid her. "I will see you in two months, at the next meeting."

They both gazed out into the ocean, but their thoughts stretched down two very different paths. The old man was settled in his thoughts. He saw the endless waves and water as evidence of the cycle of nature. The Ministry had brought peace many centuries ago, and once again, under his niece's guiding hand, the Ministry had returned to where it had begun. Celestina saw the vast ocean quite differently. It ate away at the shore, eroding and sculpting. It pounded rocks into sand. It made things that were once one thing and ground them into another. She would do the same with the Ministry. She would change it all.

She kissed him on his forehead and headed back to her shuttle.

Chapter 8
A Neighbor in Need

Bjorn spread his schoolbooks on the table, as Dylan finished putting the few dishes in the dishwasher. As usual, they had easily devoured all of the Chinese food, including all the vegetables. Bjorn opened one of his books and slapped his hand on the table.

"Ms. Arthur is the worst teacher of all time!" Bjorn announced as he set his jaw and stared directly at his brother.

"That's a bit harsh, and frankly just not true," replied Dylan.

"Seriously, Dylan, you have no idea."

Dylan, trying not to let his brother get to him, patiently explained, "I had Ms. Arthur before she moved to your school, and she was just fine."

"Well, something happened. She must have changed. I think she hates me," responded the younger brother angrily.

Dylan breathed in deeply, knowing that this argument was going nowhere in a hurry when the doorbell chimed. "Stay put, I'll let him in," ordered Dylan, as he headed towards the front door.

Dylan, opening the door, struggled to contain the smile. Standing on the porch was an impeccably dressed, slightly older, middle-aged African-American gentleman. As always, he was wearing slacks, a dress shirt, a tweed jacket, and a fedora. One hand was on a wooden cane, with a carved brass knob, but he wasn't relying on it for any support. He tipped the hat with his other hand, and in a very formal tone announced, "Atticus Freeman, at your service."

Dylan's smile widened, and he swept one arm towards the living room, inviting the gentleman into their home. "As always, my good sir, you are welcome here."

Atticus walked in, removed his hat and jacket, and hung them on the coat tree in the entryway. He leaned his cane against the wall, and turned to Dylan. "How was your day, Dylan?"

"Not too bad. Nothing all that interesting. Just another day at school," Dylan answered.

"And I assume by the scent in the air that you had Chinese food for dinner this evening?" asked Mr. Freeman.

"The Wonderful Dragon," replied the teenager with a smile.

"Best sesame chicken this side of Shanghai," stated Mr. Freeman, with an almost unquestionable air of authority to the statement.

"Yes, sir, it is," agreed Dylan, "and we also had happy family. You know, for the vegetables."

"Mr. Freeman!" piped in Bjorn from the kitchen, "How would you know it's the best sesame chicken this side of Shanghai? "

Atticus looked at Dylan and smiled. He knew Bjorn was probably feeling a little combative, which meant he had struggled with something at school. More likely than not, it was math, but that was exactly why Atticus was there.

"In Shanghai, hidden in an alley that you should never walk down alone," began Mr. Freeman, nodding to Dylan and heading into the kitchen, "is a restaurant called 'The Lonely Goose.' But I'm not here to discuss my travels with you. We can do that another time."

When Dylan returned the kitchen, after finishing some homework of his own, Bjorn's mood was decidedly improved. Atticus was explaining the steps in cross-multiplication with great patience, and Bjorn was grasping the concepts. The back door opened, and Joanna Cairbre, the boys' mother, walked into the kitchen.

"Hello, Mr. Freeman, I'm so glad to see you," she remarked with a smile.

"Ms. Cairbre, welcome home," replied Atticus.

"How is Bjorn doing?" she inquired.

"I think we may have had a little challenge with the lesson at school today, but with a little focus, he's completely grasped the concepts," answered Atticus, as Bjorn broke into a wide grin.

"You are a saint, Mr. Freeman. I don't know what I'd do without you."

"You would do quite well. I'm just glad I can help."

The Cairbre family really liked their neighbor, Mr. Freeman. He had moved into a home across the street, just a few houses down, only a week after Dylan, Bjorn, and their mom had moved into their home in Denver. Dylan had been returning home on his bike after exploring his new neighborhood when he saw Atticus, carrying a large box from his car to his front door. Dylan had quickly ridden up the sidewalk to offer Mr. Freeman a hand.

Atticus was very appreciative, especially as Dylan happily helped him unload a few more boxes from his car. When Atticus attempted to give Dylan a $20 bill, Dylan refused. He was just happy to talk to someone other than his brother, especially when he saw the laptop, iPad, and boxes with logos from Dell, HP, and Apple stacked in the living room. School would start in a few weeks, but he hadn't made any friends yet. When they'd left Tennessee, the circumstances were a bit uncomfortable, and Dylan had lost contact with all of his friends. The teen wasn't sure what it was, but he felt safe around Mr. Freeman. He was like a grandfather that the boys had never had, and from the look of things, he was a bit geeky too!

That first evening after their meeting, Atticus had brought a plate of freshly baked chocolate chip cookies over to their house. Joanna had answered the door and brought him into the living room. By the time Dylan came out of his room, it was obvious that Atticus had explained how kind Dylan had been in helping him with unloading his car earlier in the day. Dylan blushed as Joanna praised her son for his kindness and good heart.

Shortly after Dylan had helped Atticus move the boxes into his house, Dylan and his mom were working in the yard, when Atticus passed by while out on a walk. School had only been in session a couple of weeks. They all began chatting about the beautiful end-of-summer weather when Bjorn's voice broke the pleasant conversation.

"That doesn't make sense!" shouted the frustrated boy. "It simply does not work that way!"

"I got it Mom," Dylan declared, as he headed into the house. Bjorn must have been having trouble with some homework again, and Dylan would test his own patience again, attempting to help his frustrated little brother. Dylan headed inside, hoping this round would be a good one. It wasn't that Bjorn wasn't smart. He was, but he just wasn't very patient with himself.

After about twenty minutes, Dylan walked out and plopped on the bench on the front porch. His mom looked at him sympathetically. She could help her younger son with homework, but she hadn't done much math in many years. On top of that, the way that math was currently being taught was completely foreign to her. Dylan was closer to the subject and usually did a great job with his brother. Dylan cracked up and smiled.

"So . . ." his mom asked, drawing the "oh" sound out.

"He's not getting it. It's not that hard, but he's got it in his mind that he can't understand," explained Dylan.

"Thanks for trying." His mom let out a long sigh, and turned to Atticus to wish him a good day, with the intention of heading in to help her son with his homework.

"Ma'am, if I may. I spent a little time tutoring in my day. Perhaps a different voice would help?" inquired Atticus.

She began to tell him that he was amazingly kind, but before she could explain how she simply couldn't ask someone else to deal with the stubborn child, Dylan interjected, "Mom, it's a great idea!"

Mr. Freeman, beaming at Dylan, turned to see Joanna's response. She was happy to be home from work a bit earlier than usual, and she was greatly enjoying the chance to do some yard work with Dylan's help. She wanted to help Bjorn with his homework, but she knew that it might be a bit of an uphill battle since Dylan had already thrown in the towel.

"Mr. Freeman, you're very kind for offering," she began, knowing that it was probably a good idea. "Perhaps, someone else's approach may be a good alternative."

"It's always hard to say," Mr. Freeman replied sympathetically, "but often a few words from a different perspective is all it takes. I'll see what I can do."

Ten minutes later, Bjorn and Mr. Freeman came out the front door. Bjorn was beaming, obviously happy. Dylan and his mom looked at each other and then at Mr. Freeman, both revealing a bit of surprise on their faces. The young boy pumped his fist in the air, as if he had achieved some great goal, and announced, "Mom, I finished my homework. Can I please play some video games?"

"Sure, if your homework is done, you can," replied Johanna, somewhat astonished at Bjorn's positive attitude.

She turned to Mr. Freeman, wanting to ask how on Earth he had both managed to help Bjorn with his homework and improve his mood. More often than not, Bjorn was a bit cranky when he did his homework, and when he was frustrated, it was always worse.

"A smart young man you have there, Mrs. Cairbre. But I tell you, some of the methods they use nowadays to teach simply don't register as well with some kids," stated the older gentleman.

"Thank you, um, Mr. Freeman." Johanna stumbled trying to be grateful, but also wanting to know what had transpired in the kitchen.

"What did you . . . how . . . I mean, thank you for helping him, but what . . ."

"It's my pleasure," interjected Mr. Freeman, saving Johanna from tripping over her own tongue.

Dylan headed into the house to play some video games with his brother while Atticus and Joanna remained outside, chatting on the porch for some time. When she came inside, she seemed quite at ease and sat down on the plush chair in the living room, next to the sofa where the boys were intently killing aliens on the screen.

When the boys hit a good stopping point, they paused the game, knowing their mom had something she wanted to talk about. Being a single mom was not always easy, and her job required more hours at times than she wished. Mr. Freeman had offered to stop by occasionally in the evenings to check on the boys and to help with homework if they needed it. Bjorn immediately expressed his approval of the idea, especially considering how quickly Mr. Freeman had just helped him finish his homework that day. Dylan was also appreciative, especially if it could reduce his occasional frustration from dealing with his stubborn little brother.

Over the course of the school year, Mr. Freeman became a huge help to the boys, and Bjorn even asked if Mr. Freeman could get Ms. Arthur fired and take over her job. There were occasional times where Mr. Freeman would not stop by, as he loved to travel. When he would return, he would tell the boys about some of the sites he had seen and foods he had tried. Despite her best efforts, Mr. Freeman diligently and politely refused any type of payment for helping the boys with homework or checking on them, other than joining them for an occasional meal.

Over the course of the summer, Johanna was relieved to have a trusted neighbor close by in case the boys needed anything. She felt some sense of relief when he had hired the boys to mow his lawn while he was on a trip. They agreed but refused payment. After that trip, the boys continued to mow Mr. Freeman's lawn. For the Cairbre family, life seemed to be about as good as it could get. The boys were doing well in school. The family's friendship with Mr. Freeman seemed to be a real blessing. He helped the boys with schoolwork. They were able to help him around his house. It was as if his kind manner and patience had even rubbed off on the boys, especially Bjorn. Joanna had even started dating. The troubles and stresses that they experienced in Tennessee seemed to be fading into the past.

Chapter 9
It's About Who You Know

Celestina's shuttle made good time as it headed towards the Moran-Kathor Portal, through which she would travel to Zoranth. As with all of the portals, a massive city had grown up around the portal. Her captain steered the shuttle to one of the large buildings on the outskirts of the city. It was a huge hotel and entertainment complex complete with casinos, gaming centers, and experiential conclaves, which was nothing more than a fancy way of saying a place where you could experience things that were illegal, but tolerated.

The shuttle docked on the shuttle bay situated on the top of the building. Celestina instructed her staff to wait for her, as none of them were invited to this private meeting. As expected, her head of security balked at the idea of her going into the hotel alone, but she commanded him and his staff to remain with the shuttle.

As she entered the large suite, she was first struck by the astounding views. Two of the walls were solid glass, with nothing at all covering them. The view of the city and its gigantic portal facility was amazing. However, her view was partially obstructed by four massive men standing across one of the windows. They were all dressed in black. They were obviously armed. All four remained nearly motionless with faces revealing no emotion.

A much smaller, leaner man sat on an oversized, stuffed sofa, smiling at her. He was dressed in light-colored, casual slacks, and an unusual silky shirt, sporting a wild tropical design. He almost seemed out of place, with his attire and seemingly relaxed, casual attitude.

As she looked him up and down, he stood up. "Do you like my new look? I'm heading to the tropical region for a little business soon, and I'm trying to find the right look."

She continued to stare at him and then began walking into the room. She sat down on a chair and motioned him to sit back down too.

She wasn't frightened of him. She really wasn't frightened by anyone, but he was different. He was obviously cunning and smooth, so incredibly smooth. His words slipped out of his mouth with such ease, but also with such amazing control. As she had no doubt that he was a master manipulator, she simply remained cautious during the few times that they had met.

"You've never even tried it, have you?" the man asked with an inviting smile.

She shook her head, ever so slightly back and forth.

"You haven't even ever seen it, have you?" he asked, with his smile getting wider, but seeming to become more intense.

With her eyes locked on his, she reminded him, "We're here to discuss our arrangement. Nothing more. Nothing less."

With his smile widening again, he set a small box with a hinged lid onto the table that sat in-between them. He slowly opened it, revealing a number of small, flat packages, each with a bump in its middle. It was obvious that the packages could be peeled open to reveal an adhesive strip.

"You've heard about it, my dear Chief Executive Minster, but are you brave enough to try it?" He set his eyes upon her, issuing a challenge to her character with the intensity of his stare.

"Doctor Z, I have no intention of ever trying rath. You can enjoy it yourself," she responded coldly.

Chuckling, he admitted, "Opening the box is as close as I ever will get to it. It's not that I'm a prude. I just know better than messing with what I'm distributing, especially one that straight-up kills one out of a hundred that want to enjoy it. We need to add that to our agenda, along with expanding the delivery mechanisms."

She was not excited about having to deal with a man like this, but it was a necessary evil. The Ministry had its own security force, but it was far smaller than what she wanted. Eliminating two of the Ministers would significantly improve the Ministry's financial state, but she wanted to build more than just a security force. She needed a military as strong as any of the Eleven Corporations' militaries and stronger than any single country's military. To do this, she needed vast sums of money, and, more importantly, discretion in raising and spending it.

Tomar had given her the perfect way to do this. His Corporate military was toying with drugs to make its soldiers more effective. The goals were to find substances that could stimulate soldiers as quickly as possible, making them hyper-alert and giving them extra stamina.

Additionally, something was needed to counter the effects, bringing the soldiers back down and to recovery as quickly as possible. Rath was a byproduct of that research. However, it turned out to be a bit too much of a recreational drug, was mildly addictive, and killed about one percent of those who tried it.

Tomar's idea was genius. Rath was cheap to produce. Celestina had some black box discretionary funds to use. Nothing had to be declared or traced on the Ministry's books. Tomar had his military begin producing large quantities of rath and then sold it to the Ministry. While it was black box on the Ministry side, he could show it as revenue, burying it deep in the books under names of other products. The Ministry, in turn, sold it to Doctor Z's organization. It had turned into a huge cash cow for everyone involved.

"Ms. Minister, please let me put this very bluntly and openly. You came to me wanting a way to distribute a new drug, rath. My network is vast and powerful. You made a good decision. We are now in a position to greatly expand distribution, but I need a few things. We have got to reduce or eliminate the deaths. And more importantly, we need to have other delivery mechanisms, like pills, liquids, and powders. Most importantly, we need more—much, much more. You are the only supplier, and, as long as I am your exclusive distribution channel, I can make rath flow like water."

The meeting was taking an even better turn than she had expected. She was anticipating that he would want to renegotiate prices, but he didn't. He just wanted more. He was savvy, and he was making enormous profits. He knew when not to rock the boat. Doctor Z smiled in wait of her reply.

"My scientists are working on the random death aspect," she partially lied. Scientists were working on it, just not hers. "It will take a little longer to develop other delivery mechanisms, but I promise that we will have more soon. Tell me, what do you think will sell best? Pills? Liquid? We could even make suppositories if you think people would enjoy shoving it up their asses."

Doctor Z let out a huge, spontaneous laugh. "I love your style! Most people fear me, with good cause. But you and I, we see eye-to-eye. This partnership is going to be massively profitable for both of us. Ramp that production up. I'll sell every single bit that you can provide."

She was almost giddy as she headed back to her shuttle. It wouldn't happen overnight, but she would soon have a huge military under the Ministry's command. If the next Ministry meeting went as planned, she would be in complete control of the Ministry, and, therefore, its military as well.

*****

The Moran-Kathor Portal Complex was a truly vast set of buildings and stations, spread over many square miles. The portal itself, like all portals, was only a four-foot diameter opening into a huge machine. If the portal was turned off, there was nothing but internal mechanisms to see. When it was turned on, the opening was a mesmerizing shade of blue. In many ways, it was as if you were looking into a deep, vast, clear place in the ocean. The surface shimmered, but you could see past the surface, into a depth that was impossible to describe.

As beautiful as a portal was to see, this was big business, and actually seeing the portal's physical opening for more than a moment was a rarity. The massive enclosed area around the portal itself was similar to a huge train station. Instead of trains of large train cars, there were trains of long cylindrical tubes. The tubes would be blasted through the portal, as quickly as possible, one after the other. After a few hundred or few thousand tubes went through one way, the direction reversed, and tubes came flying through from the other end of the portal.

The tubes themselves were set on an intricate series of rail-like guides. Over the centuries, hundreds of different tubes had been designed, each specific for what would be carried inside. The tubes glided in and out of the gigantic building that housed the portal itself. The portal complex had a massive variety of shipping facilities and buildings spread over the many square miles. Tubes zoomed in and out of the portal building, heading to various other facilities in the complex. There were traditional train and trucking facilities that were constantly loading and unloading tubes. Huge shuttle facilities and a large seaport enabled tubes to be moved to and from the facility by air and sea. The logistics were dauntingly phenomenal.

Of course, corporations wanted the portals to be larger than the four-foot diameter, but larger portals failed. Over time, corporations had maximized the volume of what moved through a portal. Enormous quantities of goods of every type flowed through these portals, packed tightly inside the tubes. On the other end of this portal, in Zoranth, was a similar complex. Trade was good. Thousands upon thousands of companies benefited, and profits were always a good thing.

Like every other product, humans were also carried through the portals in tubes. When a portal was first set up, people could easily crawl through, and they did, until the infrastructure was in place to move the tubes on both sides.

Celestina departed her shuttle with her staff and security. Only part of them would be traveling through the portal, as she had staff and security on the other side. They headed to one of the tube stations. This particular station targeted those of significant financial means, as using these first-class tubes cost significantly more than using others. Of course, the security checkpoints were just as thorough, but the experience was more pleasant, if such a thing can be said for being packed into something that looked like a rounded coffin.

A porter took their bags and escorted them into a huge room. Row after row of tubes were lined up with walkways in between. It was more akin to boarding a ride at an amusement park, than boarding a train or shuttle. For these more expensive tube rides, each passenger had a few more inches of tube length than his or her own height. The lower portion of the tube was for whatever luggage a passenger had brought while the top portion of the tube was for the passenger. To access the inside of the tube, the top of the tube opened like a hinged, rounded box. A padded, flat bed-like surface could be lifted to reveal the luggage area below where the passenger would lie.

After packing Celestina's luggage into the lower part of the tube, the porter closed the padded, flat bed-like surface. He offered her a hand to help her climb in. Like practically everyone who traveled via tube, she hated the experience. However, it was more than worth the expense to pay for this "first-class" treatment.

Other tube stations offered significantly fewer amenities. Passenger's luggage would be pressure-packed in luggage tubes, often arriving hours or days after the passenger was transported through. In those standard-class stations, passengers were sorted by size and packed to maximize the numbers of people in the very tight spaces of the tubes. Of course, each person had his or her own space, but some tubes had been configured to stack three or even four skinny people together.

She sat on the bed surface, watching the activity around her. It was constant activity, but because of the price she paid, it was pampered, constant activity. An employee with a large pushcart came down the walkway, stopping at each tube. When she stopped in front of where Celestina was sitting, the employee, smiling, greeted her very cheerfully.

"My esteemed Chief Executive Minster, it is an honor to have you traveling with us again," the employee began.

"Thank you. I wouldn't travel to Zoranth any other way," replied Celestina.

"You are very kind. May I offer you a cocktail while you wait?"

"No thank you. It's nerve-racking enough to be closed into this tube, without adding anything to my bladder."

The employee, smiling a broad, knowing smile, affirmed, "I completely understand. Please allow me to review the safety information and your options."

She reviewed with Celestina how to lie within the tube and close the hatch if she didn't want to wait for it to automatically close. Then she confirmed that Celestina was correctly positioned in the tube for the actual ride through the portal itself. She pointed out that on the hinged side of the tube there was a handrest with a single button. If at any time, after the tube was closed, Celestina should experience any significant claustrophobia or panic attack, simply pushing the button would release an aerosol sedative near her head. One breath and she would sleep like a baby until the tube was opened in Zoranth. Speaking or yelling the word "help" would also release the sedative.

The temptation was always huge to push that button, but Celestina hated being out of control, and a sedative would do just that. She watched as the hatches on nearby tubes began to close. In the distance she heard a man yell, "I fucking hate that!" She correctly assumed it was someone arriving into the station from Zoranth.

A voice from a speaker inside her tube told her they would be departing soon. She was instructed to lie down, and the safety procedures were repeated again. The bed was padded enough to be comfortable, but not enough to ease the tension Celestina felt as the door closed. A dim light went on inside her tube, but a terrible sensation of entrapment began seeping into her mind. The voice came on again, asking if she would like to listen to any music. While she could have picked any type of music, musician, or even relaxing sounds, she declined. Closing her eyes, she made a mental note to someday find out why no one had ever thought to put windows in these horrid canisters.

The tube left the station, quickly accelerated on its way to the building that housed the portal itself, and then slowed as it entered the building. While the ride was smooth, she could still feel the tube being transferred between the rail-like guides and being coupled to other tubes.

A few moments later, the voice piped in again, “Please prepare for safety enclosure and portal transport.” Celestina felt her body clinch up as the inside of the tube began to shrink. A soft, pliable material swelled out from the walls of the tube, formfitting and pressing against everything but her face. It was like being incased in some type of foam. She could press against the material, and it would give way, but the harder she pressed, the less it gave. It was simply a shock absorber for the rapid acceleration on this side of the portal and the rapid braking on the other side of the portal.

Then it began. A momentary tug, as the tube began to move, followed by an explosion of speed. While the ride itself was only a matter of seconds, the experience of moving through the portal was different than anything else in the universe. The sensation of rapid acceleration is suddenly replaced by an eerie feeling of absolute calm. It is like floating, weightless in a vast ocean of tingling sensations. Time itself feels almost indefinable, like you have always existed, yet never been real. A wave of relaxation sweeps across your being, only to be replaced by a nearly indescribable feeling of suction. It is like you are the very last bit of a milkshake at the bottom of a glass that is violently sucked through a straw. Your body feels completely atomized and pulled through a tiny opening. Then, almost as if it had never happened, you feel the tube quickly decelerating.

About eight minutes later, Celestina’s tube door opened, and she quickly climbed out. She managed to refrain from screaming what the man on the Koranth side of the portal had yelled, but she was close. Like most, she hated the experience of portal travel. Employees were moving quickly up and down the walkways, carrying trays of shot glasses, like restaurant servers. As one came close, she grabbed one of the glasses and threw back her head to quickly swallow. The liquid had a slight burning sensation as it went down her throat, but within a minute she felt her heart rate slowing and breathing returning to normal.

Within an hour, she had cleared through security, customs, and the standard biological scans. Her shuttle was waiting and departed for the city of Dorando, the home city of Scharbigot Canchorus, one of the two Zoranth-based Ministers. Their relationship had been rather adversarial, but that was about to change. While she was to be on Zoranth for over a month, the meeting with Scharbigot was very time-sensitive.

Scharbigot Canchorus' office was a rather plain affair, situated on the eighteen floor of a reasonably nice, but affordable building in Dorando. This was to be expected. The religion that Scharbigot followed was a conservative one of self-restraint, hard work, and modesty. He had risen to power partially based on his popularity with those of his own faith, and those of similar faiths. He was seen as a dedicated family man and an advocate for the average citizen. In Celestina's mind, this would be one delicious meeting.

Scharbigot came across his office to greet her as she walked through the door. He was cordial, but weary, as he thought she was nothing more than a crafty snake. He gestured to a set of comfortable chairs and moved towards them. Once they were seated, and appropriate beverages served, he began to talk about some of the Ministry's business, but she interrupted him.

"Minister Canchorus, I have some information of a personal nature that I need to share with you. You will want to turn off any recording or monitoring devices," she stated bluntly.

He looked perplexed, but tapped a few places on a nearby table, and replied, "Okay, please continue."

She held her face completely emotionless, making sure she didn't smile. "I am sorry to bring you this news, but your son is being held at the Purostinov Justice Processing Center. His execution is scheduled for tomorrow."

For a moment, he hesitated. A look of shock swept across his face, but was quickly replaced with a false calm demeanor. "This is impossible. I had breakfast with my son this morning. He is here on Zoranth, not on Koranth. You must be mistaken."

A sinister smile crept across her face, as she pushed and swiped a device that was strapped to her wrist like a watch. A three-dimensional, holographic image of the head of a young man sprang up above the device. "No, not your legitimate son here on Zoranth, but this one."

Shock spread across his face again, and for a moment he thought that his heart had stopped beating. The image that he was seeing was indeed one of his sons. It just happened to be from another family, a secret family. His religion was quite opposed to more than one wife, as were the laws in practically every country on both planets. He closed his eyes, knowing that he was trapped and realizing that something terrible must have happened to his son.

"Your son attacked another man in a nightclub, and the other man died of his wounds. Your son is scheduled for execution tomorrow," Celestina reported.

While many would have condemned him for having two wives, he loved them both and loved all of his children. This was devastating news. He was a man of power and influence. Perhaps he could use this to change the situation and save his son. Of course, this would mean that his wives would find out about one another, along with the entire world. The media frenzy would be brutal. He would certainly lose his position as Minister, and his reputation would be destroyed. His mind kicked into overdrive, trying to figure out how to deal with everything that was flooding into it all at once.

Celestina let everything soak in for a few moments and then authoritatively offered, "There is a simple way to save your son, your marriages, your position, and your reputation."

"I doubt that. He only has one day." He paused for a moment, letting out a deep sigh, "What can be done?"

She explained, "It is very simple. One of the board members of Purostinov owes me a very, very big favor. I can simply have your son's execution delayed indefinitely. Perhaps, we could even have him transferred to a decent facility for containment."

Scharbigot closed his eyes for a moment, realizing there was absolutely nothing he could do, but trust that Celestina could help. "Please, I'll do anything to save my son. What do you want?"

The sinister smile had left Celestina's face, to be replaced by one of resolute determination and an absolute coldness that sent a shiver down Scharbigot's spine. "You'll receive two proposals that I will present at the next meeting of the Ministry. You will wholeheartedly and enthusiastically support these proposals, along with any other proposals that I present."

He understood what had just happened. She was offering him the life of his son, along with the ability to keep his life from exploding all around him. The cost was very simple and straightforward—he would have to become her pawn.

"My dear Lady Chief Executive Minister," he let out in a long sigh, "you appear to have my soul in your hands, and, with it, my vote."

Chapter 10
Paying Your Debts

Kadamba realized that he was trembling uncontrollably—like every joint in his body was being rattled against itself. His lungs needed oxygen, but each breath came in a terrible staccato fashion that simply rattled his bones even harder. It was hard to believe that he could have any tears left, but they kept flowing.

The meeting with Ocampo Rasmussen was over. In the space of a few minutes, he had decided his own fate. It was a choice of three different deaths. Nothing felt real. As his sobs began to subside, he sat up. He was back in his cell, or box, or whatever it was. The cell had returned to the stacks of other cells. It didn't seem like anyone was watching him. He tried to calm himself and figure out what had just happened.

The perky voice suddenly broke the silence. "Thank you for allowing the Purostinov Justice Processing Center to process you. Please prepare for transport."

Again he watched as the box began to move backwards out of the stacks of cells. As it had before, the box that he was in began changing and shrinking to become shaped exactly like a coffin, forcing Kadamba into a prone position. The transparent end of the box disappeared, and Kadamba simply lay there, accepting his fate. He began crying again as he felt the box shrinking even more tightly around him. Then a strange scent appeared in the air, and Kadamba became unconscious.

He awoke to two male voices. His surroundings were strange, almost feeling like a doctor's office or operating room. As the fog began to lift, he realized that he was tightly strapped down to a narrow table, only slightly wider than his body. His arms were stretched out on extensions that came out from the table. His palms were up, and thin straps tightly held his wrists, elbows, and biceps.

"Good morning," one of the male voices flatly stated. Both men were dressed in a uniform of some type. Their clothing was black and fairly tightfitting. One of the men looked down on Kadamba, trying to analyze and measure what type of person was strapped to the table.

"Seriously, Argosia, you'll owe me even more," the other man asserted. This man seemed colder. His face was slightly chubby, and his eyes seemed to have a malice about them. He stepped over and looked down on Kadamba, letting out a small chuckle. The long scar that stretched across his forehead seemed to mimic his cruel grin.

"We'll see about that," replied the man named Argosia.

Kadamba realized that he was completely naked. The processing center uniform was gone, and he was cold. He let out a shiver.

"You'll appreciate the cold in a few moments," the man with the scar noted coldly. "What did Ocampo tell you was going to happen here?"

Kadamba didn't understand. He looked at the man with obvious confusion on his face.

The man continued, "What did your processing representative tell you would happen when you got here?"

"I don't understand the question," Kadamba replied honestly, "I had three choices. This was my choice."

The man without the scar, Argosia, cut in before Kadamba could say much more, asking, "Did Ocampo explain what would happen when you arrived?"

"No, she said nothing," admitted Kadamba.

Argosia, releasing a long sigh, looked at the man with the scar, who was beginning to laugh. When his laugh subsided, he began talking again. "I told you so. That bitch is one cold-hearted monster. I like her a lot. I think she would skewer half her so-called 'clients" if they'd let her. Of course, she left out a detail or two about what happens when you arrive here. Complete disclosure wouldn't be her style. Actually, I'm not even sure that the Crime Review Committee requires what is about to happen. Ocampo probably just adds it to be cruel."

Argosia looked down at Kadamba, who began to tremble. "Hang on, kid." He reached for something, but the guard with the scar batted his hand away, pointing to the door. Argosia, shaking his head, walked out of the room.

The man with the scar looked down on Kadamba and then suddenly drove his fist into Kadamba's gut. "Sucks to be you, boy that hurt, but this is going to hurt like hell. I know you didn't know this is what would happen, but welcome to the Morphinia Containment Company, Jeorseral Facility—your prison for the next twenty-five years—although I doubt you'll make it six months, shitbag."

The man walked out of the room, leaving Kadamba completely alone. The lights went out, and for a few moments it was pitch black. He realized that the men had been betting on whether he knew what was going to happen next. Ocampo had only told him twenty-five years in prison. He knew whatever was coming would be terrible.

Then a humming noise began, and Kadamba heard something mechanical moving in the room. He let out a scream as the burning sensation hit the inside of his forearm. Looking over, he could see a laser beam burning his arm. The pain was excruciating. He was being branded by the laser. It moved down his left arm, as if it was writing something. The smell of his own burning flesh hit him. He began to heave in between his own screams, but there was nothing left in his stomach.

It went dark again, and Kadamba cried out in agony. He had never felt anything so painful in his life. The smell was terrible. He felt himself begin to sob again. Then the room lit up again as the laser burned into his right inside forearm. Kadamba released another wail. He tried to fight the straps that held his body but couldn't move. He could only screech in pain, until he passed out again.

When Kadamba awoke, it was dark. Not pitch black, but still dark. He realized he wasn't strapped down. His body was on something soft, or at least, slightly soft, like a bed. For a split second, he began to think that he was waking from a nightmare. Certainly, he must be in his own bed. As he sat up, he realized his arms felt like they were on fire. The memory of the branding came flooding back. He was in prison, obviously somewhere in Jeorseral, located thousands and thousands of miles from Stujorkian City in another country.

He was in a cell. It was much bigger than the one at the Purostinov Justice Processing Center. It must have been ten feet by eight feet, and it was obvious that he could stand up, which he did. One end of the cell appeared to have an open door, so he walked towards it. The force field covering the doorway sizzled when he hit it, sending a mild shock through his body. He sat down on the bed and tried to gingerly touch the burned places on his arms, but they were too tender. Kadamba realized there was a blanket on the bed. He lay down, covered himself with the blanket, and began to softly cry. The only thing he could think was why he didn't pick the trial and death. Maybe it would have been better.

Ka opened his eyes. He was back at Schmarlo's Landing, but completely alone. There was no one anywhere that he could see. He looked down. His arms weren't burnt. He began walking around. This was the first time he had seen the Landing without at least a hundred people here. He walked to the area that was popular with the teenagers. The silence was almost deafening. He could hear each of his own footsteps. The food vendor carts were empty. No food.

Then he thought he heard a cough, or maybe it was a sniffle. He couldn't place where it came from. Then it happened again, this time, a little louder. Ka began walking, then jogging. Hearing it again, he began running in the direction from which he was sure it was coming.

The buzzing sound awoke Kadamba, and he bolted straight up in his bed. It had been a dream. He wasn't on Schmarlo's Landing. He was in prison. The pain in his arms was nearly unbearable. He pushed back the tears, knowing he had to get a grip on what was happening. He looked around. The cell was absolutely barren, except for a single, neatly folded, red garment on the floor.

It was like the prison uniform, except that it was short-legged and short-sleeved. It didn't matter. Kadamba felt exposed. He figured at least one person had walked by the cell, and he didn't want to be naked anymore. He stuck his feet through the hole in the back, and similar to the justice center uniform, the back closed itself, and the uniform shrunk to a snug fit. Reaching around, he felt a little button at the top of the closure. He immediately thought about the pole that attached to the prison uniforms at the Purostinov Justice Processing Center that enabled the guards to move him around like livestock of some kind. He touched the button and was relieved when the back simply opened. He touched the bottom of the closure, and the opening resealed itself. Maybe, just maybe, he would not be led around on the end of pole.

Suddenly he felt a surge of current running through his body. He fell to the ground unable to control his muscles. It hurt, but it was over quickly. In the doorway was the guard with the scar on his forehead from the branding room. He looked down at Kadamba with a look of contempt on his face.

"This is going to be hell. Why didn't you take the trial and death?" the man coldly inquired of Kadamba.

Kadamba just looked at him. He knew it was probably a rhetorical question, so he did not answer. The guard simply shook his head back and forth, and commanded Kadamba to get on his feet. The guard looked around the room and ordered the bed to retract. It dematerialized into the wall. He explained to Kadamba that this was an old prison. It had been upgraded to more modern cells, with bed, toilet, sink, and shower facilities that were voice-activated, but it wasn't a truly "modern" facility. This was an actual room, built as part of the building. Newer facilities had mobile cells that were often stacked thirty to forty high. This building reached only three levels.

He ordered Kadamba to follow him. As he stepped out of the cell, Kadamba saw that he was on the second story of a long building. Prison cells lined each row of the building, with a walkway in front of the entrances of the second and third levels. It seemed there were about two hundred and fifty cells. Other prisoners were milling around. Some on the various walkways. Some in the open area below. On the bottom level were some benches, chairs, and tables. As the guard with the scar was showing him the cafeteria, a whistle blew.

"That's the signal for you prisoners to go to the playpen," the guard explained, chuckling again.

"What's that?" asked Kadamba.

"Someone somewhere decided that all prisoners deserve a little time outside. The playpen is where you get it, but this isn't going to be someplace you enjoy," disclosed the guard, his scar on his forehead seeming to share the same evil grin as his teeth.

They walked outside into a large open area. Kadamba could see that a number of similar buildings were set in a pattern around a large, fenced-in, open area. The area had some sport fields set up, some weights, tables, chairs, and benches. It was all concrete without a single plant in view. It was a dismal place. Everything seemed to be the same color. The men from his building had fanned out. Some of them eagerly joined in games while some walked around, and others were grouped together talking.

The guard walked him to a corner of the yard, where three men were sitting on a couple of benches. "Okay, scumbag," the guard declared, "this is my one favor for you. These are the scumbags you are going to end up with." He looked at them and walked away.

Kadamba sat down silently with the men. They all seemed frightened and reserved. All of them were sitting with their arms crossed. Kadamba had noticed that some, but not all the prisoners throughout the facility, had been branded. He wondered if these three were or not.

"Name's . . . name's . . . Double-Up," said one of the men, with an obvious stutter. His hair was red and wildly curly. "That's . . . That's . . . Greasy and Two-Finger." Greasy had hair that stuck to his head. It was thin and just looked dirty. Two-Finger was missing two fingers on his left hand. "You . . . you . . . might not make . . . make . . . it here too . . . too . . . long."

"Don't be so negative," piped Greasy, "This place a bitch without being scared shitless by the first people you talk too."

Two-Fingers sat with his head rocking back and forth. Kadamba looked at him, expecting him to say something.

"He ain't got no tongue no more," Greasy explained, "Jackos the Giant ripped it out." Greasy looked out into the yard, and Kadamba followed his eyes. A huge man in a prisoner's uniform was walking in their direction. Kadamba knew at once that that this was Jackos the Giant. This man was massive. He had a cold, fierce look in his eyes and was staring directly at Kadamba.

"Nah . . . Nah . . . You . . . You . . . ain't gonna make . . . make . . . it . . . it . . . here . . . " stuttered Double-Up.

"He got a chance man. He just a kid," Greasy offered.

"Nah . . . Nah . . . what . . . what . . . you done boy . . . "

"Seriously. Shut up, Double-Up. What he's saying is we can't protect you. We're the freaks. The scum. That guard throwed you with us, cause we's the worst. In prison, the ones who hurt kids or done sex crimes, they be the lowest of the low. The only reason we alive cause the prison make money on each of us. As long as we alive, we profit to them, but it don't matter how we live."

Kadamba hadn't even begun to think about the prison pecking order when he was choosing his fate, with his arms strapped to a table and Ocampo "processing" him through the "justice" system. But the closer that Jackos got to him, the more he realized that he was probably on the bottom, and this beast of a man was probably going to hurt him.

Jackos stopped about five feet from them. Kadamba could hear the air going in and out of the man's sizable lungs. The man's hands were gigantic. If he balled them into a fist, they would probably be about as big as Kadamba's head. He was a terrifying sight, and it was more than apparent that Double-Up, Greasy, and Two-Fingers were frightened.

"I see you little runts got yourself a new freak friend," Jackos announced, "Stand up! I need a look."

Kadamba stood up. He realized that he was shaking a little, but he tried to look Jackos in the eyes. If there is such a thing as a man without a soul, Jackos was it. Beyond being huge, the man exuded hate, cruelty, and perhaps pure evil. In those eyes, Kadamba saw a void, and it was truly terrifying. A slow, cruel smile began to spread across Jackos' face. A deep, low rumbling laugh began to emanate from him.

"You're a cute little flower, and that's going to work perfect for the business you and I gots to have," declared Jackos.

"I don't know you," Kadamba stated, trying to sound tough, but his voice cracked and was unsteady. "We don't have any business together. Leave me alone."

The laugh that burst forth from Jackos' lungs was enormous. Everyone in the playpen, and probably everybody in the buildings, could hear him. It was a cruel laugh, and Kadamba knew that this wasn't going to end well.

"You new here, and don't know shit. Don't know nothing. You and I got business. You owe me lots of money," Jackos responded.

"How can I owe you money if I don't even know you?" questioned Kadamba, the fear making his voice sound weak.

"You owe me 2,160 Konnary," Jackos informed him.

Kadamba just looked at him. The cruel smile on Jackos' face got wider and wider.

"I don't understand," muttered Kadamba, the fear continuing to grow inside of him.

"Hmm . . . Heard you might be a little businessman," began Jackos, with a smile. "Maybe you just a flower, but I told you, you owe me 2,160 Konnary. Didn't you understand? Doc Z always gets his."

"What are you talking about?" Kadamba felt a panic setting in. He had been taken into custody with the rath. It suddenly dawned on him that the thugs at the table in Warwon's Deli, in the sub-city, had said the same thing: "Doctor Z always gets his."

"Little Flower, since you seem so young and dumb, I'll explain," Jackos continued. "Doctor Z say you owe him 2,160 Konnery. Even though you in here and your supply be gone, you still owe. Since I am here, Doctor Z has me pay the 2,160 you owe. You good with Doctor Z now, but now you owe me."

"No, no, no this can't be. I don't have any money. I can't possibly pay you," replied Kadamba, feeling trapped and completely out of control.

Jackos let out another terribly loud, roaring guffaw and then told Kadamba, "I know you don't got no money, but we have business and you owe. We get five for every time you do a service. I keep four as my management and protection fee, and one Konnary goes towards your debt. You cute. You young. You fresh. You gonna get this paid off."

Jackos turned and walked away, laughing to himself. Kadamba looked back at the three men. They still seemed to be shaking, and none would look at him.

"Lords of the Fourth System! There ain't no fucking way that I am doing that. Screw this," declared Kadamba once he understood what Jackos intended to do with him.

Rage boiled up in Kadamba, and he began marching towards the other side of the yard, where Jackos had headed. Part way there, another prisoner stepped directly in Kadamba's path. Kadamba changed course, but the man shadowed his movement, cutting him off. Kadamba stopped. He really didn't know what to do. The momentary flash of ire had totally evaporated, and now he realized how scared he really was. He turned around, and another man struck him hard in the stomach with his fist. Kadamba doubled over in pain, as a third man kicked him in the side, sending him tumbling to the ground.

Before he could react, all three men were kicking him. He balled up, as the blows landed. He heard the men hurling insults at him, calling him "baby killer," "child murderer," and a host of other names. They had only landed a few solid blows when Kadamba felt the surge of current through his uniform. His muscles contracted hard and began to spasm. The pain was intense, but the kicking had stopped.

When the current subsided, Kadamba could see that the three men who had attacked were on the ground, along with a few other prisoners nearby. All of them had obviously been shocked too. A guard stood nearby, shaking his head. Grabbing Kadamba's arm, he forced him to walk back to Double-Up, Greasy, and Two-Fingers. The guard pushed him on the bench. For a few moments, Kadamba was able to sit, and then he fell to the ground.

Chapter 11
The First Move

Tomar Donovackia smiled. It was likely a very honest smile, as the board members sitting around his board table were still quite rattled from witnessing Greylorent Lamrainkia getting slaughtered in front of them the day before. Tomar had breakfast served before he had arrived although only a few of the board members seemed to have any appetite.

"My dear board members, let us proceed from where we were yesterday," began Tomar, as he brought up a three-dimensional representation of the galaxy. He then tapped the podium, and all the pieces of the galaxy went dim, except for the known inhabitable planets. Each planet was color-coded according to the Corporation that held the license to "develop" it. The colors were scattered about, with some Corporations having a few more than others.

"As I began to explain yesterday, we have too long lived in a world dominated by assumptions put in place before our parents or even grandparents were born. We have long assumed that having Eleven Corporations was simply the right, proper, or blessed way to live. We have placed our view of the Eleven and how the Ministry regulates the Eleven, above common sense, and above business sense, and, my dear board members, we have even put it above the potential profits that could be reaped by looking at EVERYTHING rationally and logically."

The entire board remained silent. A few of them began nodding their heads, either appreciating or, at least, understanding what he had said. There was some truth in it. On more than one occasion, the Ministry had financially bailed out Corporations that would have simply gone bankrupt or been liquated or sold in any other industry. The two worlds of Koranth and Zoranth simply assumed that the Eleven must exist. While there were no laws that mandated Eleven, or forbid discussing an alternative structure, the concept of the Eleven had become embedded in culture and society. In some ways, it was almost like heresy to talk or believe that something else was better. The worlds had simply become complacent that the Eleven simply would not be allowed to fail, and that the Ministry would simply continue with the status quo forever.

"It is time for a change," Tomar continued. "We are again at a point where the Ministry is facing a failing Corporation. The changes that are coming, and should be coming, are radical. We've grown fat and happy, sitting here on our laurels, blindly believing that things won't really change. Stameyerson Corporation is on the brink of failing. The Stameyerson board of directors and the Stameyerson family have run that company into the ground."

Tomar paused for a few moments. It had been many years since a Corporation had reached the brink. The fact that the Stameyerson Corporation was in trouble was not a secret. Every person in the room knew that it was struggling, but to what depths, of course, was not publically known.

"Every one of you sitting here, and every other so-called rational business person, believes the same thing. That is, if things get bad enough at Stameyerson Corporation, the Ministry will rescue it. Let me ask you, why would the board at Stameyerson Corporation bother to change things, to try to rescue their own company? And they aren't trying. A huge infusion of cash and support is bound to come from the Ministry. They don't believe they would be allowed to fail."

Tomar pushed a few more buttons on the podium, and only the planets licensed to Donovackia and Stameyerson Corporations hovered above the table, with Donovackia's in blue and Stameyerson's in yellow. Tomar looked around the table. Every board member was waiting for his next statement. He pushed one more button, and the four yellow planets turned blue.

Wodoval Yipson, one of the newer board members, whom Tomar had put in place, asked, "Chairman, are you suggesting that the Donovackia Corporation purchase Stameyerson?"

"No, I am not suggesting that we purchase it," Tomar responded and then pushed a few more buttons, so a small stack of documents appeared in front of each board member. Tomar paused, so that the members could quickly glance through the papers.

"Chairman, this can't be, can it? Is this even possible?" asked Wodoval.

Tomar smiled widely again. "My excellent board members, we are in an amazingly fortunate position. The Ministry has within its charter, a unique power to intervene in the Eleven. The Donovackia Corporation is very favored by the Ministry. At the next meeting of the Ministry, everything is going to change. The Donovackia Corporation will simply absorb the assets, employees, military, and all licenses of the Stameyerson Corporation. And because we were willing to step up and, in some respects, save Stameyerson, the heavy debt load that Stameyerson carries will be distributed to multiple governments, via the Ministry's authority."

Wodoval Yipson, whom Tomar had brought on board partially because of his brilliant capability regarding corporate finance, was obviously mentally running the numbers. His face went from a studious, focused look to a large grin. He burst out, "Tomar, this will make Donovackia Corporation the largest of the Eleven—I mean—of the Ten! And unless the calculations and assumptions that I'm running through my head are wrong, we will have an unmatched, unheard of cash flow and profit level."

Tomar smiled, and, as the shock of having their assumptions stripped from them faded, the rest of the board began to smile too. They all knew that Tomar was frighteningly ambitious, but this was even more than anyone had guessed. As Tomar looked around the room, he felt enormously satisfied. He knew every member of the board would now support whatever he wanted to do.

"This, my friends, is only one item on the Ministry's agenda," Tomar began again, "and it is only one of the items that will greatly expand the opportunity and profits for all of us."

The board members looked at him with rapt attention. What else was up his sleeve? What could he do to top this?

"Before, I proceed, I should share one additional detail about Stameyerson Corporation. One of their licensed planets has not been visited in almost forty years. The last reconnaissance mission revealed a world that was moving in the direction of globalization. Sadly, they had finally harnessed the atom, but as is too often the case with our human nature, they used it in a global war. Fortunately, the war had just ended when we received the return ship from that last mission."

He continued, "If the experience from other worlds holds true, then this planet's scientific and technological capabilities would have vastly expanded over these last forty years. We need to get a mission underway within two years."

Wodoval Yipson, unable to completely restrain his obvious delight at how this meeting was unfolding, piped in again, "With the new combined cash flow, we may not even need any debt financing to fund a mission. This is all such wonderful news!"

Tomar bought up another set of five planets—all colored orange and interspersed with the now eleven blue-colored planets. All of the board members watched as the orange faded to blue.

"Mr. Wodoval Yipson, I hope I am not disappointing you," remarked Tomar. "Your brilliance in finance will be needed, and we may need some debt financing for this next planetary exploration mission, and/or for the hostile takeover of the Kathor Corporation."

The board members looked stunned again. They had just had their view of the world radically shifted, and now it was being wrenched even further. Kathor Corporation had not only portals and licenses for other planets, which had just changed from orange to blue, but also owned the Kathor side of the Moran-Kathor Portal. Donovackia owned the Moran side. No single Corporation had ever owned both sides of a portal between Koranth and Zoranth. They had been built by joint ventures between Corporations, with one Corporation based on each planet. There was probably some logic in those arrangements, hundreds of years ago, not to allow one Corporation to own both sides, but it was simply one more element of the assumptions that everyone believed about the Eleven and the Ministry.

It seemed almost impossible, but Wodoval's smile grew even wider. "Sir, you are saying that we could be the first Corporation to own both sides of a portal between Koranth and Zoranth?"

"Yes, we would control both sides and a sizable portion of the flow of goods between the two worlds," stated Tomar. "While it will be a most profitable arrangement, I promise you that the Kathor Corporation has something else that we need."

Tomar brought up the two motions, one to assume control of Stameyerson and one to prepare for a hostile takeover of Kathor, for a vote. They were passed with unanimous consent. Even if there had been any reservations about changing the world in a board member's mind, the profits and wealth were just far too tantalizing to oppose—not to mention the compelling incentive offered by the lingering image of Greylorent Lamrainkia's demise.

Just as Tomar moved to adjourn the meeting, Ionia Villegas demanded to be heard. She had long been on the board of directors.

Her family's wealth stretched back generations. Tomar didn't see her as a threat, but more of an annoyance. She was a member of the board because of her family's wealth. Ionia was a capable businesswoman in her own right, years ago, when she was more involved. Today, she would simply go along with the majority of the board and spend most of her time and effort on her various social and environmental causes.

Tomar briefly closed his eyes, wondering what little animal or perceived disadvantaged group he was about to be pitched. She would certainly have a sad tale, that was, in his mind, more of a distraction than anything. Would she want money? Would she want him making some speech somewhere?

"My esteemed Chairman," she began, "as we make these moves to becoming the largest Corporation in history, I believe that we have an obligation to the people of Koranth and Zoranth. I have a few pilot programs that I sincerely believe that the Donovackia Corporation should initiate for the greater good of society. If I may have a few moments of the board's time, I would like to present these pilot programs."

Tomar had to physically fight to keep his eyes from rolling backwards. The meeting had taken most of the day, and everyone in the room was ready to move on. The thought of listening to her drone on about anything was more than he could handle.

He put his hand up to stop her from going any further. "Ionia, my respect for you and the accomplishments of your various charities and groups is immense. We have had a long day already. If you have a few small pilot projects that you wish to launch within the Corporation, you have my blessing. Should they have positive success, let us bring those results to the board, and consider, at that time, some greater expansion of the programs."

A visible sense of relief swept the room, and Ionia graciously accepted Tomar's invitation. She would proceed and return to present her programs, should any of them produce positive results.

The meeting was adjourned, and all of the members began to prepare to leave. Wodoval was the first to the door. He appeared eager to get to work on the new direction of the Corporation, but he stopped and turned around. "Chairman, pray tell, what is the name of this planet that we'll be sending a mission to within two years?"

Tomar responded, "The planet's inhabitants call it 'Earth.'"

Chapter 12
Welcome to the Darkness

Kadamba was back in his cell, sitting on his bed. Looking at the bruises on his legs, he also knew there were more on his back and sides. While they had only kicked him for a minute or two, they had certainly done some damage. The doctor at the prison clinic said that he was lucky that there weren't any broken bones or permanent injuries. However, he would be tender for a few days.

None of the guards carried any type of weapon in the playpen or in the cell buildings. Kadamba had seen outside the playpen, past a fence, that guards carried weapons, but wherever there were prisoners, weapons were not allowed. To manage them, each of the guards had the capability to electrically shock all prisoners within a small radius of the guard. The guards' uniforms had controls integrated into them that sent a signal to the prisoners' uniforms. If prisoners happened to be within the radius, they were going to be shocked. That explained why Kadamba, the men beating him, and a couple of other nearby prisoners were all on the ground in the playpen.

Kadamba lay down and pulled the blanket over himself. Every part of his body seemed to hurt. The doctor had given him a mild sedative, and he quickly drifted into unconsciousness.

He realized that there was color all around him again—trees, grass, and shrubs. He was all alone on Schmarlo's Landing. Again, it was completely empty of people and totally silent. Kadamba looked for the bruises and the branding; they were gone. Time seemed to slowly crawl as he walked around. There was no one near the food vendors and no food either, just the carts and kiosks.

Then he heard the sound again—a child sniffling or coughing. He couldn't place from where the sound emanated, but he began jogging, then running, desperate to find the child. Suddenly, he found himself in the playground. Only a few feet away was Alorus—standing, looking at Kadamba, with panic in his eyes. He was holding his throat, as if he were choking. Foam began to slowly seep from the corners of his mouth.

Kadamba ran to him to try and help, but the moment that he reached the child, Alorus fell to the ground. Kadamba dropped to his knees, in a panic. He had to help. Panic and dread began flooding through every vein in Kadamba's body. He didn't know what to do. He screamed, "HELP!" as loudly as he could, but no one came. He screamed again and looked around, hoping for someone, anyone, who could do anything. Then he looked down, and Alorus was gone.

Terror began to set in. He jumped up and began running around the Landing, desperately trying to find the boy. He had to be there, somewhere. There had to be something that he could do to help the child. Suddenly, he thought that he heard him again, and Kadamba ran as fast as he could.

He returned to the playground, and Alorus was standing in the same place as before, looking at Kadamba with an expression of fear and helplessness on his face. This time, the foam pouring out of his mouth was tinted red with blood.

As Kadamba stepped towards Alorus, the boy collapsed to the ground. Kadamba screamed again for help, rushing to the boy. He dropped down and scooped Alorus into his arms. "Please stay with me! Please don't die! I am so sorry. Please stay with me!" When Alorus looked up at him, his body began to convulse. Kadamba could see the fear and alarm in the boy's eyes. "Please don't go! Please don't die!"

A buzzing sound ripped Kadamba back into consciousness. He was covered in sweat and breathing very hard. Ka realized that he was shaking and tried to control it, but just couldn't seem to get it to stop. Feeling his face, he wiped away the tears that were falling from his eyes. Alorus' image was stuck in his mind. There was nothing he could do. Ka knew that he was the lowest of the low, the scum, and he began to think that all the bad things happening to him, and those about to happen, were all things that he deserved.

He pulled himself out of bed, showered, and when the buzzing sound began again, he stepped onto the walkway. All of the prisoners were coming out of their cells, heading to breakfast. He marched along with them, afraid at every step that he would again be knocked to the ground and beaten mercilessly.

For part of the morning, the prisoners were allowed to mill about the building. There were a few guards around, and Kadamba stayed close to one of them as he tried to learn the new world that he was in. He tried to keep the panic at bay. He wasn't sure how he would survive. He did learn there were more than just cells in the building. The bottom floor had a room with a monitor in it and places to sit and watch movies or news or whatever was playing on the monitor. There was another room with old-fashioned paper books and places to sit and read.

A cold dread began to move across Ka's mind. Looking around, he realized that no guards were anywhere near him. He felt a giant hand cover his eyes, as a massive arm wrapped around his throat quickly and tightly. He knew it was Jackos the Giant. He felt himself being picked up and carried somewhere. He wanted to scream but couldn't get any air to come out of his lungs.

Within a few moments, the Giant's grip loosened, and then Ka was dropped onto the floor. He opened his eyes to find that he was in another room. He knew that it had to be in the building, but he had no idea where he was. Scrambling to his feet, he realized there were a number of other prisoners in the room with him, eyeing him with cruelty and hatred. Jackos was smiling viciously at him.

"You ready to start working off your debt, little flower?" asked the massive Jackos.

"No, not like this, I won't. NO!" screamed Kadamba, not sure if he was panicking or getting angry. Jackos simply began to laugh. Kadamba knew that he wasn't getting out of this, but he wasn't ready to give up. "I'll scream if you don't let me out of here. I'll scream so loud every guard in every building will hear me!"

"Little flower, you can scream, but ain't no one coming to help you, even if they hear you," explained Jackos, snickering.

Kadamba knew that the situation was hopeless. Adrenaline began flooding his system. He couldn't run. There was nowhere to run. This room had a true door, not a force field, and the room was full of prisoners glaring at him and laughing at him. Instinct seemed to take over and he felt his hand tighten into a fist as he began to swing at Jackos.

Everything began moving in slow motion. One of Jackos' enormous hands caught his fist, before it got even close to landing. The

Giant's other massive hand quickly wrapped tightly around Kadamba's throat, lifting him into the air. As hard as he could, Kadamba kicked a leg out and brought it back as hard as he could, slamming into Jackos' thigh. Jackos barely grunted and then emitted a sarcastic, "Ouch."

The hand that had grabbed Kadamba's fist was now coming at Kadamba's face. The pain was excruciating. Kadamba flew backwards, landing on the ground. Jackos stood there, peering at him, as a wicked smile spread across his huge face.

"Training time, my little flower," Jackos informed Kadamba and then looked around the room, "Okay, boys, time for him to start paying off his debt."

Kadamba fought back, kicking and thrashing, as hard as he could, as the men began to attack him. They managed to rip his prison uniform off, but he wouldn't yield. The harder he fought, the harder they hit and kicked him. Eventually, they got the better of him, held him down, and subjected him to what they wanted. Ka was barely conscious when they were all done with him.

What happened next was almost more humiliating and degrading than the attack itself. The medical staff at the prison's clinic was completely devoid of any compassion. There was no acknowledgement that he had been victimized. He was treated as if he had been a willing participant in his own gang rape.

Back in his cell that evening, Kadamba was trembling. He couldn't control it. His world was spinning even more out of control. A darkness was beginning to grip him, with icy claws. He could almost visualize the emotions that were beginning to overwhelm him. It was like standing alone in a dimly lit forest. The black mist of self-hatred, mixed with depression and anxiety, moved of its own accord through the trees, coming for him, trying to find its way to overtake him. Each direction he moved to avoid the blackness, allowed it to get closer, until finally it overtook him, pushing itself into his lungs to stifle his breathing, blinding and burning his eyes, and wrapping him in a panic and pain that he simply couldn't escape.

"Little flower," whispered a voice that he recognized and feared.

Kadamba opened his eyes to see Jackos the Giant's enormous shape filling the opening of the doorway to his cell. His eyes seemed to peer into Kadamba, making him feel naked and exposed. "Go away!"

"You did good today, Little Flower," Jackos asserted.

"Get away from me!"

"You and me, we partners, and you have a debt to pay," the giant told him.

Kadamba pulled his knees to his chest, as he sat on the bed, alternating between glaring at Jackos and looking away in fear. Pulling his legs tight made many of the bruises hurt even more. The inside of his arms still burned from the branding. Jackos chuckled as he watched Kadamba struggle. He just stood there, staring with a wicked smile on his face. "Business was good today. You knocked seven Konnary off what you owe me. Heal up. I give you a few days. Next time, maybe you decide not to fight so much."

"Fuck you," replied Kadamba.

Jackos began to chuckle. "I'm not the one getting fucked."

"I'm not an animal! You can't do this!" cried Kadamba.

Jackos stepped into his cell and dropped to one knee in front of Kadamba. His eyes were full of malice and hatred. Before Kadamba could react, one of those huge hands caught Kadamba's neck, twisting him and forcing his head to the mattress. Jackos brought his face close to Kadamba's. The stench of his breath was rancid, and Kadamba could feel the air hitting his cheek each time Jackos exhaled. "If you was an animal, I'd treat you better."

Long after Jackos left, Kadamba didn't move. He just remained motionless, lying on the bed. The darkness began seeping back into his mind, pushing itself into the few corners that Kadamba tried to protect. He eventually stopped struggling. He deserved this. He probably wouldn't make it long and figured the misery of his life was not going to stop. Even through the physical pain and darkness creeping through his mind, he could still feel one emotion more than any other—guilt. Here, in this prison, he would die, and then his soul would descend into an even worse hell. He deserved it all.

The lights in the prison went dim. Night had come, but Kadamba still barely moved. Eventually, he pulled the blanket over himself and curled into a ball. It hurt. Everything hurt. As the hours ticked on, sleep was not his friend.

The next day was a fog. He knew he was walking from place to place. The cafeteria. The playpen. His cell. Nothing was real. The few bites of food he put in his mouth didn't have any taste. The words people said to him didn't make any sense. Reality was there, but it seemed just out of reach. As night came again, he waited. The darkness invaded deeper and deeper. He could feel it flow through his veins, invading every inch of his body.

His eyes were still open when the morning buzzer shrilled. The fog was deeper. Kadamba could see those around him, but they seemed to be far away, as if he was peering down a tunnel. He knew that he had left his cell, but didn't know where he had gone. Or had he even left his cell? He looked at the bruises and branding. He knew that they hurt, but was it him that hurt, or simply a vision of him that hurt? He wasn't sure, but it didn't matter. Night came again.

Once again, Kadamba realized that there was color all around him. There were trees, grass, and shrubs. Was this reality? Was all this real? He was all alone again in Schmarlo's Landing. He knew he had been here before. Where was the creeping darkness?

Suddenly, he heard the cry. He broke into a sprint and ran straight to the playground. Alorus was standing there, but there was no foam coming from his mouth. He just stared at Kadamba.

"Do you know what you did to me?" asked the boy.

Kadamba took a few steps towards the boy and fell to his knees, sobbing and trying to get the words to form.

"Why did you kill me, Ka?"

"I'm so sorry," Kadamba cried out, "Please don't die! Please stay with me. I am so sorry! Forgive me. Please, please forgive me."

The child simply looked at Kadamba. He wasn't saying anything, as a trickle of blood began flowing from his mouth.

"No!" Kadamba cried out, "Please no! Don't die again. I'm sorry!" He dropped his face into his hands. He kept crying. His hands became wet from the tears that flowed. He began to beg for forgiveness again and looked up, but the boy was gone. He could feel the tears beginning to form again and began to drop his face to his hands, but stopped in horror. His hands were covered in blood.

The shrill morning buzzer ripped him back to consciousness in his cell. He was shaking again. A guard was standing at the doorway. "You have to come out of your cell today. You have to eat."

Kadamba followed him to the cafeteria and managed to eat a little bit. It was flavorless, but he ate anyway. The guard walked him back to the open, three-level area that served as a common area, and put Kadamba in a chair.

Kadamba looked at the cells. He looked at the men. He knew he was alive but wondered if this wasn't actually hell. His body hurt, but he ignored the physical pain. It hurt more inside, deep inside. He couldn't take it. He looked at his hands again. He wasn't sure, but maybe there were bloodstains on them. He looked up, and not that far away stood the Giant. A strange clarity came into Kadamba's mind. It was like he was having a vision. Jackos was holding him high above his head, like a weightlifter who had snatched up a huge barbell. Rage was painted across the Giant's face, and he yelled as he forcefully pulled the body of Kadamba from its height, dropping one of his knees out to slam into Kadamba's body.

Kadamba understood the vision. Jackos was here to help him end his own misery. Jackos could take his life, with almost no effort. He was a beast. He was a monster. All Kadamba had to do was to enrage the beast, and then he could die. It would all be over soon.

He felt himself come out of the chair and break into a sprint. The Giant's back was turned. Kadamba focused on the small of his back, leaping into the air, and landing both feet as hard as he could into Jackos' spine. Jackos fell forward, stumbling to keep his feet. He bellowed a mighty roar into the air, as he spun around, his eyes on fire with rage and hate.

Kadamba bounced himself back onto his feet and charged at the beast, diving to tackle him as hard as he could. He stopped in midair, as the Giant simply caught him with one hand on his shoulder and one around his neck. With every ounce of strength that he had, Kadamba pulled both legs upward and struck out as hard as he could into Jackos' groin. The beast bellowed again as pain washed across his face, but was rapidly followed by a rage Kadamba had never seen. Suddenly he found himself above Jackos. His vision was true. Jackos would break him across his knee, and everything would be over.

The air went rushing past Kadamba's face, but he wasn't moving downward. As his body spun through the air, he realized that Jackos had thrown him. He saw the chairs stacked like dominos against the wall, where he knew was going to hit. The stack erupted and scattered as Kadamba slammed into them.

Jackos took two steps towards the Kadamba but fell to the floor before reaching him. Jackos, and the men around him, convulsed and shook on the floor as the current flowed through them. Current flowed through Kadamba too, but he didn't feel it. He didn't feel a thing.

Chapter 13
Turkey on the Beach

Tim Parnell was at the Cairbre's dinner table for the fifth Sunday in a row. Joanna and he had been dating now for over six months, and the chemistry was electric between the two of them. Both Dylan and Bjorn were happy to see their mom so relaxed and enjoying herself. For some kids, it is hard to see a parent happy with someone other than their birth parent, but for Dylan and Bjorn, life was not all white picket fences.

Dylan knew his father's name, but he hadn't ever met him. His mom had met him in a coffee shop where she worked when she was in college. He was a little bit older than her, and already out of college. When she found out that he was married and that she was nothing but a fling, she vowed never to have anything to do with him again. When she discovered that she was pregnant, she changed schools and moved across the country.

Dylan barely remembered Bjorn's dad. He was a small child when Joanna started dating the guy. He was from Sweden and apparently had swept Joanna off her feet. He lived with them for a few years, and Joanna gave birth to Bjorn during that time. Dylan had vague memories of the fights before he left. The man wanted to travel the world and thought Joanna should go with him. He argued that the brats could just be left with Joanna's mother. Of course, he eventually took off, and the last anyone heard was that he had been kicked to death by an ostrich somewhere in Africa.

After the Swede bailed on them, Joanna's mother had described the situation in the old woman's typical, crusty manner. "Your man-picker's done busted." Grandma was pretty accurate. Joanna dated a few more men, but nothing seemed to click until she met Tim. It had only been six months, but he seemed to be a wonderful guy, and the boys liked him too.

After they cleared the dinner dishes, Tim high-fived the boys, telling them he would see them soon. He was heading to Seattle to close a deal for his company. He was a salesman or something for some trendy, corporate social media company. The boys didn't totally understand what he or the company did, but it sounded pretty cool. Plus, he seemed not to worry too much about money.

Dylan poked his head around the corner and saw exactly what he thought those noises were. His mom and Tim were locked in what was obviously a very passionate kiss. "Gross" was the first thought that flashed through Dylan's mind, as he headed back into the kitchen to help Bjorn with the dishes. Watching your mom kiss someone was awkward at best, but he was happy she had found a decent guy that was so good to him and Bjorn. Truthfully, he was a little curious. He'd kissed the girlfriend that he had during the last school year, but it wasn't anything like the kiss that he had just seen.

"Bjorn and Dylan," called Joanna after Tim left, "could you guys come in here, please?"

The boys looked at each other with a knowing glance. That was mom's "let's have a talk" voice, which usually ended with additional chores, or some other, less-than-thrilling impact on their lives. She had them sit on the sofa and looked at them for a few moments.

"So what do you boys think of Tim?" she asked.

"He seems pretty cool," Bjorn blurted out, happy that the first words out of her mouth were not about something she needed help with around the house.

"Dylan?"

"Mom, he seems like a pretty nice guy."

"I agree with you both. He is a nice guy, and he treats us all very well. He's just made us an offer that I want to talk with you guys about," she shared and then paused looking at the boys' faces.

Dylan first thought was that, of course, he had wanted to move in, or something even more permanent, but something was very coy about the way his mom was approaching this. He could tell that she seemed genuinely excited about something, and was trying to pop some big surprise on them.

"Okay, Mom! What is it?" Bjorn asked impatiently.

"This almost seems too real to be true, but … Tim has a condo near Playa del Carmen, and he's asked us to spend Thanksgiving in Mexico with him!"

Both boys' eyes grew wide, and they eagerly listened and discussed plans for the trip. They would both have to miss a couple days of school, but they both absolutely agreed that it would be worth it.

Chapter 14
Cogs in the Machine

Captain Tristanidad Luciano stood a few feet away from the Colonel's office for a moment, lost in his thoughts. He knew he should say something to the Colonel. It was the right thing to do. In many ways, it would also cover his own ass. As the Captain of the Elite Forces of the Donovackia Corporation's military, he could never have anyone say that he suspected something, but did nothing.

"Come in, Captain," the Colonel declared, without even lifting his eyes from his desk. Captain Luciano walked into the office and crisply saluted.

"At ease, Captain, please sit down."

"Thank you, sir. May I please close the door, sir?"

The Colonel agreed and bid the Captain to sit again. Colonel Jecamiah Agastya had expected to see the Captain this morning. The morning's command briefing memo had mentioned gearing up for the next planetary exploration mission. It had been over a decade since Donovackia Corporation had launched a mission, and the Captain would certainly be excited, as he would be assembling and training part of the mission team. However, there was a troubled look on his face.

"Sir, may I speak off the record and in confidence with you?" asked Captain Luciano.

"Captain, please, what troubles you?" replied the Colonel.

"Well, you know that I help as an instructor at the Gorgano Martial Arts Academy when my time allows it."

"Yes, I've seen your 11-year-old son compete. He'll be kicking your butt within a few years," noted the Colonel.

Both men laughed. It was probably true. The kid was good, but concern was apparent in the Captain's eyes.

"Tristanidad, what is it you want to talk about?" inquired Colonel Agastya.

"I'm not sure exactly how to say this or even bring this up," began the Captain. "One of the students, and one of my son's friends, is Mungo Chaldea, the General's son. Lately, he's been having some serious trouble with some of the kids his age, at school. His mom recently approached me. She wouldn't say much, other than there was some trouble at home. She asked me to just be a friend to the boy. She told me he needed a strong, stable, but compassionate, male influence in the boy's life."

"I can certainly see why she would turn to you," affirmed Colonel Agastya. "You're a good man, and a fine role model. I'm sure you would be there for the boy regardless of whether or not Camdrin Chaldea had approached you about her son or not."

"Well, sir, that's part of the problem." The Captain hesitated and then decided to continue, "I know there is some secret or secrets that this family is concealing. I don't mean to pry into others' business. It's just . . . I pulled Mungo aside to just let him know that he had a friend if he needed it. Tears flowed from his eyes like a river. He doesn't say much. He's come over to play with my son, and a few times, he has crawled into my arms and just cried. Camdrin has become more and more evasive as I try to talk to her. I don't know what to do. He's a good kid, but something is going on."

The Colonel released a deep breath. "Tristanidad, I know more than I can say. Please understand this. The boy obviously needs a friend, right now. I don't believe that he is in any danger. He's not being abused. Right now, he just needs a friend. Please just let him spend as much time as possible with your family. It may be important right now for Mungo to have an emotionally safe place, with a family that functions and to have as much love as yours does. You're a good man for stepping up, but please, don't ask any more questions. The issue hopefully will be resolved for the Chaldea family soon."

The Colonel maintained his look of calm and compassion as he talked to the Captain, but inside he could feel the frustration rising. How the hell did the General get to his station in life? That pompous, sexist, self-righteous, judgmental idiot should not be in command. The Colonel knew who the General really was, and what he was really like. He was rotten to the core. The Chaldea family absolutely loved the illusion of the perfect General and his perfect family. He portrayed the perfection well, but every bit of it was a façade hiding the truth. This wasn't the first time there was an issue, and he was afraid it wouldn't be the last.

Colonel Jecamiah Agastya was fond of the young Captain. It really wasn't a surprise that they were having this conversation. They were both military men. Both had been tracked young into command school and elevated at young ages. Colonel Agastya had recognized years ago that Captain Luciano was a man of depth. He was an outstanding officer, an excellent leader, and amazingly cool under pressure. However, unlike so many who were drawn to the military, he was also a man of deep and complex emotion. He hadn't become cold and emotionally stunted, like so many others in the military. It was about fourteen years ago, when they were both younger and in more forward-combat roles, that he watched Luciano heading down a path he had already tread. While the Colonel couldn't roll back time and undo his own regret, he had kept Captain Luciano from heading down the same path.

Tristanidad Luciano had been madly in love. Kalila was a wonderful young woman, full of life and as madly in love with Tristanidad as he was in love with her. When Luciano was scheduled to be deployed on a very dangerous mission, he made the decision to end their relationship. He simply couldn't ask the woman that he loved to sit by and wait for a potential call about his death. Better that he set her free then, than have her lose him later.

The night before he planned to let her go, he confided his plans with his superior officer, Jecamiah Agastya. Agastya had done the exact same thing, five years before that, and regretted every moment of it since. The woman he loved with every ounce of his being was gone, and he was afraid that he would never be able to fall in love again. Agastya convinced Luciano not to end the relationship. If they were truly in love, then they should be together. Their union had gone on to produce three wonderful children and, in so many ways, had made Luciano a better man.

The Colonel's secretary interrupted the men, reminding them that the General's briefing was in five minutes. Both officers headed towards the Executive Command Briefing Room with anticipation, joining the other eighteen senior command officers for what was sure to be the announcement of the initial orders to begin preparations for the next planetary exploration mission.

The room was arranged like a small auditorium. Three long, elegant tables sat, one terraced above the one before it. In the front of the room was a podium, where General Swinton Chaldea stood, waiting for the officers to assemble.

"Members of the Donovackia Corporation Military Command Staff, welcome on this excellent day," began the General. "While we have significant, ongoing business to attend to, let me start with the news that all of you already know, as I issued it in this morning's briefing memo. The Donovackia board of directors has initiated plans for the next planetary exploration mission. Ladies and gentlemen, we have two years to prepare for this mission."

A rumble went through the officers, along with questioning looks and perplexed gestures. One of the other officers expressed the sentiment in the room. "General, sir, two years? Every mission I have ever heard of takes at least three to five years of planning. The Donovackia Corporation doesn't even have a spaceship under construction, and that takes a minimum of three years to build. Could you please clarify and provide details on how this can possibly proceed on a two-year timeline?"

"Excellent question, and I am afraid I don't have a clear answer for you," replied General Chaldea. "I was briefed before this meeting by Chairman Donovackia, himself. He has assured me that there will be a ship ready for us. I do not know how, but he ordered us to initiate planning and preparation.

"I do know this much. It will be a twelve-man, standard crew, with an estimated travel time of two to three years. The return vessel will also be a standard, unmanned vessel, bringing back only artifacts and crew reports.

"For the twelve-man crew, the Corporation will be supplying six non-military crew members. There will be two global logistics and trade experts. Their job will be to analyze the planet's capability to globally move goods around the planet. There will be two infrastructure and technology experts. They will focus on understanding the planet's technology, and should the planet be close to ready for development, they will work with the other experts to identify a location that has sufficient electrical power for a portal and access to global trade routes. The final two will both be experts on identifying and validating Transprophetics.

"Our military will supply six crew members. Obviously, we will supply the crew commander and vice-commander. Ultimately, the six men we supply will serve as security for the experts. Each soldier will be assigned to one of the experts.

"This is a standard mission. The ship will be landed covertly on the planet, and the return vessel hidden. The transport ship will be destroyed, and the crew will deploy across the planet to complete their various tasks and analyses. In six months' time, they will regroup at the hidden return vessel, complete their final reports, load the return vessel with artifacts and reports, and send it home.

"As everyone in this room knows, once that ship leaves our solar system, they are on their own. There is no two-way communication capability once they break the light barrier. They are on their own, and they will be stranded on that planet."

The meeting continued as all military meetings do, with roles, tasks, and responsibilities assigned and distributed. The Donovackia Military Command was excellent at doing its job, even if Colonel Agastya had significant reservations about the character and capability of the General. Those issues could be managed and dealt with if needed. The meeting was adjourned, with the Donovackia Military machine energized for this major undertaking.

As he walked back into his palatial office, the General waved his hand, and the doorway disappeared, sealing the man in privacy. He walked to the bookshelf behind his desk. It was made of multiple woods, highly crafted and handsome. He'd commissioned the work himself and worked closely with the artisans as they crafted it. He ran both hands across specific places on two different shelves. Two other shelves shifted, and a secret compartment was revealed.

General Swinton Chaldea pulled one of the four bottles from the opening and examined the contents. It looked like water. He opened the bottle, holding it to his nose and breathing deeply. It barely smelled at all. Did he love this, or did he hate this? He wondered why someone had ever thought to ferment the bulbous roots of the portano plant and drink it. He chuckled. It really didn't matter. This was his secret friend. It helped him get through the day.

Of course, it had been a challenge last year when his wife had discovered his secret. As if it made any difference in the world that he had been drinking a little rodka each day. He could afford it. She didn't need to know, and no one else needed to know either. It wasn't a problem. She'd made him take a personal two-week "vacation" to a so-called "spa." He played the game, pretending that he had a problem and would work to never touch it again.

Chapter 15
Dynasty of Power

Celestina ran her hand across Tomar's chest. He let out a small moan in his sleep. She found herself drawn passionately to him. He was powerful. His rise to Chairman of one of the Eleven had been meteoric. To command that type of power so quickly was erotic and sensual. He was handsome and well-built, in every aspect. Their desire was mutual and intense. In bed, their time was volcanic. It was rough and even violent at times, but it satisfied each of their deepest sexual needs and desires. During those times, lying in each other's arms in pure bliss and absolute exhaustion, they discovered that each of their lusts was beyond just sexual. They both obsessed about power, wealth, and fame, and shared their secret dreams of their own manifest destiny.

She felt the silky sheets that wrapped around her body, touching her everywhere that she wasn't touching Tomar. She let herself enjoy the sensations. Soft silk. Warm skin. It was so much better than traveling through those damn portals. Only that morning, she had been encased in one of those coffin-like tubes to be blasted back to Koranth for what would be a historic meeting of the Ministry of Interplanetary Corporate Relations. Everything was about to change.

After she arrived, she headed straight to Tomar. She needed his touch. She needed release. She needed to dominate and be dominated. As always, he obliged, as he needed and wanted the same. Of course, she also needed to make sure he was ready. Everything was about to change radically. He assured her that his board of directors was ready to make Donovackia Corporation the largest Corporation in history. His military was already quickly expanding and preparing for the next planetary exploration mission. The confidential information she had supplied about this planet called Earth, held by the Stameyerson Corporation, and the fact that the Kathor Corporation already had a ship under construction was perfect. Everything was underway as planned.

Their other business was going well also. Tomar had a surprise for her. It was almost like he had sat in on her meeting with Doctor Z. They'd been able to make rath a bit more "safe" and reduced the potential near-instant deaths to a quarter of one percent. Moreover, rath was now available in a pure powder form. He was ramping up production as quickly as he could. Within days, they would be able to supply the Ministry with thirty-five times the amount of rath that they were currently supplying. She could begin growing the Ministry's security force into a mighty military, in its own right, within weeks.

She realized Tomar's breathing had changed. Before she could even finish processing the thought, he rolled her onto her back and was inside her. She let out a deep moan, as every bit of air escaped her lungs. His thrusts were rough and deep, driving her into the bed, as he bit into her neck, not hard enough to break the skin, but enough to cause erotic pain. She was overwhelmed at the intensity of the sensations ripping though her body. She barely realized when he lassoed her hand with the silk strap tied to the bedpost. As he tied her other hand to the other bedpost, she knew that he was about to absolutely ravage her. She had done the same to him a few hours before. This was a spectacular way to prepare for tomorrow's meeting.

*****

A few hours before the Ministry's meeting was to start, Celestina released to the media one of the proposals she would bring to a vote that day. Analysts in every form of communication on both planets went into overdrive. Some believed that this new, young Chief Executive Minster was the salvation of a regulatory body that needed an overhaul. Others condemned her for pushing changes on a body that seemed to function so well. Everyone agreed that it was a radical idea to trim the Ministry to three Minsters from five. It didn't matter what audio, visual, or holographic medium that anyone tuned in to, the press coverage was extensive, ongoing, and live.

When the Meeting was called to order, it was a media circus both inside the Ministry's meeting hall and outside. Most pundits had predicted that the motion would fail. At best, Celestina would only garner her uncle's support. Most, mentioning his health and frailty, were surprised that he had even attended this meeting. Debate had been significantly limited, and when the motion was brought to a vote, shock went across both planets. It passed 4-1. Even Celestina was surprised. Merniva Golackick, the other Minster from Zoranth, had voted for the reduction of the Ministry to three Minsters.

As part of the proposal, the Ministry would vote immediately for the three members who would remain as part of the Ministry. After Celestina Wiroviana, Hareold Wiroviana, and Scharbigot Canchorus voted themselves as the three ministers, Merniva Golackick had to be removed by force from the proceedings. She went out screaming that the system was rigged and that she should be one of the three.

Celestina quickly moved into action. The Ministry's rules and guidance documents were amended, and two very significant announcements were made. Effective immediately, the Donovackia Corporation assumed control, and would absorb, the failing Stameyerson Corporation. Additionally, the Donovackia Corporation could begin proceeding with a hostile takeover of the Kathor Corporation. Within hours, the Donovackia military seized control of the assets of the Stameyerson Corporation. Now the Eleven were Ten. Within weeks, it would be Nine.

"My esteemed Minsters," Celestina began as she rose to her feet. "There is one final proposal that I will put to you today as we close this historic meeting. It is one of simple honor; it is a simple symbolic gesture to a grand servant of the people of our planets. Hareold Wiroviana, my uncle, has served his country, his planet, and the Ministry for the whole of his life. While his seat is coming up for election in two years, I move that we make his appointment a lifetime appointment."

The crowd in the official meeting room stood in ovation. It went without saying that Hareold Wiroviana was a respected civil servant, and sadly, it was clear to those who saw him, and those that knew him, that he would be unlikely to be alive in two years. This seemed a befitting honor.

The official paperwork was brought forth. Hareold abstained from the vote, and Celestina and Scharbigot passed the motion. To Scharbigot's eyes, the stack of paper seemed awfully large for such a simple motion, but Celestina claimed that most of the great accomplishments of her uncle were listed and spelled out in the motion, as a testament to the greatness of the man.

Later that evening, Scharbigot would take the time to read the motion in detail. His signature and official seal were on it. It was unquestionably now the rule of law that would stand, unless the Ministry vacated it at a later date, which would never happen. How can a father not do everything he could to save his son's life? As much as he hated Celestina for blackmailing him, he had to admit that she was cunning. Buried deep in the motion was an ascension clause. When Hareold died, his seat, with its lifetime term, would pass to his next of kin. If the next of kin was part of the Ministry, the seats would be folded together, carrying both seats' votes. She had effectively created a monarchy for herself.

Chapter 16
Compassion in the Darkness

"Do you believe in miracles, son?"

Kadamba could hardly make out the face of the person talking to him. As his eyes began to focus and he awoke, he realized that he was back in the prison's medical clinic. He supposed they would accuse him of being a clumsy bird. They certainly wouldn't consider him anything other than a small portion of their profit. Something that simply needed to be fixed up, so that he could be counted when the government paid each month.

"Mr. Vorhoor, can you hear me?" the voice spoke again. This time Kadamba focused. He did know the face. It was one of the many guards that worked at the prison.

What would he want? Was he there to taunt Kadamba for attacking Jackos? The reality of it hit him. He was still in the prison. Jackos hadn't killed him. He stared at his hands. There had to be blood on them. Then he looked at the brand on his left arm. It was two simple words in Lamaratian, the dominant language on Koranth. Maybe others couldn't see the blood on his hands, but they could read those two words, "Child Murderer."

"Kadamba, I need you to listen to me now. I don't have much time," the guard stated.

If Kadamba could have laughed, he would have, but he could feel the darkness quickly creeping through him. Maybe here in the clinic he could finish what Jackos had failed to do. Maybe he would end his misery with a scalpel or inject himself with something. Anything. Anything at all to end this pain and guilt.

Kadamba saw what looked like a gun in the guard's hands. A sense of relief swept over him. He wasn't going to have to try. He looked into the guard's eyes, almost wanting to see the hatred and disgust that this man certainly held for him. It would be the final validation that he deserved to die. But the guard's eyes were wrong. "Doesn't he hate me like everyone else does?" thought Kadamba, as he searched the man's face for signs of contempt or something that would validate why the gun was in his hand.

The injection stung as it went into Kadamba's neck. It wasn't a laser gun or energy blaster, it was a gun-shaped syringe. "Kadamba, this is the only time I can talk to you, so you have to listen, and you have to remember what I tell you. You will not live if you don't."

"I don't want to live" Kadamba responded, as tears began to streak down his cheeks.

The guard looked at Kadamba and let out a knowing sigh. "You're a kid. You screwed up as badly as you possibly could. You have to live with that, but that doesn't mean you have to die. There is always hope. Listen to me now. Do NOT forget what I am saying. I won't talk to you or even acknowledge you, once you are out of the clinic. However, if you stay close to me when you are out of your cell, I can protect you somewhat. Jackos won't do anything if you are near me or another guard. When I'm not there, watch the guards; we have patterns that we walk. If you learn those patterns, you can keep yourself within twenty feet of a guard throughout most of the prison."

"Jackos will simply get me in my room," Kadamba muttered.

"You can be safe in your cell," the guard maintained. "When you go into your cell, place your left hand on the wall and say, 'Seal.' That will make the force-field door close, and only a guard can open it from the outside. Never tell anyone how you learned this or how you do it, as management has decided that this should not be known."

Tears began to well up in Kadamba's eyes again. This was the first moment of compassion that he had experienced since the justice enforcement officer had shot him on Schmarlo's Landing. He tried to get words to form, but his tears choked them off.

The guard put his hand on Kadamba's shoulder. "Son, I can't undo what you have done. You made a horrible mistake. You will have to come to terms with that someday. I may work in a prison, but that doesn't mean that I don't believe in humanity and treating others as human beings. I'll do what I can to help you."

They both saw the medical staff person coming, and the guard's face hardened. It was like he had pulled on a mask. He looked down at Kadamba, giving him a small nod. As he walked away, he rudely let his shoulder bump into the staff person. He could hear the man in the white coat mutter, "Fuckin' asshole," under his breath as he returned to his duties.

"Prisoner Vorhoor," began the medic, "it's a damn miracle that you are alive, much less in as good of shape as you are. What did you think you were, a stupid bird?"

Kadamba could hear the coldness in his voice, as the medic told him how lucky he was. He had only suffered a concussion and a dislocated shoulder. He would need a sling for his arm for a week or so, and his headache would eventually go away. He was scheduled to be in the clinic overnight, and would be returned to the general population the next day.

That night as Kadamba lay in the dark, he realized that something had changed. The creeping darkness didn't seem to have as strong of a life of its own. As a matter of fact, it had subsided some. The guilt and self-hatred were still there, but the blackness that covered him seemed less intense. That guard must have given him some type of powerful antidepressant.

He found himself on Schmarlo's Landing again and immediately began jogging to the playground. As he suspected, Alorus was there, standing and looking at Kadamba with condemning eyes. Kadamba walked up to him and waited.

"Do you know what you did to me?" asked the boy.

"Yes, I do. I am sorry. I would give my life to undo it," Kadamba admitted, as tears began to drip down his face.

"Why did you kill me, Ka?"

"I never meant to kill you. I should have never sold you the rath. I can never say how sorry I really am for what I did."

"But I'm dead, Ka. I don't have anywhere to go."

"You can sit down here with me. I'm not going anywhere either."

The guards at the Morphinia Containment Company were distant. They never really interacted with prisoners, except to keep the peace. The guard who had visited Kadamba kept his word. He barely acknowledged that Kadamba existed. He treated him just like any other prisoner. On rare occasions, they would make eye contact, and Kadamba could see a compassion buried deep under the cold, expressionless mask that the guard wore.

After leaving the clinic, Kadamba focused on the guards' movements. Sure enough, there were specific patterns they walked. It had been carefully choreographed to provide maximum coverage of the population with the fewest number of guards. Kadamba learned to move with the guards, following one for so many paces, and then changing direction to move across the path of another, and then walking towards another. In many ways, it became a game.

Jackos had visited Kadamba a couple of weeks after he left the clinic. He stood outside his cell smirking. He had given Kadamba time to recover from his wounds, and now it was time for business to begin again. Jackos, understanding the guards' patterns too, had timed his visit to give himself ample time to reacquaint his "business partner" to his role in paying back the debt that Jackos had been forced to buy from Doctor Z.

Kadamba watched with an absolutely expressionless face as Jackos smacked into the invisible force-field door. He wanted to laugh but knew that Jackos' anger and rage would grow every day that he couldn't pimp Kadamba out for sexual services. So, he simply curled up on the bed and pretended to sleep while Jackos cursed and threaten him from the walkway outside his door.

Jackos' rage and anger did grow by the day, and Kadamba had to be increasingly careful as he moved about. More than once, Jackos managed to get a hold of Kadamba, but both were shocked before Jackos could drag him off to a more secretive place. Getting shocked hurt, but nothing like what Ka had endured already. As time passed, his wounds healed, the bruises faded, and the brands stopped burning and simply became scars.

Between his past and the well-known rage that Jackos held for him, Kadamba made no friends in prison. Even Double-Up, Greasy, and Two-Fingers were afraid to be near him. The guilt that he carried was so nearly overwhelming at times that he wondered if it was destroying him, but at least he wasn't being physically abused. Isolation is a frightening thing on its own, but sometimes, isolation, when you are surrounded by people, is even worse.

Kadamba endured, not really knowing what his life was about. The only thing that he really had was Alorus. He wasn't going crazy or having hallucinations. He simply carried Alorus with him. He was there in his dreams, both at night and during the day. It wasn't that Alorus kept him company or needed anything; he was simply there.

One day, Kadamba stuck his head out his doorway, ready to duck back and seal it if it wasn't safe. As he looked down the walkway, he saw something that he had never seen before. The guard who had showed him compassion—more than that really—the guard who had saved his life, was walking towards him on the walkway. The truly unusual thing was that the guard was smiling, and the smile widened when he saw Kadamba. As stepped out of his cell, Kadamba didn't know what to think, but the mere act of seeing someone smile towards him was like a light breaking through the darkness. For a brief moment, an emotion that was long-gone reappeared. Kadamba was eager to see another human being.

Time seemed to nearly freeze, as Jackos stepped out of a cell directly behind the smiling guard. Before Kadamba could even register that it was happening, the sharp point of something came bursting forth from the guard's chest. A spray of blood shot out of the guard's mouth as his last breath wheezed from his lungs. Jackos picked up the guard like a rag doll and tossed him over the railing where he landed with a thud on the floor below. The Giant turned and began running towards Kadamba. The force-field door barely closed in time.

Kadamba felt a horrible rage ripping through him, as he stood looking at the grinning, angry giant through the force-field door. It was rage unlike anything that he had ever felt before. It didn't matter that people hated him. He had done something horrible. But this guard was something different. He was a good person. He didn't deserve to die like that. As Jackos began to laugh, Kadamba fell to his knees. The man had died because of Kadamba. He knew that the guard was coming to see him, to tell him something good. Now not only would Kadamba not know what he wanted to say, why he was smiling, but he also had died because of him.

Kadamba was still on the floor when the force-field door opened. It was two guards. They had to pick him up off the floor. He was almost comatose, but he could walk. Were they taking him to feed him to Jackos? He could hear their words, but his mind was too jumbled to process what they were saying, so he just walked with them. They left the building containing Kadamba's cell, walked through the playpen, past another building containing cells, and into a much nicer building than anything that he had seen in a long time. There were offices lining the corridor and more cells.

They pushed Kadamba into one of the cells, and the doorway sealed shut. A monitor appeared on the sidewall, with a perky smiling face. It was that same damn woman from the Purostinov Justice Processing Center. She must get rich doing all these recordings, Kadamba thought, as he slapped her image. "Thank you for your stay at the Morphinia Containment Company. It has been our pleasure to serve you while you served your term of incarceration. Please prepare for transport."

He slapped the wall again. It was infuriating to have this pesky, perky nitwit giving instructions. He looked around the room. Nothing. There wasn't one item in the room other than him. Then a box materialized out of the wall.

"So, here we go again, you smiling bitch!" shouted Kadamba.

"Please remove your clothes and place them in the bin," ordered the recorded voice, as the image of the woman smiled.

Kadamba knew he would be shocked if he didn't comply. He tossed his uniform into the box, and it was gone within seconds. "So, what do you want me to do now?"

Almost on cue, a shower stall and toilet grew out of the wall.

The image of woman began talking again. "You have fifteen minutes to complete all personal needs. Please shower and note that transportation time may be extensive, so please use the facilities before you depart."

Kadamba quickly used the toilet and stepped into the shower. It seemed a little bit odd, as it wasn't as rushed as it had been at the Purostinov Justice Processing Center, and certainly wasn't as degrading as the first time that he had to deal with the perky monitor woman. A warm, but strong air current dried him, and a door in the back of the cell appeared. He stepped through it and realized he was standing in a large bay that was obviously used for deliveries by truck. There was only one truck in the bay. Its flatbed trailer was stacked with large closed tubes that looked like tubes that were used at the portals. One of the tubes was on the ground, with a man laughing beside it.

"I guess they ain't joking. This is for real," he declared, as he motioned for Kadamba to come over to him. "Well, you're in for a new experience. I was surprised to see this particular type of tube loaded on my truck. Generally, these are first-class tubes for the portals."

"Is this for me?" asked Kadamba.

"Well, I guess it probably is," the man replied.

"I can't pay for it."

"Suppose you can't, unless you gotz some money shoved up somewhere. Uh. Hang on a minute." The man climbed into the cab of the truck and came back with a pair of underwear and a t-shirt. "Sorry, this is all I got. Don't seem right just transporting a man buck-naked."

Kadamba thanked the man and put on the clothes. He looked at the tube container. He wasn't too sure; it looked kind of like a coffin.

"Someone wants you transported petty badly although starting way out here ain't too classy. It'll take about five hours for us to get to the Kareenet-Pooshz Portal Complex. I can't tell you how long it will take after that." Then, in a somewhat muted voice, he looked at Kadamba, urging, "Son, don't panic, but quickly get into the tube and close that lid. I'll take it from here."

As Kadamba crawled in and lay down in the tube, he saw what prompted the man to hurry him along. He thanked the man and pulled the lid closed. Inside he experienced a very trapped sensation. He felt the tube being lifted and assumed it was being placed on the truck's trailer. A pleasant voice came on, explaining the safety procedures.

The guard, with a long scar across his forehead came marching up, cursing, as he walked. "Dammit, that just ain't right! Bring that boy back down here. We ain't done with him."

"Sorry sir, once the tube's loaded and locked, it ain't opened until the other side," replied the driver.

"Son of a bitch, you mean that shitbag is going to Zoranth? What in the hell is going on?" demanded the guard.

"Don't rightly know," the man responded, as he climbed into the cab of the truck. "All I do is make the pickups and deliveries. It's a good living, and I sure as shit don't ask too many questions."

The truck pulled out of the bay, went through security, and disappeared as it headed out. The guard with the scar watched for a moment and then stomped back over to the only other guard in sight. "Don't even think I'll be paying you, Argosia. This is crap. His sentence was twenty-five years."

"Well, a bet's a bet. You bet he wouldn't live for more than one year here in prison. You even helped Jackos find a secret place to 'train' the boy. You're a real piece of work, and you owe me," Argosia asserted.

"Fuck you. I don't owe you nothing. I'm heading to the manager. We need to get that little flower back here where he belongs. I didn't even get a piece yet," argued the guard with the scar.

Argosia looked at the man. The scar was bright red, and his eyes were full of hate. Argosia had watched him abuse prisoners, smuggle drugs into the prison, help set up beatings, killings, and prostitution in the prison, and he was sure that he gave Jackos the shank for the latest murder of a guard. The truth was that the man belonged in prison, but he'd never be there. No matter what system of justice is set up, the system usually becomes more important than justice. And sometimes, the system is run by people with their own agendas, and then there isn't any justice at all.

"You know, you belong inside these cells, not guarding them. It's time that I'm done with you, and done with this place," Argosia told him.

"Good. You ain't got the balls for this place, Argosia. You're a flaky, wimp-ass pussy. You ain't got what it takes," asserted the cruel guard.

Argosia watched as the scar exploded into a million pieces, along with the guard's entire skull. Argosia holstered his laser gun. It was a sloppy weapon, but sometimes it just felt good to do the right thing. To actually see something just in an unjust place, and do it with pizazz.

Chapter 17
Truth behind the Mask

The command came for Colonel Jecamiah Agastya to report at once to General Swinton Chaldea's office. Rather than simply using any of the advanced communication available, the General had sent his secretary running through the hallways of the vast command center building. The Colonel shook his head, as the out-of-breath junior officer worked to get air into her lungs. Colonel Agastya ordered the secretary to get some water and to take a few moments before returning. He would announce himself to the General when he got to the General's office.

"That absolute cunt!" shouted the General, as Colonel Agastya walked into his office. The General waved off the Colonel's salute, as he continued his tirade. "What in the hell does she think she is doing? That stupid, mindless, liberal, save-the-bargabuko, feed-the-homeless, pain in my ass!"

Colonel Agastya looked at the beautiful bookshelf behind General Chaldea's desk. He saw that two of the shelves were shifted from their normal positions. Apparently, the General's so-called vacation had not produced the hoped-for results. In actuality, it was slightly impressive, in a twisted kind of way. It was not yet lunch, yet the General showed only the slightest signs of his secret. While his thinking was clouded, his emotions twisted, and his judgment impaired, the man could continue to function, where others would simply pass out on the floor.

The General slammed his hand on his desk. "She is absolutely out of fucking order! She is out of her league! She is clueless as what it takes to maintain military discipline! She will ruin what has become the largest military force on the two worlds! We are six months into preparation for a planetary exploration mission, and her damn high-

and-mighty holiness drops this crap on us. We don't have time for this, and who gives a fuck anyway?"

"General, sir, you have me at a disadvantage," stated the Colonel, trying not to let his feelings of annoyance show through.

"Sit down, Colonel," ordered the General, as he gestured to the chairs directly in from of his desk. "That Ionia Villegas, our esteemed board member, just lights my fuse!"

The General tapped a few places on his desk, and a monitor appeared with the image of a young man.

"This right here. This is the problem," asserted the General as he pointed at the image of the young man's face. "He's been drafted. We have to take him. He is on his way to initial training camp as I speak. I am the top military officer in the largest military ever conceived, and that stupid woman forces me to accept him into our ranks. A piece of shit scumbag that should be dead, or at least suffering his ass off in prison somewhere, but no . . . we're stuck with him."

The Colonel let the General pitch his fit and move through his tirade. Interrupting or asking for clarification would only further infuriate the irrational man. Colonel Agastya looked at the image on the screen. He looked to be of the right age. He was a good-looking kid. There was nothing about the image that would cause the outrage that the General was displaying.

The General paused to take a deep breath and then continued, "What you're looking at is a monster, a drug-dealing, child-murdering beast. I won't have him in my military. Apparently, Ionia Villegas, that overly social activist board member, wants to help young people in trouble, and she has decided to use my military as the tool. It's some damn pilot program that has Chairman Donovackia's personal blessing, if you can believe that shit."

"Sir, let's just let him wash out, or have him 'suffer' from some 'random accident.' Various programs like this have produced various results," suggested Colonel Agastya. "Some kids that come through these programs are okay. Others, we just get rid of. In any event, right now, we are ramping up our numbers significantly. We need bodies."

"We can't touch this one," stated General Chaldea.

"I don't understand, sir," replied the Colonel.

"Ionia Villegas' grandnephew worked at the Morphinia Containment Company as a guard, if you can believe that," began the General. "He was trying to protect this particular shitbag of a prisoner. I guess he told his Great Aunt Ionia about the boy, and her liberal heart bled for him. She promised her nephew that she would personally pull the boy into her damn program. The dumb nephew got killed by another prisoner when he went to retrieve the boy for transport. Ionia is treating this as the man's last request. She'll see that her beloved nephew's pet prisoner is saved. Colonel, we can't directly hurt this boy, but I order you to make sure that this boy fails. It has to be so damn subtle that no review would ever turn up anything. Make his life hell. Make sure he fails."

Colonel Agastya returned to his office and pulled up the boy's file. He was of age, barely. The record seemed scant. There was no medical record, or other records from the prison that he could access; they were blocked. He couldn't even see which of the Morphinia Containment Company's facilities had detained the boy. The record held nothing but basic information, such as his date of birth, height, and weight. This was concerning, but not surprising. The General's hand was in this. Muddled thinking. The military training camps weren't even within the Colonel's chain of command, but he would take care of it anyway. This Kadamba Vorhoor probably wasn't military capable anyway.

With a few conversations, word was out. This new cadet was to be run out of the military, but no one was to be able to trace any inappropriate behavior. It really wasn't that difficult. Given Kadamba's background, he'd be hated anyway. Initial training camp would be a living hell. Certainly, the boy would prefer to return to prison where he belonged.

A message flashed across the slim device strapped to his wrist. It was from Captain Tristanidad Luciano. He wanted to have a drink and maybe dinner at the Boatyard Grub and Pub after work. Considering how his day had been, Colonel Agastya readily agreed. Plus, it was his favorite place.

The Captain was already at the bar when Colonel Agastya arrived. The bartender, Earmon Terman, signaled him to the bar and placed a rocks glass in front of him.

"You're a good man, Earmon," the Colonel said, as he sat down on the stool next to the Captain Luciano. The bartender poured the golden colored liquid into Agastya's glass and headed off to help other customers.

"Do you ever drink anything else?" Captain Luciano asked.

Agastya held the glass up, admiring the golden, yellow-brown color. He swirled it a bit in the glass, took a deep sniff, and then took a sip. He could taste the slightest hint of melons and other sweet fruits, coming across the smoky, slightly burnt taste of the barrel in which the liquid had aged. He set the glass back on the bar. "Certainly, I like others, but this is my favorite. And there's just something about walking into an establishment like this one and having the bartender pour your drink without your asking."

Both of the men laughed and toasted Earmon Terman. Captain Luciano began to say something. It appeared something serious, but the Colonel stopped him and motioned to a monitor above the bar. An old film was playing.

"This is the best part," noted Agastya.

*

The scene was set in a bar. The main character had walked into the bar and realized that there were two other men in the bar, waiting to kill him. A third assassin, having followed the main character in, blocked the way out. The protagonist walked up to the bar, looked the bartender in the eyes, and said, "Make it a double Grenadines Special."

The bartender pulled a glass from under the bar, already full, and set it in front of the main character. He threw his head back and sat down on a barstool. "Give me another." The bartender obliged, setting another full glass in front of him.

The camera panned to the three assassins. They were smiling as they watched the bartender set a third and fourth drink in front of the protagonist. When he stood up from the bar, he staggered a little, muttering something incomprehensible. The assassins sprang to life, ready to slay their apparently inebriated prey. The man, pivoting, dropped the first guy with a solid right punch to the jaw. He flipped the second onto a table, breaking it. Finally, as the third assassin charged, he spun, grabbed a bottle, and smashed it across the assassin's head.

The protagonist walked back up to the bar, just as the bartender set two glasses on the bar. He poured two drinks, from a bottle identical to the one Earmon had poured for Agastya. The bartender and the protagonist raised their glasses, and the bartender toasted, "Here's to the Grenadines Special."

*

"I just can't help but love that scene," Colonel Agastya confided.

"And you drink the same drink," noted Captain Luciano.

"But, of course, can you imagine anything less?" replied the Colonel, with a smile.

Both men raised their glasses again. Colonel Agastya knew that his younger friend needed something. As he was beginning to ask, Earmon came up to the two of them. "The corner table is available."

"Perfect timing as always, my friend," replied Agastya to Earmon, as he picked up his glass, which the bartender had just refilled. "Sometimes, I think you read my mind."

They sat down at the table. Captain Luciano prefaced things, as he often did, that what he was about to share was off the record. The Captain was more and more concerned with the General's son, but was relieved that the boy was able to spend as much time as he had recently with the Captain's family.

"Tristinidad, I've known you a long time," Colonel Agastya patiently told him. "I can tell when you are hedging and failing to get to the point. What's the real problem here?"

The Captain looked down, as if he was contemplating whether to say anything or not. His face firmed with resolve, and he began. "The General's wife, Camdrin Chaldea, broke down while she was picking up Mungo last night. We were outside, and no one else was around. She was obviously upset. I asked what was wrong, expecting her to say nothing as she usually does."

"And last night, she finally said something?" asked Colonel Agastya.

"She said that the General forced himself on her the night before," revealed Captain Luciano.

"He raped her," stated the Colonel, without much surprise in his voice.

"I tried to tell her to call authorities, but she quickly recanted her story. She said that she must have been delusional. I don't know what to do."

"There's little you can do, Tristanidad, especially if she won't do anything for herself," Colonel Agastya responded, sympathetically. "Rape is a terrible thing within a marriage, and way too often it goes unreported. Just keep being a friend to Mungo. I am going to share a few more things with you about the General. You can't share this with anyone."

Colonel Agastya told his young friend many of the things that he knew about the General. He had cheated and done a crazy amount of illegal drugs while in infantry school. He was known as a problem.

Even after he met his wife, he continued to party. Eventually, he married and began to create a grand illusion. A bit of undeserved luck on the battlefield launched his command career.

Sometime, a dozen years or so before, he began to drink. He and his wife had their first two children, a boy and a girl. Life seemed good from the outside, but they wanted a third child, and the General couldn't perform well. The pressure of a growing command career was weighing heavier on him than he could handle. He turned to the bottle to drown the emotions. Oddly, even though he had been a party animal in his youth, he hid his drinking. They would even hold formal dinners at the house. He would serve alcohol, but would rarely have very much, at least, where people could see. He had managed to hide the drinking from everyone, including his family.

The truth was that he really was an emotional midget to begin with. He rarely talked to his own kids. From the outside, he appeared to be an involved father but had nearly nothing to do with their upbringing. No matter what they did, it wasn't good enough for him. He would pass his edicts of how life should be through his wife. The oldest son was forced into the same infantry school that his father attended. The boy hated it. When he finally followed his own passion, which was science, the General would prance about like it was his idea, stating that it was his amazing upbringing and genes that created such a fine young man.

The boy had completely lost his temper at a graduation ceremony a few months before. He told his father that he was useless and that he could simply go straight to hell. The boy hasn't spoken to the General since. The daughter had a similar experience. She was also forced to attend infantry school, but she went AWOL last year. The last that anyone knew was that supposedly she became a mountain guide on the other side of the planet.

Two years ago, everything fell apart for the General. Camdrin, his wife, found him at the bottom of the stairs passed out. She tried to get him help. He would pretend, get treatment, and play along, but the drive to suckle on that bottle was just too much. She threw him out last year. When she finally let him move back in, she experienced the same thing she just had just described to the Captain.

"So, the man really is a monster?" asked Captain Luciano.

"Pretty much so," replied Colonel Agastya.

"Why is he in such a position in life?"

"Some people are masters of illusion, and General Chaldea is one of them."

"He really shouldn't be in command, or be married, or have children!" declared Captain Luciano.

"Captain, we need to be very careful. He has many friends, most of whom know nothing of his secret. Those that do know are being very compassionate, as they truly know so little of the man. He is digging his own grave. Of that, I am sure. I'm just working to minimize the collateral damage. Please just be a friend to Mungo. He needs that right now."

"What about Camdrin?" asked the Captain.

"Sadly, until she decides to do something, she's stuck," Colonel Agastya admitted. "She has to get the strength to leave him on her own. It's not right. It's not fair, but it is what it is. Just be patient. He'll eventually destroy himself."

Chapter 18

A Painful Way to Meet

Bjorn could hardly contain his excitement. He was bouncing off the walls. Their flight left in the morning for Mexico, but his mom had still insisted that he complete his homework before they left. This seemed completely ridiculous to him. He could do the homework in Mexico, or on the plane, or when they returned, but his mom had demanded that he have it completed before they left.

The knock on the door was a bit of relief. As Joanna opened it, a smiling Atticus Freeman was standing there, well dressed, and, as always, carrying his cane.

"Oh, Mr. Freeman, I am glad that you are here, but I am afraid this could be more of a challenge than usual," she confided.

"I imagine the young lad is a tad bit overly excited about his trip?" Atticus inquired.

"Yes, he certainly is," replied Bjorn's mom.

"We'll make sure to wrap this up as quickly as possible," Atticus assured her, as calmly as if he had expected a challenge before he had even arrived. "He is a good boy, and a vacation like this one is so very exciting for him."

Atticus headed into the kitchen, where Bjorn was struggling to focus on his homework. Joanna stood outside the entryway to the kitchen, just out of sight. She was amazed at the very nature of Mr. Freeman. He connected with Bjorn and seemed to calm the boy's spirit by simply walking into the room. It seemed to her that Mr. Freeman had an infinite well of patience on which to draw—which, at times, was very fortunate.

Dylan came down the stairs from his room, chuckling. Joanna looked at him, wondering if she should ask what was so funny, or if she should just leave it be. In many ways, he was a typical teenager, but in many ways he wasn't. He was gentle and kind, almost to a fault. He had been born this way. Her mother, even as crusty as she was, would often say that an angel must have given him some additional grace, on his way down from heaven. She couldn't imagine a better big brother for Bjorn. She disliked the fact that she was often required to work late at the law firm where she was the office manager, but it paid well enough and enabled her to provide for her sons.

Before she could decide if it was a text from a girl that might be amusing Dylan, or something else, he began to speak. "Mom, I think Bjorn might need a little extra help packing. We are both packed, but it looks like he may have decided to bring a few extra things to the beach."

"Okay, Dylan, I'll have a look, and give him a hand," she said.

They both headed back up the stairs. Bjorn's bag seemed to bulge oddly. Joanna picked it up and laid it on the bed. When she opened it, both she and Dylan laughed. Right on top sat three official dodgeballs.

"Your little brother sure does love playing dodgeball, doesn't he?" she commented.

"Bjorn is a wicked player and loves the game," replied Dylan. "It just totally figures that he wouldn't go for soccer or baseball or some 'traditional' sport. It's just not his style."

Dylan thought back to how they had discovered Bjorn's love of the game. They had just moved to Colorado and neither had made any new friends. They went to a nearby recreation center to shoot some hoops and maybe swim. Dylan left Bjorn in the gym for a few minutes, and when he returned, he was happy to see Bjorn talking with some kids his own age.

Apparently, the boys were on a dodgeball team that had a tournament in the recreation center that day, and one of the players had suddenly become ill. If they couldn't round up another player quickly, they would have to forfeit. Bjorn was thrilled to be invited to play. The boys on the team were even more thrilled once the games started. Bjorn was deadly with a dodgeball. Halfway through the games, the boys started calling him Beckham, because he could "bend it like Beckham." It seemed an odd reference since this was not soccer, but Bjorn loved it.

Bjorn continued to play with the team after the tournament and had become quite a crafty little sniper. He would hide in the back, waiting for an opponent to become vulnerable. He would then launch a ball, and if you didn't know better, you would think he was bending the ball around other players.

Dylan picked up one of the balls, but before he could walk out of the room, his mom snatched it from his hands. "Nice try, but I saw that look on your face, and you're not going down there to bean him with this," his mom announced, holding the ball up.

"So close!" Dylan laughed, as he headed out of the room. He turned and looked at the wall. "Guess we should be glad he didn't try to take that too,"

Bjorn's bow was still hanging on the wall. Both boys loved archery, after finding an indoor range near the rec center. At first, Joanna wasn't too excited about the idea of her boys shooting things, but a conversation with Atticus had made her change her mind. There were many worse things in the world than dodgeball and archery. She may have hoped that Bjorn would have been into more traditional sports or activities, but each of us has our own path to follow.

*****

The condo was in a large complex right on the beach in Playa del Carmen, Mexico, complete with swimming pools, hot tubs, tennis courts, and a basketball court. The beach was in a protected little cove with inflatable bouncing structures floating in the water and sea kayaks and paddle boats for wandering about. The condo itself had more than enough bedrooms, a beautiful modern kitchen, and an ocean view balcony five stories above the ground. It was peaceful, and all four of them were having a wonderful time.

On the second day of their vacation, Dylan and Bjorn decided it was time to explore a bit outside of the complex. While Joanna was a little apprehensive, Tim was more open to the idea and gave them some clear instructions on where they could go and where to avoid. There was a nearby street with many merchants and stores, a local park, and a few interesting neighborhoods.

The boys set out, both enjoying the warmth of the Mexican sun, especially considering the unusual ice storm that they were missing back home in Colorado. Before long they found the local park. A group of kids was playing a pickup game of soccer, and both Dylan and Bjorn were drawn to watching the game. The skill of some of the younger kids surpassed most of the kids Dylan had played with through the years. He was amazed at the ease of the footwork and how relaxed they were as they played.

Then Dylan noticed her. The whole world suddenly shrunk down to nothing but one girl. He couldn't even see anything else. He wasn't even sure that he was breathing. She moved with grace and confidence with the soccer ball like no girl that he had ever seen. As she came closer, his heart may have stopped beating. Her long black hair was tied back in a ponytail, revealing the soft features of her face. He watched her execute classic soccer moves like the Roulette, Cryuff, and the Rivelino like she wasn't even trying. It was as if she were dancing with the ball.

He was mesmerized by her. The closer she came, the more he felt frozen in place. Even when she planted her left foot solidly and began moving through what would be a very powerful strike, he couldn't move. The ball was sailing low through the air, and he knew it was coming in his direction, but he could not unlock his eyes from hers. She was looking right at him. He felt like she might even be looking right into his heart, knowing that he couldn't see anything but her.

The ball struck him full force, right where no male of any species wants to get hit. He felt his legs lift up as his body crumbled to the ground. He heard himself let out a long, low moan as he cupped his hands between his legs. As he lay there, he could hear Bjorn laughing hysterically, along with most of the other kids that had been playing.

Another teenage girl came trotting up, rainbowed the ball into her own hands, and looked down at him on the ground. "Guess you got what you deserve!" she sassily snapped at him in a thick Spanish accent, "Don't be perving on us, you dumb gringo!" She yelled something in Spanish to the kids, and the laugher seemed even louder.

After dropping the ball, she dribbled back towards the giggling group of kids. The girl who had just crunched his manhood stood about twenty-five feet away. Her face seemed to be alternating between a giggle and something of a compassionate look. He couldn't really tell, as his eyes were watering a bit. He wasn't crying, but he sure was close.

She walked over to him and held out her hand. "Sorry about that," she offered in nearly flawless English. "I really didn't mean to peg you there."

Trying to roll up into a sitting position, he painfully managed to say, "That's okay. I'm Dylan. I think I will sit here a minute."

She withdrew her hand, smiling. "I'm Adelita."

For a moment, their eyes locked again. Dylan found himself speechless, as did Adelita. Both of them found smiles forcing their way onto their faces, but neither seemed to be able to find a word to say. The world unhinged itself from the two of them, and they just froze, focused on the look in the other's eyes.

Bjorn had partially regained his composure but was still bright red from laughing so hard. He looked over at the two of them, rolled his eyes, and spouted out without thinking, "Geez, so, you gonna ask her to kiss it better, or what?"

The moment was shattered, and both Dylan and Adelita blushed, as their eyes rapidly widened in embarrassment. Dylan's head spun towards his brother, and he snapped, "Bjorn! Shut the hell up!"

The girl, who had first spoken to Dylan, yelled out to Adelita in Spanish, calling her back to the game. Adelita looked down at Dylan and spoke softly, "Sorry, I gotta get back. I hope you're not too hurt, Dylan." Their eyes met again, and both of them couldn't help but let small smiles spread across their faces. She turned and jogged back to the game that had started up again.

Bjorn was still having trouble regaining his composure. This was funny, damn funny, and Bjorn knew that he was funny too. He was stuck in one of those moments where just he couldn't stop laughing. Looking over at his brother, Bjorn forced a goofy compassionate look on his face.

"Do you need me to go get you a shovel to dig your nads back out?" asked Bjorn, and he lost it again, laughing out loud as tears came from his eyes.

"Bjorn," Dylan stated, as sternly as he could, "I'm going to kick your ass." He then realized he was still partially slumped over in pain. The whole scene probably had been amusing to watch, but he still wanted to smack Bjorn.

Eventually, Dylan was able to get up, and Bjorn mostly regained control of his giggles. Dylan knew he'd probably be teased by his little brother for quite a while on this one, but it didn't really matter. He'd come back to this park tomorrow, hoping that Adelita would be there again. Even if he was embarrassed, he really didn't want to leave the park right at that moment, but it was closing in on dinnertime. Tim wanted to take them out to a local restaurant that he claimed had the best tacos el carbon anywhere on Earth.

As he and Bjorn walked away, he looked back. Adelita was looking his way. He brought his hand up about chest high, giving a tentative wave in her direction. She returned the wave, and he could see her smile. Dylan knew he was coming back to this park tomorrow.

"Dude, she's way out of your league," Bjorn offered, as he playfully pushed his brother towards the path that led out of the park. "And I'm hungry and pissed off! Let's go!"

"Bjorn, why are pissed off?" demanded Dylan. "The only thing 'off' is how hard you've been laughing your ass—off."

"I'm pissed cause I forgot to have my phone out," replied Bjorn smartly. "Do you have any idea how many hits I could get on my YouTube page if I had that scene on video?"

"Shut up, Bjorn!"

Chapter 19
A New Direction

The ride was surprisingly smooth inside the tube for Kadamba, and the hours passed quickly. As the driver had promised, they arrived at the Kareenet-Pooshz Portal in about five hours. He could feel the tube being hoisted from off the truck and expected to have the lid opened at any minute. Instead, he felt the tube whisking about on rails, then being coupled to other tubes. He'd seen the process in documentaries at school and at home, but he'd never been through a portal before. He was tempted to simply say, "Help," and let the aerosol sedative knock him out, but he was too curious.

The tube was still for a few moments, and then a voice broke the silence. "Please prepare for safety enclosure and portal transport." Kadamba felt a pliable material press against his body as the tube began to rapidly accelerate. Time seemed to freeze, and then his body felt as if it had been sucked through a tiny opening and shot out the other side. The tube slammed to a stop, and Kadamba almost screamed.

For the next few minutes, he felt the tube whizzing through the Pooshz Portal Complex. He had no idea where he was going or why. Being in jail had truly been a terrifying experience, and the thousands of miles between prison and his home in Stujorkian City seemed so far. As he lay in the tube, it dawned on him that this was different. He was on another planet. He didn't know anyone here. The more he began to think about it, the more his anxiety level began to increase. He wanted out of the tube. He wanted to run. The sensation of being trapped and completely out of control began to overwhelm him. He began to panic. All of a sudden, he couldn't get any oxygen into his lungs, even though he was breathing faster and faster.

The lid popped open, and Kadamba jumped out, falling flat on his face. He just lay there for a moment, until he felt the boot kick into his side. Not hard, but hard enough to get his attention.

"Stand up, cadet. We don't have all day."

Kadamba slowly rose to his feet, scared, but wanting to see what was happening and where he was. Standing before him was a large, extremely muscular man in a camouflage military uniform. The man didn't look angry, but he was obviously not happy to be where he was.

Kadamba looked around. He felt as out of place as he had anywhere. This was obviously a first-class tube station. There were well dressed employees rushing about, and all of the tube passengers appeared to be rather well-off in life. The man in the military uniform did seem out of place, but not nearly as much as Kadamba did. He was standing in the underwear and t-shirt that the driver of the truck loaded with tubes had kindly given him.

"Follow me, cadet," ordered the uniformed man, as he began making his way through the passengers who were also getting out of tubes. Kadamba followed, not knowing what else to do. For a few moments, he thought about running. He wasn't in prison anymore. He was just following this uniformed military person, and there were just a few random security personnel about. Would they try to stop him?

Before he could decide, an employee stopped him. "My dear sir, our apologies if the tube trip was unsatisfactory," the woman offered, as she handed him a long robe. He stopped, and quickly put on the robe. Maybe she thought that he had vomited during the portal passage and had abandoned his clothes. He didn't really care. He felt much less exposed in the robe.

"Thank you, ma'am," the uniformed man said, as he motioned Kadamba towards the door. A military vehicle, with another uniformed man, was waiting outside the door. The man, obviously a driver, held the door open for the two men as they approached the vehicle. Kadamba climbed in, realizing that his opportunity to make a dash for it was probably gone.

They were dropped off at a military shuttle facility. Within a few moments of arriving, they boarded a shuttle and were airborne. Kadamba felt small and out of place. The shuttle was very nice, and the seats were large and accommodating. The uniformed man who had met him at the tube portal handed Kadamba a glass of water. The man looked at him intently. Kadamba couldn't tell if he was angry, or disgusted, or what. It was almost a look of curiosity and pity.

"You sure as hell haven't said much since you flopped out of that tube. You can speak, can't you?" inquired the soldier.

"Yes," replied Kadamba.

"I suppose we should be relieved about that," the solder said, with a smile.

"Where are we going?" asked Kadamba.

"You don't know where you are going?"

"No. No one told me anything."

The uniformed man just looked at Kadamba for a moment with a look of shock on his face and then slowly shook his head back and forth. "Nothing? You have no idea what's happening? You haven't made any decisions? You haven't signed any paperwork?"

"No, sir," replied Kadamba, scared that all of this was a mistake. "This morning I was in prison. They stuck me in a tube on a truck, and now I'm here. That's all I know."

The uniformed man kept shaking his head slowly back and forth. It was obvious that he had expected Kadamba to know something, but he knew nothing. "Okay, then. I'm Lieutenant Mittelwert Padda, Commander of the Donovackia Second Brigade Initial Military Training Facility, Zoranth Division. You were identified as a potential candidate for military service. You were to have been briefed before you got here, but obviously something went wrong. So, let me put this very simply: You can either sign in for initial training for the Donovackia Corporate Military when we land, or I can send you back to prison."

"I'll join the military, sir. Please," responded Kadamba.

"This is very simple, Cadet Vorhoor. If you fail to complete your initial training and to serve a term of ten years of military service, you will be transferred back to prison. I understand that you have not had a chance to think about this and that you didn't even know about it. Someone very important and very influential plucked you out of that prison. Given your crimes, you should be left to rot and die, but someone has twisted the strings of fate on your behalf."

The lieutenant left Kadamba alone and headed to another room on the shuttle. Kadamba wasn't sure what to think. He rolled up the sleeve on his left arm and looked at the scar again. Child Murderer. He thought about his mom and his dad and his sisters. Did they know what had happened to him? Did they even know where he was? He remembered that his birthday had passed while he was in prison. Anything resembling control in his life had been swept away. The one person who had shown him mercy and compassion was dead, killed by that monster, Jackos. For months and months, the Giant had hunted him in the prison, trying to get him, but he had been protected by a guard. He realized that he didn't even know the man's name.

Ka looked down at his arm again. There were no scars. He was back on Schmarlo's Landing. He walked to the edge of the landing and stood looking out at Stujorkian City. Everything seemed so quiet, so peaceful.

"What are you doing, Ka?"

He turned to see Alorus standing nearby. The boy's face looked a little different. He didn't look like he was as hateful. There wasn't any foam or blood around his mouth. He looked exactly like he did when he'd bought the rath from Ka. A tear began to form in Ka's eyes. "I'm so sorry, Alorus. I wish I could undo everything I did."

"I know, but what are you doing here?" asked Alorus.

"I'm just looking at the city. It's peaceful here," replied Ka.

"You're not in prison anymore. Where are we?"

Kadamba looked at the boy closer. He knew he wasn't real, but in so many ways he was. He was part of Ka's life. "We're on Zoranth now. I'm joining the Donovackia Corporation's military."

"Is that fair? Should you be out of prison?" asked the boy.

Tears began to run down Kadamba's face. He looked out at the city again, trying to find the building that was home. He couldn't see it anywhere.

"I don't know. But I don't think I will ever see Stujorkian City or home ever again."

Hearing a video monitor turn on, he opened his eyes to see the lieutenant watching some news program. He was shaking his head back and forth as a woman on the screen, standing at a podium, was making what seemed to be an important speech.

"My dear citizens of Koranth and Zoranth, today the Ministry of Interplanetary Corporate Relations is happy to announce a complete ceasefire in the war between Iguran and Paknorta. This war has been waged for too long, and too many lives have been lost. Through diligent and painstaking negotiations, we have dissolved the governments of the two nations, and created a new, more peaceful, single country."

Kadamba looked at the Lieutenant. He appeared to have a very pensive look on his face. He turned back towards Kadamba, noting,

"Everything is changing so quickly, and I'm not always sure it is for the best."

"Wasn't that Celestina Wiroviana, the Chief Executive Minister?" asked Kadamba.

"Being in prison, I guess you aren't too up on current affairs. The ministry has effectively taken over five countries," explained the Lieutenant. "The Ministry's military is now the sixth largest military on the two planets. Some people think it is a good thing. She preaches peace. She's stopped multiple wars, but recently, she's done it using her new military might. I don't know that much about politics, but I guess I should be happy. The Donovackia military is the largest and strongest military ever."

They chatted for a few more minutes, until the shuttle began descending for the Donovackia Second Brigade Initial Military Training Facility. Kadamba moved to window, and the Lieutenant pointed out various buildings, training areas, and places in the huge training complex. The facility was the only thing Kadamba could see. It was completely isolated from any cities or towns. Kadamba was happy to be out of prison, to be given this chance, but there was a little piece of him that had hoped to see an option—maybe someplace he could run, if he had too. There was nothing anywhere near the massive facility. Kadamba just hoped life would be a little less painful here.

He was quickly processed, assigned to a unit, and in many ways a new life began. It was difficult, but he wasn't being brutalized. Because of the scar and the stigma attached to it, he was ostracized by the other cadets. It didn't matter that much, as no one was trying to beat him or pimp him out. He often thought that he was being singled out for additional work, assignments, or more difficult tasks, but it was okay. He would do anything needed not to have to return to that prison.

In many ways, he started to become a soldier. He could use multiple weapons, and he loved the hand-to-hand combat. The physical training was excruciating, but rewarding. He was in the best shape of his life.

He often thought about heading to the communications depot to call his parents, but he never did. At times, he would convince himself that it was best to let them think he was dead. Perhaps they made up some story about him wandering off into the world, or perhaps dying in an accident. When he thought of how terribly disappointed they must be in him, it was easy to just let them believe he was gone forever.

Chapter 20
Mission Clarity

Commander Conall Bornani sat outside Tomar Donovackia's office, waiting for the Chairman of the most powerful Corporation in the two worlds to call him into the office. It was uncomfortable. Commander Conall Bornani was a soldier, through and through. He was about to be promoted to the rank of Captain when an opportunity arose to take command of the next planetary exploration mission to a planet known as Earth. He leapt at the opportunity. He had been orphaned at a young age and had recently lost his wife. He had little left but his military career.

Tomar's office was too plush and palatial for Commander Bornani, but he forced himself to appear comfortable while meeting the most powerful man on the two worlds. Tomar was gracious, offering the Commander a seat in an area overlooking Stujorkian City. "Commander, I appreciate your taking the time to come and see me. I have a number of things that I want to discuss."

"Of course, sir. This is an exciting and important mission, and I am honored to be a part of it," answered Commander Bornani, trying to sound humble.

"Please give me an assessment of your crew," Tomar requested. "This is likely a one-way mission, and I need you to be sure you can accomplish the goals of quickly and thoroughly assessing the planet's readiness for invasion and development. Of equal, and perhaps even greater importance, is discovering if any Transprophetics have appeared in the population."

Commander Conall Bornani gave Tomar a thorough assessment of the five other soldiers, the two infrastructure and technology analysts, the two global logistics and trade analysts, and the two experts who would be working to discover if the planet had any Transprophetics. With just over a year left to prepare, the Commander was very confident that his crew would be one hundred percent ready for the mission.

Tomar had, of course, been involved in the selection of the six experts on this mission, but he had been less involved in selecting the soldiers. That was General Chaldea's job. He had faith that his military would provide the best possible warriors for the job. This was the first planetary exploration mission to launch since he had taken over. While he was extremely busy with growing the Corporation, he absolutely wanted to make sure that this mission was successful. "Do you understand, Commander, exactly how the experts will proceed to root out Transprophetics?"

"They will be dispatched into the planet's population to try to find anyone who claims to have the powers to move objects, the ability to move through space without being seen, or any of the known capabilities of Transprophetics," explained Commander Bornani. "They will scour whatever news and research resources that they can discover. If they find a potential candidate, they will interview the candidate to ascertain whether or not the person is, in actuality, a Transprophetic, or simply a charlatan playing on the gullibility of others."

"And what happens if they discover a true Transprophetic?" Tomar knew the answer, but he wanted to see how the Commander would approach and handle his response.

"They will kill them."

"Yes," Tomar replied, satisfied that the Commander understood. "And if we are unable to validate that any Transprophetic exists on Earth, then what?"

"The remaining four experts in infrastructure, technology, logistics, and trade will make an assessment of whether the planet is primed for development. That assessment will be sent back, along with various planetary artifacts, via the return vessel," responded the Commander.

"Very good. Are you prepared to send back a report that states a planet is not ready, knowing full well that you and your crew will likely spend the rest of your lives on that planet?" Tomar inquired.

"I and each of my crew members are absolutely prepared for that option."

"Do you understand what you and your crew will be tasked with, at that point?"

"Yes, sir. We will fan out across the planet, continually looking for Transprophetics. If we find any, we kill them. If we are extremely lucky, we might someday run into a future crew from Donovackia. If, as the years have passed, we have found a Transprophetic, then we inform the future crew."

Tomar and the Commander continued to talk for some time. Tomar was comfortable that this was the man for this mission. He had a clear grasp of what needed to happen on Earth. While Tomar absolutely wanted to hear that Earth was ready for development, he would rather that the mission find the planet needing a bit more time. Tomar could wait. He had absolute control of his Corporation, and many plans that would take him even further than he had already come.

The Commander left Tomar's office and returned to the former Stameyerson Corporation's launch facility. Of course, now it was the Donovackia Corporation's launch facility. What was once Eleven Corporations was now Nine, and there were rumors that another Corporation was being targeted for acquisition by Donovackia. It really didn't matter to Commander Conall Bornani. He would only be here for one more year, and then his fate was on Earth.

*****

Tomar began to prepare for the last meeting that he had that day. Spending any time with Scharbigot Canchorus, one of the now-three Ministers, was more of an annoyance than anything else. Celestina was firmly in control of the Ministry. Her uncle's health had further deteriorated, and his vote was absolutely hers. Scharbigot had simply become a figurehead. He still performed Ministry duties, but Celestina ran the show.

The communication device on his wrist vibrated. It was Celestina. She had tears in her eyes, but also seemed to be smiling at the same time. He swiped his finger across the device, and a live holographic image of her appeared in front of him.

"Celestina, what is the matter?" asked Tomar.

"My uncle is dead. He passed away a few minutes ago."

"I'm very sorry to hear that. He was an amazing man and was so wonderful to you. And I suppose congratulations are also in order. His seat in the Ministry has now passed to you. "

Celestina smiled, answering, "Yes. It is true. I now have complete control of two of the three votes in the Ministry. I've already passed my first new rule since my uncle passed. I've granted Scharbigot a lifetime seat on the Ministry's board. In return, when he passes away, the seat becomes mine."

Tomar began to laugh. "You are such an evil genius."

"I know," she replied, her smile growing.

"Have you contacted Scharbigot to tell him the news?" asked Tomar.

"Not of yet. I believe you are meeting with him in a few hours, so perhaps you could share his good fortune and lifetime appointment with him?"

Tomar laughed. "I'd be more than happy to let him know that for the rest of his life, he is a Minister."

Chapter 21
Set Up to Fail

Donovackia Board Member Ionia Villegas sat comfortably in the chair in General Swinton Chaldea's office with a wide, gracious smile on her face. "My dear General, you are a man of my own heart," she began. The General focused all of his energy on not leaping across his desk and strangling the overbearing, liberal woman with his bare hands. "I am here to personally thank you for working with me on my pilot projects to help troubled youths find direction in the wonderful military organization of our Corporation."

"Of course, ma'am," the General managed through partially clinched teeth. He was working as hard as he could to sound friendly and not let Ionia Villegas know how he really felt about her. He hated her. He hated all her social and environmental causes. He wished she were dead.

"In particular, I wanted to thank you for accepting Kadamba Vorhoor into the program. It means so much to me that I could honor my murdered nephew, by helping a young man that he believed deserved a second chance."

The General's face continued to show calm, but at the mention of that person, he could feel his blood pressure rising. He would just have to keep cool, at least, until after she left. "Of course, ma'am, I've heard your nephew was a true humanitarian. His death was a tragedy. May the Lords of the Fourth System have mercy on his soul."

"Thank you, General. He was a good man. Kudos to you for continuing and building upon what very well may become his legacy. I will be presenting these pilot programs to the board of directors of the Donovackia Corporation in the coming year. All twenty of the youths that we placed in various training camps have successfully completed and passed their initial military training. It's very exciting, wouldn't you say?"

"Of course, ma'am," affirmed the General, hoping his face wasn't turning red.

"Once each of them has completed the next round of training and has been placed in active roles in the military, we shall declare this pilot program a complete success!" declared Ionia Villegas.

Standing, the General showed the Minster to the door. The entire time he'd held back a nearly overwhelming desire to pick her up and smash her into the ground. It would be so easy. She was old and just beginning to become slightly frail. He could crush the life out of her, and the whole universe would be better off.

Sealing the door behind her, he strode over to his bookshelf. He opened the secret compartment and pulled out one of the bottles, unscrewing the top quickly and putting the bottle to his lips. The liquid had a slight burn as it went down, but it had only a slight taste. He sat down in his chair and pulled up Kadamba Vorhoor's record. The little bastard had scored above average in his initial training. He took another long draw from the bottle.

The record seemed fairly stark. There was nothing that really stood out one way or another. In some respects that was good. The General still intended to get rid of Kadamba, and that absolutely nothing was amiss in the records was positive. He sat back in his chair to finish the bottle.

It was time for an ass-chewing. Someone needed to feel his fury. He slammed his hand into the desk, and his secretary's voice came through. "Sir?"

"Run your cute little butt down to Colonel Jecamiah Agastya's office and bring his lazy, worthless ass back here, NOW!" commanded the General.

The General smiled and laughed as he threw the bottle into the trash. He grabbed another from the secret compartment and took a long drink. He was going to enjoy this.

As usual, the Colonel made the General's secretary sit down and get a drink before heading back to the General's office. This time, he told her that when she caught her breath, that she was dismissed for the day. She should go home. He would tell the General that he had sent her to train a new secretary and that she wouldn't be returning until tomorrow.

Colonel Agastya took his time walking to the General's offices. From the look in the General's secretary's eyes, the Colonel could tell that the General was very likely to be in a monstrously foul mood. "Let him stew a little and get himself really worked up," thought the grinning Colonel as he walked to the General's office.

"Are you the MOST incompetent second-in-command this military has ever had to suffer through?" yelled the General as Colonel Agastya walked into his office. "I ordered you to get that drug-dealing, child-murdering son of a bitch out of my military during his initial training! You failed!"

"Sir, with respect, your orders were followed, as were mine," replied the Colonel. "It was kept completely under the radar, and no one could suspect that we sabotaged his training. He had the hardest tasks, the dirtiest assignments, the worst opportunities. The kid made it through the training in spite of our very covert attempts to run him out. He passed."

The Colonel met the General's icy gaze with stoic coldness in his own eyes. The General would never behave like this around others. It was only those who were close who got to see the real person that he was. He was a bully. He was a true jerk of a human being. He liked to intimidate others with his rank, making them feel small. It made the General feel better to tear others down.

"That wretched woman was here again today," stated the General with disdain, "gloating over the success of these damn criminals she wants to save with my military. She wants to turn my military into her personal social cause. She'll have us all overrun with gangsters, murders, and rapists, if the likes of you can't do your damn job!"

"Sir, I am very familiar with her program. It is very selective. Kadamba Vorhoor may be an unlikely candidate, but he passed initial military training, even with obstacles that should have stopped him," Colonel Agastya responded.

"If you can't do your damn job, then I will!" The General sat back down at his desk and started thumping buttons, bringing up a screen with the testing results from Kadamba's initial training. It was actually impressive that he had done as well as he did. The Colonel's orders were clear. Make him miserable, and try to make him wash out. The cadet had been mostly ostracized by the other cadets and hadn't even known that he had it harder than anyone else, but he still had passed.

The General began changing the scores in Kadamba's record.

"What are you doing, sir?" asked the Colonel.

"If this little fucker wants to be in the military, I'm going to show him what it is really like," chuckled the General.

The Colonel watched as the General upped all of Kadamba's scores. He moved the cadet from above average to excellent. He flipped to the next screen, which held Kadamba's post-initial training camp assignment. He changed it to Elite Forces Training.

"Sir, what the hell are you doing? He's not good enough for Elite Forces," asserted Colonel Agastya, stunned at what he was seeing.

"You and I know that, you dumb son of a bitch. Tell Captain Tristanidad Luciano that a new cadet has been assigned to his command. And make sure he understands that this little fucking shitbag is to fail, or better yet, die!"

Glancing at the trashcan, Colonel Agastya was unsurprised to see the bottle. The secret compartment in the General's bookshelf was obviously getting lots of use, as scratches now showed where the door opened. Today was just another episode in the twisted thinking of a man completely hooked on rodka. As he walked back to his office, he began to think about the General. Agastya had attributed part of the General's thinking and behavior to the addiction, but that was only a small part of the truth. The man was simply a complete asshole. The rodka just helped him cope with those around him who were disgusted with his being an asshole while, at the same time, it gave him the courage to be the asshole that truly he was.

Chapter 22
Revealed

Tomar led Scharbigot Canchorus into a plush seating area near some floor-to-ceiling windows in his office. The Minister was presumably there to talk about the Donovackia Corporation's latest acquisition target. Scharbigot had publically staked out a position on keeping the remaining Nine Corporations intact, not allowing any more mergers, acquisitions, or takeovers. Scharbigot knew it was only for show. Celestina had been in complete control ever since she revealed that his son, from his secret marriage, was scheduled for execution. At least, Celestina had kept her word. The young man's execution had been indefinitely delayed.

"My esteemed Minister Canchorus, how are you today?" came the greeting from Tomar.

"Good, but let's cut the formalities. You're planning another hostile takeover. I know you have the means, but at some point, you have to stop. Your Corporation is bigger than any Corporation in history. It's time to rest on your laurels," Scharbigot asserted.

"Did you hear that Minister Hareold Wiroviana has died?" Tomar asked, completely ignoring what the Minister had just said.

"No, this is news to me. What a shame," Scharbigot expressed. "He was a rare man, especially in these days."

"Yes, indeed, he certainly was, and I must congratulate you also."

"Why on the two worlds would you say that?"

Tomar smiled. "Hareold's seat has been folded into Celestina's. Her first act was to vote to convert your seat into a lifetime appointment, just like Hareold's had been. Congratulations."

The Minster sat with a stunned and disappointed look on his face. He had planned to retire and completely disappear from public life when his term expired. The Ministry had become a sham. Celestina was completely in charge and now had an unnecessarily massive military.

Tomar watched Scharbigot's face for a moment and then looked across the room. On his desk sat a meter-long cord of rope. He had impressed himself recently with his ability to manipulate the rope with his mind. Previously, he only moved things about, but now he had discovered that he could fold paper, tie knots in a rope, and even pour a glass of water. The more he worked his skills, the more impressive and powerful they became.

He still had not revealed to anyone that he was a Transprophetic, not even to Celestina. He loved having the secret, and he now knew that it had its uses. He would reveal to Scharbigot what he was capable of doing.

"Do you personally know any Transprophetics?" Tomar asked the Minister.

"I've met one once, but she was a bit of a religious fanatic. She believed herself to be divine and her so-called powers to be divine in origin. Of course, it's nothing but simple biology, anatomy, and physics," replied the Minister.

"Yes, it is a simple thing, but it is almost divine, wouldn't you say?" asked Tomar. "It's the ability to do so much more than others."

Tomar brought the rope into the air behind the Minister's back. He tied a slipknot, leaving a large loop. As the Minster began his reply, telling Tomar that simple evolution didn't create more divine or superior people, the loop slipped over Scharbigot's head and Tomar pulled it tight around Scharbigot's neck. Tomar focused his mind as intensely as he could on the loose end of the rope. He pulled it harder and harder and higher and higher. Scharbigot scratched at his own neck, trying in vain to get his fingers under the tightening cord.

For a few brief moments, Tomar could see nothing around him, but the end of that rope. He kept pulling with his mind, focusing with every bit of energy he could muster. Scharbigot, unable to fight the force, eventually found himself hanging in the air, with the rope becoming tighter and tighter, spastically fighting for his life. His face turned red. For a moment, he looked at Tomar, not understanding why. Tomar responded with a cruel smile as he watched the Minister's life fade away.

Chapter 23
To Become a Killer

Kadamba looked at the list displayed on the monitor in the hallway of the Donovackia 2th Brigade Initial Military Training Facility, Zoranth Division, command building. He couldn't believe that he had been assigned to Elite Forces. His expectation was to be assigned to infantry or transportation. He knew that he had performed well in the initial training, but he didn't think that he had performed that well. Being named to Elite Forces would be a prestigious assignment; however, receiving this assignment felt absolutely impossible. Ka was sure that there were other soldiers, better soldiers, ones who didn't carry his scars that would be more likely to get this honor.

He took a deep breath. The last couple of months had been extremely hard, physically, mentally, and emotionally. He hadn't made any friends, but as far as he knew, he hadn't made any enemies either. He continued to be an outcast because of the scar on his arm and what that scar told people. He looked at the screen again, expecting it to change at any second, assigning him to some horrible assignment. Then a terrible thought occurred to him. What if the assignment was simply a ruse? What if he was just going to be sent back to prison?

He looked up and down the hallway; he was still alone. He touched the screen just to make sure that it was real and stared at the list. All of the members of his unit that had completed training had assignments. Most of the assignments seemed to be somewhat aligned with the capabilities of the men with whom he had trained. However, there wasn't a single name on the list, other than his, that was assigned to Elite Forces. That was it. It was someone's idea of a sick joke. In his gut, he knew it. He was going back to prison or someplace far worse.

Kadamba's mind shifted into overdrive. This was a military training camp. It was not a prison. There were not multiple fences with barbed wire, no guards wondering about with guns, and the truth was, that there was no one forcing him to stay. He made a quick inventory in his mind of the things that he would need. He would be heading into the woods tonight, going AWOL. A comfort began to sweep across him. No prison. No military. It would just be him and a planet to discover. He would live off the land for a few years, not that he really knew how, but he was confident that he could figure it out. He took another deep breath and began consider how to secretly start gathering the supplies that he would need.

"Cadet Vorhoor," the voice broke his concentration.

"Yes, sir!"

"I'm sorry to startle you, son," Lieutenant Mittelwert Padda remarked. "I see you have been looking at the post-training camp assignments."

"Yes, sir," replied Kadamba, fearing that the look on his face would give away his plans of living life on the run.

"It appears we have a common destination, cadet. I've been transferred to Elite Forces. I will be taking charge of their training program and facilities on Koranth. The shuttle leaves in two hours. I'll see you on the platform."

"Yes, sir," replied Kadamba.

Kadamba watched as the Lieutenant walked down the hallway. Two hours would not be enough time to gather what he needed to head into the woods. If he wasn't on that shuttle platform before the Lieutenant, he knew that a contingent of soldiers would begin looking for him. Even if he could slip away from the training camp, he would be captured before the end of the day. He wouldn't be sent to a military prison. No, he would be sent back to prison with Jackos, where he was sure he would die.

Then another thought crossed his mind, "What if the Lieutenant was simply escorting him back to prison?" He had been the one to pick Kadamba up and bring him to the military training camp. Kadamba realized that he was trapped. The only real option was to be on that platform and hope that he really was heading to Elite Forces training.

The shuttle departed on time. Rather than a typical military transport, this was the same shuttle that had brought him to the camp. Kadamba imagined that it was an executive shuttle. The seats, large and comfortable, were arranged in seating areas, rather than just rows. He felt out of place, as the Lieutenant walked into the section of the shuttle that he had been told to sit in. Like the prior trip in this shuttle, there was no one else around.

Lieutenant Mittelwert Padda sat down across from Kadamba. While the Lieutenant had brought Kadamba to the training camp, Kadamba had seen little of the commanding officer since they had left the shuttle. It felt odd again, to be on the same shuttle, heading once again to the Kareenet-Pooshz Portal, with the very same soldier who had picked him up just a few months before. The Lieutenant studied the newly graduated cadet for a few moments.

"Are you surprised to be on this shuttle with me again?" asked Lieutenant Padda.

"Sir, yes, sir," responded Kadamba, "I didn't expect to be assigned to Elite Forces, but I am grateful."

"You know your scores weren't good enough to get into the Elite Forces?" stated the Lieutenant.

"Sir?"

"With your past, son, and the fact that you were mostly a loner, you didn't score high enough to get into Elite Forces. You simply didn't make the cut," stated the Lieutenant.

Kadamba swallowed hard. This was it. Kadamba just knew that the Lieutenant was about to tell him that he was going back to prison. He tried not to panic. In his mind's eye, he could already see Jackos laughing and telling him to get ready to complete the "business" they had together.

"Son, what I am about to tell is strictly off the record. I will deny this conversation," Lieutenant Padda informed him.

"Yes, sir," replied Kadamba. The sense of dread began filling his insides. He could taste the acid from his stomach working its way into his throat. He wanted to vomit, but he held his composure, at least on the outside. He watched as the words formed on the Lieutenant's lips, knowing his life would soon be over.

"Your scores were artificially reduced while you were participating in training. No one wanted to give you the scores you deserved. No one wanted to give you the scores you earned. And it is simply because of that brand on your arm," the Lieutenant stated, in a very matter-of-fact manner. "It is this simple. The world will always look at you as a devil. Our job here was to make you fail. Everyone will deny that, but it is the truth. You were given the worst assignments, the hardest jobs, and put in situation after situation that would have broken many men. Yet you survived, and even excelled."

Kadamba searched the Lieutenant's face for a twisted smile, for an evil grin, for anything that would let him know that the man was playing him and making fun of him. The next statement had to be about going back to prison, back into the domain of Jackos.

"Cadet, I am a man of honor. I don't much follow politics or the whims of society. I measure a man by what I can see with my own eyes. I see the brand on your arm. I know what the words mean, but I don't know, and I don't need to know, the details. What I have seen is a man set up for failure, set up to be ruined, yet a man who refused to give up."

Was this a compliment? The Lieutenant seemed to be showing something like respect to Kadamba, and he didn't know exactly what to do. He just looked at the Lieutenant and listened, not knowing what the next words would be.

"I don't know who, son, but once again, someone has twisted the strings of fate on your behalf. Your scores from training camp were changed. Someone, with some serious influence, has given you the scores that you actually deserved. I have no idea whether they knew what they were doing or not. Your assignment to Elite Forces surprised the hell out of me, but you are capable of this assignment."

"Thank you, sir," replied Kadamba, not knowing what else to say. The vision of Jackos faded quickly from his head, as he realized that this wasn't a ruse. He really was going to Elite Forces training.

The Lieutenant looked at Kadamba for a long moment, as if he was trying to see inside of him. "I don't know what it is that keeps you going, but you will need it for this next year. For every ten men that go to Elite Forces, four drop out. That's four people without any stigma. You're going to have one hell of a difficult time at training. I imagine that it will be similar to initial training. You will be given the toughest tasks, the hardest jobs, and you'll have little or no support. I can't promise to make it any easier on you, but I will be watching."

The Lieutenant stood up and left. Kadamba just sat in that comfortable chair, not sure what to think. He would be leaving Zoranth in a few hours. That meant a ride in the tubes again. He wasn't scared to ride in them, but he wasn't looking forward to it either. Actually, he'd rather ride around in the tubes all day than ever see Jackos again. He realized that his entire body was still tense. He closed his eyes, breathing deeply, forcing himself to relax.

The sun was shining brightly, and Ka looked around. Everything seemed perfect, as it always did here on Schmarlo's

Landing. The trees, shrubs, and grass were green. The sidewalks were swept, and trashcans empty.

Ka walked to the playground. The sand was perfectly flat and level, as if no one had ever touched it. He stood for a moment, regarding the spot where Alorus had died. It almost seemed too perfect of a place for anyone to experience any pain, but he knew better.

There wasn't a cloud in the sky, as Ka walked to the very edge of the Landing. A small half-wall and guardrail stood at the very edge of the building. Some people couldn't get very close, but Ka walked right up to the wall, reached out his hand, and felt the force-field cover that protected the Landing. He wondered whether it might not have been better for there to be no force-field cover. Maybe he could have run to the wall and jumped over before Alorus had died. Maybe he could have fallen off before he had sold the rath to Alorus.

"Why are you here, Ka?" asked the boy.

He turned to see Alorus standing behind him and looking at him intently again.

"I don't know," Ka answered him.

"How come you and I are the only ones here on the Landing?" Alorus inquired.

Ka looked at the boy. He wished with all his heart that he could undo what he had done. A tear began to run down the boy's face. Ka stepped towards the boy, but the boy took a step back.

"Ka, why isn't there anyone else? Why is it just you and me here?"

"I don't know why, Alorus. It just is."

Ka walked over to a nearby bench and sat down. Alorus followed but stood a few feet from the bench.

"Where are we going, Ka?"

"Back to Koranth."

"Are we going home?" asked the boy.

"No. I've been assigned to Elite Forces. I'm going to training," stated Ka.

"Do they like to have guys that are real killers in Elite Forces?"

Ka's face dropped into his hands, and he began to cry again. Maybe there was something to the boy's insight. Maybe he would be good for a place that trained soldiers to be the best. To kill on command. Maybe he was nothing more than a killer.

The shuttle landed with a jarring bounce, waking Kadamba. He looked around, almost expecting to see Alorus standing there, looking accusingly at him, but there was no one but the Lieutenant signaling him to the door.

"This portal trip will be a little different than your last," chuckled the Lieutenant. "You're not going first-class this time. This is true military portal transportation. Welcome to the Pooshz Rapid Transport Facility."

They placed their bags on a conveyor belt and watched them zoom into a hole and out of sight. They were surrounded by all sorts of military personnel. They were waved through and headed into a large, open building with a maze of walkways. The employees of this facility were obviously military and simply fulfilling their duty, which was packing the passengers as efficiently as possible into the tubes.

Lieutenant Padda and Kadamba were directed to the same tube, as was a third soldier. Little was said as the men were stacked into the tube. While each had his own space, it was even more claustrophobic than before. The space was tighter, and the surface was harder. However, it was the same calm voice that came on in the dimly lit space to review the safety instructions. This time, Kadamba pushed the button and felt the gentle spray of mist hit his face. With the next breath, he was unconscious.

Chapter 24
Lost Love

The smell of the barbeque filled the air. Captain Tristanidad Luciano stood near the grill on the deck in his backyard, wearing casual clothes and holding a pair of tongs, as Colonel Jecamiah Agastya walked around the house and greeted his young friend. The Colonel, also dressed casually, took a deep breath. "Oh Lords of the Fourth System, what are you cooking? We're going to have to fight off your neighbors!"

Captain Luciano smiled. He was happy that his mentor and friend would join him on an off-duty day. The Captain's children played in the yard, laughing and enjoying themselves. As was often the case, Mungo Chaldea, the General's son, was playing with them. The Colonel smiled as he watched the kids, and Luciano handed Agastya a dark glass bottle without any label.

"Brewed it myself," confided Luciano, as Agastya studied the bottle.

Agastya sniffed the opening of the bottle, and his eyes widened as he smiled. He could smell the strong hops' scent, but he also could smell a familiar, citrusy aroma. He tilted the bottle back and took a long draw. "Amazing, my friend. You certainly have a talent for food and drink."

"Do you detect a hint of any fruit?" asked Luciano.

"Sayangfruit, from the tropics, I believe," Agastya suggested.

"Very good," replied Luciano. "What do you think of it?"

"I think you better have more than one bottle set aside for me this evening!"

Both men laughed as they looked out in the yard, watching the kids continue to play. The Captain's wife, Kalila Luciano, came out the backdoor, holding a large tray. Luciano kissed her as she handed him the tray.

"I know you two boys forget the vegetables, if someone doesn't put them in your hands; all you two do is eat meat and drink beer!" she joked, as she hugged Agastya and whispered into his ear. "We're so glad you decided to join us this evening. It means a lot to Tristanidad and to me." She kissed Luciano again and headed back inside.

"What's this about?" Agastya asked Luciano.

"Fifteen years ago today, my friend," replied Luciano, "you kept me from making a terrible mistake. I was ready to let her go, but you persuaded me otherwise. I'll never be able to repay you for that."

The Colonel smiled and nodded. He was happy for his young friend. Out in the yard, the kids were laughing and running around without a care in the world. The Captain's kids had a wonderful family. They were growing up in a fine home, with two parents that loved each other and loved their children without conditions. He was proud of his friend for also being so supportive of Mungo. The boy was spending more and more time at the Luciano home. While the boy's home was less than ideal, at least he had a place where he could feel loved and safe.

*****

Earmon Terman watched as Colonel Agastya walked in the door of the Boatyard Grub and Pub. Reaching below the bar, he brought up an empty glass, setting it on the bar in front of the seat that he was sure the Colonel would use. He turned around and selected the tall bottle from behind the bar. As he poured the golden-colored liquid into the glass, the Colonel sat down.

Agastya studied the glass for a few moments and then took a small sip. The bartender nodded and went to wait on other customers. It was late, and the bar wasn't as busy as it had been earlier in the evening, but Earmon left the Colonel alone in his thoughts while he finished his drink. As the Colonel emptied the glass, the bartender returned, looking intently at the Colonel.

"It's a rare day that I have to ask you for another round," the Colonel remarked rather flatly.

"Is that what you really need?" replied Earmon.

The Colonel, chuckling, divulged, "I've known you for almost twenty-five years. You scare me at times with your ability to see into my soul."

"You're wrong," the bartender announced, as he placed a folded photo on the bar in front of Agastya. "Your mind tells you that too many years have passed, but your heart will never let go, until you know."

Earmon walked away, and Agastya stared at the folded photo lying in front of him. He knew what he would see without even unfolding the photo. He'd left it on this very bar, about twenty years before. It was almost inconceivable that it was sitting in front of him again. So, Earmon had picked it up off that bar and kept it for all these years, just waiting for this moment to put it in front of him again.

He picked up the photo, holding back the tears that were fighting to burst out of his eyes. It had been a wonderful evening with the Luciano family. The food and drink had been wonderful, and the company even better. Tristanidad and Kalila Luciano were two of his best friends, but they had something that he would never have. He was glad for that evening so many years ago when he'd convinced Tristanidad not to let Kalila go.

He unfolded the photo. He was so much younger in that picture. He was so happy. Aridatha Dolce had her arms around him, holding him tight and smiling. She had been the light of his life. She was so perfect. They were so in love, but he had broken her heart. He was so convinced, all those years ago, that she would be better off without him. He completely believed that his military career was simply too risky for him to make her wait for a call that might have come. He might have died in a battle somewhere, and she would have been left alone.

As he looked at the photo, he knew he'd been so wrong. Twenty years had passed, and that call would have never come. He was still alive; she was still alive, but he was all alone. Placing the photo back down on the bar, he walked out the door.

Chapter 25
Tacos and Tennessee

The evening breeze coming off the Caribbean Sea was cool, but the air continued to be warm and comfortable. Since the restaurant was only a few blocks away, Tim, Joanna, and the boys decided to walk. Bjorn had moved on to other things by the time that the boys had walked from the park to the condo. Dylan was happy that Bjorn's hadn't announced to everyone, including his mom and Tim, that he had been flattened to the ground by the most beautiful girl in the world.

As they approached El Pescado Dorado, the smell of the air was intoxicatingly full of delicious scents of Mexican fare. The smell of chilis, garlic, cumin, and cinnamon mixed with the sea breeze, and both boys attempted to speed the group up. They were already hungry, and the smell made them even hungrier.

The restaurant was a fairly large affair, with huge windows, covering much of the walls, which were opened to allow the air to circulate. The tables and chairs were carved with elaborate tropic scenes of parrots, plants, and fruits, all painted in bright, vibrant colors. It was crowded, but because Tim had reserved a table, they were seated fairly quickly. The boys ordered one of their new favorite drinks, a Sidral Dundet, an apple-flavored soda while the adults ordered traditional margaritas.

The conversation was light and happy. All four of them were smiling and happy. Then Joanna noticed that Dylan seemed a million miles away. He was staring towards the entrance, almost in a trance. "Are you okay, Dylan?"

"Uh, yeah, uh, uh, I'm fine, I mean—uh, I'm good," replied Dylan. He pulled himself back to together, unable to contain the smile that was spreading on his face.

Joanna and Tim both looked at each other and then to where Dylan had been looking. Tim chuckled, eyeing Dylan with a smile. Joanna blushed just slightly. She immediately realized what that look was on her son's face. Bjorn had been distracted and was playing with his straw when he realized that everyone at the table had goofy looks on their faces. He was perplexed for a moment, then looked around, and started giggling.

"Hey Dylan, there's your girlfriend!" he announced in an annoying, sing-song voice.

"Shut up, Bjorn," Dylan snapped back.

Tim looked at the boys quizzically, inquiring, "Do you actually know her, Dylan? She's beautiful."

Bjorn simply couldn't contain himself any longer. Dylan began to blush and shake his head up and down, knowing he was about to relive this afternoon's scene in the local park.

Bjorn began to laugh. "She about knocked Dylan's balls clean to Cuba this afternoon with a soccer ball! My dingwit brother just stood there like an idiot while she pounded that soccer ball. WHAM! Right in the NADS!"

Bjorn fell into another uncontrollable giggle festival. He tried to say more but couldn't get the words to form because of how he was cracking himself up. Dylan tried to explain what had happened, without sounding like he was some dumb, love-struck, gawking imbecile, but both his mom and Tim were having trouble not cracking up too. Then suddenly the adults both had more serious, but smiling expressions descend upon their faces.

Dylan turned his head, knowing what he would see. She was standing right there, in a flowing yellow sundress. Her dark hair, slightly wavy, appeared to shimmer and throw off reflections of different colors. With her hands clasped low and slightly drawn up, it seemed like she was a little timid or embarrassed.

Tim began to stand up and gently cleared his throat. Dylan, appreciating the hint, quickly stood to greet her. Joanna's smile widened. She was happy that Tim was teaching the boys a bit more about proper etiquette and manners. At times, it seemed a tiny bit forced and foreign in today's world, but watching her son stand and greet this beautiful young woman like a gentleman was truly heartwarming.

"Hi Dylan," Adelita spoke softly, "we met at the park today."

"Hi Adelita. Yeah. Uh. Glad to see you again," he replied, trying desperately not to trip on his own tongue.

"I just, um, well, I wanted to . . ." Before she could finish her thought, Dylan swept his arm towards his mom. "This is my mom, Joanna. And her boyfriend, Tim, and you know my little brother, Bjorn." The adults made their polite greetings while Bjorn, a little belatedly, rose to his feet to greet Adelita.

Adelita smiled at Bjorn and whispered to Dylan, but not quietly enough so that everyone heard, "Your little brother is sooo cute."

It was Bjorn's turn to blush, but always the comedian, he quickly commented, "That was a hellava shot this afternoon. Dylan's still walking funny and bowlegged!"

Before Dylan could tell his brother to shut up, Joanna piped in, "Bjorn, we need to go wash our hands before dinner." She turned to Adelita, declaring, "It was wonderful to meet you. I hope we see you again soon." She then scooted Bjorn towards the restrooms.

"I'm so, so sorry about this afternoon," Adelita offered, turning to gaze into the teenage boy's eyes. As much as he was taken with her, she was feeling just as intensely towards him.

"I think I need to go to the bar to check out the tequila selection," Tim explained, as he gave Dylan a quick wink and headed towards the bar.

Dylan looked back towards Adelita but really didn't know what to say. He was completely at ease yet completely terrified, standing there with her. Adelita was struggling to try to get a conversation going, hoping that it would tame the butterflies going wild in her stomach. All at once, they both noticed the growing commotion near the bathrooms.

An obviously drunk tourist was waving his finger at Joanna and Bjorn. He appeared to be having trouble standing, and it was apparent that he was mad at Bjorn and Joanna. Bjorn's face was clinched in rage, and his hands balled into fists.

"You little punk! Don't even try to tell me to leave her alone!" The drunk man's words were slurred and angry. "She wants to come home with me, and I'm taking her!"

All of a sudden, it felt like the building trembled. It was an eerie and frightening feeling. A huge vase, filled with a gigantic plant, rattled and fell off the shelf above the man. It came crashing down on his head, and he toppled completely unconscious to the floor.

Activity burst throughout the restaurant, and Dylan began moving towards his mom. He saw Tim push through the crowd and signal towards the entrance. Tim scooped up Bjorn, grabbed Joanna's hand, and headed towards the door. Dylan was only a few paces behind, and when he got outside, Bjorn was nearly hysterical. He was crying and kept repeating, "It followed me! It followed me!" Within a few moments, Joanna had calmed the boy, but he was visibly shaken.

The manager came out the door a few minutes later, looking very shaken and apologizing over and over. Tim pulled him aside, and they launched into a rapid conversation. Neither seemed exactly sure of what had happened, but the manager was reassuring Tim that it was all the drunken man's fault. Some patrons had seen him grab Joanna roughly, so Bjorn had pushed him away and tried to pull his mom to safety. Bjorn was a hero, and the manager assured Tim that the drunken patron would be arrested.

Adelita came out of the restaurant, with a slightly older couple. Dylan knew at once that they were her parents. It just made sense. The Asian man was handsome, tall, lean, and dressed impeccably. He was holding his wife's hand. She was elegant and moved gracefully. Her long hair and high cheekbones were very similar to Adelita's. He could see the resemblance at once. Dylan wasn't sure if she was Hispanic or maybe Spanish, or even Greek. They were both very kind and concerned with what had happened. Bjorn was still rattled. He held his mom's hand and kept himself very close her. Adelita's father managed to bring a bit of comfort to the boy with his praise of the boy's bravery.

Bjorn just wanted to go back to the condo, and Tim and Joanna decided that was the best plan. Adelita's parents offered to have Dylan stay. Perhaps, the two teenagers could even get their own table for dinner. The manager, who was talking with the police, overheard, and interjected that he would be honored for them to stay and that dinner would be his treat. Dylan was torn. His little brother was so shaken up, and Dylan was often the one to care for him. Both his mom and Tim urged him to stay, and, after a few moments, he decided that he would. Adelita gently placed her hand on Dylan's elbow as a happy smile spread across her face.

Dinner was like a dream for the young couple. While the circumstances weren't necessarily "traditional," it was still both of their first dates at a nice restaurant, eating at their own table. They found many commonalities. Both loved soccer, but Dylan had moved on to other sports in high school and admitted he was never even close to as good as she was. They were both 15, loved some of the same TV shows, disliked chemistry class, and even shared a desire to skydive, which none of the parents would allow. Adelita's father owned a company that had property around the world in various resort communities. They were living here because the company was building a new hotel.

Living here had one other big advantage for Adelita. Her mother's sister lived here with her uncle, Hector Morozea. He was a scuba diving instructor and guide. They decided that it would be fun to have Uncle Hector take the two of them on a dive.

When Dylan returned to the condo, his mom was curled up in Tim's arms on the couch. It was obvious that she had been crying. Joanna, pulling herself up, asked how the rest of Dylan's evening was. Of course, it had been like a dream, better than he had ever expected. Both adults were very happy for Dylan and very pleased that his evening had gone so well. They told him that Bjorn had eventually calmed down and was already asleep. They had come back to the condo and had a quiet dinner.

"I told Tim about Tennessee," Joanna confided to Dylan.

"Snotty, self-righteous, small towns aren't always the American dream," Tim asserted, with a very compassionate voice.

Joanna and the boys had moved to the small town, to live with her mother, as the grandmother's age was beginning to weigh heavily. It had seemed so idealistic, at first. It was small-town America, with good schools, a five-block long downtown, and friendly people that all seemed to know each other.

Then the trouble had started. In some ways, it was a bit unreal. No one really believed in ghosts or the supernatural, but strange events began to happen in their home. A toy would go flying across a room. A book would fall off a bookshelf, seemingly of its own accord. The house seemed to shake at times, rattling dishes and pictures on the wall.

Joanna had been lost, at first, on what to do. She didn't want to seem crazy, but she eventually confided in the wife of the minister of the church that they occasionally attended. The woman had been compassionate, and in many ways she and Joanna became friends. In truth, she really didn't believe Joanna, at least in the beginning. Then one day she while she was visiting, the television remote fell off the table and rolled across the floor, right in front of her.

Soon afterwards, the rumors began. It was subtle, at first. There would be a strange look from someone in the grocery store, or a car would drive past the house more slowly than usual. Then it began to grow. Joanna overheard that her mother's house might be haunted by a demon or a poltergeist. Some of the boys' friends didn't come over to the house anymore and even began avoiding them at school. It was uncomfortable, and the family began to feel isolated.

Of course, there were a few people who were compassionate. They tried to be kind, but it was always from a distance. In a town like that one, conformity and having a place to belong were important. No one was comfortable with being seen as bucking the social norms or the prevailing perceptions of those who were the most vocal in town. Sometimes, Joanna would wonder if any of these nicer folks were trying to talk sense into those who had come to the judgment that the devil had moved into her house on Oak Street. She knew better. It would be easier for her to move away and let the rumors die down, but her mother had become very ill. She had to hold on.

Sadly, within a few weeks, Joanna's mother passed away from a heart attack. It was apparently evidence enough for the minister's wife to decide that an exorcism was in order. She showed up on a Saturday morning to piously let Joanna know that her husband and a few elders would be coming by to rid the house of the evil spirits.

She and Joanna were standing in the living room arguing when Bjorn walked in on them. The woman tried to reassure Bjorn that the house would soon be rid of the evil poltergeist. Joanna demanded that the woman leave and not to bother coming back. At that moment, a picture fell off the wall. Even though it was a few feet from the woman, it landed at her feet, cutting her legs in many places. She left in a hurry, blathering on about Satan and demons and unclean spirits.

Things got even worse after the woman wrote an article in the church newspaper about the devil moving into a local home. Even the tiny local paper picked up the story and ran an article. It was more that anyone should have to take. Joanna moved the boys to Denver, and they severed contact with everyone they knew in Tennessee.

Chapter 26
An Illusion of Compliance

"General, in less than one month, the Donovackia Corporation will launch this vessel into space," Tomar Donovackia declared, as he looked down onto the gigantic spaceship that sat in the middle of an even more enormous building. General Swinton Chaldea stood beside him on the walkway that circled twenty stories above the vast open space of the building.

The Donovackia Corporation launch facility was not quite as big as the portal facilities that linked various planets together, but it still was the size of a small city, with dozens of buildings and tens of thousands of people working towards getting the crew and the ship ready for the one-way trip to Earth.

The men began walking back to the bank of offices and meeting rooms that hung in one corner of the huge space, much like an insect nest. Tomar loved spending time in these offices, looking down on all of the activity. This would be the first of many space launches, and, over the last few months, he had become more involved with the process. His first priority was the overall health and growth of the corporation, but this launch was an intense passion.

"Is Commander Conall Bornani living up to your expectations, sir?" asked the General.

"Exceedingly! Thank you for putting him at the top of the list. I believe he can handle the delicate and difficult challenges that face the crew in the next few years," Tomar answered.

"If I may ask, sir, what do you think the chances are that this 'Earth' is ready for development?"

"Good question," responded Tomar, "and one I have asked myself and dozens of others, over and over, for two years now. The truth is that we don't know and won't know until the return vessel comes back. The likelihood is not good. They only harnessed the atom about forty years ago. The last mission revealed no Transprophetics. The best guess is that it will probably be another 20 to 40 years before Earth is ready."

"Excuse me for asking, sir, but why not wait another 15 to 20 years?"

"General Chaldea, it is, of course, because of the less public aspects of the exploratory mission. When a crew finds a planet not yet ready, they stay. Everyone knows this. What is less common knowledge is that every crew member, civilian and military, is extensively trained to hunt and kill Transprophetics. No matter what stage a planet is in, in terms of economic and technological development, we must keep them from advancing as they would with the discovery and scientific validation of a Transprophetic. We want a planet to build out infrastructure, technology, and global trade on the most massive scale possible, without risking our capability to invade and dominate."

"Of course, sir," the General agreed. He knew this, but struggled to make small talk with the most powerful man on two worlds. Tomar was intimidating, and it had been hours since the General had a chance to relax—with his secret friend. Beginning to feel frayed, he needed a little help to stay balanced and focused.

As they walked into the entryway of the hanging bank of offices and conference rooms, the shrill voice of Ionia Villegas broke the General's concentration on that clear liquid that he loved so much. "Just the two gentlemen that I was looking forward to seeing!" The General wanted so badly to grab the woman, walk back out to the walkway, and toss her to her death. They exchanged pleasantries and headed into a conference room.

"General, did our dear Chairman tell you that we would be meeting today?" asked Ionia to the General.

"Ionia," interjected Tomar, "the General and I have been throat deep in extremely important matters today. I simply forgot to tell him that we would be getting together."

The General worked to keep the bile from running up into his mouth. He hated this woman but greatly respected Tomar. What on earth could the two of them have to talk to him about together? Tomar got things done. Ionia Villegas simply meddled, annoying everyone with her social and environmental fixations.

"General," Tomar began as they all sat down. "My military has been expanding at an enormous pace. Our normal recruiting efforts are not keeping up, even when we factor in the addition of the

Stameyerson Corporation and the Kathor Corporation's militaries. We need more bodies, faster."

"Yes," interjected Ionia. "And the pilot program that you and I have begun, General, has already produced results. It's time to expand it exponentially!"

The General looked at the both of them, trying to muffle and disguise the shock of what he was hearing. He couldn't believe that the Chairman could buy into the crap that this horrid woman was hawking. She would ruin the military with vagrants and criminals.

"One of the twenty pilot subjects is back in jail," the General noted. "He couldn't seem to control his desire to steal and brutalize others."

"Yes, but eighteen have completed their secondary training and have been permanently placed," Tomar responded. "The economics are also good. We buy these kids from the justice processing companies or the containment companies at a factored discount to what the companies would get from the government over time. We've worked a deal with multiple governments to repay that discount with an added margin to more than cover any training that we provide. Everybody wins."

A smile began to wash over both Tomar and Ionia's faces. The General forced a smile to appear on his face, despite his disgust. These scumbags that Tomar and Ionia wanted in his military were people who had screwed up in life. Why should they be allowed in society?

"To make this even better," Tomar continued, "the Ministry's military is also growing at a terrific pace. Because we have the best training infrastructure in the galaxy, we've struck an agreement with the Ministry's military to provide trained soldiers for its infantry and transportation units. We make a profit on buying the bodies out of the justice and containment facilities and training them, and then we make another round of profit selling them to the Ministry. We have to source more bodies, and this will be an excellent source."

The General's mind went into overdrive. He had to sink this plan. How could he have let it come this far? "We still have one test pilot subject who has not completed his training," the General blurted out.

"Yes, my dear Kadamba Vorhoor," Ionia added, "that boy is absolutely proving the value of this program. In a few months, he'll graduate from our military's Elite Forces training. My nephew would be so proud. He was right. The boy deserved another shot at life."

Tomar laid out his vision for the military's recruiting expansion, including a healthy budget to begin buying candidates out of the justice processing companies and containment companies. The General had no choice but to pretend that he was on-board with the programs. Inside, he felt himself growing angrier and angrier.

Chapter 27
A Question of Perception

Captain Tristanidad Luciano and Lieutenant Mittelwert Padda came to attention as Colonel Jecamiah Agastya stormed into the conference room and sealed the door behind him. He had been pulled from an important meeting regarding security at all of the Donovackia Corporation properties during the exploratory space launch that was now only two days away.

"This had better be damn . . ." began the Colonel as he looked at the men. "What the hell happened to you, Lieutenant?"

"That's why you're here, sir," Captain Luciano answered. "We have a very serious issue on our hands."

The Colonel signaled his junior officers to have a seat. He looked across the table at the Lieutenant's blackened eye. He knew this man to be one significant soldier and knew he had to be quite proficient at hand-to-hand combat. For someone to take a swing at the Lieutenant was pretty brave or pretty stupid.

"Alright, Lieutenant, explain," commanded Colonel Agastya.

"Sir, I'm not sure . . ." began the Lieutenant.

Captain Luciano interjected, "General Chaldea hit him."

"I did not defend myself or retaliate," the Lieutenant added, with a mix of honor and regret.

"Whoa, whoa, whoa," the Colonel asserted, stopping the obviously agitated men before him. "Slow it down, and explain exactly what happened."

Taking a deep breath, the Lieutenant began to explain what had happened. He had been called to headquarters from Elite Forces training by the General himself. The General was extremely irate about one of the cadets, Kadamba Vorhoor. The Lieutenant explained that for the last year of Elite Forces training, they had made the cadet's life absolutely miserable. He had the worst tasks. He went days without sleep. He was shorted on rations on long jungle missions. Every covert means had been attempted to get the kid to wash himself out, but he wouldn't give up.

The General, in a fit of fury, had accused the Lieutenant of insubordination. For almost twenty minutes he yelled and screamed at the Lieutenant, eventually coming from behind his desk and striking the man.

"Then what?" asked Colonel Agastya.

"He started throwing up in his trashcan, and I went to Captain Luciano's office," Lieutenant Padda stated.

"You've had this kid through both initial training and now Elite training. I personally discussed with you the need to secretly make this kid miserable enough to wash out. What happened?" Colonel Agastya inquired.

"Kadamba wouldn't give up. We made him miserable, as you ordered Colonel, but he simply took whatever was thrown at him and just kept going," the Lieutenant explained.

"Why don't you go ahead and show the Colonel what you showed me," Captain Luciano suggested.

The Lieutenant tapped a few places on the table, and a shrunken, three-dimensional scene rose from the table. The men stood up to look at the image. It was of a hilly wooded area, and soldiers were grouped in various places.

"Capture the flag," the Colonel noted, "still one of the best training games ever."

The Lieutenant began to explain the nuances of this particular version of the game, including the fact that it was being played with energy blasters set to stun. If you got hit, you wouldn't die, but you would have one hell of a bruise. As always, the goal was to capture the other team's flag and bring it safely back to your own team's base. There were three teams. He pointed out the miniature image that was Kadamba, marking him in red. He then pointed out Kadamba's team commander, marking him in yellow.

The Colonel watched as Kadamba's team commander made mistake after mistake. He strolled into an ambush, and Kadamba tackled the commander, rolling and firing at an enemy position. The enemy dropped, and Kadamba pulled himself into a tree, taking out a second enemy while his commander obliviously yelled at him.

By the end of the game, it was obvious that Kadamba had led the commander to an enemy flag and single-handedly repelled six of their soldiers while the commander grabbed the flag. On the return trip to Kadamba's team's base, the incompetent commander stepped into the open and began waving the flag as he ran up to the his base. Kadamba, seeing the enemy soldier taking aim, sprinted forward between the commander and the incoming blast. Kadamba, hit by the energy blast, slammed into the commander, sending him falling forward into the grass. The commander crawled into the base, winning the game while Kadamba rolled in agony on the ground.

The Lieutenant continued to bring up scene after scene of training scenarios where Kadamba was put at a disadvantage, abandoned by his teammates, or directly set up to fail something. In each scene, Kadamba never gave in or gave up.

"Short of shooting the man," stated Lieutenant Padda, "I'm not sure how we could have stopped him. He's shown more courage, bravery, and honor than any cadet I've seen in a long time. The thing that makes him even more impressive, from my perspective, sir, is that he didn't have a single friend the entire time he has been both in initial training and Elite Forces training. No one seemed to be able to do anything but focus on that scar on his arm."

The Colonel began to rub his chin, looking at both men. The General's behavior had been getting worse and worse as of late. Just that morning, the Colonel also had to endure another one of the General's tirades regarding Ionia Villegas. All of his yelling and screaming was almost tolerable, but striking another officer was not.

He ordered Captain Luciano to accompany Lieutenant Padda to the medical clinic to document the injury. Military Justice Officers would meet the men at the clinic to get full statements on the assault. The Colonel ordered additional Military Justice Personnel to meet him at the General's office. It was now time to end the illusion and charade that was General Swinton Chaldea.

The two Justice Officer's came to attention as Colonel Agastya approached the door to the General's office suite. Inside, the General's secretary snapped to attention as the Colonel came into the room.

"I'm sorry, sir," the secretary began, but before she could finish, a second voice interpreted her.

"I am Counselor Dominisk Nortoe," the man began as he held out his hand to the Colonel. "I am legal counsel for General Swinton Chaldea."

Agastya simply looked at his hand and then stared directly at the man. He had no intention of shaking his hand. He was not here to play games. It was time for the General to face reality.

Dominisk Nortoe put his hand back to his side and began explaining that the General had left the command center to attend personal business and that he would be unavailable and out of touch for the next three weeks.

"You mean he is checking into another rehab facility to pretend to deal with his problem?" barked Colonel Agastya. "Does that son-of-a-bitch really think he can blame his addiction for his recent actions and not be held accountable?"

The Colonel turned to the two Military Justice Enforcement Officer. "Get this man out of this building before I throw him out a window!"

*****

The glass was already sitting on the bar that evening when Colonel Agastya walked into Boatman's. As he sat down, Earmon Terman began to pour. The bartender looked at the military man with sympathy. "You've had a rough day, my friend."

The Colonel chuckled as he shook his head affirmatively and took a long sip from the glass. It burned slightly on his tongue and his throat, but the flavors and the intensity of the drink were compelling. He sat the glass on the bar and studied it. Why was it that he and so many people could simply enjoy the taste and even the physical and psychological effect of this liquid while others became overwhelmed and lost control of their very lives to it? Was it as simple as the difference between want and need? He desired to blame the character of the person that let the liquid control his life, but he knew that wasn't true. He knew too many good people who had succumbed to addiction to simply blame someone's character.

He saw the finger pointing at his glass before he realized that it was Captain Luciano. The man pulled up a barstool and thanked the bartender as he poured another glass and refilled Agastya's.

"Make any progress?" asked the Captain, after taking a sip.

"The General has been ordered to return within seven days," replied the Colonel.

"He won't be allowed to return to his home. I talked to his wife, Camdrin, and she's done with him," stated Captain Luciano.

"Good for her. She deserves much better than that bastard."

The men sipped their drinks, trying to unwind after their stressful day. They both agreed that it was an amazing amount of restraint and control that Lieutenant Padda had exhibited after being attacked by the General. Neither of the men believed that they would have been able to hold back if the General had taken a swing at them. However, by not becoming physically engaged, the Lieutenant had made the case against the General stronger. Unfortunately, they both knew that General Chaldea was a very powerful man, so bringing him down wasn't going to be as easy as they hoped.

Their conversation was interpreted by the vibration of the devices on their wrists. "Well, so much for wrapping up this day," the Colonel remarked. "Back to headquarters we go."

"I've got to hit the head before we leave," Captain Luciano declared, as he got up from the bar. "Pay the tab, and I'll settle with you later."

Colonel Agastya turned back to the bar to call for the bill, but Earmon was already there, holding the folded photo in his hand. "Drinks on me this evening, Colonel," the bartender announced, "but only if you take this with you."

He handed the picture to the Colonel, who opened it up and looked at it again. Aridatha Dolce's smile was exactly like he remembered. Even after twenty years, he could still remember how her lips tasted and the way she smelled. He still dreamt of those mornings when he would wake up in her arms, and the entire world was only the two of them. He looked up at Earmon, trying to find the right words to say. The bartender simply looked him in the eyes.

"It's time for you to have her picture close to you again," began Earmon. "In this life, my friend, there are some regrets you may be forced to take to your grave. But others, we can choose to die with those, or not."

*****

Chairman Tomar Donovackia was on the large screen in the Executive Command Briefing Room when the two officers walked in. Most of the Donovackia Military Command was already assembled, and the last few stragglers arrived within a few moments.

"Thank you all for arriving so quickly," began the Chairman. "Today has been a significantly challenging day for our organization.

As some of you already know, General Chaldea has a personal family issue that requires his absence for a short period of time."

Agastya and Luciano looked at each other, forcing themselves not to let others see their eyes rolling.

The Chairman continued, "Unfortunately, we've had an even more significant crisis this evening at the Donovackia Corporation launch facility."

Beside the image of the Chairman, a video feed came up of a small bus driving across a large tarmac at the launch facility. Without warning the bus exploded, and its burning wreckage was scattered for hundreds of feet. "On that bus was the backup crew for the exploration mission to Earth, and one member of the crew."

Over the next couple of hours, the assembled military command, the Chairman, and other officials debated how best to proceed. It was agreed that it was fortunate that none of the civilian experts were lost, and while tragic, it was neither the commander nor the vice-commander that was killed in the blast. The decision was made that security would be massively boosted at the launch facility and that the mission would proceed as planned. The weather forecast was perfect, and with some experts predicting solar winds and significant solar flares within a week, it seemed the best solution.

As acting commander of the Donovackia Military, the job of finding a replacement for the dead crewman fell on Colonel Agastya.

"Colonel Agastya, the launch is in less than 48 hours," Chairman Donovackia reminded him, as all eyes turned to look at the Colonel. "Are you absolutely certain that you can find a replacement crew member?"

The Colonel, looking at the screen, answered, "Yes, I am sure we can."

Chapter 28
An Honorable Farewell

Kadamba watched as the shuttle approached and landed at the Elite Forces training center. It was the same shuttle that he had been on before, but this would be his last time. The door opened and Lieutenant Padda stepped out and beckoned Kadamba aboard. The shuttle was airborne in moments.

The seats were as plush and as comfortable as Kadamba remembered them, and an attendant served him a drink. It was a stark change from the last year of training. He'd endured countless hours of physical and psychological drills. While it had been extremely tough and there were so many times that he wanted to give up, he continued to remember the terror of being in the containment facility. No matter how miserable he seemed, he was better off suffering with a weapon in his hand than being abused by Jackos the Giant.

The Lieutenant sat across from him, studying him intently. He'd watched this boy become a soldier and, in many ways, become a man in the last year and a half. Society's norms would likely condemn Kadamba forever. It wouldn't matter what he did or what contribution he might make to the two worlds. He was branded and forever would be seen as less than human.

Somewhere there was a family that had lost a child to the actions of the man sitting across from him. Lieutenant Padda pondered that thought for a while. Did they still hate Kadamba, did they even hate him to begin with, or did they even know him? It was difficult to ponder what it must be like to lose a child. It had to be an experience like none other. Padda was torn in many ways as he looked at Kadamba. Yes, he'd done something terrible, but what the Lieutenant had seen was not the monster that the world wanted Kadamba to be, but a tenacious, honorable soldier.

"Son, are you sure you want to do this?" asked Lieutenant Padda. "You haven't had much time to think about this."

"Yes, sir," replied Kadamba. "I am sure that I want to do this."

"Alright," replied Padda. "You know that this is the third time that we've been on this shuttle together. And this is the third time that I've watched the strings of your fate be twisted in a direction that I would have never guessed would happen."

"Sir?" asked Kadamba.

"I am your commanding officer, but I am at a loss at what to say now. This world would condemn you and damn you forever. I don't know you that well personally, but I know what I have seen. You've never given up, even in some extremely tough circumstances, with many things and people weighing against you. I think it will serve you well, whatever the future holds for you"

"Thank you, sir," Kadamba responded, honored by what the Lieutenant had just said.

"Get some sleep, son, we'll be at the launch facility in the morning."

Kadamba looked out the window of the shuttle. They were high in the sky, so he couldn't see the ground. Late the night before, he had a holographic conference with Colonel Jecamiah Agastya. As he walked to the conference room, it had seemed very odd to him. He had only just finished training. He wasn't really that important, but the acting head of the Donovackia Military wanted to talk to him.

Kadamba had accepted the Colonel's offer without a second thought, but that was last night. Today, he was still confident that he wanted to go, but he thought about his family. Over two years had passed. Had they forgotten him? Did they still love him? Should he try to contact them before he left? It was all too much to think about right now. He could stay awake for hours and hours thinking about it, but it was time for sleep.

Ka took a deep breath. The air was clean, almost sterile. As always, everything was perfect on Schmarlo's Landing. The grass and shrubs and trees were all green. Not a speck of litter was anywhere to be seen.

Ka, looking down, realized he was still in his uniform. It felt odd to be dressed like this, rather than in the clothes he was wearing the day Alorus died. He walked around the Landing, looking for the boy but couldn't find him. The playground was perfect as always, without a speck of sand out of place.

Ka walked to a bench at the edge of the Landing and looked out at the landscape. The sky was black and grey in the distance, with clouds looming large on the horizon. The sun, close to setting, cast an eerie glow across Stujorkian City.

"A storm is coming," the boy announced.

Ka spun around, almost grabbing for the weapon that should be at his side. He knew it was Alorus, but he had been startled by the boy.

"Ka, do you see the storm in the distance?"

"Yes, I see it," replied Ka.

"Will it be a bad storm?" asked the boy.

"I don't know, but I think we're safe here in the Landing."

Ka walked over to a bench and sat down. He looked out at the storm, watching the lightning between the clouds, and felt the tears welling up in his eyes. Why did he have to say that? The Landing would be unaffected by the storm, but that didn't mean it was a safe place.

He gestured to Alorus to join him on the bench, knowing that he wouldn't. He'd been here on the Landing so many times in the last couple years, so he knew Alorus wouldn't get too close. He wasn't sure why he always ended up in the Landing with Alorus, but he did. Over and over and over again.

"We're in that shuttle again, aren't we, Ka? Where are you going?" asked Alorus.

"Someplace called Earth."

"Ka, I don't want to leave Koranth again. Do I have to go with you?"

"I'm afraid we don't have a choice."

As dawn broke, the shuttle touched down gently, and Kadamba continued to sleep as two men walked into the room. They both looked at him, but one of them was shaking his head. "Are you sure this is the best you could do, Lieutenant?" asked Commander Conall Bornani. "We launch this afternoon."

"I think this kid will surprise you," replied Lieutenant Padda.

"A drug-dealing, child-killing, untrained thug?" asked Commander Bornani.

"He's trained. He passed Elite Forces military training under circumstances that most men would crumble under."

"Maybe you're right, Lieutenant," Bornani stated. "The training is excellent, but I wish he had some real experience."

"Commander, we found a replacement crew member for you in a matter of hours. He's here, and the launch will remain on schedule," the Lieutenant ordered.

Bornani began to chuckle under his breath. "You know, you are right. I've got a trained Elite Forces soldier who already has a taste for blood. He'll be pared with Dr. Nahash Tarea. He's one of the Transprophetic Experts. They'll probably love hunting their prey."

Chapter 29
A Nightmare Begins

The day following the incident at the El Pescado Dorado restaurant, Dylan, Joanna, and Tim were sitting at the table, lazily enjoying a late breakfast. They could hear Bjorn in the bedroom, occasionally giggling, but since they were on vacation, they just let him relax. Eventually, he came into the living area with a monstrous grin on his face. For a boy who seemed so scared and shaken up the night before, he sure was in a jovial mood this morning. Bjorn was like that. He could switch from one emotion to another on a dime. Sometimes it made sense; sometimes it was just best to accept it for what it was.

Everyone looked at him, just waiting for the announcement that they all knew was coming. Unsurprisingly, Bjorn played it up, dragging out the obvious anticipation that was building. He set his tablet computer on the table.

"Dylan, I'm sorry that I didn't have my phone out to take a video of Adelita mashing your junk with a soccer ball. You'd be famous on YouTube too."

Everyone looked at Bjorn quizzically. He tapped a few places on his tablet, spun the screen towards them, and announced, "I'm a supernatural rock star!"

The title of the video Bjorn opened was "Supernatural Rock Star Kid Smashes Vase on Drunk A**hole's Head."

Everyone watched as the scene from the previous evening played out on the small screen. None of them had noticed the night before that someone was recording the events on a phone. The drunken man had tried to stop Joanna as she was heading towards the bathroom. She brushed him off, but he became extremely belligerent, very quickly. The scene showed Bjorn taking a step towards the man, his face burning with anger. Whoever posted the video had added some visual effects that made it look like Bjorn was sending out waves to the vase.

The vase tumbled, smashed the man on the head, and then the video cut to a stadium view of a crowd exploding in cheers.

Everyone was quite for a moment, not exactly sure what to say.

"Don't mess with me! I'll kick your butt!" Bjorn exclaimed as he struck a pose like a bodybuilder and growled. "Brainwaves baby! I gotz dem brainwaves!"

The night before, Joanna and Tim had convinced Bjorn that it wasn't a poltergeist or demon. More than likely, it was a tiny earthquake tremor, or even more probable, it was one of those trucks that loudly rumbled through the streets. Perhaps it had bumped into the building. Bjorn had agreed with them last night and let his fear go. Today, he was in quite a happy mood, especially since he was the star of a trending, popular video on the Internet. Even better, but slightly annoying as the day wore on, was that he could say, "Brainwaves baby! I gotz dem brainwaves!"

Adelita joined them at the condo in the afternoon to swim and play in the ocean. To anyone watching the scene, the growing infatuation between Dylan and Adelita was very obvious. Adults on the beach and at the pool smiled when they saw the young, awkward couple. To make it even more adorable, they had a little wingman, whose goofy antics never seemed to completely stop.

The next day, the boys walked to the park again to watch Adelita play soccer. There were even more kids playing soccer and playing in the park than the day that they had met Adelita. It was pretty crowded.

"I think I will wander around and see if I can get myself a girlfriend too," Bjorn announced in a smartass tone, "but I won't have to get my nuts crushed to do it!"

Dylan cracked up and told him to stay in the park, where he could see him. Bjorn zipped off, and Dylan found where Adelita and her friends were playing soccer. As he came towards the group, she looked in his direction and then came bolting towards him. He was surprised, but happy that she was so eager to see him. Suddenly, he realized she was yelling and pointing at something behind him. He turned in time to see two men dragging Bjorn into a van and speeding away.

Chapter 30
Once a Coward

The video feed of the Donovackia Launch Center Mission Control Room was still abuzz with activity three days after the successful launch of the mission to Earth. Colonel Agastya watched the large screen as he sat alone in the Executive Command Briefing Room. He had just finished running another briefing for the Donovackia Military Command. He was exhausted, but satisfied. The launch had gone off without a hitch, and as equally important, those responsible for the bus explosion had been captured. They were nothing but some fringe, radical, political group that wanted attention.

He tapped a few places on the table in front of him, and a screen appeared over the table. He began scrolling through his messages, working to sort the important from the less important. It always seemed a nearly impossible task, but a necessary one. The image of his secretary appeared in the corner of the screen, and he swiped it to cover the entire screen.

"I'm sorry to interrupt you, sir," began the man, "but the housing authority needs your authorization to provide an apartment for General Chaldea. He is back, but his wife won't let him back in the house."

The Colonel chuckled. If he didn't authorize this, the General would be homeless. Of course, that wasn't true. He would find someplace while his administrative review was held. This whole process was going to be so painful. The illusion that the General had created was believed by so many. His character, Captain Luciano's character, and even Lieutenant Padda's were being quietly attacked. This whole damn thing would probably turn into an intolerable circus.

"Authorize the housing request," replied the Colonel as he closed the session, and the screen disappeared. He watched the large screen on the wall of the briefing room again for a while. Tomar

Donovackia had returned to the Mission Control Room. He didn't provide any real value, but he was the Chairman, and this was his game.

The Colonel pulled out the picture of Aridatha Dolce. He must have looked at it a thousand times since Earmon made him take it. Her smile was still the most beautiful thing he had ever seen. He could almost feel her arms around him as he looked into her eyes. Earmon's words keep playing over and over in his head.

"In this life, my friend, there are some regrets you may be forced to take to your grave. But others, we can choose to die with those or not."

He pulled the screen back up from the table and did something that he had vowed to himself that he never would. It wasn't that he couldn't, but he just never thought he could handle knowing what happened to her. In his position, it would be so easy to find where she went, what she did, who her friends were, and so much more about her life. It was just too painful for him to know. He always hoped she had found love again, but then again, he hoped that she was missing him as much as he missed her.

The picture that appeared on the screen was as beautiful as ever. Age had touched her, just like it does to all of us, but for her, it made her even more beautiful. Agastya struggled to hold back the tears as they tried to push themselves from his eyes. Why had he left her? Why had he never tried to find her and tell her what a stupid fool he had been? He flipped through the pictures, landing on one of her sitting on a beach, looking out to sea. He read the words that had been superimposed towards the bottom of the photo and then touched a few places on the screen. A physical copy of the photo appeared on the table. He folded it, put it into his pocket, and headed to Boatman's.

*****

Earmon was waiting at the bar as Colonel Agastya walked into Boatman's Grub and Pub. The Colonel smiled to his friend, but the bartender didn't smile back. Agastya walked up to the bar and sat down. Earmon simply looked at him with a nearly expressionless face.

"Good evening, Colonel," began Earmon as he pulled a glass that was already filled from under the bar. "Your usual sir, a double Grenadines Special." The Colonel looked at the glass. He wanted this to be a joke, but he knew the bartender too well. It wasn't a joke. There was someone, or more likely, more than one person, in this bar that wanted to kill the Colonel. He took the drink, and downed the entire thing in one gulp. It was sweet, but had no sting to it at all.

Earmon pulled another already filled glass from under the counter and set it in front of the Colonel. "Rough day running the whole military?"

"Probably not as rough as my night might become," replied Colonel Agastya.

"I think it will be an easier evening than you thought. It's always good to have friends," assured the bartender as Captain Luciano sat down next to the Colonel.

"Give me a double Grenadines Special," Luciano stated, without missing a beat.

The Colonel and the bartender looked at the Captain with surprise on their faces, as Earmon placed a filled glass in front of Luciano. "I am the senior officer of the Donovackia Military's Elite Forces. I am trained to know when things are not how they should be." The Captain paused and looked at the Colonel. "For example, there are four men at the second booth from the far wall that shouldn't be here."

Earmon shook his head affirmatively and pulled a bottle from under the bar. "I think the two of you will probably finish this, and it looks like everything is under control."

"How did you know to be here?" ask the Colonel.

"Earmon messaged me about twenty minutes ago," began the Captain. "I have no idea how he got my contact details, but he did, and he told me that you would need me here this evening."

As the Colonel affirmatively shook his head, the Captain laid what looked like a pen on the bar. The Colonel picked it up and studied it. It wasn't a pen. It was smooth and blunt on both ends. There were no markings, and nothing happened to it as the Colonel tapped it on the bar.

The Captain took it back and began to twirl it though his fingers. "It's my new toy. Looks like I will get to show it off later tonight." The two men continued to drink the sweet juice, pretending to become intoxicated. They laughed and joked while the four men at the booth occasionally stole glances in their direction. After a couple of hours had passed, the officers' plan was set.

Colonel Agastya stood up from the bar stool and slapped the Captain on the back. He took a few steps, then staggered back, and said his goodbyes. Appearing to be unsteady on is feet, he headed for the door. Once he was outside, the four men in the booth stood up and followed. Captain Luciano was a few steps behind them.

Outside, Colonel Agastya leaned his hand on the wall of the building and began to cuss in a slurred voice. “Crap, I shoulda hit the damn head before I walked out. Oh well, fuck it, the alley works too,” he muttered, as he pushed himself up and headed into the darkened alley.

The four men spread out as they entered the alley, knowing their prey was compromised and alone. The man who appeared to be the leader stepped deeper into the alley and called into the dark. “You traitorous son of a bitch! Now you get what’s coming to you!”

“Four against one doesn’t seem fair,” came a voice from behind the men. Captain Luciano stood at the opening of the alley, still twirling the small pen-like object in his fingers.

“Get out of here, dumbshit, and live to see another day,” called the leader.

Luciano stood there, continuing to twirl the object through his fingers. The largest of the men stepped back towards Luciano and began to take a swing. As the man’s arm moved through the air, the object in Luciano’s hand suddenly swelled and expanded into a six-foot long staff, glowing blue at each end. Before the man’s fist landed, the staff spun through the air, redirecting the blow harmlessly past Luciano’s face. With the brute off balance, Luciano stepped back, dropped low, and struck the staff across the man’s midsection. As the man began to double over in pain, Luciano came upright, bringing the other end of the staff hard across the man’s head. Without a word or utterance, the man flailed out and collapsed on the ground.

The next two men were already moving towards Luciano, who reacted quickly, with fluid, graceful movements. Within a few seconds, both men were sprawled on the ground unconscious. The leader took a step in the direction of Luciano, drawing a laser gun. Luciano spun the staff to a vertical position holding it in front of him. The two blasts from the gun were absorbed by an energy shield that emanated from the tips of the staff, protecting the Captain.

“Boo,” asserted Colonel Agastya, who had quietly slipped a few inches from the leader’s back. As the man spun, Agastya leveraged the man’s weight, twisting and breaking his gun arm. The man crumbled to the ground in pain.

Agastya picked up the laser gun and shoved it in the man’s face. “Time to start talking.”

Over the next few minutes, the man explained that he and his fellow attackers were infantry soldiers and that General Chaldea had convinced them that Colonel Agastya was the lead traitor in a conspiracy bent on destroying the Donovackia military, the Corporation, and even the Ministry itself. The men's task was to kill Agastya and then kill his traitorous accomplice—Ionia Villegas.

"What now?" asked Captain Luciano.

"I need you to get these men into military detention immediately," replied the Colonel.

"What are you going to do?"

"I'll have Military Justice meet me at the General's apartment," Colonel Agastya replied, "and by the way, I like your new toy."

*****

The Colonel waved his hand over the lock to the General's door, and the door swung open. General Chaldea rose from the couch in the middle of the room where he was sitting, dropping the bottle that was in his hands. "What in the hell do you think you are doing, Colonel?"

"It's over. For you, it's all over now," Colonel Agastya stated.

The General, stepping towards the Colonel, began to take a swing at his face. Without hesitation, Agastya blocked the punch and drove his knee hard into the General's groin. "That was for your wife, Camdrin," remarked the Colonel, "and this is for your kids." The upper cut came solidly through the General's bent-forward face, sending him backwards, crashing over the couch.

Colonel Agastya could hear him fumbling around behind the couch. The telltale buzz of an energy blaster being powered on from behind the couch caused Colonel Agastya to dive to the side as two Military Justice Enforcement Officers decked out in battle armor stepped into the apartment, drawing their sidearms.

Agastya heard the energy blaster fire as he hit the ground and waited for a blow that he was afraid would hit him or near him.

"Sir," called out the Military Justice Enforcement Officer.

Agastya rolled over and stood up. The blood spatter on the far wall told the Colonel that it truly was over for the General. Walking over, he looked on the floor behind the couch. The General's body lay on the floor. The back half of his head was missing, and the energy blaster that the General had stuck in his own mouth was still in the General's hand.

*****

A few days later, Earmon Terman set three empty glasses on the bar counter. It was early afternoon, and there were no customers in Boatman's Pub and Grub. He headed back into the kitchen to help with getting ready for the evening crowd, knowing he would come back shortly for a toast.

When he returned, Colonel Agastya and Captain Luciano were just pulling up their stools in front of the three glasses. He walked over, selected the appropriate bottle, and poured. "Here's to the Grenadines Special," announced Earmon, as the three men lifted their glasses and sipped some of the golden-yellow liquid.

"Alright," Captain Luciano added, as he looked at the liquid in the glass, "I don't know if I'll ever be able to enjoy this as much as you, but I am beginning to appreciate it."

"Some say it's an acquired taste," began the bartender. "I think it has something to do with the whole experience of it." Earmon finished his drink and headed to help the other customers that were beginning to come into the bar.

"How's Camdrin and her boys?" asked Agastya.

"They seem to be doing okay. None of this is easy, but I think they will be good in the future. Right now, my wife is at their house, helping them pack. They are all three heading to the other side of Koranth to try to find the boys' sister," explained Captain Luciano. They both agreed that it was good for all three of them to go find the daughter and hoped that they could find closure and peace together.

"Have you made a decision yet, Agastya?" asked the Captain. "Will you accept the promotion to General?"

Colonel Agastya slowly pulled a folded picture out his pocket and laid it on the bar. Captain Luciano looked at the photo and immediately knew that the woman sitting on the beach was Aridatha Dolce, the Colonel's lost love. He knew that he owed much to her. Without the Colonel's regret of letting her go, Agastya would have never stopped him from making the same mistake. He read the words on the photo and looked at this friend, not knowing what to say.

They looked up as Earmon began refilling the three glasses on the bar. He raised his glass, and the two officers did the same. As Earmon looked down at the picture, he began his toast, "In this life, my friends, there are some regrets you may be forced to take to your grave. Here's to those that we choose not to."

After finishing their drinks, they said their goodbyes. As he walked towards the door, Jecamiah Agastya, looked at the picture and read the words at the bottom one more time, before folding it and placing it back in his pocket.

Even today, my gaze falls over the waves
For far away what my heart so deeply craves
On a distant shore, I can only hope to pray
That my true love will come and finally stay

Chapter 31
Lost in the Mountains

Commander Conall Bornani scanned the screen that hung in the air of the bridge of the spaceship. They had slipped the ship into orbit around the planet called Earth, and the ship's systems continuously scanned for a perfect landing spot. He was excited to be so close to finally reaching their destination and was confident that his crew would do their jobs well.

The last two years aboard the ship had been a completely new experience for Kadamba. He'd spent much of his time, previous to boarding the ship, in the outdoors, training for the military. At first, he had felt like a trapped animal. He couldn't get out, but over time that had faded. Compared to the rest of the crew, he was completely unprepared. The other eleven members of the crew had two years to prepare for the mission before they actually launched. Kadamba had nothing but a few hours of preparation right before the launch.

At first, the crew had been very distant from him. He could hear the rumblings about his past and what he had done. He focused his efforts on learning what the others knew of this planet called Earth, immersing himself in learning a predominant language called English. He scoured and studied all of the information that he could about the planet. The last exploratory mission had discovered a planet that had emerged from a second global war. A country called the United States of America had entered the war late, but had led its allies to victory. That was some forty years before. He tried to imagine what the planet would be like when they arrived. What would have changed? Would this United States still be dominant? Would more wars have erupted?

Kadamba learned the details of how their mission would proceed. It was fairly straightforward on its face. Part of the crew would study the planet's technology, infrastructure, and trade. They would make an assessment of whether a planet had developed to an optimum point for invasion and "development." It became a fairly simple two-part question in Kadamba's mind. First, could the planet provide enough goods and products to make putting a portal in place profitable? Second, could the planet provide the power and infrastructure required to get a portal running once it arrived?

That was only part of the equation, and Kadamba was not to be included in making those assessments. He was simply a bodyguard for the less palatable part of the mission—discovering whether the planet had any Transprophetics and killing them. Eventually, humans would evolve to have members of their population develop certain characteristics, like the ability to move things without touching them. Once scientists on a planet validated and understood Transprophetic capabilities, everything would change fairly quickly. He'd studied these Transprophetics in school and had seen them in various media, but he'd never met one in person. What would they be like? Would they somehow be different?

Kadamba didn't really like the man that he would be protecting, Dr. Nahash Tarea. He wasn't a medical doctor; the title was bestowed on him because of some very non-medical advanced educational degree. Apparently, it had something to do with religions and the foundation of truth. The man was wiry, and his hair reminded Kadamba of the man called Greasy that he'd met in prison. His hair was thin and just looked dirty in the way it clung to his head. When he spoke, the words seemed to come out in a hiss. No matter what he said, Kadamba always felt like the man was talking down to him, trying to make Kadamba feel small, unimportant, and insignificant.

Their job on the planet seemed fairly black and white, at least on the surface. They would simply be there to discover whether any Transprophetics had appeared. Kadamba hoped it was a simple question to answer. He hoped that when they arrived on Earth that there would be Transprophetics on the planet's media, and maybe even that Transprophetics would be leading governments and religions. The doctor had explained that it was unlikely that it would be that easy of a job. Human nature, as it is, will reject that which is different. Those with Transprophetic abilities may hide their abilities for a generation or two out of fear. A few may try to exploit their abilities, but only if they understand that they have them. Often the first few generations of Transprophetics can't control their abilities. That's where Tarea's expertise would come in most useful.

According to the doctor, they would most likely find a Transprophetic in one of two places. Almost every culture on every planet had some type of "magic." It was part of human nature to want to hope that the abilities of a Transprophetic were real. Paradoxically, Transprophetics that sought to hide their skills would often hide them in plain sight. Often those would be magicians that performed shows. That was an easy place for a Transprophetic to hide and to use his or her talents with people believing that it was nothing more than illusions and trickery.

The second place where Transprophetics might be found would be around religion. A person who was a little different often could seem to be divine. When strange things happened around a person over which they seemed to have some influence, a god or gods were often given credit for the unusual capabilities.

When they neared the planet, they began picking up the planet's broadcast signals. Kadamba had been disappointed that Transprophetics weren't anywhere obvious. If they did exist on the planet, it might take a bit of work to find one.

"Commander has called a meeting in 15 minutes," Dr. Nahash Tarea announced, as Kadamba watched a video that the ship's systems had recorded. "I don't know why you need to be in this meeting, but apparently you do."

"I'll be there," replied Kadamba.

"What are you watching?" asked Dr. Tarea.

"Apparently, it is a comedy show," replied Kadamba. "Actually, it is pretty funny. It's about . . ."

"Just be at the meeting," interrupted Tarea, as he walked away.

Kadamba returned to watching the show. He wondered if it really was how some of these Earthlings might think about aliens. It seemed terribly odd to Kadamba. He was a human, but he would be an alien here on Earth. He'd watched a few shows about aliens that the ship's systems had captured as they approached Earth. Some were serious, but this one was funny, especially the alien.

Growing up in a world that knew there was life on other planets was all Kadamba had known. But on Earth, no one knew whether there was life or not on other planets. If there was, no one knew what it would be like. That made this show even more intriguing. The female lead on the show knew that the alien, named Mork, was from another planet, but he was human, just like everyone everywhere. The alien tried to understand Earthling behavior and fit in, usually with humorous results.

Kadamba stopped the video and headed to the meeting.

*****

Aerial photos and maps were appearing, slowly moving, and disappearing on the walls of the spaceship's meeting room.

Commander Bornani began to speak once all the crew members were in the room.

"It's hard to believe, at times, that we're so close to Earth," he began. "After all the years of preparation and travel, we're almost there."

He tapped a few places on the conference table, and an image of the planet appeared. They all watched as the planet began to spin, zooming into the planet's surface, and creating a three-dimensional map on the table's surface.

"The ship's system has identified the most ideal landing point for us," he noted, pointing to a small canyon-like feature right by a lake. "This is Fat Bottom Lake, in the Rocky Mountains. It is secluded. We'll land here near the lake in this canyon. Our home, this ship, will be destroyed after we land. The return vessel can easily be submerged in this lake, as it is very deep and murky. The only thing that will be hidden will be a small remote that will resurface the return vessel."

"What about this small building over here?" asked one of the other soldiers, pointing to a small structure away from the lake and canyon.

"As best as we can tell, it is a small dwelling that is currently occupied," replied the commander. "Hopefully, it is. When we land, we'll need supplies and some intelligence to get us started. If there are inhabitants living there, we'll have a place to start."

The final preparations were put in place to land the ship. Kadamba looked over the map multiple times, as did the other military members of the crew. They created multiple scenarios for what would happen when they landed. The one assumption that Kadamba hoped was true was that no one on the planet would know that they were there. The technology from Koranth and Zoranth was far superior, so landing the ship undetected on the planet should be easy.

"I know I probably don't have to say this," began the Commander as the meeting was winding down, "but nothing, absolutely nothing from Koranth and Zoranth, aside from the return vessel, can come with us."

He turned around and opened a box on the floor behind him and passed out clear, sealed bags with each of their assigned clothing.

"Leave the bag sealed. After we land, we'll each walk out of this ship naked, with nothing but the clothes that are in the bags. I will personally leave your dead body on this ship if you try to bring anything with you."

After the meeting adjourned, Kadamba returned to his quarters. It was very small, but it was space that was his alone. He'd been in the quarters of the other members of the crew. He knew all of them had brought things from home. In some ways, he was now glad that he hadn't. Every one of them would be leaving something behind that would be destroyed with the ship. He curled up in his bunk, trying to put his excitement aside and get to sleep.

The sky was grey above the Landing, and Ka walked quickly to the edge of the building to look out across the city. Rain was falling in the distance, and his view was obstructed by low clouds. He sat down on the bench to wait.

After some time had passed, Ka stood up and began walking around. This wasn't like Alorus not to show up at some point. Usually, he would appear shortly after Ka arrived. Even during these two years aboard the spaceship, Alorus remained distant.

Ka began to walk around the Landing. Alorus wasn't in the playground or near the lifts. The storm seemed to grow closer as Ka wandered around, looking for the boy. As he was passing the food vendors, he thought he heard a sniffle. He opened the door to the small kiosk that sold the Freezies that Stelky had loved so much.

When he looked inside, he found the boy curled up in a corner of the small building. "What are you doing, Alorus?"

"I'm scared, Ka," confided the boy. "The storm is almost here. Why did you have to kill me and bring me with you? Why did they let you get away and come to another planet?"

Ka stepped into the little building and sat down on the floor. Alorus pulled himself up farther into the corner, sniffling as if he had been crying.

"You know I am sorry, Alorus. I wish I knew what else to say."

They both sat on the floor, waiting for the other to say something. But neither of them spoke. Ka wished that Alorus wasn't with him, but that just wasn't an option anymore. Wherever Ka would go, Alorus would always be with him.

The gentle ringing of his alarm awakened him shortly before dawn. The landing went perfectly. They were now safely on Earth. It was now time to disembark the ship and start the next phase of their mission.

Standing in the middle of his quarters, Kadamba began to laugh. He threw his shirt against one wall. He removed his pants, wadded them up and tossed them on the bed. He was already barefoot, so all that was left was his underwear. He looked at the wall opposite the door, staring for a few moments. He almost wanted that perky, smiling, recorded talking head of a woman to show up one last time. He would laugh out loud at her, for she had no power over him and never would again.

He dropped his underwear to the floor and stepped out of it, leaving it where it landed. He gestured, and the far wall became a mirror. He looked at himself. He wasn't the boy that had killed that bargabuko in Mr. Lormate's class. His body was lean and muscular, a man's body. He'd religiously worked out in the small gym aboard the ship, keeping himself fit, and practicing the various martial arts that he had learned in military training. As he was admiring himself, his gaze hit his arms. He would live with those words branded onto his arms forever. He took a deep breath.

"Come on, Alorus," he spoke to himself, "let's go find out whether either of us can find some peace on this planet."

He tucked the clear package containing his clothes under his arm, walked down the corridor, and stepped out of the ship. The smell was the first thing that hit him. He didn't yet know, but the scent was of clean mountain air and pine trees. Closing his eyes, he breathed in deeply, becoming lost in the fragrance. He heard what had to be birds chirping in the distance. This place felt right, just right.

"For the love of the Lords of the Fourth System, would you please get dressed?" barked the Commander.

Kadamba looked around. All of the crew had disembarked the ship and were putting on the clothing from their packages. Kadamba did the same and watched the Commander walk to the ship, swipe his hand across a panel, and press a few buttons. A panel opened and the

Commander pulled out a remote that was about twice the size of his hand. He retracted the ramp, and the door sealed itself shut. A large hatch on the bottom of the ship opened, and the return vessel slowly descended.

The return vessel was dark and shaped more like a torpedo. In its center cargo section, three men could easily fit, but would be unable to move about. It was designed for a fast return to Koranth with the reports and artifacts from the planets. While the trip to Earth had taken two years, the return trip would take less than one.

The Commander maneuvered the return vessel over the lake, and within a few moments, it was submerged out of sight.

"Two hundred feet down," the Commander announced a few minutes later. "Only two more things left to do."

Everyone turned and looked at the spaceship. It had been their home for the last two years. On this planet, it was the only craft capable of manned, interstellar travel, but it had been severely compromised by the trip and especially by coming into the Earth's atmosphere. Kadamba realized that he didn't exactly know what would happen next. He only knew the ship would be destroyed.

The Commander tapped a few places on the screen of the remote, and the crew watched as the ship slowly dissolved to ashes.

"Well, damn," began Dr. Nahash Tarea, "that was about as ceremonial as getting your shoes shined."

"No use in being ceremonial," replied the Commander, as he walked the crew over to the canyon wall. He made a few marks on the wall and then hid the remote under a stack of rocks a few feet away.

They were all standing looking at the wall, when they heard the voice. "What are y'all doing there staring at the canyon wall?"

They spun around to see a portly, older man in faded khaki work pants and a flannel shirt. He was holding a shotgun in his hands, but had it pointed at the ground. The inquisitive look on his face deepened as they all turned around to stare at him. They all had prepared for their first contact with an Earthling, but this wasn't what any of them had imagined. He easily could have been the grandfather of half of the crew, but his holding that weapon made all of them realize they were unarmed and potentially in danger.

"Are you y'all lost?" the man asked.

"Actually," Kadamba responded, "we're aliens from the planet Ork. We're here to study you. Na-Nu Na-Nu." Kadamba then held up his hand and separated his middle and ring fingers. The old man burst out laughing. Not knowing, exactly what else to do, the rest of the crew also began to laugh.

"You are completely lost, aren't you?" asked the man again.

"Yes, sir, we certainly are," Kadamba affirmed. "Our transportation broke down, and we are stranded."

"You shoulda stayed on the road, rather than wandering into the woods," the old man advised. "Well, come on then, Margaret and me have a little place not too far from here. I guess the hunting can wait until tomorrow. By the way, I'm Jerry."

The man gestured with his hand for everyone to follow him, and the whole crew began following. Within a few moments, the Commander and Vice-Commander were walking beside the man, talking about the beautiful day. They could see the small dwelling in the distance. It was the same one they had studied back on the ship. Before the old man knew what was happening, he was face down on the ground with the shotgun pointing into his back.

For the next few days, the old couple remained tied up in the living room of their cabin while the crew constantly questioned them about life on Earth. A small television, radio, books, and magazines also provided the crew with additional information and current events. The crew ransacked the cabin, finding a few more guns, some clothes, money, and other supplies they needed.

Kadamba was uncomfortable with the treatment of Jerry and Margaret. He tried as best as he could to ease the misery that they were suffering. It wasn't that they were being physically abused; it was just that they were being treated as if they weren't really human. Kadamba knew what that felt like.

A travel guidebook that Dr. Tarea had found on a bookshelf seemed to intrigue him. It was a book filled with hotels, attractions, and events for a country called the United Kingdom. Something about a show called "Garret Greyson—Master of Illusions" captivated the doctor. He decided that it would be the first place that he and Kadamba would need to go. There was something about the show's description that made him think that there might be more than just illusions about Garret Grayson.

Kadamba was standing outside the cabin on the day that he and Dr. Tarea were to leave. The old couple only had a pickup truck, so the expedition crew had left in waves. The Commander had already driven most of the crew to various destinations, where each pair had headed off in separate directions. In six months' time, they would all meet back up, finalize their reports, and send the return vessel home. Kadamba, closing his eyes, listened to the birds again. He liked this place. He had never really spent much time outside Stujorkian City. He'd been to beaches and the ocean but never in the mountains back home. He wondered if they were as peaceful as it was here in the Rocky Mountains.

The blast shook Kadamba out of his trance, and he turned to run towards the cabin when a second blast stopped him in his tracks. He was sure that he knew what it was, and when Commander Bornani and Dr. Tarea walked out of the cabin laughing, he was certain. One of the experts on infrastructure and technology followed them out. She had been paired with Commander Bornani and was as cold-hearted as Dr. Tarea. She was furiously wiping blood spatter off her arms. "You asshole," she whined to the Commander, "was it really necessary to fucking blow their brains out all over me?"

Kadamba stared at the three people walking towards him and the pickup truck. He would be stuck with Dr. Tarea for the next six months. How was cruelty, and even death, so easy for these people? How had they managed to see Margaret and Jerry as something other than human? He tried hard to put his head around it and understand. They were here on a mission. This was another planet. He guessed that there was always a threat that the humans on this planet could evolve to the point where those on Koranth and Zoranth had. If that happened, would the Earthlings invade his world? Was that how these crewmates of his thought? He shook the thoughts from his head. He wasn't here to be a philosopher; he was now an Elite Forces soldier, responsible for protecting Dr. Tarea. He would do his job, however distasteful it seemed.

Chapter 32
Lords of the Fourth System

Celestina relaxed in the enormous chair behind the even grander desk in her new office. Once Minister Scharbigot Canchorus had passed away, in such an untimely manner, she decided to consolidate the Ministry's administrative functions in one location. Multiple buildings in the central city of Stujorkian City had been acquired and retrofitted to her needs. Her new office suite occupied the entire 187th floor of the building. The panoramic views were stunning.

She looked across the plains to the mountains far in the distance. Somewhere far over those mountains, her uncle rested at peace in what was now her estate in Beliasium, situated right on the ocean. She was looking forward to next week when she and Tomar were planning a few days away to plot their next moves. The Ministry was firmly under her control, and with proper planning, there would be only one Corporation for the development of other worlds.

The buzzing sound from one of her secretaries shattered her relaxation, and she returned to the present moment, eager to attack another day.

"Chief Executive Minster," came the voice from the holographic head that rose from her desk. "We may have a little bit of an issue. I am not sure how to proceed, but please look at the lobby."

A screen rose up next to the holographic head, showing the giant lobby of the new headquarters of the Ministry of Interplanetary Corporate Relations. An old man, dressed in worn clothes that seemed to be of a tropical, but native pattern was seated near the security desk. On his lap was a long crystal box. Even from a distance, Celestina could tell that the box held a sword of some type.

"What's the issue?" demanded Celestina.

"He claims he is the Ministry's last archivist, and he demands to speak with the Chief Executive Minister," replied the secretary.

"He looks like a crazy man," Celestina noted, with disdain. "Send him away."

"Madam, the problem is that he claims to be an employee of the Ministry. He told the security guard to enter his name into the system and validate him."

"And?" demanded Celestina. "Is he an employee of the Ministry?"

"We don't know," the secretary replied hesitantly, "All that came up with his name was that he was the head of the 'Endowment of the Archive, Guardians of Sabro, The Frozen.' That in itself might not be interesting, except that when the guard tried to access the associated files, the system returned a noncompliant warning. These files haven't been accessed in over six hundred years."

Celestina looked at the old man in the lobby. Her curiosity was piqued. This could make for an interesting start to her day. She bid her secretary to have the man escorted, along with his box, by heavily armed security personnel to her office suite. She now had a mystery to start what was sure to be another grand day.

The old man was seated in the comfortable couches in an area near the windows. Four brutish securities guards stood watch as Celestina greet him. "Welcome," she began, "I am Celestina Wiroviana, Chief Executive Minister for Interplanetary Corporate Relations. You have us at a disadvantage, as we know so little about you."

"My thanks for your time to receive me," the old man answered. His voice was weak, and Celestina could see that many, many years weighed heavily on the man. "I am here to fulfill the promise of my house. Without an heir, I return Sabro to the Chief Executive Minister."

Celestina looked at the crystal case in his hands. The sword was not what she had expected from seeing it on the security screen. It was not of a metal that she could describe; she wasn't even sure whether it was metal or not. It seemed to shimmer, with flecks of bright strands and waves moving through the blade in random patterns. In one moment, the blade would be a soft, whitish color, and in the next moment, translucent. It was magnificent and memorizing to behold.

"So, this is Sabro, the blade in this case?" she inquired.

"Yes," he replied, "in the case where we hope and pray it will remain for all eternity."

Sitting herself down across a small table from him, she bid him place the case on the table. He reluctantly held the case in his lap. She glared at him for a moment, reveling in the mystery that this was becoming. "And why, my dear sir, should this blade remain encased?"

"Only the bloodline of the true chief of the Burongi may handle the blade," he explained, looking at her and wondering what kind of woman she was. Like generations before, he was separate from this world. He cared little for what happened outside the jungles and rain forests of his homeland.

"Okay, I'll take the bait," she remarked to him. "Tell me who you are and why this sword is in my office."

"Will you, as the Chief Executive Minster, take back Sabro?" the man asked, as a terrible coughing fit began to rack his body. "You must keep it safe and pray it is never needed again." The coughing became worse and worse, and man seemed unable to control it. Celestina ordered medics and instructed that the old man be taken to the Ministry's private medical clinic for treatment and observation.

Unable to speak much at all, he placed the case on the table. As the medics placed him on the hovering medical transport board, he managed to utter, "There is no other."

She studied the case on the table. The case itself was magnificent. She was practically giddy like a schoolgirl. A mystery had been given to her. She summoned her staff, who in turn summoned various experts in history, metallurgy, and computer science.

The files related to the Endowment of the Archive, Guardians of Sabro, The Frozen, were completely corrupted. The team searched archives and files across the two planets but came up empty on any references to an Endowment or Sabro. Almost as intriguing, was that no one could identify the material of the case or guess at the material of the sword. Despite scans of all types, no hinge, lever, lock, mechanism, or even crack could be found in the case. It was as if the case had grown around the sword, except that it appeared perfectly carved on both the outside and inside.

After days of research, nothing could be found. The old man had lost consciousness on the way to the clinic and slipped into a coma. He was dying from something the best experts could not identify or understand. Everything about this sword intrigued Celestina more and more. She had it placed in her office and studied it every day. In her heart, she knew that she would eventually understand it, but what she really wanted to do was wield it.

Late in the evening, she was studying the case and the sword again. She knew so little, and it was eating at her. She ran her hands along the lines of the case. Over and over she caressed it, her fingers hoping to find something that so many experts had missed. As she was about to give up, she felt a surge of icy coldness. There was a cold spot on the case. It began to move, and her hands traced the path. Suddenly, the top portion of the case began to slide open. She gently set the top portion aside. She had done it. She stared into the case. The sword was hers to wield.

The moment she touched the sword, the old man in the clinic sat up, awake from his coma and screaming. "Don't touch Sabro!" he screamed, but blocks away, Celestina could not hear his warning as she gripped the handle.

Celestina screamed as her skin came in contact with Sabro, and she jerked her hand back violently. Her fingers felt as if she had dipped them into something colder than the coldest thing she had ever felt. The joints in her hands immediately locked up, and a frigid, icy coldness began making its way up her arm. She felt as if each nerve was being sliced open and burned with frozen fire.

As she looked at her hand and her arm, she could see the arteries and veins in her arms turning a brilliant white, and then bluish-black as the brutal chill moved up her arm. She tried to step backward, away from that cursed blade, but she only crumbled to her knees, screaming as the sensation felt like her arm was being pulled into a frozen wasteland. In her mind's eye, she could see a vast, lifeless, frozen landscape. She felt naked as she was sucked into this frigid reality. Icy, howling winds ripped at her exposed soul, peeling away strips of her very being. Sheets of ice crashed down unimaginably massive mountainsides, shaking the frozen tundra into which her spirit was slowly sinking. Her screams alerted her diligent secretary, Besnik Treowe, who would always work late whenever she did. He immediately summoned security and medics. Within minutes she was evacuated to the Ministry's private medical clinic. Her arm was completely immobile and frozen solid. They wrapped her in heating blankets, unable to determine what had happened or why.

She drifted in and out of consciousness for days, often mumbling about the cold and the wind and the ice. The doctors struggled to keep her body temperature from falling. Over the course of a few days, she began to stabilize, but the arm would never be the same.

The doctors were completely unable to ascertain what had happened or why. Her arm had begun to regain functionality, but the bluish-black tint to her veins and arteries remained. The lines fanned out from her shoulder to her fingers and pulsed with a lighter hue with each beat of her heart.

With her arm in a sling, she walked to the room where the old man was dying. He had become weaker and weaker while she struggled with the effects of touching the blade. More than once his heart had stopped, and the doctors brought him back.

A doctor was tending to him when she entered the room. He appeared to be asleep, and his face was even more gaunt than when she had met him.

"Give him something to wake him up and make him alert," she commanded the physician.

"Yes, ma'am," blurted out the physician, "I'll be back in a few moments."

She stood watching as the doctor returned and injected a stimulant into the IV line running into the man's arm. As the stimulant hit him, his eyes popped open wide, and he bolted into a sitting position.

"Only the bloodline of the true chief of the Burongi may handle the blade," he warned as he collapsed back into the bed. "You should have never touched the blade. It is a relic from a long lost time, and you must pray it is never needed again." He looked at her with a piercing intensity that almost frightened her. Then he blinked, and the milky cloudiness of his ancient eyes returned.

"What happened to me when I touched Sabro?" she demanded.

"You must understand, that only the bloodline of the true chief of the Burongi may handle the blade," repeated the old man, sighing heavily, "Only he is capable of wielding this weapon."

"We can't find anything about you, or Sabro, or any endowment for an archive," she accused him, the frustration growing in her voice. "By the Lords of the Fourth System, who are you and what does this blade have to do with the Ministry?"

"I am the last Archivist of the Ministry. Without an heir, I have returned the blade," he repeated, as his eyes seemed to drift into a trance. "I pray we never again see the Lords of the Fourth System."

"What are you talking about?" she demanded.

"Do you even know where the phrase, 'Lords of the Fourth System,' comes from, Chief Executive Minister?" the old man asked, with a seriousness that made her shiver.

"It's just a phrase," she replied. "It's been around forever."

The old man coughed, but more gently than before and looked at her questioningly, as if he was trying to decide whether he should say something or not. He was being well cared for by the medical staff, and they would ease his passing. Sadly, the doctors believed that he would die within the day.

"It's more than a phrase; its meaning has been hidden in history," the old man told her. "My father and his father before him and his father before him have kept the secret alive and guarded the blade. For generations, we have lived a simple life in the jungle, fulfilling our duty."

"Okay, tell me the story, so that I may protect the blade and its secret for you," she suggested.

The old man relaxed, and his eyes glazed over as his mind drifted into the past. "Do you know what the Fourth System was that men from Koranth invaded?" he asked.

"Not off the top of my head," she replied.

"It was the Twelfth Corporation that installed the portal on the Fourth System," he began.

"There have always been Eleven until recently," she interrupted, declaring that he must be wrong.

"Please listen to my story," he commanded, "and I will tell what the Ministry itself hid in history over seven hundred years ago."

He began his tale, explaining that after the Exorthium Colonial Wars, the Ministry had been formed, and it was to monitor Twelve Corporations, not Eleven. As planets were identified that contained life, missions were sent, and eventually portals were opened to three other planets. The profits and riches that flowed were enormous. A mission, to the fourth planet that had been discovered by the early explorers from Koranth and Zoranth, found a planet with vast cities that were frighteningly similar to the metropolises of Koranth and Zoranth, with one exception—there was not a living human on the planet.

That first crew visited many of the giant cities, finding nothing but nature taking over what once had been built by the hand of man. There was one striking similarity in each of the cities. A huge pyramid had been built on the south end of each city that was grander than anything on either Koranth or Zoranth. The base of each pyramid spanned well over a square mile. The walls rose quickly to over two thousand feet. The top revealed a massive courtyard with nine buildings in a horseshoe. In each city, it was the same.

The largest of the buildings atop these pyramids was at the top of the horseshoe. On each side of the horseshoe, four temples stood, with towering columns supporting high roofs. In every one of the buildings, massive amounts of jewels, coins, and objects of rare metals were piled in gigantic heaps. The walls were stacked deep with bars of rare, shining metals. The amount of wealth in each of the buildings was impossible to calculate.

However, that largest building at the top of the horseshoe was very different. A flight of a hundred stairs led to a single door, well over two stories tall. Opening that door revealed an enormous throne room encompassing nearly the entire building. The ceiling, floor, and walls were decorated with fine tiles, adorned with gems and rare metals. Statues of grotesque beasts that were abusing and consuming humans lined the walls, gilded with thick layers of precious metals, and adorned with gemstones larger than the fist of man. The throne itself was raised above the floor of the room by many steps, with each of the steps, covered in razor-sharp spikes of gemstones of a thousand different hues. The throne itself was made of a material that no one had ever seen. It was pure white, but light seemed to pass through it, sending off bursts of brilliant colored lights. The wall behind every throne exhibited a macabre mosaic of blackened human skulls, stretching up for over five stories.

Behind each of the thrones, in the middle of the wall of skulls, was a passageway, a long corridor that sloped downward, deeper and deeper, winding into the very heart of the pyramid. The walls of the passageways were lined with countless human bones and skulls. Splitting off from the main passageway were more rooms filled with treasures. The passageways all ended in a large room that should have been pitch dark but was not.

In each corner, a large caldron of oil burned. The oil seemed to be fed slowly from an unknown source. A few of the caldrons had flames running down their sides, as the oil fed slightly more quickly than it burned off. In the middle of each of these fire-lit rooms lay a massive, stone sarcophagus.

The first crew was wise enough, or perhaps superstitious enough, to leave the sarcophaguses as they were. They believed that whatever was in those sarcophaguses had probably sat on the thrones. They dubbed them the "Lords of the Fourth System." They sent their reports and artifacts back to Koranth in the return vessel, and within a few years a ship returned with a portal. A large hydroelectric station near one of the cities was brought back online, and Koranth was connected to the Fourth System.

Celestina watched as the old man began to cough again. The telling of the story was obviously difficult in the man's condition, but when doctors came to tend to the man, she ordered them to give him another stimulant and sent them away. She wanted to hear the entire story as quickly as possible.

"I can't believe that we've never heard any of this," remarked her secretary, Besnik Treowe, who had accompanied Celestina to meet with the old man.

"No, my friend, the Ministry has long been a powerful organization," replied the old man with another cough. "What I have told you and what I will now tell you was erased from history to protect all of us." The old man continued the story.

Once Koranth and the Fourth System were connected, the Twelfth Corporation's military flowed through the portal as a precaution. Experts were sent to study the planet and, moreover, to study the grand pyramids. They were declared some planet-wide religion. Of course, as is the reality of human nature, one of the sarcophaguses was opened.

Inside the sarcophagus was something like a man, or perhaps it was a god. It was hard to tell. Its skin was almost translucent, but light seemed to be lost into the surface of its skin. It was clothed in very royal, but functional, almost warrior-like clothing. Upon its head lay a crown of gems welded together somehow, as no metal or other material was apparent.

As that first scientist gazed upon the being, its eyes opened, and a cruel smile spread across its face. It rose from the sarcophagus, climbing out, but seeming to float and barely make contact with any surface. It stood before that poor scientist who was transfixed by the creature's presence. Those who saw the event said that the caldrons all began to burn brighter as the being stretched out its hand and touched the scientist's face. The scientist screamed as his entire body erupted into flames. A nearby soldier opened fire with a laser gun, but only managed to end the scientist's suffering.

Energy blasts, lasers, and projectiles seemed to only pass through the being as it came up the passageway, turning each person it touched into a human torch. Within hours, the Corporation had exhausted every weapon in its arsenal, trying to stop the being. But nothing seemed to work. Knives, rocks, and sticks seemed to pass through what looked and moved like a large man. Over the next few days, the few humans left on the Fourth System retreated to the portal, pursued by this terrible being. When the last of the humans on the Fourth System perished, the creature stepped through the portal to Koranth.

"How can this be?" asked Celestina. "I've never heard of anything like this."

"Of course not," replied the old man. "Your own Ministry never wanted you to hear of this ever." After another cough and drink of water, the old man continued to tell his tale.

As is still the case, portals are dangerous devices. The Twelfth Corporation had placed the Koranth side of this portal in the remote jungles of the country of Zuoruntu. Unbeknownst to the Ministry or the Corporation, the portal had been placed near a sacred site of the Burongi.

When the being came through the portal, it massacred everything the Corporate military could throw at it. It simply walked up and whomever it touched burst into flames. It was a terrifying death, but what came next was even worse. Some of the Burongi had been watching what was happening. They were still mostly a tribal people, living in the jungles and the mountains at that time. They witnessed the creature's destructive nature and then watched as the beast began to gnaw on the burned bones of the dead.

A young warrior chief among the Burongi was outraged at what was viewed as sacrilege. He traveled into the scared site, where a warrior king of old was buried. The Burongi believe that this king of old had fought demons of some hell with a weapon from the gods—Sabro. The chief retrieved the blade from the burial tomb and returned to fight the being.

"The blade passed through the creature, just as every other weapon had. For a mere second, it appeared the creature would be unaffected, but then its scream shook the trees. Much like Celestina's arm, the creature was frozen.

A scientist, who had hidden in the jungle, began to examine the being. He was frozen solid, but within a few hours, the Lord of the Fourth System began to thaw. Fortunately, one of the Ministry's Ministers had come to the site. Upon seeing the creature beginning to move, he ordered it thrown back through the portal. The creature, that Lord of the Fourth System, was returned to his own world and within a few minutes the portal was powered down.

The Ministry moved quickly to absorb the Twelfth Corporation and all its assets. A large stone temple was built over the portal, and within a few years, the jungle reclaimed the evidence of our so-called advanced human activity.

Celestina watched as the old man worked through another terrible coughing fit. It was obvious that he was in great pain. She felt some pity for him but wanted a few more answers before she left him. She summoned the doctor, commanding him to administer another dose of whatever stimulant was keeping the old man alert.

"So the Ministry actually absorbed the Corporation and took its rights to this planet of great wealth?" she asked.

"Yes," he replied, "but only to power down the portal and make sure no one ever opened it again."

"So, your family long ago was entrusted with the sword and the story. Who else knows?" asked Celestina, hers eyes getting wider and wider.

"Chief Executive Minister, the people in this room are the only ones," replied the old man, as yet another wrenching coughing fit gripped him, and he began to choke.

She glared at him, until the fit ran its course. He stared at her with blank, empty eyes. She cared little, as she only had one last inquiry. "Pray tell me then, old man," began Celestina, with a greedy glint in her eyes, "where is this portal hidden?"

Celestina let out a scream, as the old man's head slumped and his eyes glazed over, staring into a distant place from which he would never return. He was dead, and any secrets from the Ministry's past vanished as the final bit of air escaped from his lungs.

Turning to her longtime, trusted secretary, Besnik Treowe, she declared, "You've just been promoted. I don't care how long it takes, or what resources you need, find me that portal!"

Chapter 33
Master of Illusions

Kadamba stood on the balcony and looked out over the Thames River. The sun had been down for a few hours, and the air was brisk and cold. He could hear the muffled sounds of Dr. Tarea and the woman who owned, or maybe just used, the rundown apartment. It wasn't pleasure that came from them. It was more animalistic. They were using each other—she wanted money and Dr. Tarea just wanted to get off.

The last few weeks had been so different than anything Kadamba could have ever imagined. The mission seemed twisted and warped. Kadamba understood that they didn't have resources here on this planet. They had to steal them. Cash had worked great in the United States. You could get anything you wanted. Then came the challenge of leaving the US. Something called passports were needed.

Dr. Tarea and Kadamba had made it to Washington, DC. They had stolen a few cars and robbed a few gas stations. It was even easier than either had expected. The further east that they traveled, the more money Dr. Tarea decided that he wanted. Cheap motels were no longer good enough for the doctor; he wanted to stay in nicer and nicer places. The food here was different. You could get things cheap at fast food joints and diners, but Dr. Tarea discovered he enjoyed nicer restaurants.

The two of them had been casing a gas station in a less refined part of Washington, DC when Kadamba saw the exchange. He recognized it. He'd done the exact same thing years before. It was a small-time drug purchase.

Kadamba followed the older one, who was obviously the seller. He wore all black leather and dark glasses that hid his eyes. He ducked around a corner and was trying to unlock a door in the alley when Kadamba approached him.

"Sir, I saw you sell that kid some drugs," Kadamba informed him.

"Yo," replied the dealer as he pulled his glasses off, "you didn't see shit, motherfucker!"

"I don't want to cause trouble. I just need some help. Please?" Kadamba disclosed.

"And that honky motherfucker standing behind you is what?" the dealer asked, pointing to Dr. Tarea. "Your seeing eye dog?"

Kadamba saw the man reaching into his pocket to pull out a small revolver. Before the man could completely raise the weapon, Kadamba took him to the ground, disarming him and poking the gun into his temple.

"I don't want any trouble," began Kadamba, "if I did, you'd be dead. I need help, and I am thinking you probably know someone who might know someone who could help."

The man was obviously angry. "Fuck you, asshole, I ain't doing shit for you."

"Listen," Kadamba commanded, as he cocked the revolver's hammer back, "I need to buy passports for the doctor and me. Can you help me?"

"What, motherfucker! You want papers! Do I look like a passport office to you?" defiantly barked the dealer.

Kadamba pushed the barrel of the gun harder into the man's temple, as Dr. Tarea walked over to them. "Just blow his brains out. He can't help."

"Okay! Okay! I know a man!"

Kadamba helped the man to his feet, pocketing the gun. They walked for many blocks, and the farther they went, the more rundown the neighborhood became. They climbed up onto a loading dock of what looked like an abandoned warehouse, and the drug dealer knocked on the door.

A small metal window on the door slid open at the same time that Kadamba realized that there were three men across the street, standing on the loading dock of another warehouse. The three men had automatic weapons trained on Kadamba and Dr. Tarea.

"Fuck you want, Lippy?" came a voice through the small window, which now had the barrel of a handgun pointing through it.

"Got some buyers for Daddy Rings," answered the obviously nervous dealer. "The brother here and his honky be lookin' for papers."

"You a dumb motherfucker," came the voice as the window slammed shut. The door began to open, and two men holding small automatic weapons stepped out.

They looked Kadamba and the doctor over. One of the men gestured for them to go inside. Once they walked through the door, they found themselves against a wall, being frisked, and everything they had with them was taken. They were walked down a long corridor and brought into a large room.

Music with a deep, thumping bass played somewhere in the distance. The room, furnished with old sofas and beanbags, was lit by some twenty or so lava lamps that were spread about on small tables and shelves. About a dozen people sat around the room, half of them smoking joints. At one end of the room was a very large sofa with an equally large man sitting on it. Two men stood at each side of the sofa, dressed in black, holding what Kadamba knew to be Uzis, nasty projectile weapons that were difficult to control. None of them moved as the three men were brought in front of the sofa.

The large black man on the sofa removed his dark glasses. All of his fingers and each of his thumbs were adorned with heavy gold rings set with huge jewels. Around his neck hung thick braided chains of gold, and a few of the necklaces had huge rings dangling from them. He threw the glasses onto the sofa and stared intently at the dealer, who Kadamba now knew was nicknamed, "Lippy."

"Da fuck you thinkin'?" demanded the man, in a voice as deep as his size, as he rose from the sofa. He was tall and thick. Kadamba watched as the huge man looked Lippy up and down, with an obvious look of disdain on his face. The man wasn't quite as big and muscular as Jackos the Giant, but he was every bit as intimidating. Lippy was shaking as the man strode two paces and landed his fist with a terrible blow into Lippy's gut.

Lippy drop to the floor on his knees, crying and apologizing. "They dropped me man. I ain't have no choice. They wanna buy papers. I ain't know what else to do."

"Da fuck you think bringin' 'em here?" Daddy Rings repeated, as he kicked Lippy, sending him flying across the floor.

Kadamba's hand shot out to grab Dr. Tarea's arm when he heard the doctor begin to speak. Kadamba knew that this had to play out before they could say anything. The best thing in the world was to shut up and wait.

Daddy Rings bent over Lippy, warning, "You best hope they ain't nuthin' but buyers, or you won't be seein' yo momma ever again."

Daddy Rings stepped back to Kadamba and Dr. Tarea, "Da fuck you two want in my house?"

"We need passports," blurted out Dr. Tarea before Kadamba could say anything.

"You best shut yo' mutherfuckin' honky-ass mouth fo' I string a noose up and light yo' ass on fire," Daddy Rings declared.

"It's all cool," Kadamba assured Daddy Rings, as calmly as he could. "We're in your house, man. We'll follow your rules. We're just trying to find someone we can buy some passports from. Ain't no disrespect. We just here needing help. Didn't give Lippy much choice."

"I don't do business with the man," announced Daddy Rings, looking at Dr. Tarea. Then he looked back at Kadamba, "and you probably a brother who sold out to the man."

"Nah, crazy circumstance stuck us together," replied Kadamba. "We ain't the man. We on the run, and we need to buy passports."

"Don't be such a jive-ass mutherfucker," came a female voice from behind them, "Figure out if they legit or not, and do business—or don't."

Kadamba turned to see the most beautiful sight he'd seen in long time. She was tall and thin, wearing a dark-orange, leather jacket, that was open and revealing an amply-filled, black leather bra. Her pants were black leather, flaring widely at the opening of the legs. She had high cheekbones and piercing black eyes. Her large Afro shimmered and seemed to have as much personality as her sassy attitude.

"Girl, get the hell out of here. This ain't yo' business," commanded Daddy Rings, as the young woman started walking towards Kadamba.

"Business be family business, brother, and you caught yourself a cute one right here." She swept her hand across Kadamba's face, as she stepped by them and playfully slapped Daddy Rings on the arm. "Why you be actin' the shit and everything?"

"Damn, if you wasn't my sista," replied Daddy Rings, "I'd backhand yo' black ass across the room."

"Brother, let's just see if we gotz a couple of players or what," she suggested. "You two mutherfuckas better not be narcs."

Stepping back over to Kadamba, she put both her hands gently on his face. She even smelled intoxicating, like the Rocky Mountains, except there was something sensual about it too. She looked deep into his eyes and smiled. If he could have controlled his reactions, he would have, but he couldn't. He blushed and smiled, looking back into her eyes, feeling like a little boy being held safely by his mother.

"Okay, Rings," she announced, without breaking eye contact with Kadamba, "you find out if that honky is on the level, and I'll check everything out about this brother." She ran her hands down his arms, interlocking her fingers and hooking one of his hands with hers. She began to walk towards the door, with Kadamba obediently following along.

"Have a seat," ordered Daddy Rings, gesturing to Dr. Tarea to sit in on the sofa. Dr. Tarea sat, not knowing what else to do. Daddy Rings sat next to him, still towering over the wiry, little man. He put his arm around the doctor, inquiring, "You ain't no narc, is you?"

"No, no, I'm no narcotics officer," replied the doctor, his voice cracking with fear.

Daddy Rings looked him in the eye, as a tall coffee table was pushed in front of the seated pair. "We'll see about that." On the table sat a mirror, lying flat, a small vial, a razor blade, and a small straw.

Dr. Tarea looked at Daddy Rings with apprehension. The man's giant hand picked up and opened the vial, tapping the open end on the center of the mirror. A white powder formed a small pile. The doctor stared at the substance, knowing what it probably was, but afraid it might be something else.

"I don't do drugs," whispered Dr. Tarea, his voice getting hoarser and weaker.

Daddy Rings chuckled as he used the razor blade to spread the powder into a line on the mirror. He picked up the straw, holding it out for Dr. Tarea. "This part is simple," Daddy Rings explained, "either you ain't no narc and you do this here line, or you is a narc and you don't."

His hand trembling, Dr. Tarea took the straw from Daddy Rings and placed it in his nose. He bent over, snorting in as he moved the straw down the line of cocaine. He sat up and looked at Daddy Rings, who was smiling.

Daddy Rings took the vial again, tapped out another pile, and used the razor blade to form another line. "This shit be real good. You best try it on the other side too."

Dr. Tarea put the straw to his other nostril and snorted in the second line of cocaine. He closed his eyes for a few moments. When he opened them, Daddy Rings was smiling. The whole room seemed to be brighter. Someone had turned on a large boombox in the corner, the beat filling the room. Dr. Tarea started bobbing his head side-to-side, biting his lower lip. "Fuck me . . . Wow!" were the only words that Dr. Tarea could manage.

Daddy Rings started to laugh, "Nah, just yo' friend be getting' fucked. You get to party. Silly-ass honky."

Someone handed Dr. Tarea a joint, and he took a deep drag on it, holding it in his lungs. Maybe these drugs weren't quite as bad as the ones on Koranth decided Dr. Tarea as his body started gyrating to the beat of the music.

*****

Kadamba was mesmerized as the beautiful woman led him down the corridors and up staircases in the warehouse. He wasn't sure where he was, and he couldn't seem to take his eyes of her. After she closed the door behind him, he looked around. It wasn't what he expected. It was clean and bright. The walls appeared to have been painted, and a desk, a dresser, and bed were in the room. He realized it was a bedroom. "Are we still in the warehouse?" he asked, as he peered around.

"We sure are," she replied. "It ain't much, but it's home."

Holding his hand, she put her other hand on his face. He trembled as she ran her fingers along his check. Looking at him quizzically, she asked his name.

"Kadamba," he replied, not even thinking to use anything else and not really being able to think at all.

"Where'd you get that name?" she asked.

"My parents."

"Duh," she teased him, "Where's a name like that come from?"

"It's a very long, long ways from here. What's your name?"

"Violet."

She pushed him onto the bed, where he sat looking up at her. She slowly pulled his shirt off and pushed him onto his back. She crawled on top of him, straddling him as she pulled off her jacket and bra. She ran her hands over his chest. "Damn, you one strong boy."

She traced the outlines of the muscles of his chest and shoulders. He shivered at her touch, not knowing what to do. She looked him in the eyes, and he saw a compassion and kindness that seemed so rare in his world.

"You've never done this before, have you?" she asked.

He looked away, shaking his head side-to-side slightly.

She smiled as she looked down on him and kissed his nose. She looked into his eyes again. "I can tell you want this, don't you?"

This time he looked her in the eyes, slowly shaking his head up and down in affirmation.

"Then let's make this something you'll remember forever," she suggested, as she pressed her lips to his.

She was gentle, kind, and patient. The minutes merged into hours, and Kadamba lost track of time, spinning in a world of pleasure and ecstasy. Hours later, he awoke, realizing that she was in his arms. It was dark. He didn't know what had happened to Dr. Tarea, and in that moment, he didn't really care. He pulled Violet closer and drifted back to sleep.

The room was bright when he awoke again. She was gone, and he was alone, naked in the bed.

"Come on, lover boy," a man's voice stated. He rolled over and saw one of the thugs that had been standing by the sofa staring at him from across the room. "You wanna do business or not?"

Kadamba quickly pulled on his clothes and followed the man back to the room where he had first met Violet and Daddy Rings. Dr. Tarea was curled up on a sofa, with his head tucked under a cushion.

"Your honky friend can party," Daddy Rings declared, sitting on the large sofa with Violet by his side. "She says you ain't no narc or trouble of any kind. We can do business with you and the honky. It ain't gonna be cheap, but since I got yo' money, I know it ain't no problem. Good thing Violet like you. Otherwise, well, you don't even wanna know."

Another man handed Kadamba the items that had been taken from his pockets the day before. The wallet still seemed to have all the money that he brought with him.

"It all there," Violet assured him. "That a lot of cash to be carrying."

Kadamba put everything back in his pockets, as Dr. Tarea began to groan. "Oh, fuck me," he muttered, as he sat up, putting his hands to his head. "What a night . . ."

A number of the people in the room began to laugh, including Daddy Rings. "Your honky friend found a few things he never try before. I think he be likin' 'em a lot."

"Daddy Rings," Dr. Tarea announced, as he stood up unsteadily, "I think you're my new best friend."

As the laughter began to recede, the door opened, and another black man stepped into the room. While everyone in the room was dressed casually and comfortably, the man who walked into the room was wearing a suit.

"Good morning, Ernest. Good morning, Violet," the man stated in greeting, looking at Daddy Rings and Violet. "I understand we have some new customers."

Dr. Tarea snorted a little laugh, "Daddy Rings sounds a lot more like you than Ernest does!"

"Still better than 'Nahash,'" replied Daddy Rings with a chuckle. "You can go by Dr. Tarea, and I'll be Daddy Rings."

Kadamba realized that Violet had hardly taken her eyes off of him since he walked in. He looked around at the room. It wasn't someplace he ever imagined himself standing or a situation he could have ever dreamed of being in, but it was okay. While he'd been intimidated and scared last night, today, he felt more relaxed. With the guns and the dark clothes, it was easy to see these people as thugs or villains, but they were just people.

"I'm Owen Johnson," the man in the suit said, extending his hand to Kadamba and Dr. Tarea. "I'll be helping you with your current dilemma. Please come with me."

The two men followed Owen back into the corridor that wound through another set of hallways and stairs. Eventually, they came to a room that looked like an office. A camera was set on a tripod, pointing towards a light-blue screen against a wall. Each of them took a turn getting their pictures taken, and then Owen walked them back to the room where Daddy Rings was still seated on the sofa.

"Come back in five days. We'll have papers for you then," Owen promised, as he walked back out of the room. Kadamba turned and handed Daddy Rings a stack of bills. The large man thumbed through the bills with his ring-laden fingers. He smiled at the two of them. "This ain't the way I usually do business, but it all good."

He put his hand out to the side, and another man placed a vial in his hand. He smiled and looked at Dr. Tarea. "Here a lil gift from me to you." Dr. Tarea took the vial and smiled at the Daddy Rings. "That be a gift from me to you, Nahash," the man continued in a serious tone. "When you want more, just come on by, but don't forget your wallet. You'll have to buy it next time."

Kadamba took a deep breath. This scene felt a little too familiar. It seemed drug dealers had some common traits, no matter what planet they were on.

Two days later, Kadamba and Dr. Tarea were back. This time they brought more cash. Dr. Tarea had gone through the cocaine that Daddy Rings had given him and wanted more.

Back at the hotel, Dr. Tarea tried to get Kadamba to try some.

"I'm just not interested," Kadamba responded.

"Look boy, we've got a flight booked. We're doing our job. Come on out and have some fun tonight," declared Dr. Tarea.

"You go have fun. I'll just hang out here at the hotel," Kadamba told him.

Dr. Tarea slammed the door as he left. Kadamba wasn't interested in seeing the man again, but knew he would be back at some point, but probably not soon.

After Dr. Tarea left, Kadamba headed back to the warehouse. He knocked on the door. The little window slid open, and then the door opened. "Back so soon?" asked the man.

"I was hoping I could see Violet," replied Kadamba, hoping the man didn't hear any desperation in his voice.

"Head on back," the man directed, "She with Daddy Rings."

The room was lit by the lava lamps, and Daddy Rings was sitting on his sofa. Music blasted from the boombox again. A number of people, including Violet, were dancing, gyrating to the pounding beat. Violet smiled when she saw him, pulling him into the group. His awkward movements made her laugh, and she whispered in his ear, "Guess you haven't done this much either."

She pulled him towards the door, back to her room. He was more confident this time, and they both found passionate pleasure in one another's arms. They talked all night long. Kadamba learned that Ernest and Owen were her older brothers. They'd moved from Mississippi with their mother when they were kids. She'd worked three jobs to send Owen, the oldest, to college, but when he graduated, he couldn't find a job. Ernest had figured out how to make money on the streets, and when their mother died young of cancer, all three siblings went into business together. The streets weren't kind, but they made a living.

The next day, Kadamba returned to the hotel to find Dr. Tarea passed out in the bed with a prostitute. The next two nights were the same. Dr. Tarea would go out and party, while Kadamba spent time with Violet. In her bed, he began to think about what it might be like if Dr. Tarea were dead. Kadamba's skills could probably be of use to someone like Daddy Rings. Violet cuddled in close to him, and he began to drift off.

The grass was as green as always, as were the shrubs and trees. Ka looked around the Landing. It was as quiet and still, as always, but rain was bouncing off the force-field cover that sheltered the Landing. The sky was dark grey, and lightning bounced between the clouds.

He walked back to the Freezies vendor, expecting to find Alorus hiding from the storm, but he wasn't there. Ka walked to his favorite bench and sat down. He wasn't even sure why he'd checked on Alorus. Maybe he was worried. Maybe he just didn't want the boy to be scared.

"Does she have a little brother?" asked Alorus from behind Ka. He walked up, looking accusingly at Ka. "Think she'll mind if you sell him some rath?"

The next day, Kadamba left the warehouse and then returned with Dr. Tarea to get their fake passports. Violet was gone. Kadamba knew it was probably for the best. Saying goodbye would be too hard, and he could never stay. His short stint as a drug dealer hadn't turned out so well for him.

*****

Dr. Tarea stepped out onto the apartment balcony in London. "That hooker reminds me of that girl you were banging back in DC, probably not quite as sweet, but . . ."

Before Dr. Tarea could say anything else, Kadamba brushed by him, stepping back into the rundown apartment. "Get your ass in gear, doctor. The show's over in twenty minutes."

They'd already been to the small, dingy theater where Garrett Greyson, Master of Illusions, put on his cheap show. As far as Kadamba was concerned, it was a pathetic show, by an even more pathetic man. There was a woman in a box who was sawed in half, and other tricks and illusions that one could see at any traveling carnival sideshow. The show was nothing special, and Kadamba pressed Dr. Tarea on why he thought this man could be a Transprophetic.

Dr. Tarea had explained that it was the lameness of this show that made it stand out. There was nothing new in the show. Even on this planet, magicians strived to perform more complicated tricks. "He's not doing anything new. He can use his skills, make money, and no one knows. If he was making waves and coming up with new 'illusions,' people would take notice. He's just too ordinary to actually be ordinary." It seemed a weak explanation to Kadamba, but he wasn't the expert.

Kadamba stood in the alley behind the theater. They had watched the show the night before and knew that Garrett Greyson would leave the building long after the crowd had left. The pistol Kadamba jabbed into the man's side made him shriek.

"The take's already gone," Garrett Greyson began to plead, "The manager—he takes it with him. There's nothing left."

"Unlock the door. We're going back inside," ordered Kadamba.

The man fumbled with his keys, finally opening the alley door and stepping inside the building. The hallway was littered with props, and Kadamba pushed the man through, telling him to go to the stage.

Dr. Tarea was waiting on the stage when Kadamba and Garrett pushed through the curtain. A single chair sat in the middle of the stage, and a spotlight shone brightly on the chair.

"Tape him to the chair," commanded Dr. Tarea, gesturing to a roll of duct tape on a small table in front of the chair, lying next to a feather and a large knife. The man looked around frightfully, as Kadamba pushed him into the chair. Within a few moments, Garret Greyson's legs were both taped to the chair's legs while his hands and arms were secured to the chair's back.

"What is it you want?" begged Garrett, "Billy's been paid. I don't owe anyone else, I swear."

Dr. Tarea chuckled, "This has nothing to do with any of that. We're here to see a magic show."

"I don't understand," responded Garrett.

"Oh, I think you do. You do one every night and play it off as illusions, but I know what you really can do," Dr. Tarea told him.

"My God, what in the bloody hell are you talking about?" asked Garrett, sounding more and more panicked.

"So this is a Transprophetic," thought Kadamba. He seemed more of a scared stage performer than any harbinger of change. He took a step back, wondering how the doctor would prove that this pathetic man was anything more than what he claimed he was.

"You see the feather, there," Dr. Tarea pressed him, as he picked up the knife. "All you need to do is move it, or I'll cut you open."

The man looked at Dr. Tarea, shaking his head. "I can't do that. I make illusions. It's not real."

"You see, Kadamba," the doctor noted, as he held the knife to the man's cheek, "he wants to hide what he really is, but here's the truth. The more intense the emotion, the more likely he'll reveal his talents. And what better emotion to use than fear."

The scream was deafening as Dr. Tarea drew the knife across the man's cheek and then pulled it across his other cheek. "I'm going to skin you alive unless you move that feather."

The man begged and tears began to roll down his face. "I'm just an illusionist. No one can do what you're asking. It's not possible."

The blade dug into the man's shoulder, and he cried out in pain, again.

"One last chance, or it gets personal," chuckled Dr. Tarea, as he ran the blade up the inside of the man's thigh.

The man's face was red, and veins popped out on his temples and forehead as he strained to move the feather, using only his mind. The feather remained exactly where it was on the table. The doctor pushed the knife hard into the man's groin, and the man began to shake. "I can't do it. It can't be done."

"Oh yes, it can, you just have to try harder." The doctor raised the knife, stabbing it into the man's leg, narrowly missing that which made him a man. Garret, screaming out in pain, started blowing in the direction of the feather. It wobbled a little on the table.

"Nice try, you damn fraud," Dr. Tarea said, as he pulled the knife out and handed it to Kadamba. "I guess this one is nothing but a fake. A fake who knows your odd name, Kadamba. I'll leave the honors to you. You haven't had a chance to kill since we left Koranth. Enjoy yourself."

Kadamba stood on the stage looking at the bloody knife while Dr. Tarea began to whistle, walking off the stage, through the seats, and out the door. He didn't know what to do. This was terrible. He looked at Garret Greyson. There were tears in the man's eyes.

"I'm sorry." The words came out of Kadamba's mouth before he knew it. He stepped over to the man and began to cut through the tape.

"So, it's all come to this?" Garret questioned Ka.

"What?" asked Kadamba.

"I'm killed as a freak, all because I wanted to entertain and do magic. I wish I could have moved the feather for your friend. I've always wished I could do real magic."

"I'll get you out of here."

"It's too late," Garret uttered softly, his head dropping to his chest.

Kadamba looked down and realized the stage was a pool of blood around the chair. Dr. Tarea had severed the man's femoral artery in his leg. He'd bled out before Kadamba could do anything. Kadamba stood and looked at the man, as a tear ran down his cheek. So this was it? This was how they would find if this world held any Transprophetics. His stomach knotted and emptied its contents onto stage and the table. He stood there for a few moments, looking at the body of Garret Grayson, wishing that all of this had been an illusion.

"Nice job, killer," yelled Dr. Tarea, as he walked back into the theater and strolled quickly down the aisle, through the seats to the stage, "but it's time to leave."

A rolling wave of smoke hit the stage as Dr. Tarea tossed his Zippo lighter to Kadamba. "The lobby is already blazing. Light that curtain on fire, and let's get out of here."

A few blocks away, they turned and looked up. The low clouds reflected the orange and yellow of the roaring fire that destroyed the theater, covering their tracks.

Chapter 34
A Flower from Heaven

The smog was thick as Kadamba walked the back streets, late in the evening in Bangkok. The streets were crowded with foreigners from many different countries, who had come to this city, well-known for being a destination for sex tourism. Everywhere you turned was another hawker of some sleazy establishment trying to persuade visitors to come inside and see what the place had to offer. Drugs and sex were on display everywhere, and Dr. Tarea was like a kid in a candy store.

Maliya was her name. She was only nine years old. The monks at the Tao Wong Wa shrine declared that she was the incarnate rebirth of some long lost deity—one who could move objects using her thoughts alone. Apparently, these monks followed some long-lost mix of Buddhism and Hindu traditions. Kadamba didn't really understand that much about the history or the belief system, but it seemed like something that should pique the interest of a man with an advanced degree in religions and truth. However, Dr. Tarea seemed only barely interested in anything other than spending his evenings getting strung out, watching bizarre sex shows, and hiring underage prostitutes.

After a week of indulging, Dr. Tarea decided that it was time to get serious about their mission. In an abandoned warehouse they set it up with the few items that would be required to confirm whether Maliya was a Transprophetic or not.

While the monks of the Tao Wong Wa shrine certainly wanted to protect the young girl, they were woefully unprepared for someone like Kadamba. Having slipped into their residence during the middle of the night, Ka had little trouble kidnapping the child. Within a few hours, she was taped to a chair, looking at a small table with a flower, known as a "hidden lily," resting on it.

"Pick it up," insisted Dr. Tarea, as he looked at the child. He made various gestures to try to get the girl to understand what he wanted, but she only stared at him. Over and over, and in multiple ways, Dr. Tarea tried to get the girl to understand what he wanted her to do. Tears ran down her face, as she replied in Thai.

Kadamba paced the room, telling himself repeatedly that he was an Elite Forces soldier and his job here was to protect Dr. Tarea. Evidence that Transprophetics existed on this planet would change everything. He tried to reassure himself that what he was doing was in the best interest of his people, in the best interest of the mission, in the best interest of Koranth.

The little girl looked at him, her eyes begging him to do something. He'd learned a few words and phrases in the last few days, and he understood that every time she said, "Ch̀wy c̄hạn d̂wy," she was asking for help.

"I guess talking and being kind just aren't going to work," Dr. Tarea muttered. "It must be time for a little more fear in this child's mind."

Dr. Tarea unsheathed a large knife, holding it in the air in front of the girl. He pointed again at the flower, demanding, "Pick up the fucking flower before I skin you alive!" The little girl began to sob and struggle against the tape that held her to the chair.

"Wait!" Kadamba asserted, more forcefully than he expected to say it.

Dr. Tarea looked at him and laughed. "I suppose you want in on playing with this little precious thing."

"H̄yib mạn k̄hụ̂n mā," Kadamba spoke quietly to Maliya, pointing to the flower. "H̄yib mạn k̄hụ̂n mā pord."

The girl's sobbing stopped, and she looked at Kadamba. "Pick it up, please," he repeated again in Thai. She looked at him, and he nodded his head up and down, trying to make his face smile.

Maliya, looking at the flower, began to concentrate. Dr. Tarea stood as still as a statue, his eyes fixed on the flower. For a moment, nothing happened. Then the flower began to rise, hovering in the air over the table.

"Lords of the Fourth System, this little creature is a Transprophetic!" declared Dr. Tarea. He began to laugh. He even danced around a little.

"You know what this means, don't you boy?" asked Dr. Tarea. Kadamba stared at the doctor, trying to share in his excitement, but the acid in his stomach was boiling.

"We'll be rich and famous!" declared the doctor. "Once a portal is open here, we'll be heroes. We'll be the ones who identified the best timing to develop this planet! Tomar Donovackia will shower us with wealth!"

The flower dropped back to the table, and Dr. Tarea looked at the little girl. Her face showed nothing but confusion. Dr. Tarea pointed at her, "You've made me very happy today, my little Thai flower!" His smile went crooked, and the girl's expression changed from confusion to fear. He stood over the girl looking down on her soft features. "I wonder if she would have become something more than an oddity for some random monks."

"She might," replied Kadamba, as he walked up and stood by the doctor, knowing exactly what was going to happen next.

"It's almost a shame that she has to die," stated Dr. Tarea, but there wasn't anything resembling compassion or regret in his voice.

Kadamba held out his hand, and the Doctor looked at him, snickering. "I guess this is the part you like, the killing." Dr. Tarea placed the large blade into Kadamba's hand.

Kadamba's fingers slid into each of the form-fitting indentations on the handle. He spun the knife in his hand, so that the blade guard rested on the bottom of his hand, and his fingers slid once again into the indentations. His arm dropped, and he felt the point of the blade graze across his elbow, just like the blade that he had used to kill that bargabuko in Mr. Lormate's class.

That bargabuko had died quickly from the powerful blow that Kadamba had inflicted. He hoped that the next blow that he would deliver would bring death just as quickly. He brought his arm up, across his chest, and took a deep breath. With every ounce of his strength, he drove the blade home. He felt the blade guard smash into flesh and bone, as the knife's blade buried itself completely. He let go of the knife, knowing that everything in his world had just changed.

Dr. Tarea looked at Kadamba for a moment with shock in his eyes. Then the doctor, who supposedly knew so much about religion and truth, looked down at the handle of the knife, sticking out from his own chest. He staggered backwards, falling into a pile of tarps that had been sitting on the floor.

“I’m sorry you had to see that,” Kadamba apologized to the girl, as he freed her from the chair.

He held out his hand, and she put her hand into his. Within a few minutes, they were in a crowded Bangkok street. Kadamba saw the police officer in the distance and pointed to him. Maliya shook her head affirmatively and started running towards the officer.

Kadamba saw the officer step towards the child, and he knew she would be okay. When Maliya turned and pointed, trying to explain to the officer what was happening, Kadamba was long gone.

Chapter 35
No Peace in the Mountains

Kadamba looked up the long gravel drive to the cabin. He could see the yellow plastic tape across the door. The last time that he'd stood looking at that door, two blasts had taken the lives of two innocent people. He thought about Jerry and Margaret. They were just some old couple enjoying their last years in this majestic setting.

Pulling the police tape off the door, he went inside. Everything was mostly how he remembered it, except for the dull brown spatter stains on the wall. Some things had been rearranged, but he was surprised by how much hadn't been. It would likely be a few days before his crewmates arrived, and he was happy that there was still canned food in the pantry. He could stay here in the mountains and not worry about having to go into town. No one had seen him come, and he'd prefer if no one saw him go.

The old couple had a spare bedroom, and Kadamba made himself at home there. As he sat in the bed, he realized how different his life had become. Here he was completely alone, without obligation or confinement. He'd been in prison, the military, on the spaceship, with Dr. Tarea, and even with Violet, but he'd never been free like this. He wasn't sure what the future would bring, but he was sure what would happen in the next few days.

Even though he knew it was a dream, coming to the Landing had its benefits. For one thing, it was always the same. The grass was always green. There was never any trash. Outside the Landing, the weather might change, but inside, it was always the same.

The sun was shining brightly, and Ka began to walk around. As always, it was almost completely silent, except for a distant squeaking sound. There really only was one living thing in the Landing, and that was Ka.

Ka saw Alorus in the distance. He was swinging on a swing in the playground. Ka moved stealthily, getting closer and closer to the boy. He wanted to see the child's face when the child didn't know he was nearby. It was the same, nearly emotionless face that Ka had come to know all too well.

"I see you, Ka" the boy cried out, as he stopped pumping his legs and allowed the swing to begin making smaller and smaller arches. Ka walked into the playground and leaned back on the backrest of a nearby bench and watched the swing slow itself.

When it finally stopped, Alorus looked at Ka, like he was trying to figure him out.

"You didn't kill the little girl," said Alorus, stating it almost like a question, but also more like a fact.

"No, of course not," replied Ka.

"Why not? Aren't you here on a mission? You're supposed to hunt and kill these Transprophetics," Alorus reminded him.

"If these Transprophetics had been adults and maybe been a real threat, then maybe I could have killed them, but she was just a scared little girl. I simply couldn't kill an innocent kid."

Alorus just looked at Ka. It wasn't an accusing look; it was more one of confusion. Ka, expecting the boy's usual accusation, was prepared to hear him say something like, "Well you killed me."

But the boy didn't say anything. He just started pumping his legs again, pushing the swing higher and higher.

The morning sun was bright, and the air was brisk. Kadamba was happy to be in the mountains. He walked to the lake again. It was peaceful here. He closed his eyes and listened to the birds while breathing in the clean mountain air. He sat on a boulder for a while, wondering if there were places like this back on Koranth.

He slipped into the small canyon and found the remote for the return vessel. The surface of the lake was absolutely clear as the return vessel broke free of the water. Kadamba swiped and tapped a few places on the screen, then looked up and watched the spaceship dissolve into ashes that fell to the surface of the lake and began to spread out. With a few more taps, the ashes of the remote drifted away in the light breeze.

He walked back over to the boulder and sat down again. A single mountain towered on the horizon. Before they had betrayed the man, Jerry had called it Wóablakela Peak, and he challenged them to find it named that on any map. He had claimed that it was the name given to the mountain by a Native American medicine man. The medicine man would climb to the peak to seek inner peace and find strength to serve his people. The mountain had a more Western-sounding name now, but Kadamba like the way Wóablakela Peak sounded.

Hearing the sound of a vehicle approaching, Ka released a loud sigh. He wished he could have just come down from Mount Wóablakela, at peace with himself and willing to serve his people. But he was not at peace, and the will of his people was not what he could serve.

She'd complained once about the blood that spattered on her from Jerry and Margaret, so it was almost like a favor. The bullet passed through her head, spattering Commander Conall Bornani, before Kadamba turned the gun on the Commander. Both lay dead a few feet from where they had stepped out of the car and greeted him. It was unceremonious. He didn't say a word. He simply drew the gun and shot them both before they could react.

He looked at the bodies, as they lay on the ground, and he wanted to feel remorse. He couldn't get a day to go by where he didn't think of Alorus. That boy didn't deserve what had happened to him. He thought of Garrett Greyson and how his own inaction had let the man bleed out on that stage. He wished that he could have stopped Dr. Tarea, but it had been too late. As he looked at his crewmates on the ground, he didn't feel guilty. He wasn't sure in that moment that he felt anything at all.

Over the rest of the day, the remaining members of his crew from Koranth returned to Fat Bottom Lake in pairs. Each of them met the same fate as Commander Conall Bornani. Kadamba wrapped each of their bodies in a tarp, a blanket, or a bedspread. He stacked them in the living room of the cabin. The pile reminded him of the stacks of firewood outside the cabin that Jerry and Margaret would never get to use on cold winter nights.

He walked through the house with the can of gasoline, emptying it on the stack of bodies. He stood outside the door, looking at Dr. Tarea's Zippo lighter. In some ways, he wished that Dr. Tarea's body was in that stack. It would be fitting for that cruel bastard to burn with the other crew members.

"Every religion I know on this planet and others has some words that are said for the dead. Words that are usually meant to give comfort for those left behind." He looked closely at the stack of bodies. "I have no words for each of you. You died to your family and friends when you left Koranth. Whatever words were said there are good enough."

The lighter seemed to float in the air as it sailed towards the stack of bodies. As it landed, it appeared like a candle in a dark church—one small flame burning in the blackness, pushing back the ominous emptiness of the dark. Then in the space of time it takes to blink, roaring flames engulfed the pile.

Kadamba closed the door of the pickup truck. It wasn't the old truck in which he first left Fat Bottom Lake, but it was close enough. He pulled out the stack of airline tickets that he'd purchased and the new passports he'd acquired. Lhasa Gonggar Airport was his final destination. He hoped that in the mountains of Tibet there would be another Wóablakela Peak where he could go and find peace.

Chapter 36
Revelations of Truth

Sirens blared as the Mexican police cars arrived at the park. Joanna and Tim were there within a few minutes too. Everything was a blur to Dylan. Why had he let his little brother wander off? Why in the hell had those men grabbed Dylan and shoved him into that van?

Dylan sat down on the park bench between his mom and Adelita. Joanna was obviously in a state of shock, but still trying to comfort her older son. As the last police officer walked away from Tim, Dylan watched, as Tim took out his smartphone and started walking towards the public restrooms.

"I gotta go to the bathroom," Dylan explained, as he got up and followed Tim, hoping not to be noticed. Rather than going into the restroom, Tim went behind the building. Dylan stopped before he came around the building. He quickly poked his head around the corner and saw that Tim was right there, holding his phone up, obviously on a video call.

"Mr. Parnell, how's your vacation going?" asked a young woman on the other end of the call.

"Terrible, Kaylee. I need your help."

"Okay, what can I do?"

"Kaylee, please don't hang up," Tim asserted into the phone. "My girlfriend's son has just been kidnapped. I know that you're connected to GAPN. I need to talk to Sebastian, please."

"Mr. Parnell, I don't know what you're talking about. I'm sorry, but I don't understand."

Tim, releasing a deep breath, continued, "Kaylee, a few weeks ago, I came up behind you while you were working late. I saw what you were doing. I could have fired you on the spot, but I didn't. It wasn't all that long ago that I was a kid too. And I was a hacker too. I was one of the original members of the Legion of Doom. I was known as Rudianos."

He paused for a breath, and Kaylee tentatively inquired, "Okay, what does this have to do with me?"

"I need you to connect me with Sebastian, as quickly as possible. I think he can help," voiced Tim.

"Okay, Tim, hang on."

Tim sat down on a small retaining wall behind the bathroom, letting out another deep sigh. "Dylan, come on around here." Dylan tensed up. He thought he had been quite stealthy, but Tim obviously knew he was there.

"What's this all about?" Dylan asked Tim.

"Do you know what my company does?" Tim asked him.

Dylan looked at Tim, realizing that he didn't have a clue about what the guy really did. "Not really."

"It's really fairly simple," Tim explained. "We take direct data feeds from over two hundred and eighty-two social media-enabled companies around the world. Facebook, Twitter, YouTube, Flickr, and hundreds more. Many of these feeds are from private social networks, corporate networks, government networks, you name it. We've worked a deal to get the data, protect privacy, and extract the intelligence that our clients need. We aggregate the feeds, slice it, dice it, and analyze it a thousand different ways."

"That's pretty cool," Dylan remarked.

"Kaylee is a system administrator that we hired about a year ago. I caught her trying to hack into the systems that aggregate the feeds. I could have fired her, but that would have been a little hypocritical on my part, as you already heard. I was a hacker in my younger days. More importantly, I saw some value in watching her. If she could hack in, we were vulnerable. I had her checked out by a friend of a friend who happens to be FBI. She's got connections to a group called GAPN."

"What's GAPN?" asked Dylan.

"Global Anonymous Pirate Network. It's a loosely affiliated group of hackers, anarchists, conspiracy theorists, and the like. They made big news recently by releasing a trove of secret government documents from the United Kingdom, France, Germany, and the Netherlands."

"Oh right, I heard about that. They can't find the guy that got into the European government systems," Dylan mentioned.

"That's right," confirmed Tim, "The guy's name is Sebastian Twyman—a former MI6 operative. Rumor is that he never left London. It's the most monitored city on Earth, and no one has seen him, even though he supposedly uses the Underground to visit his favorite coffee shops."

"What's all this have to do with finding Bjorn?" asked Dylan.

"The police are doing everything they can here, Dylan. I don't know if I can help or not, and I'm risking a lot if I get to talk to Sebastian, but I think he can help find Bjorn."

When Tim's phone began to buzz, he quickly swiped the screen. Kaylee's face appeared, and her voice was shaky. "Okay, Tim, this better not be a setup."

"On my life, it's not," Tim swore.

The screen split, and Kaylee's face moved to the bottom half of the screen. The top half of the screen was fairly dark, but a man's face was apparent.

"Hello, Tim Parnell," the man on the screen greeted him. "Or should I call you—Rudianos?"

"Mr. Twyman, thank you taking my call," replied Tim.

"So I guess you know what Kaylee has been up to at your company?" inquired Sebastian. "Is that what this call is about?"

"Partially. I need your help," Tim began.

"The missing boy in Mexico?" asked Sebastian. "I'm in London. You're in Playa del Carmen. I am sorry, but I doubt that I can help you, Tim."

"It's rumored that you like to have a mocha latte at 150 degrees while riding on the London metro system. It helps you relax and think, right?" Tim put forth.

"Sure," replied Sebastian, "but what does that have to do with all of this?"

"The Underground stations are a panopticon. It's no secret that the Metropolitan Police and other government agencies are using facial recognition, scanning every face that comes into the subway, and your face is one of the top ones they are looking for. With more than 11,000 cameras in the London Underground alone, you should have been spotted by now."

"Well, I guess they'll have to try harder," Sebastian responded, with a tone of annoyance starting to creep into his voice.

"Let me put it all on the table, Mr. Twyman," Tim disclosed. "I believe you've hacked, compromised, and probably copied and reverse engineered every facial recognition system in and around London. You've made it, so that you can move around undetected by the cameras. Your teams probably know more about their systems than they do."

Sebastian began to chuckle. "Oh, do go on."

"I think you planted Kaylee at my company to get a direct feed on every social media site. I don't know the exact reason why," Tim admitted, "but I think if I give you access to the feed, you could help me find Bjorn."

Sebastian's face became motionless and absolutely silent. Tim was right. Sebastian was trying to get access to that feed, and he had the capability to scan every word, picture, and video for whatever he wanted. If there was a picture or video of Bjorn on a social media site, he had the systems to find it. He just didn't have the feed.

"I'm impressed, Tim," began Sebastian, " but I won't confirm or deny anything you just said."

"Sebastian, I don't have time to dance around. If I give you pictures of Bjorn, descriptions of the van, and every bit of social media data from the last few hours, can you scan it and find him?"

"Open the gates to that feed, and if he's anywhere on any picture or video, we'll find him. But what's in it for me?" asked Sebastian.

"Help find the boy, and we'll figure something out that more than compensates you," Tim promised.

Tim passed his personal username, password, validation code, and access window to Kaylee. Within a few minutes, a massive stream of data was flowing into Sebastian's network from every significant social media site on Earth.

Tim and Dylan walked back to the park bench, where Joanna and Adelita were still sitting. The police, having fanned out, seemed to be interviewing everyone in the park. In the distance, Dylan saw a man walking with a cane. He seemed to be heading towards the bench.

"No way," Dylan uttered, and everyone turned to look when the man got close. It was their family friend, Atticus Freeman.

"Mr. Freeman, what are you doing here?" asked Joanna.

"A friend of mine has a condo in Cancun," replied Mr. Freeman. "He invited me down the day you left. I thought I would come down here and surprise you. The front desk of your condo building told me you'd be here."

They filled Mr. Freeman in on what had happened to Bjorn, and he did his best to try to provide some comfort to Dylan. One of the police officers approached them and suggested that they return to their condo. He would be in touch as the investigation proceeded. There seemed little to do other than follow his suggestion.

Back at the condo, time seemed to slow. Every second that ticked by felt like an eternity. The air felt thick. They tried to make conversation, but nothing could lighten the weight that felt like it was pressing down heavier and harder on all of them. Each of them wanted to do something, but what was there for them to do?

The knock on the condo door made them all flinch. "That's my Uncle Hector," Adelita assured them. "We were going to talk about maybe going scuba diving tomorrow. He's just here to pick me up and take me to my aunt's and his house. My parents had to go to Rome."

Adelita answered the door and introduced Hector to everyone. He looked the typical part of a dive instructor—tanned, long hair, sandals, shorts, and a loose t-shirt advertising a dive shop. His dive knife was even strapped to his leg.

Atticus stood up to shake his hand, and, like a flash of lightning, Hector's dive knife was at Mr. Freeman's throat. Joanna shrieked.

"Kadamba Vorhoor, where's the boy?" demanded Hector to Mr. Freeman.

"What the hell are you doing?" screamed Adelita at her Uncle. "He's a family friend."

Mr. Freeman seemed unfazed by the knife at his throat and simply looked at Hector. "How would I know?"

"I never thought that I would meet the poster boy, himself," continued Hector. "Tell me where the boy is now, or I'll run you through."

Tim and Dylan began to move, but Mr. Freeman held a hand out, indicating that they stay put. Before Hector could react, Mr. Freeman twisted Hector's hand causing him to drop the knife. One of Mr. Freeman's legs shot forward, as he extended Hector's arm back, furthering the twisted position of the hand that had held the knife. Mr. Freeman's other hand came up and across Hector's chin, knocking him backwards and causing him to fall across Mr. Freeman's outstretched leg.

"Holy shit," blurted Dylan, as the younger man hit the ground.

Hector quickly rolled away and popped back to his feet.

"STOP!" yelled Joanna, "Someone, tell me what in the hell is going on here?"

"Has this man told you who he really is?" Hector demanded, without taking his eyes off Mr. Freeman. "Has he explained that scar on his arm?"

Everyone looked at the inside of Mr. Freeman's arm. Dylan realized that this was the first time he'd seen Mr. Freeman in more casual clothes—a Panama hat, casual pants, and a short-sleeved, guayabera shirt. The scar was obvious on his arm, once it was pointed out, but it just looked like random markings.

"Tell them, Kadamba," Hector commanded, with sneer in his voice. "Tell them who you really are. Tell them what that scar on your arm means."

"It's obvious that I could ask you where the boy is," Mr. Freeman offered, "especially since you *can* read the words on my arm."

Mr. Freeman, sitting back down, began talking to Hector in a language that none of them could understand. Adelita's face looked surprised as Hector began conversing with the older man in the same tongue. It was obvious that whatever Mr. Freeman was telling the younger man was making sense. The tension level began to recede.

"Okay, will you please explain what the hell the two of you are talking about and what it has to do with Bjorn?" demanded Joanna.

Mr. Freeman, rolling his cane between his hands, took a deep breath. "You're going to have trouble believing what we're about to say."

"My son is missing," replied Joanna, "I don't care. If it helps find my boy, I'll believe anything."

"My given name is Kadamba Vorhoor. Hector and I are not from this planet. We came here on separate exploratory missions from our planet. I arrived over thirty years ago, and Hector came about a decade ago. Both missions had the same goal—to discover if Earth was ready, essentially ready, for our planet to invade."

"It sounds like bullshit to me," Tim commented, "but what does it have to do with Bjorn?"

"Part of these missions is to understand if a planet has any *Transprophetics*," Mr. Freeman went on, "people with, what you might call, telekinetic or paranormal abilities—like the ability to move things without touching them. It's nothing more than an evolutionary step, but when it happens, everything changes. The people of our planet want to invade before scientists on this planet can validate a Transprophetic."

"The vase," Dylan noted. "It was all over the Internet. Bjorn is one of these Transprophetics, isn't he? You saw it. That's why you're here."

Mr. Freeman looked at Dylan, nodding his head slowly up and down, "Yes, I came here to try to protect him. I didn't know if anyone else had come from Koranth, my home planet, but I knew if they did, they would come after him."

The men from Koranth explained more details of their missions and what they were attempting to accomplish. Both explained that they had each forsaken their missions, instead deciding to just build a life here on Earth. Hector's mission had been unable to validate any Transprophetics, so they sent their return vessel home with reports saying that Earth was very close, but not quite ready. That was ten years ago. Like, Kadamba, Hector had been in the Corporate military. He was basically a bodyguard to a logistics and trade expert. He and the expert had been in a car accident that killed the expert and left Hector in a coma for months. After his recovery, Hector decided to abandon his mission and just make a life on Earth.

Hector had recognized the words in Lamaratian on Kadamba's arm. Unbeknownst to Kadamba, now Atticus Freeman, he had become the poster boy for the Donovackia Corporation's prison recruiting efforts.

Both Joanna and Dylan couldn't help but be panicked and cry as Mr. Freeman explained that part of these missions was to find and eliminate any Transprophetics. The stories these two men were telling were beyond fantastical—nearly impossible to believe—but if they were true, it was terrifying. It meant that either someone from Hector's crew, or someone from a new mission, might have kidnapped Bjorn, believing the boy to be a potential Transprophetic.

Mr. Freeman looked at his neighbors—the woman who had become his friend and the teenager whom he had grown so fond of. He knew that they would feel nothing but betrayed. More than anything in the world, he wanted Bjorn to be sitting in that room. He would have traded his life at that moment for the boy's safety.

"What does that say on your arm?" asked Dylan.

Mr. Freeman looked at the words that he had lived with for more than thirty years. The scar on his skin stopped hurting so many years ago, but the wound in his own heart refused to heal. The pain just never stopped. Alorus was always with him. Dylan watched as a tear formed in the man's eye. It ran in a single streak down his cheek as he answered, "Child Murderer."

A single second of silence can echo through the soul louder than any scream. In that brief moment, Kadamba could feel the horror of watching Alorus die, the pain of the laser burning into his arm, and the terror and torture of being raped in prison. It washed across his soul, weighing down even more heavily now that those close to him, those who had entrusted him with the young boy, knew this piece of his past. Even though he had done nothing but try to protect Bjorn, he could feel the accusations in their eyes. It was as if he were responsible for what had happened to Bjorn.

The buzz from Tim's phone broke the painful silence. He picked it, swiped the screen, and Sebastian's face appeared. "I think we found the boy."

"Where?" asked Joanna quickly.

"I'm not sure," replied Sebastian. "The picture we found was of some teenage girl making that stupid duckface, but in the background there is a van and what looks like two men leading a child with a bag over his head into a building. No GPS with the photo, but it's from a Mexican social network."

Tim's phone beeped, indicating that he had received a message. He flipped the screen to the messages, pulling up the photo from Sebastian.

"Do you know where this is?" he asked, holding the phone out for Hector to see.

"It's only two blocks away," replied Hector, as he looked at the blurry picture of a van, with a man pulling a child with a bag over his head into the building. "It's an old warehouse."

At once, all six people in the room were heading to the door. Within a few moments, they were in front of the warehouse. Hector turned to Adelita, realizing they were acting without thinking. "Stay here. Call the police."

The door screeched on its rusted hinges, as it swung open, and they walked into a small, dark room. Another door across the room led to a staircase, and they quickly headed up the stairs, emerging into a dimly lit, large room. They stopped in their tracks as a man across the room leveled a submachine gun in their direction. "Come on in," he greeted them. "Wrong place, wrong time for all of you."

Mr. Freeman felt the point of the gun as it pressed into his back. Out of the shadows, an old man emerged, pushing Mr. Freeman forward. His face was ragged looking, and his grey hair seemed thin and greasy as it stuck to his scalp and forehead. Laughter seemed to seep under his breath. "For most of the nearly thirty years I spent in prison, I dreamed of meeting you again, Kadamba—to kill you for putting that knife in my chest, instead of into that vile little Thai girl."

"Dr. Tarea," stated Mr. Freeman flatly, "you should be dead."

"Should be, but it didn't work out that way. The Thai police found me in that warehouse. I spent months in a rundown, nasty hospital and then decades in the hell they called a prison. I'm going to enjoy killing you. Turn around."

Mr. Freeman turned to look at Dr. Tarea. The years and time in prison had worn on him heavily, but the evil look still remained in his eyes. He was a cruel soul, and his crooked smile began to spread as he looked at Mr. Freeman.

Dr. Tarea began to lift the gun, bringing it chest height, only a couple of feet from Mr. Freeman's chest. "I'll put this hole right where you should have driven that knife." Dr. Tarea began to laugh, as the perverse joy of finally killing Kadamba swept over him.

The blur of Mr. Freeman's cane as it spun into Dr. Tarea's knuckles resembled an airplane propeller. The solid maple cracked as it hit bone, and the gun went sailing across the room. Dr. Tarea looked in shock, as the cane spun again and flew across the room. Everyone's heads spun as the solid maple hit a large metal barrel, sending a gong-like sound through the room.

The grunting "ugh" that gushed from Dr. Tarea's lips turned everyone's attention back to the doctor. The brass handle of the cane was firmly in Mr. Freemen's hand, and blade that was hidden by the maple was buried in the Doctor's chest.

"Stay dead this time," commanded Mr. Freeman, as Dr. Tarea fell backwards, landing with a thud on the hard floor.

"Perfect throw, Hector," Mr. Freeman remarked, peering at the stunned members of the group.

"Huh?" replied Hector as he felt for the knife at this thigh. The man in the back of the room had dropped the submachine gun and was staggering backward. His face showed a look of utter terror, as the handle of the dive knife protruded from his throat.

A scream of pain alerted the group to the fact that there were others in the far room. They all scrambled for the door, and Hector rudely yanked his knife from the dying man's throat as he ran past him.

Chapter 37
Brainwaves

Bjorn felt the powerful grip of the man holding him in place. The bag that was slipped over his head was dusty and smelled of burnt oil. The vice-like grip on the back of his neck tightened as the van accelerated. Bjorn wanted to scream, but was too scared to even form the sounds needed.

Wherever they went had been fairly close by. Bjorn's feet barely touched the ground as they walked him into a building and forced him up a flight of stairs. Not a word had been said in the few minutes since he was snatched out of the park. He was roughly pushed into a chair and could hear tape being ripped from the roll.

His legs were taped to the legs of the chair, and his arms taped to its arms. The adhesive, pulling tightly at his skin, hurt. The minutes seemed to tick by. He could hear whispers nearby but couldn't understand the language that was being spoken. Then there was silence. He couldn't tell if anyone was in the room or not. Bjorn tried not to cry, but he couldn't help it. He wasn't sure how long he had been taped to the chair when he heard the sounds of the men's voices again.

The light was dim in the room when they pulled the bag from his head. Four men, with one significantly older, stood regarding at him. They stared for a minute, not moving, not saying a word. They just peered at him with cold, uncaring eyes. Tighter and tighter, the fear gripped Bjorn, making him wonder if he would ever see his mom and Dylan again.

"What do you want?" begged Bjorn when he couldn't stand the silence anymore.

The older man sneered at him. Bjorn hated this man from the moment he'd seen him. He reminded Bjorn of some of the homeless men that would panhandle and hassle the kids on the busy street near his home. He looked gaunt, and his greasy hair clung to his head.

Another of the men began to chuckle. "Do you realize that we have members of three exploratory missions here in one room, and we've got a potential Transprophetic right here in front of us? What are the odds?"

Bjorn looked around, hoping to find something that would give him some clue as to what was going on. The room was obviously in some type of industrial building. The ceiling was high, and the few old sodium lights that still worked barely lit the room. There were empty shelves along one wall, a stack of rusted 55-gallon drums, and doors on each end of the room. In front of the chair, where he was tied, stood a small table with single rose and a large, unsheathed survival-type knife.

"As the senior member, Dr. Tarea, do you want the honors?" asked one of the younger men.

"Tempting for sure. I'd love to see what this little boy is made of," replied Dr. Tarea, "but I'd also like to see if you young guys have any new tricks up your sleeve, Commander Fahey."

The Commander gestured to another of the group, "Dr. Nadina, please, proceed."

Dr. Nadina took a step towards Bjorn, slapping him hard across the face. "Do you want me to hurt you little boy?" he asked.

Bjorn began to cry. "No, no, please don't hurt me."

"I'm going to carve your fingernails off of your thumbs if you don't do exactly as I tell you. Do you understand?"

"Yes, I'll do anything." The tears were streaming down Bjorn's face.

"Lift the rose," commanded Dr. Nadina.

Bjorn looked at the man, wondering what he meant. "I can't. I'm taped to this chair."

"Just lift it with your mind, or I'll cut your ears off and feed them to you," threatened Dr. Nadina.

Bjorn looked at the man, the fear beginning to be replaced with curiosity and indignation. Could this guy be that stupid? "Untape me, and I'll dance around with the rose," Bjorn offered coldly.

Dr. Nadina put his hand on Bjorn's shoulder and, in a very gentle and calm voice, told Bjorn, "You have the capability to lift that rose using nothing more than your mind. You can do this. I don't want to have to carve you up. Just lift the rose."

"Okay," replied Bjorn as he began to focus on the rose. He looked at the red petals of the flower, then the leaves, and then the stem. He knew that he would have to lift it by the stem. He focused, but nothing happened.

"Believe that you can do this, and you can, little boy," Commander Fahey assured him. "We don't want to hurt you. We just want to see if you are as special as we think you are."

Bjorn looked at the men in the room. They were all staring at him intently. "They must be insane idiots," thought Bjorn, "How can four grown guys actually think that I can do magic?" Inside he chuckled to himself. "They'd all crap their pants if I actually made that rose fly into the air." Looking at the rose again, he imagined how funny it would be to lift it. In his mind's eye, he put the rose into the air.

"Lords of the Fourth System!" gasped the fourth man in the room as he watched the rose rise into the air. "A Transprophetic has evolved on this planet."

"You stupid fucks," snapped Dr. Tarea, "I told you that I found one thirty years ago in Thailand. This has been a waste of time. We need to get to your return vessel and let the Donovackia Corporation know that it is time!" He turned to the fourth man in the room, admonishing, "Gomarha, you and your crew should have found at least one ten years ago when you were here."

"Yes, it is time," Commander Fahey agreed. "Our return vessel leaves from Fat Bottom Lake in two days, and we now have proof that Transprophetics exist on this planet."

The sound of a door squeaking on its hinges alerted them that someone had come into the warehouse. Commander Fahey gestured to Dr. Tarea to come with him. Pointing at Bjorn and then looking at Dr. Nadina and Gomarha, the Commander drew one finger across this throat.

Bjorn watched as Gomarha walked to the table. As he reached out for the knife, Bjorn visualized it flying away from the man's hands. Gomarha cursed as the knife shot away, leaving his hand grasping at air. Dr. Nadina walked towards the door, opposite the one that Commander Fahey and Dr. Tarea had slipped through. "I'm heading out. We're not risking all four of us. Kill the boy and catch up if you can."

Bjorn, holding the knife in the air, began to move it around. He found that if focused on what he wanted the knife to do, rather than on just the knife itself, that he could move it easily. Gomarha grabbed for the knife, as Bjorn floated it in front of him. Bjorn shot it across Gomarha's face, leaving a gash across his cheek.

Gomarha spun trying to follow the knife's flight. He shot out his arm again, and the knife slashed across the top of Gomarha's hand, opening another wound. He spun towards Bjorn. "I'll just strangle you, stupid kid."

Bjorn, spinning the knife in the air, brought the point it into Gomarha's butt. It took every bit of focus Bjorn could muster, but he pulled the knife out of Gomarha's butt, spun it in the air, and then drove it into Gomarha's thigh. Gomarha grabbed the handle of the blade, wrenching it from his leg. Holding it up, Gomarha stepped towards Bjorn, sporting a cruel, angry grin.

Bjorn visualized the knife stabbing into the man's shoulder, and Gomarha shrieked in pain as his own arm flailed, making him stab himself.

The door that Commander Fahey and Dr. Tarea had left through burst open, and Tim and Dylan ran into the room, followed by Joanna, Mr. Freeman, and Hector. Gomarha turned and ran through the other door, hoping he could catch up to Dr. Nadina.

"I've got this," Hector announced, as he bolted after the escaping Gomarha.

The rest of the group ran to Bjorn, freeing him from the chair. Tears flowed freely down everyone's faces as they reunited with the little boy. The nightmare was over. The little boy was reunited with his family. He was happy to see that Mr. Freeman was there too.

"Mom," Bjorn said, as the group began to regain its composure.

"Yes, my precious angel."

"There was never a poltergeist, and I *was* the one who made that vase hit that man," the little boy confessed, with another tear streaking down his face.

Joanna, reaching out, wiped the tear away. "I know, son. We have a lot to talk about."

A smile crept across the boy's face, and he turned to his brother. "See—brainwaves, baby. I gotz dem brainwaves."

*****

Gomarha, having misjudged the stairs at the back of the building, stumbled and fell. The wounds inflicted by the knife, wielded by the boy Transprophetic, had made him weaker than he had anticipated. He pulled himself upright, trying to stand, but realized that he had injured his knee in the tumble down the stairs.

Hector, slowing, walked down the stairs when he saw that the man was unable to stand without the support of the wall.

"Commander, you're alive!" Gomarha explained, as Hector descended the staircase. "We found one. Upstairs. There's a Transprophetic. We'll all be rich heroes!"

"Gomarha," replied Hector, "ten years is a long time. What have you been up to?"

"It doesn't matter. I found the next crew that came here to Earth. One of them is already on his way to Fat Bottom Lake. Their return vessel is hidden in the same place as ours was, and the crew's before that. Crazy. Their return vessel leaves in two days. We could be home within a year."

"Can you walk?" asked Hector

"No, I think I broke my leg or maybe my knee," replied Gomarha.

"Too bad. I guess only one of us will be a hero when we return to Koranth," Hector declared, as he drove his dive knife blade low into Gomarha's gut, pulling it upward until he hit the bottom of the man's ribcage. He stepped back as Gomarha slumped to the ground.

"Why, Commander—why?" Gomarha pleaded.

Hector looked down at the man, as blood began to pool around his body from his already blood-drenched shirt. A crooked smile spread across Hector's face, and he turned and headed back up the stairs.

Chapter 38
Actions and Consequences

It was late in the evening when the group finally arrived back at Tim's condo. The police had grilled them for hours, and they were repeatedly chastised for not allowing the police to do their jobs. The three dead bodies were eventually taken to the morgue. To keep from being kept in the local jail, all of them relinquished their passports until they would be allowed to leave the country. Their simple vacation had transformed into something that none of them could have ever imagined.

Before the police had arrived at the warehouse, the adults of the group told Bjorn not to share any of the unusual happenings of the day. The ability that he had was something that absolutely needed to be kept secret, at least until they were cleared of any wrongdoing and allowed to leave Mexico. It would simply be too sensational otherwise. Tim also texted Kaylee, asking her to let Sebastian know that the boy was safe and he could stop searching.

As the seven of them sat around the table, Mr. Freeman placed a cup in the middle of the table.

"My young friend," he said to Bjorn. "You will need to learn to use your abilities, so that you can control them."

Bjorn was exhausted. He simply made the cup go up a few inches and then set it back on the table. Joanna looked at him and sent him to bed. Tomorrow would be a better time to help the little guy begin to deal with all of the things that had happened to him during this traumatic day.

Tim looked intently at Atticus and Hector. "The events of today make me think your story of being from some other planet isn't as much bullshit as I thought this morning," he confided. "So, what happens now?"

"My best guess is that the one guy that got away, this Dr. Nadina, will head for their return vessel," began Mr. Freeman, "Bjorn said he remembered one of the men saying that it would be leaving in two days. If the return vessel gets off this planet, it would take about one year for it to make it to Koranth. Then, if a spaceship and a portal were ready, it would take two years to return. However, it is unlikely that a ship and portal are just waiting. They would likely take a couple of years to prepare for the mission back to Earth. Regardless of when they return, within a week of the portal being activated, Earth will be invaded."

"So how do we stop them?" asked Dylan.

"I wish I had an answer to that," replied Mr. Freeman. "If we could find and destroy the return vessel, then it might be another five to twenty years before another exploratory mission is sent again to Earth."

"Where is the return vessel?" asked Dylan.

"Dylan, I wish I knew. Mine was hidden in the mountains, deep in a body of water called Fat Bottom Lake. Theirs could be anywhere on Earth," Mr. Freeman conveyed.

Joanna held up her hands, and everyone turned to her. Everyone had been talking about the big picture, saving Earth, but she was focused elsewhere. "What about Bjorn?" she questioned, "What happens to him?"

Mr. Freeman explained that Bjorn still was a normal kid. He just happened to be able to do some things that others couldn't. The abilities that Bjorn possessed were not unnatural, just simply the ongoing evolution of the human species. Mr. Freeman proceeded to share a little of the history of Transprophetics on Koranth and how they changed everything in almost every scientific field.

What Mr. Freeman could not predict was what would happen to Bjorn if the world found out that he was different. The Transprophetic that he had found in Thailand completely disappeared, and despite his searching for years, he was never able to find her or any other Transprophetic. He'd spent years looking for them.

He went on to explain that if scientists here on Earth studied Bjorn, it would take at least a few years, but everything would very likely begin to change on Earth. That's what the Corporations from his world feared. However, he wasn't convinced that it would be more than an annoyance at this point for the mighty military machines of Koranth or Zoranth. The truth was that they simply didn't want to risk a planet taking any technological leaps before the planet was under the control of a Corporation. For Bjorn's safety, it was probably best that his abilities remain absolutely secret. Once the Donovackia military arrived, they would be looking for Transprophetics, so they would likely kill him in order to keep Earthlings from studying him.

Joanna continued to look at Mr. Freeman, unable to hide her mixed feelings about him. That scar on his arm seemed to scream at her. If this man's own planet had rejected him for killing a child, had her sons been safe around him?

"Explain this to me, Mr. Freeman," she asked coldly, "if you've spent so much time looking for them, how did you somehow end up my neighborhood?"

"Joanna," began Mr. Freeman softly, sensing the mistrust in her voice, "I happened to be passing through a small town in Tennessee. I picked up the local paper, and there was an article about a haunted house in that town. A very pious woman was also having lunch at the diner where I was eating. Apparently, she'd written the article for her church newspaper, and the paper's editor, who was also a member of the church, decided to publish it in the town's paper. She had all kinds of things to say, including how a wall-hanging picture flew off the wall and nearly hit her."

"So you tracked us down?" asked Joanna.

"Yes," replied Mr. Freeman, "I'd spent years looking for Transprophetics, hoping to be able to protect them from any future missions from Koranth. Bjorn was the closest thing that I found, and I just decided to base myself out of Denver to watch him. Most of my trips have been to see if I could find any others."

"Did you ever find any others?" asked Dylan.

Mr. Freeman, turning, looked intently at Dylan. His gaze made Dylan feel uncomfortable. It wasn't an accusatory look, but rather like Mr. Freeman was trying to look inside of Dylan. "In all my travels, Bjorn is the only Transprophetic that I am sure is aware of his own abilities," replied Mr. Freeman, maintaining the direct gaze.

A silence settled over the table. Everyone was emotionally drained and physically exhausted. With only two days until the return vessel departed, and a truly unbelievable story, it was unlikely that anyone at that table could change the direction of fate. Even as they each sat thinking about it, the weight and complexity of it all felt overwhelming.

Hector had remained silent through most of the discussion. His mind had raced back to the auto accident that left him stranded alone on Earth. He had never really thought of trying to find the next crew. It was best just to make a life here on Earth. He always thought that if he lived to see the invasion of Earth by Koranth, then he would simply return to his planet a hero, and, until then, he would just live here. Now, he knew that in two days a return vessel would leave Earth, and it wouldn't be three to six years before he could go home. It would be less than a year.

In the time since Kadamba had left Koranth, Tomar Donovackia had absorbed all the other Corporations. He alone was free to direct the development of other planets. Rather than launch every mission from Koranth, Tomar had begun moving the parts for spaceships through various portals and assembling them on other planets. He had simply begun using a hub-and-spoke model. The trip from Aechmea, the nearest hub planet to Earth, had only taken two months for Hector's crew.

While portals still couldn't be sent through a portal, Tomar began sending spaceships with portals to these hub planets. It made it easier and quicker to get a portal to a new planet, or add a portal to an already developed planet. Tomar was even setting up portals between other planets. No one had ever even dreamed that portals would lead anywhere but to Koranth and Zoranth.

"Hector, where was your return vessel hidden?" asked Dylan, his mind still struggling to figure out how to stop the coming invasion of Earth.

"Uh, what?" replied Hector, lost in his own thoughts.

"You're spaceship. Where did you land and hide your crew's return vessel?" repeated Dylan.

"Oh, that's a good question, we hid it really well. It was, well, um, it was in the Appalachian Mountains, at a place called Saint Julian Lake," Hector reported.

"Do you think we should have someone check the two lakes where your crews hid your ships?" asked Dylan to Mr. Freeman and Hector.

"Who would we get to do that—and how would they do it?" interjected Tim. "Anyway, the latest crew probably has theirs hidden somewhere else."

With the weight of the evening getting heavier and heavier, they all decided that it was time to call it a night. Tomorrow they would try to figure out if there was anything at all they could do other than help Bjorn hide his abilities and wait for the coming of the Donovackia military. While it seemed hopeless in the long run, the fact that Bjorn was okay and back with them seemed all that really mattered.

Hector took Adelita home to her sister's and his house. They would all touch base tomorrow. Perhaps not all was lost; maybe they could salvage some of the vacation and go for a scuba diving session.

A room was arranged in a nearby condo for Mr. Freeman. While he actually did have an acquaintance in Cancun, it would take a few hours to drive to there, and it was very late. Atticus settled into the room and headed to bed. The events of the day continued to play through his head over and over. The future seemed always so uncertain. We do so many things to try and guide the strings of fate, but they don't always twist in our favor.

The cane was back in Ka's hand as he walked along the path on Schmarlo's Landing. The sky was clearing from a recent rainstorm, but drops of water still ran down the force-field cover that protected the Landing. He headed to his favorite bench, looking off in the distance at the city that was once his home. After all these decades, he rarely thought of the city itself. Alorus was really the only thing from Koranth that was with him day and night.

He looked at the cane in his hand and then pulled out the hidden, white blade. Dried blood spotted the sharp dagger in many places. The blade was made of bone, and the bloodstains seemed to penetrate the blade. Ka let out a heavy sigh. He'd bought the bladed cane years before, when a simple injury required a little assistance. Somehow, it became to be part of his image. He didn't need it but liked having it. The more he thought, the more it was good that he had it, because he did need it when he'd met Dr. Tarea again.

"Ka, will Dr. Tarea be joining us here on the Landing?" came the child's voice from behind him.

Ka looked at his hands. They weren't the hands he had when he last visited the Landing in his waking hours. They were hands of an older man. He hoped that the hands belonged to a wiser man than the teenager that he had been.

"Alorus, Dr. Tarea will never be here on the Landing," replied Ka.

"You've killed a lot of people, Ka. Haven't you?"

"I suppose."

"How come I'm the only one here on the Landing?"

"I don't know. Maybe, it's because you were the only child whose life was stolen by my actions."

"I guess that makes sense," the boy confirmed, as he sat down on the bench next to Ka. "Am I the only one that you regret?"

"That's a difficult question to answer. I wish that I'd never taken anyone's life."

"But if you hadn't, Bjorn would be dead."

Ka looked at the boy, as the child stood up and walked to the playground. Alorus climbed into one of the swings and began to swing back and forth.

Chapter 39
Duty-Bound

Hector lay in bed next to Adelita's sister. He'd fallen in love with her the moment that he saw her. She was a radiant beauty on a vacation in paradise. They'd connected on a scuba diving trip when he was her instructor. She'd made him laugh. She'd made him smile. She'd made him forget that he had been the Commander of an exploratory mission to Earth from a planet far away called Koranth. She'd returned multiple times to see him and then eventually moved to Mexico. They had a good life together. They were happy.

In the dark, he wondered what would happen to Earth. He knew the basics of bringing and powering up a portal, but what would the invasion actually be like? He would know soon enough, and he knew it wouldn't be pleasant.

He rolled over and stared at his wife as she slept. He wished this day had never come. His crew had found the planet Earth not quite ready. He hoped that he would just live out his days and be in the grave before Earth was invaded. But it was a dream. He was a Commander of a spaceship in the Donovackia military.

He slipped out of the bed and into the closet, retrieving the old revolver that he kept in a shoebox. He watched his beautiful wife as she slept. This would be painless, he told himself. She won't feel a thing. He pointed the revolver at her head and pulled back the hammer. His finger was on the trigger, but he just couldn't pull it.

His mind raced looking for a reason. He knew who he was and what he needed to do. His crew had identified a perfect spot for the portal. He would just make his way to that spot and wait. He would be a hero as he helped his fellow soldiers prepare for the invasion. All he needed to do was pull the trigger and free himself from the one thing on this planet that tied him to it. He could go home a hero. He lowered the hammer carefully. He realized that he had forgotten about Adelita sleeping in the next room. The gunshot would wake her.

The teenage girl looked so peaceful sleeping in the guest bed. She was like a miniature version of her sister. He'd always liked her. She'd taught him the game of soccer, spending hours with him in the park. He let out a deep sigh. He couldn't do everything that he really needed to. Killing his wife would untie him from this world, but he just couldn't do it.

The minutes ticked by slowly as he returned to bed, torn as to what to do. "Shhh," she whispered as she ran her hand up his bare chest. "Adelita and I are going to breakfast in a little bit, but I have something for you first." He felt her leg move across his legs, as she crawled on top of him. How could he do this? The gun was now in the drawer by the nightstand. She was the one thing that kept him tied to a life on Earth. He had to be free.

His mind was torn to pieces as her hands ran over his body. In his mind, he could see himself, the hero returned to Koranth—the wealth, the glory, and the honor. But his body said otherwise and reacted as a man does to a sensual woman's touch.

After they were both satisfied, he listened to her shower, wanting to join her. He pretended to sleep when she came back in and gently kissed his lips. As he heard her car pull away, he crawled from his bed, duty-bound to free himself from this life on Earth and return to his home world.

Chapter 40
Defending the Nation

The next morning, Bjorn was sitting at the table with his mom while Tim fixed breakfast. In his usual indomitable style, Bjorn was cheerful and grinning with a smile that can only come from the face of a child. He was happy. He was special. He had dem brainwaves! At first, Tim wanted to make Bjorn stop moving things around on the table, but Joanna, in her gentle way, relaxed the man, allowing the boy to play.

In so many ways, it was unreal to watch. Bjorn quickly figured out that he could manipulate more than one thing at a time. He lifted his spoon, then his fork, and then his knife and plate. With a giggle, he lifted the piece of toast that Tim had set in front of Joanna and dropped it quickly onto his own plate.

"I didn't do nothing," he declared, trying to look innocent.

"Ladies first, young man," declared Tim, in a mock voice of authority. "Serve your mom before you serve yourself."

The three of them laughed, and Joanna said, only half-jokingly, "You know what would be impressive, Bjorn, is if you could butter the toast for me."

Bjorn's smile widened, and his brow furrowed as he focused. At first he focused on trying to mentally grip the handle of the knife, but it clattered to the table. Before anyone could react, it was in the air again, with Tim and Joanna mostly ignoring the profanity that had slipped from the boy's lips. Relaxing, Bjorn focused again. In his mind, he told himself not to focus just on the knife, but rather focus on what the knife needed to do. He took a deep breath, and the blade slipped through the butter, cutting a perfect pad.

He breathed a "yes," and then the knife flicked the pad of butter sending it through the air. Reflexively Bjorn reached for the butter, even though it would sail past his hand by a few feet. It stopped in midair, not far from his hand, but the knife clattered to the table again.

"Not bad, kiddo," Tim noted. "Alright, let's just eat now."

"I'm not done," replied Bjorn stubbornly as he moved the butter through the air. He closed his eyes for a moment, then waved his hand, with the palm down in the same motion that a knife would make to spread butter. The butter, having hit the toast, spread itself across the slightly brown surface.

Joanna picked up the toast and regarded it. "Perfect," she exclaimed, as she nodded to Bjorn and bit into it.

Mr. Freeman's knock on the door awakened Dylan. He had slept late, after having serious issues falling asleep the night before. On her way to bed, Joanna had checked on him and found him struggling to get to sleep. She sat on his bed for some time, trying to get her oldest son to understand that he couldn't save the world. But the weight of the day had fallen heavily on Dylan. He hadn't been able to protect his little brother. In so many ways, Dylan was a truly amazing big brother for Bjorn. That was impossible to deny, but for Dylan, having his brother snatched away was more than he could handle. He didn't know how, but he swore he would do everything he could to protect the little guy, especially when the invasion began.

It was hard for Joanna to watch her son be so hard on himself, but she understood. He loved Bjorn with all his heart, and, with a heart as big as Dylan's, she was sure that he would do everything in his power to take care of his younger sibling.

"Good morning, Dylan," said Mr. Freeman, as the teenager walked into the kitchen, still in his t-shirt and underwear with his hair completely a mess.

"We have to stop that return vessel, Mr. Freeman," Dylan announced.

"Oh, I wish we could, but I don't know what we could do," replied Mr. Freeman.

Before he could continue the conversation, Dylan's phone rang.

"Whoa!" exclaimed Tim, "a phone call and not just a text. Probably a telemarketer. I'm not sure teenagers know that those devices also make calls, not just texts." All of the adults shared a chuckle that quickly evaporated as they watched the concern grow on Dylan's face.

"Have any of you guys seen or heard from Hector this morning?" Dylan asked.

None of the people in the room had heard a thing from him. Everyone just assumed that they might see him later, perhaps even go scuba diving.

Dylan, setting the phone on the table, sat down. "He's gone. Adelita and her aunt went out for breakfast this morning. The aunt's debit card was denied. They paid with cash and went to the bank. Hector cleaned out the account while they were eating. They rushed home, but he and a bunch of his stuff is gone."

"Did they check his work?" asked Tim.

"Yes. Video from the marina shows that he took off in one of the company's boats early this morning. Either the GPS tracking that the company uses failed, or he disabled it. His cell phone is also just rolling to a prerecorded message. Adelita's sister is a wreck. It looks like he has skipped out."

Joanna looked accusingly at Mr. Freeman again, and the older man appeared to feel around for his cane. He would often roll it in his hands when he was thinking, but, of course, the Mexican police had taken it.

"Atticus, what aren't you telling us?" she asked, even more bluntly than she had meant to.

"There's nothing more that I know than you do," Mr. Freeman responded as gently as he could. It hurt to feel the anger in her voice. She wasn't hiding her feelings of betrayal as well as she wished she could. Mr. Freeman looked at Bjorn and Dylan. What mattered most to him was that the boys were safe. He didn't know if he could protect them from the coming storm, but he would do his best. Hopefully, Joanna would eventually come to understand that he wasn't the monster branded on the inside of his forearm, but he understood her concern. She was a good mom.

"Then why has he bailed out on everyone?" she asked again, almost sounding panicked.

"I really don't know," replied Mr. Freeman.

"Maybe he knows something about Mexican justice that made him run off," added Tim.

"I doubt it," said Mr. Freeman. "If he did, then he would have skipped out last night."

"Oh!" exclaimed Bjorn, "I know where he might be! Chubby Butt Pond!" Everyone flinched as the plate Bjorn had been levitating crashed, shattering on the tile floor.

"Seriously, Bjorn!" snapped Joanna, "we're going to need some ground rules around these abilities of yours, and number one is no messing with anything that is breakable."

"Sorry, mom," the boy replied sheepishly, "it's just those guys only mentioned one place last night. Maybe Hector knows about it and is going to get them."

"Chubby Butt Pond?" asked Dylan. "Where's that?"

"I don't know," stammered Bjorn still feeling like he was in trouble for breaking the plate. "It was just the only place they mentioned that I can remember."

Dylan looked at this little brother for a moment. The wheels in his brain were spinning in overdrive. Of all the people in the world, Dylan knew the little guy best. He grabbed his phone and started rapidly tapping away with his thumbs. "Hector lied, Bjorn could be right," Dylan announced.

"Okay, Dylan, slow down," Mr. Freeman responded. "You've totally lost me here."

Dylan picked up his brother's tablet, tapped a few places on the screen, and then spun it around. "There's no St. Julian Lake in the Appalachian Mountains. That's where Hector said his return vessel was hidden. There's no St. Julian Lake at all in the United States," explained Dylan as he pointed to a map on the screen. "However, there is a Lago San Julian here in Mexico. He was lying last night. He needed a place but couldn't think of anything off the top of his head in the US that wasn't too obvious."

"I'm a little lost here," Tim admitted, "Catch me up."

Dylan looked at Mr. Freeman. "All three ships from your planet went to the same place. That could be why Hector skipped out. He knows where the return vessel is."

Dylan turned to Bjorn, "You heard them say the place last night, goofball. It wasn't Chubby Butt Pond that they said."

"Nope," replied Bjorn smiling, "It was Fat Bottom Lake."

They began hashing everything over. Dylan was probably correct. Mr. Freeman's return vessel had been hidden in Fat Bottom Lake. The likelihood that Dylan was correct about Hector continued to grow, as Tim searched online, trying to play devil's advocate and disprove Dylan's theory. Bjorn, having heard the men talking yesterday about a return vessel and Fat Bottom Lake, simply further reinforced the idea that all three vessels had used the same landing place. More than likely, the return vessel from the latest crew was sitting at the bottom of that lake, but it would only be there for about twenty-four more hours before it departed Earth.

"This is all irrelevant," declared Mr. Freeman. "Even if we weren't stuck here in Mexico on travel restrictions, it would be impossible for us to get a flight and get there."

"But we live in Denver, right at the base of the Rockies," Dylan voiced. "Certainly, there is someone that one of us knows that could help?"

Unfortunately, there seemed little that they could do, and the discussion turned to protecting Bjorn. He was less than impressed that everyone wanted to hide his amazingly cool new skills, but he mostly understood the danger. After yesterday, he didn't want to relive anything like being kidnapped again. Dylan excused himself and headed out onto the deck. A gentle rain had begun to fall, and he just wanted to be alone and watch the ocean.

Tim's face grew grave as his phone began to ring and vibrate. He picked it up, excused himself, and headed into one of the bedrooms, closing the door. He wasn't sure how this would go, but he needed to figure out how to handle Sebastian and limit the damage that had been done to his company and career. He'd laid in bed the night before trying to sort out how on Earth he could compensate Sebastian. Without him, they wouldn't have found Bjorn. More than likely, Bjorn would be dead. Tim may have been one of the founders of the company, but that really didn't matter. There was no way he could give a known criminal access to their systems, without risking everything. The truth was, he was probably already at risk of losing his job, losing his company stock, and going to jail. It was worth it, but he wasn't sure how to wrap this up.

Mr. Freeman watched Dylan as he leaned on the railing of the balcony. He knew Dylan well enough that he didn't need Joanna to tell him that the teenager was struggling with a huge amount of guilt over what had happened to Bjorn. Mr. Freeman excused himself and headed out to the balcony, leaning on the railing next to Dylan.

"I love watching the rain on the ocean," Mr. Freeman confided, "It's mesmerizing."

"Will it still rain like this after your planet invades us?" asked Dylan.

"When I left Koranth, we had some ability to modify the weather, but not as much as some would like. As far as I remember, it wasn't something that we messed with on other worlds."

"I won't be able to protect my brother when they arrive, will I?"

"If he keeps his abilities hidden, they're unlikely to find him," Mr. Freeman assured him.

"There's no way that Bjorn can keep this under wraps. I'd bet within a couple of years that he's on TV doing tricks. It's just too tempting for him. He'll be famous before they get here, and it won't take anything to find him." Dylan sounded both defeated and angry.

"We don't know what the future holds, Dylan, but we can only do what we can do," Mr. Freeman shared, trying to sound compassionate and understanding, but knowing he probably sounded more patronizing than anything. "There are many things that could delay or maybe even stop the Donovackia Corporation from coming here. There is only so much we even know. Try not to worry, son."

"You're right, Mr. Freeman," Dylan agreed, looking more optimistic than he had before. "We only know certain things, and we can only do what we can do. We have to stop that return vessel from leaving this planet."

"Dylan, there is nothing that we can do," replied Mr. Freeman sympathetically.

"Oh yes, we can," the teenager asserted, as he turned and ran back inside.

*****

As Tim closed the bedroom door, he reluctantly answered the video call, and Sebastian's face appeared on the screen. "Hello Rudianos," said Sebastian smiling. "I am truly glad that you were able to find the boy."

"I'm not sure how to thank you, Sebastian," Tim began, but before he could finish his thought, Sebastian interrupted.

"Please, it has been an honor to be a part of saving the boy. Now that the boy is safe, I can only imagine that you are worried about my compensation."

"Yes, I don't know how to go about compensating someone like you, for something like this. It's just . . ."

"Tim, let me explain a few things first," interjected Sebastian, "and as you said, let's not dance around. I am an internationally wanted criminal, or so various governments would like everyone to believe. Money for me is not an issue, so don't worry about that."

"Okay," replied Tim, "I had a feeling that we wouldn't be talking about money. I can only imagine that you want ongoing access to my company's aggregated social media feed, but I don't know how to accomplish that."

Sebastian shook his head in agreement. "Even if you left the pipe open for me, eventually you'd be caught, and more than likely, you'd end up in some dark room being interviewed by people claiming to have nothing but 'national security' interests at heart, as they repeatedly violated your civil liberties and perhaps tortured you."

"Yes, those thoughts have certainly gone through my head. At this point, I am not sure that something like that might not happen anyway," Tim admitted. "What I've already done is unlikely to go unnoticed."

"You're completely safe at this point, Tim. Let's make this simple. All that you owe me is a favor," Sebastian told him.

"I'm not sure what you mean, Sebastian. What favor do you want?" replied Tim, both confused and grateful.

"I'm not sure. Just a favor in the future when I need it," Sebastian explained. "No one will ever know that I was in your systems. Your server logs have been cleaned. All of your monitoring systems, from bandwidth to performance metrics, have been reset to show no additional activity while data flowed into my network. We even hacked into your dark fiber provider and erased all traces of the additional data flow."

"Holy shit," replied Tim as he stared at the phone, almost unable to believe what Sebastian was saying. It wasn't that he didn't believe Sebastian's group had the capability to do what he'd said; it was that Sebastian did all those things to protect Tim. For all practical purposes, Sebastian had helped find Bjorn for little more than a promise. "I don't want to appear ungrateful at all, sir, but . . ."

Before Tim could finish his thought, Sebastian interrupted again, "You could have fired Kaylee. You could have even had her arrested. But honestly, this isn't a tit for tat. A boy's life was at stake, and you and I had the means to make a difference and do something right. Not every hero wears a white hat, my friend."

Tim looked at the image of Sebastian on the screen. He was a daunting character that was beginning to become larger than life to many people in the world while, at the same time, he was being more and more vilified by those governments whose dirty secrets he was exposing. It was daunting to know that he would owe this man a favor, especially one that could be anything. However, Bjorn was alive and that was good enough. He would just hope that the favor wouldn't "cost" too much in the future.

"One other thing, Tim," said Sebastian. "Kaylee will no longer be working for your company. If you're ever asked, please give her a positive reference."

"That will be easy to do," replied Tim, relieved that it wasn't anything more significant than that.

As the men began to say their goodbyes, Dylan burst into the bedroom.

"Sebastian, we still need your help," Dylan blurted out. "This isn't over yet. Please."

"Dylan," responded Tim, "Sebastian has done his part. We just need to say thanks and get focused on life."

"Let the boy speak," Sebastian answered. "If his little brother is now safely back with you, why isn't this over?"

Dylan sat down next to Tim, looking at the screen. The light was slightly better wherever Sebastian was calling from, and Dylan saw that Sebastian was very much what he expected. The man was the legendary image of an MI6 agent—handsome and rugged, with cold, steel blue eyes, and a strong jawline. It was almost as if you could see the experience and intelligence in his face. A small smile crept across Dylan's face. Dylan had a mission and was about to talk to someone who knew real risk and how to get things done.

"I know you're affiliated with GAPN," began Dylan. "Do you have operatives in the United States, ones that could carry out a mission to stop an alien ship from leaving this planet?"

Sebastian looked at Dylan for a few moments without saying anything. Dylan realized that he probably sounded a little bit crazy even asking such a question, but it was the only way he could think of to get someone to Fat Bottom Lake to stop that return vessel from leaving Earth and bringing back a military force that would want his little brother.

"Kiddo, I've heard a lot of crazy things in my time, but . . ." Sebastian responded, hesitating before he completed his own thought.

"Mr. Twyman," began Dylan again, "five years ago no one knew who you were. The news says you were an MI6 agent that went bad, but many people don't agree. Maybe you did steal all the documents and other stuff, but something made you do it. You've gone from being super-spy, super-patriot for your country, to the top of the world's most wanted list. You heard something or saw something that made you decide that things weren't as they seem."

Tim put his hand gently on Dylan's shoulder. "Dylan, I think Sebastian has done more for us than we could ever ask. We need to say thank you and goodbye."

"The boy's right," Sebastian affirmed. "Things aren't always as they seem. Okay, Dylan, I obviously don't know what all is going on, but let's hear a little more before we say goodbye."

Mr. Freeman, Joanna, and Bjorn had also slipped into the room after Dylan. Within a few minutes, they had outlined to Sebastian how a giant Corporation from Koranth and Zoranth had sent missions to Earth to see if it had advanced enough to invade. They explained that they believed that the latest mission was set to send its return vessel back to Koranth tomorrow from a remote place in the Rocky Mountains called Fat Bottom Lake. Most importantly, they emphasized that this return vessel would carry a report stating that Earth was now ready to be invaded. Of course, they left out the part about Transprophetics, and especially, the fact that Bjorn happened to be one.

"So, no little green men?" asked Sebastian when they finished. "They all look like this Atticus Freeman beside you?"

"No," replied Dylan, "they look like all of us . . . Can you help? Please?"

For a few moments, the silence was deafening. Sebastian's face revealed that he was lost deep in thought. "I am sure you all realize how fantastical this all sounds," began Sebastian. "Alien invasions aren't exactly my specialty. Not that long ago, I would have said you are all suffering from some group hysteria, but after what I've found in various documents that I have acquired from multiple governments, including your own, I am finding myself more and more open to things I once thought impossible."

"So—you can help us?" Dylan inquired, again.

"Let me explain a few things first," Sebastian answered. "GAPN, the Global Anonymous Pirate Network, is a very, very loose association of all kinds of people and organizations—hackers, militants, revolutionaries, criminals, and even teens downloading movies. The only thing that kind of binds everyone is a distrust of the status quo. While there is sort of a hierarchy and sort of a managing structure, it is very loose. As such, affiliations, partnerships, and projects dynamically happen, and often among people you would never associate with outside the Network."

"Oh," Dylan expressed, disappointingly, "so—you're not the man in charge?"

"No, I am not; no one is in charge of GAPN. I have a few people that work directly with me, but I don't have a global network of operatives, like some news outlets might lead you to believe."

Sebastian began to chuckle a little as he saw the despondent faces on his smartphone's screen. "That doesn't mean that I can't help. It just means that I'll have to do a little networking to see if I can find someone to help us."

"Thank you, thank you!" Dylan expressed. "I knew you would help us!"

"One thing, kiddo," Sebastian added. "If we find this alien spaceship, you owe me something."

"What?" Dylan asked.

"The truth. I can tell that you've left something extremely critical out of your story. Also, if we find this spaceship, GAPN keeps it, and you have to promise to tell me what it is you've left out," Sebastian stated.

A dead silence fell over the condo bedroom, as everyone looked at Dylan. He stared directly at Tim's smartphone, looking Sebastian directly in the eyes. "Deal."

Twenty minutes later, Tim's smartphone buzzed with a message. Tim grabbed his laptop, and everyone gathered around it as he logged into a private teleconferencing site. In a corner of the screen, Sebastian's face appeared, with a slightly smug smile. Below him, a video feed opened showing a large man with a huge handlebar mustache, wearing a worn camouflage shirt.

"Major William Daniel Adams, Commander of the Fourth Brigade of the Rocky Mountain Freedom Militia, at your service!" announced the man in rather gruff tone, with a slightly Southern accent. "My comm-patriot from the other side of the pond tells me that the United States government has been complacent in allowing aliens to use our mountains to hide their spaceships."

Sebastian's eyebrows visibly lifted as the man was talking, as if to say, "Just go with it." Major Adams was obviously unimpressed with United States government in general and the fact that it had failed to act on the potential of an alien invasion was more than the man could handle. He assured the group that his brigade could take care of the problem.

"Vern!" the Major yelled, as an aerial photomap of Fat Bottom Lake and the surrounding area filled the open space on the screen. "Explain to these good people what the plan is."

Part of the face of an older man, obviously trying to use the mouse on the Major's computer, filled a section of the video feed. "So, I understand that the ship is likely in the lake. When they bring it up, they'll likely set it here, as that's the end of the lake closest to the road and that old driveway. See here on the opposite side of the lake, that's probably a duck blind. Leading away from it is probably a trail, maybe a game trail, but it looks big enough for a motorcycle or ATV."

He went on to explain that the brigade had twelve men that would split up. One group would come up from the road while the other group would come up the trail on ATVs. They would surprise the aliens and have them pinched off.

Considering the options, everyone who was stuck in Mexico agreed with the plan. There just didn't seem much else to do. Major William Daniel Adams, Commander of the Fourth Brigade of the Rocky Mountain Freedom Militia, assured everyone that he and his men would defend their country and planet. They already had men loading vehicles as they were speaking, and they would be able to make it to Fat Bottom Lake by mid-morning the next day.

Sebastian was rubbing his chin when the Major's video feed cut off. His face filled the screen, and he was obviously trying to choke back a laugh. "Like I said, GAPN has all kinds of people and organizations. You don't always work with the people you'd expect."

"It's better than nothing," Dylan admitted. "Thank you."

"Ya, thanks!" piped in Bjorn.

"Hello, Bjorn," said Sebastian, who really hadn't had a chance to even meet the boy he had helped save. "I'm glad to see that you're doing well."

"I am. Thanks for the all the help, spy-dude!"

"It is my pleasure," responded Sebastian with a chuckle.

"Can I ask you a question?" asked Bjorn. Everyone else in the room's eyes got a little bit bigger. There was just no telling what was about to come out of the boy's mouth.

"Of course, you may," Sebastian assented, with a smile.

"Why do people in England like tea so much?" asked the curious boy.

Sebastian laughed. "That's actually a much better question than most Americans ask me," he replied. "It's actually very ingrained in our culture. Hopefully, someday you can come to the UK and experience it yourself."

"So, do you like tea?" inquired the boy.

"Well, not that much, to tell you the truth," Sebastian admitted with a smile, "I prefer coffee."

Bjorn scrunched up his face a little. It appeared he was sizing up the man on the screen who had held up a white paper cup with familiar green markings. "Well, do you have a Walther PPK?"

Sebastian smiled at the young boy again. "I hate to disappoint you, but I like the SIG Sauer P220, but if it makes you feel any better, you already know how I like my martinis prepared."

Bjorn smiled, nodding his head appreciatively. There really wasn't much else to do, but to wait until tomorrow. Hopefully, Major William Daniel Adams and the Fourth Brigade of the Rocky Mountain Freedom Militia would achieve some success.

Chapter 41
Clarity of Truth

As the day wore on, the visitors to Mexico decided to spend some time on the beach. There was little else they really could do. They decided to try to make the best of the circumstances and do what they could to act like they were on vacation.

Tim and the boys headed into the protected cove on sea kayaks while Joanna and Mr. Freeman sat under a cabana on the beach, enjoying a drink served in a coconut. Mr. Freeman was again dressed in a short-sleeve shirt, and Joanna had trouble keeping her eyes off of the brands on the inside of his arms.

"They are frightening, aren't they?" Mr. Freeman remarked, as Joanna seemed lost in thought, gazing intently at his arm.

"I'm sorry, what?" she replied with some surprise.

"The scars on my arms," he said.

"Mr. Freeman, I am sorry for my coldness the last few days," she began. "I just don't know what to think."

"It's quite alright. You're a mother, with two boys, and just discovered that someplace in my past lies something quite horrible. Along with everything else that has happened in the last two days, you are right to be apprehensive," Mr. Freeman told her.

"I just feel as if I passed judgment on you without knowing anything. I try to be a better person than that. All I know is what the scar says. I don't know what it means."

Atticus, looking at his arm, remembered how the searing heat of the laser burned his skin. His mind flashed to the moment he saw Alorus struggling for life on the playground, to the terror of Jackos the Giant, to the isolation of military training, and to the sense of vile disgust of having been paired with Dr. Nahash Tarea. He closed his eyes as a tear forced its way into the corner of one eye. All he could see was Alorus, lying in a pool of his own blood. How many times would he have to ask himself why it couldn't have been himself rather than the boy?

"Mr. Freeman," Joanna said softly, a compassion flowing from her that he had never felt, "please tell me who you really are. I need to know the truth."

It wasn't an easy story to tell, but he told her of the foolish teenage boy that he was, who got mixed up with a powerful drug dealer. He was young and stupid, he should have never sold the rath to Alorus, but he did, and it cost the boy his life. He told her of being stunned and arrested, the brutality of the justice processing, and the horror of prison life. There was compassion from a guard whose name he never knew, an isolated military life, and the opportunity to come to Earth. He told her of the time he betrayed his own people and thought that he had killed Dr. Tarea, and then went on to kill of the rest of his crew.

He'd spent a year wandering through the mountains of Tibet, then another year wandering through Asia, and another year in Europe. He didn't know if he was looking for something, just exploring, or just hoping to find peace. Eventually, he returned to the United States, having decided that he never wanted the people of Koranth and Zoranth to invade. He got into computers and spent much of his time trying to find Transprophetics. He even returned to Thailand but never could find any trace of the girl, Maliya. He'd traced hundreds of potential Transprophetics but was mostly able to prove to himself that they were fakes, without resorting to any of the horrific procedures that the supposed experts liked to use.

In some ways it was ironic. He had become a Transprophetic hunter, like the horrid Dr. Tarea, but he was different. He had always hoped that he would find a second Transprophetic, and then he would simply wait and watch. If another mission from his world found the Transprophetic whom he was watching, he planned to simply kill the team. But he never found another Transprophetic, despite all the years of searching.

He left few details out. She deserved to know. He was from Koranth, and he had been involved in her children's lives. He was responsible for taking the life of a child, a burden he would carry forever. He just hoped she believed that her sons were never in any danger from him. When he was done, he looked at his arms again. The paradox was so real. The scar had defined so much of his life, but it wasn't who he really was.

For Joanna, it was a hard story to hear. He really wasn't that much older than Dylan when he had sold the rath to the little boy. His life was nothing that she could even really imagine. She looked at him, as he stared at the scars on his arms, and saw the man that he was. He may have had a terrible past and done some terrible things, but the man she saw under the cabana had been there for her sons. Some people can never put the past aside, but she decided to believe what she had seen with her own eyes—the man who had cared for her boys. He had befriended, comforted, and tutored them. He'd put his own life at risk to save theirs. He was their family's friend, and in her heart, she knew he always would be.

"Atticus," she said softly, not knowing how the next words would even come out of her mouth. "You are our friend. Please help protect the boys."

"Of course, I will," he assured her. "I don't know if I know how to do anything else. Whether today or tomorrow, a storm will come, and I will do everything that I can to help all of you."

They sat and watched as Tim, Dylan, and Bjorn splashed each other with the kayak paddles. Their laughter could be heard above the gentle waves that spread onto the sandy beach. If it weren't for the events of the last two days, it would be hard to believe that this wasn't just a wonderful family vacation.

"Can I ask you one other thing?" Joanna added.

"Of course, I have little left to hide," replied Atticus.

"Have you forgiven yourself?"

It was a thought that had become so foreign that it barely entered his mind. "No," he replied slowly, "I wouldn't even know how."

"Atticus," she said, trying to keep herself from crying too. "You have to eventually. You are a good man with a good heart. It was so long ago. I know that it has shaped much of your life, but it doesn't define who you are. I hope you can find a way to finally let it go."

Chapter 42

View from the Duck Blind

The next day, Tim answered the call and quickly opened his laptop computer. Both Sebastian and Major William Daniel Adams' faces filled the screen. Everyone in the condo gathered around the monitor, hoping for good news.

"Well?" demanded Dylan, as the two men on the screen seemed to be hesitating.

"I ain't never seen nothing like it," Major Adams began. "We managed to sneak up on them, and, sure as hell, there was some type of spaceship. It wasn't that big, and they were loading stuff in it. I had old Vern hold back in that duck blind with a video camera."

The two men's faces shifted to the corners of the screen as a video began playing. The quality wasn't great, but it was still good enough. Across the lake, a handful of people were loading things into the ship.

The first shots from the militia caught two of the Donovackia crew, dropping them to the ground. The other four or five crew members scattered, as the militiamen opened fire. Everyone in Mexico watched as the hatch on the ship closed, and the return vessel lifted up from the ground. The camera followed it as it hovered about fifty feet above the ground. Then it rotated and shot into the sky.

When the camera pointed back towards the far side of the lake, gunfire could be heard. The video closed, and Sebastian and Major Adams' faces grew to take over the screen.

"Dammit!" proclaimed Dylan. "So, it got away!"

"It was one hell of a sight. If we didn't get it on camera, I don't even know if I'd believe what I saw," Major Adams admitted. "It was real, and we failed to stop it."

"The crew," interjected Mr. Freeman, "did you capture any of the crew?"

"Sons of bitches were armed to the teeth and put up one hell of a fight," replied Major Adams. "Three of our guys came home in body bags; three others are in pretty bad shape. We killed six of them bastards, but I can't say with absolute certainty that others didn't get away. But we got nobody alive."

Major Adams switched the screen to show the faces of the dead men. A silent, but collective sigh went out, as not one of them was Hector.

"Did you find a remote?" asked Mr. Freeman. "That ship had a remote that launched it."

"I'm still trying to get my head around everything," Major Adams replied. "There wasn't no remote. There wasn't no goddamn alien thing up there. We stripped their bodies and went through everything. There wasn't a damn thing you couldn't buy at a Walmart Super Store. If I hadn't seen that ship blast into the sky with my own eyes . . . well, goddammit, I really just don't know what the hell to think."

Sebastian thanked him for his help and promised to be in touch in the near future. The Major signed off, and Sebastian's face filled the screen. Everyone was silent for a few moments. It was still almost impossible to believe.

"Okay, I'm still not sure what to believe," began Sebastian, "but this isn't something trivial. Major Adams buried six people near that lake that he says were completely human. We all saw that spaceship shoot into space. Where the hell does this leave us?"

Mr. Freeman again explained how he believed that the ship would take about a year to reach Koranth. Then within two to maybe up to five years, a ship carrying a portal would come to Earth. Once the portal was in place and powered up, the invasion would begin. Earth would become just another resource from which the Donovackia Corporation sucked goods and products to sell on Koranth and Zoranth.

The one thing that was clear to everyone was that there really wasn't any proof of any of this. The only thing they had was the video of the spaceship. Revealing that would only rile up conspiracy theorists, and, more than likely, give authorities the ability to track down Major Adams. At this point there was little they could do, but wait until they got out of Mexico. Sebastian promised he would begin trying to figure out what to do, and they'd all be in touch again soon.

Chapter 43
Path of the Medicine Men

Atticus Freeman adjusted the strap on his backpack, as he looked at the remains of the cabin in the predawn light. He didn't need the sunlight to tell him what was there—ghosts. Maybe not ghosts that would haunt the living, but ghosts that he, Kadamba Vorhoor, had put there.

He never knew if authorities had found the cabin that he had burned to the ground with the crewmates that he had killed, some thirty years before. He didn't know if their bodies had turned to ash and become part of the landscape. He really never wanted to know. It was something that he had done and thought little of. In many ways, he had done it in a fog. At the time, it was the only way to keep Maliya, the beautiful little Thai Transprophetic, and everyone else on planet Earth safe from the Donovackia Corporation. Perhaps as much as that, it had been the only way that Kadamba could keep himself safe.

All of that barely mattered. They were ghosts that haunted nothing but their own pasts and could do nothing in the present. But the past was the reason that Atticus was here, and he headed towards Fat Bottom Lake. Across the lake, he could make out the duck blind from which the video of the return vessel had been filmed. Even though it had only been a month, it almost seemed like a lifetime ago, maybe even someone else's life.

Atticus, Tim, Joanna, Dylan, and Bjorn had spent another two weeks in Mexico as the Mexican officials investigated the events of the day Bjorn had been kidnapped. Under pressure from the US State Department, they had been allowed to return to the United States.

The two weeks in Mexico had actually been fairly fun, aside from the almost daily questions from investigating officials. They had spent significant time on the beach and had eaten at a few tasty restaurants. They even decided to test whether Tim was right or not. Did El

Pescado Dorado actually have the best tacos al carbon? A few other places gave Tim's favorite a good challenge, but in the end, El Pescado Dorado's tacos were declared the winner.

Atticus headed part way around the lake and into the woods. The going was easy, and Atticus picked up a game trail, which he followed for a while. Eventually, he came to a large meadow and found a boulder on which to rest. Off in the distance, he could see his goal—Wóablakela Peak. He hoped that when he made his way to the top, he, like the medicine men of old, would be able to discover some inner peace and find the strength to serve.

By late morning, he was at tree line. The view of the surrounding mountains and valleys was unreal. A few wispy clouds moved across the sky, and the day was warm with a gentle breeze. Over the next two hours, the desire to give up weighed heavier and heavier on Atticus, as the going became more and more challenging.

At one point, he came to what seemed to be the end. He had been climbing over and through boulders, with the air getting thinner and thinner. He would jump to one boulder, climb another, and then have to catch his breath. Now he stood at the bottom of a cliff. Whatever birds made these high places their homes had a haunting cry that seemed to warn him to turn around.

Making his way along the bottom of the cliff, he found a crevasse and began working himself up the narrow crack. Once he was up about twenty feet, he found he could move out onto a shelf. From there, the climbing was easier. Another long boulder field awaited him, which he slowly made his way through.

The peak of the mountain began to narrow, and suddenly Atticus realized he only had a couple of feet to each side of him. Over the edge, on each side of him, the drop off appeared to be nothing but a sheer cliff, falling over a thousand feet to the valleys that he could see far below on each side.

A huge boulder that looked like an egg standing on its end blocked his way. He thought he was near the top, but he really had no idea how much farther that he would have to go beyond that egg-like boulder. A small ledge led around the base of the boulder. As he crawled through, his backpack bumped the boulder. He took it off and took a large drink, leaving his pack behind.

Crawling on his belly, he made it around the boulder. The fear that was growing within him became even deeper as he got to the other side of the boulder. Forty feet in front of him was a small cliff, not more than eight feet high, but the path up to that little cliff was only five feet wide. Taking a few steps, terror gripped him. Both sides of the path fell away sharply, and he could not see anything but the ground over a thousand feet away. He dropped to his hands and knees, crawling like a scared infant to the base of the little cliff.

The air was thin, and what little oxygen that he could inhale came in small gulps. The true risk of where he was and what he was doing became more real than he could handle. Would he tumble down the mountain if he fell, with his body occasionally smashing into the mountainside, or would he just fall the thousand feet to his death? How on Earth could the native medicine men of old climb this mountain and find peace and serenity?

He steeled his nerves, standing and pulling himself up a couple feet on the little cliff. He could see the summit. It was only another thirty feet or so away. He was so close, and yet so far. The path that he would have to traverse between the top of the little cliff and the top of the mountain looked like the edge of a knife. He couldn't do it. He couldn't overcome the fear. Death was a certainty if he fell from up here. For Atticus, the mountain was a disappointment. He would not find peace.

A light breeze blew across his face, and he closed his eyes, clinging to the rocks and trying to find the strength to crawl back down the mountain in defeat and failure. Maybe this was a stupid idea. A myth and a dream lost to time. Did he really deserve to find peace anyway?

In that moment, a vision of Bjorn taped to that chair came into his mind. He could feel the fear in the boy again. Maliya's face flashed through the vision—the terror of the abuse that Dr. Tarea was pouring upon her. All he knew was that he wanted to help them. He wanted to serve these people of Earth, his home. They were his people, but how could he do that if he failed to overcome the fear that was making him cling to these rocks, especially this close to his goal?

He felt the surge of energy and determination ripple through his muscles, pulling his body to the top of the little cliff. He took the first step onto that edge of the knife, fighting back the fear and hysteria exploding inside. When he couldn't take that next step, he fell to his knees, beginning to crawl on his belly. The mountain widened slightly, and he stood up, crawling to the top of the boulder that was the summit.

The world was below him. He was on top of everything. It was like nothing he had ever seen, felt, or experienced. There were no words to describe the moment or the emotion, but it changed him. As he stood on the summit, he realized how peaceful he felt. In that moment, he knew what those medicine men of old had experienced.

The boulder had an indentation, shaped like a reclining chair. He sat down, laid his head back, and watched the few wispy clouds floating overhead.

The raindrops felt foreign, hitting him in this place. It was a gentle rain, and he could feel a slight breeze in the air. The force-field cover was gone from Schmarlo's Landing. Ka, walking towards the playground, realized the grass, shrubs, and the trees weren't as green as they once were. Something felt different.

He turned and instead walked to his favorite bench, and sat down, looking out across where the city should be, but it wasn't there. It was nothing but a vast plain, with mountains in the distance. The rain felt good, like it was washing old grime away.

Ka headed back towards the playground, looking up and around. Schmarlo's Landing was midway up the Schmarlo Tower, but there was no tower rising above the landing. He changed course, moving to where the food vendors were. The kiosk that held the Freezies and all of the other vendors were gone.

Turning, he walked back to the playground. Alorus was swinging again. He looked so young and so innocent, like a child should look. Ka sat down on a bench and watched the boy. Thirty-some years had passed. Ka had changed, but Alorus was still the same—frozen in that last moment that Ka had seen him. The way the boy looked never changed, except that today—Alorus was smiling as he pumped his legs back and forth.

"Hello Ka," said Alorus, as he sat down next to Ka on the bench.

"Hello, Alorus," replied Ka.

"The rain feels good, doesn't it?"

"Yes. It feels like it is washing everything clean."

The boy looked up at Ka, smiling. A small tear ran down Ka's cheek, and the boy nodded his head up and down, as if acknowledging something unsaid.

"I have to say goodbye," Ka told the boy.

"I know," Alorus replied.

"I just don't know how to say I'm sorry and make it real, but I have to let you go now."

The boy stood up and began walking away. He turned, looked at Ka again and smiled and nodded his head. Ka let a smile begin to creep across his own face, despite knowing that this was the last time that he would ever see Alorus. The boy, waving, walked out of sight.

The rain grew heavier and heavier, and the breeze turned into a wind. Ka stood up and walked to the elevator. Every time he had come to the Landing, the elevator was here, but he had never used it. Today, he would. He stepped into the clear enclosure and shook off the water as the doors closed. It was quiet. The air was still. He felt the tiny jolt as the elevator began to move. He left Schmarlo's Landing for the last time.

Atticus opened his eyes. Perspective, was it the perspective of being up here that changed everything inside of him? Maybe it was. Or, maybe this really was a spiritual place. Feeling at peace inside, he knew that he would come down from the mountain a different man than the one who had climbed it. He may not have been born on Earth, but it was home, and he would defend it and all of its people.

Chapter 44
A Secret to be Kept

Only a couple of months after Mexico, Atticus saw Dylan on his bike and was surprised to see that Bjorn wasn't with him. With his bow strapped to his back, Atticus was sure that Dylan was heading to the nearby indoor archery range where the boys had a membership. Bjorn almost always tagged along with Dylan, but not today. As it was only a few blocks away and a sunny Colorado day, Atticus decided to walk to the range. It might finally be time to have the serious discussion that he needed to have with Dylan.

The adults had spent hours trying to sort out the future and how to deal with the invasion. In many ways, they were trapped in a catch-22. The only thing that they had that might be considered proof was Bjorn's abilities. However, the more people that knew about Bjorn's talents, the more the boy was at risk when the invasion began. It was frustrating and overwhelming, but at the same time completely surreal. It was hard to believe that there even was another world that would invade Earth.

The range was empty when Dylan arrived. The clerk greeted him and bid him to have some fun with the range to himself. He walked through the retail space of the store, barely glancing at the products, making his way into the enclosed range. The space itself was nothing more than an old warehouse that had been converted into an indoor archery range. A few fake trees and shrubs had been placed in various spots to give some minor illusion of the outdoors, but the bullseyes placed a few feet apart on the far wall were the reason that people came.

Atticus came into the back of the range and quietly sat down. Dylan didn't notice that his family friend was in the back watching him. Dylan filled three of the tubes for holding arrows with six arrows each.

The first target was at twenty yards, the second at thirty, and the fourth at forty yards.

He started at the twenty-yard mark. The first shot was sloppy. It hit the blue outside ring of the target, and Dylan cussed at himself, demanding that he focus. Taking a deep breath, he set his stance. He let the bow hang by his side for a moment, making sure he was gripping it in the correct place. He raised the bow and notched the arrow. In a fluid motion, he pulled back the arrow, his hand coming to his jawbone. Focusing on the target, he released the arrow. It hit the target with a thud, barely outside the yellow bullseye. The next four arrows flew true, each landing within the small yellow bullseye.

Dylan stepped back to the thirty-yard mark. Atticus remained still, and Dylan didn't notice the man as he began the same routine, shooting at a new target thirty yards away. The six arrows scattered across the target, but all in all proved a decent set.

Dylan, having stepped back to the forty-yard mark, notched another arrow. In rapid succession, he let all six arrows fly. Each one smacked into the yellow bullseye of the target, crowding the center of the plastic sheet. Dylan walked up to the targets and pulled all eighteen arrows out, refilling the six tubes. As he finished placing his arrows in the last tube, he realized that his friend was sitting and viewing him. He smiled and trotted back.

"Hey, Mr. Freeman," Dylan greeted Atticus. "I didn't know you were here watching. How long have you been here?"

"It's good to see you, Dylan," replied Atticus. "I've been here for a bit. Go ahead and shoot your next set."

When Dylan moved over to the twenty-yard mark, only three of the arrows found the yellow bullseye, but the others were close. He moved to the thirty-yard mark, only getting one of the six arrows into the bullseye. The first two arrows from the forty-yard mark were wide when Dylan felt Mr. Freeman's hand on his shoulder.

"Put the last four into the bullseye again," Atticus told him. "I want to see you do it again."

Dylan looked at Mr. Freeman, not sure what to think. The man had come to his brother's aid in Mexico and killed one of the men who were likely going to kill Bjorn. In many ways, Atticus was like a grandfather that Dylan never had. He didn't know what the coming days would hold, but he felt like he would need Mr. Freeman's help. Closing his eyes for a moment, he knew that he could trust the one person he knew from the planet of Koranth.

Dylan spun and released the three arrows one after another at lightning speed. Each of the arrows slammed into the yellow bullseye with tremendous force. Dylan and Mr. Freeman both stood for a minute, looking at the target.

Dylan was notching the last arrow when he felt Mr. Freeman's hand on his shoulder. Mr. Freeman took the last arrow from Dylan and studied it. Looking back at Dylan, he said, "Do this one without the bow," and then tossed it into the air.

The arrow ripped through the air, sending a shrill sound through the room. Its point drove through the nock of one of the arrows in the bullseye, splitting the shaft in half and burying itself deep in the target.

"How long have you known, Dylan?" asked Mr. Freeman.

"For over a year," replied Dylan. "I'm sorry I didn't say anything."

"That's okay. Does your family know?"

"No one knows, except for you," replied Dylan, relieved to finally have let this secret out, but starting to shake a little. "When I started to figure it out, I was like, 'Whoa, this is cool!' But then I watched how a couple of the kids at my school are treated. They are different."

"Dylan, it's all okay," Mr. Freeman assured.

"Everything was so wrong in Tennessee. For a while, I thought maybe I was the demon that everyone was so scared of. What if it was all me? I don't want to be a freak. My brother can pull this off like no one else. I can't. I just want to fit in. I don't want people to think of me as a freak."

"I understand, Dylan," Atticus offered compassionately, as he put his arm around the teen's trembling shoulder. Dylan's sniffle turned to tears. The teenager began to sob a little bit harder, and Atticus held him tighter.

"You don't understand, Mr. Freeman," Dylan choked out between the sobs. "I killed that man. It was me, not Hector."

"I know," replied Atticus.

"What? You knew?" asked Dylan.

"Well, up until a few minutes ago, I had a strong feeling that it wasn't Hector, but was you," Atticus confided. "He just looked too shocked in that moment after I killed Dr. Tarea. Someone else in the room had to have the focus and determination to protect us. It wasn't Hector. Plus, whoever it was, had to get that knife out of Hector's belt and put it into that man's neck. I just had a feeling it was you."

"Please, don't tell anyone," Dylan pleaded, as he began to regain his composure. "I have to protect Bjorn, and it might be useful that I can do what he can do. But I don't want anyone to know."

"I think for now," began Atticus, "that might be a very good idea."

"Thanks. And, um, sorry for crying. I didn't mean to."

"You are one of the most determined, brave souls that I have ever met. I am your friend, and I will be here for you, no matter what," Atticus swore. "You are an amazingly strong young man. I can't predict the future, Dylan, but I do know this—the strength that you have will be needed, by your brother, by your mother, and possibly—by everyone on Earth."

Chapter 45
And Now it Begins

Commander Shakastan Zuaberi stood up smartly, as he climbed out of the tube. He'd ridden through the accursed things many times and was well versed on how many people would vomit and be weak after being transmitted from one end of the galaxy to another. He was no different. Traveling between portals in the tubes was miserable, but as he stood up, his iron will commanded his body to ignore the effects.

The Wooranti Portal on the planet of Aechmea had been in place for well over a decade, and the infrastructure had been built out as magnificently as any portal on Koranth or Zoranth. Today, Commander Shakastan Zuaberi stepped onto the first-class platform and declined the employee's offering of a shot of Coronit to calm his nerves. Usually, he would be stepping out into the military transport facility, which was far less posh than this facility.

He pushed a junior officer, who looked lost in the elegant surroundings, out of the way, and strode back to the tube that was arriving directly behind his. As the hatch on the tube popped open, Commander Zuaberi held his hand out, locking it with Tomar Donovackia's. He helped the Chairman out of the tube.

Tomar released a loud laugh. "You bastard! You look as if you actually enjoy having your soul sucked through space on these damn tubes!"

Commander Zuaberi chuckled in response, "No, sir, I'll be much happier to be on my spaceship traveling through space without feeling like I'm being pulled inside out."

Tomar Donovackia threw back the shot of Coronit, enjoying the stinging sensation as it moved down his throat. "Every portal offers a different shot when you arrive," noted Tomar. "This Coronit they serve here is a bit harsh, but I like the aftertaste."

Tomar stood for a few more minutes, letting his body recover from the tube ride. Through the decades he'd taken thousands of trips to dozens of planets. In his mind, they were all his planets, and he was about to have another one. He loved this part—launching the mission that would invade another planet, so that he could begin to "develop" it.

His research department had scoured the reports and artifacts sent back from Earth. The planet had an ample and widely varied supply of products, and an infrastructure to support global trade. In addition to the profit that would be made from Earth's products, it was simply exciting to try new things. He looked forward to products called *coffee*, *chocolate*, *beef*, *truffles*, *mangos*, *chicken*, and *potato chips*. Over the last decade, he'd created new revenue streams—planetary tourism and planetary settlement. He'd launched more portals to every planet and even connected distant planets with portals that didn't lead to Koranth or Zoranth. When he had taken over the Corporation, distant planets were only suppliers of products. He had changed everything. Trade flowed in every direction, and he had a little piece of it all. Of course, all of that meant an enormous expansion of his military machine.

He kept an iron like grip on the Corporation and his military. On distant planets, he'd meddled more and more with the politics and governments, and in many cases, he simply installed his own government. The Donovackia Corporation had become the quintessential essence of business perfection—and it was all his.

Commander Zuaberi and Chairman Donovackia boarded a shuttle and settled in for the long ride to the Marator Space Station, orbiting the planet. The days of launching a deep space mission from a planet's surface were long gone. Various parts of a spaceship were ferried through the portals from Koranth and Zoranth, where shuttles would take them to orbiting space stations for assembly.

Only a few decades before, a single ship would leave Koranth with a portal, and that one ship would slip into a planet and power up the portal. Now, a portal might come from Koranth to a planet like Aechmea on a single ship, but the invasion was different. A dozen ships could be built on Aechmea to accompany the portal-carrying ship from Koranth. Additionally, a matched set of portals might be built on Aechmea, with one portal staying on Aechmea and another being installed on another planet. For the last two decades, Tomar had built a network of portals between planets.

For this next invasion, which was, of course, still called "planetary development," eight ships, in addition to the portal-carrying ship from Koranth, were being prepared.

The Marator Space Station was, for all practical purposes, a city in space. "It makes me feel as if I am a boy again," Tomar remarked, as he looked out the window of the shuttle. "Every time I travel to one of my space stations, the sense of wonder and exploration explodes inside of me. It is such a thrill to know there is so much still to be discovered and conquered."

"Yes, sir," Commander Zuaberi agreed. "It is impossible not to be awed and excited as you step into the station and see the activity and preparation."

"And, how goes the preparation?" asked Tomar.

"Right on schedule. We are two days from launching," replied Commander Zuaberi.

"Outstanding!" proclaimed Tomar. "I am eager review the final preparations and give my send-off speech."

The shuttle landed in the open bay, and the force field closed behind it. Tomar marched onto the landing zone, eager to begin his tour and confer with the invasion force commanders. As with each previous invasion, this one was bigger and grander than the previous. Part of the fleet would begin attacking one part of a planet while the portal-carrying ship slipped onto the planet to install the portal. It was a simple matter of distraction. Once the portal was installed, the Donovackia military machine would pour through the portal like water.

An entire landing bay had been converted into a banquet hall for the final night before the fleet departed. Tomar had decided that he would address all of the soldiers who were part of the invasion and have a grand feast. Food and drink were served, and speeches were made, with Tomar addressing the invasionary force with his usual flare and circumstance. The atmosphere was like a festival, with everyone having a grand time on the evening before the fleet would leave to invade the planet called Earth.

A recent book that he had read from another planet had convinced Tomar that he should occasionally mingle with his soldiers, even though he found them to be terribly common. After the meal and the speeches, many of the soldiers stayed to enjoy a final round of Coronit or other beverage.

As Tomar and Commander Zuaberi approached the huge bar that had been set up for the event, Tomar grabbed the Commander's arm.

"Lords of the Fourth System!" declared Tomar quietly pointing to one of the soldiers, "That man is freakishly gigantic!"

"Yes, he does catch the attention of those who see him," replied the Commander. "He's a bit of a unique case. It took him many, many years to qualify for the program, but he is one of the many prisoners that converted his containment sentence to military service."

"Now that I look at him, he is a bit older. And what is his role in this mission?" asked Tomar.

"He is simply part of the defensive detachment that will protect the portal. Often we need to subdue the locals without revealing any advanced weaponry while we get the portal up and running."

"I can completely see how a man like that would be useful," Tomar agreed. "I would be absolutely frightened to face that man in any type of confrontational situation."

"Yes, indeed," replied Commander Zuaberi. "I pity any man on Earth that has to face Jackos the Giant."

FROM THE AUTHOR

Thanks for reading my first published novel. I hope you enjoyed it. Would you please take a moment and offer an honest review and rating? The book is on Amazon.com and Goodreads.com. Thank you!

ABOUT THE AUTHOR

Shea Oliver lives in Niwot, Colorado, near the base of the Rocky Mountains. He can often be found wandering through mountain forests and alpine tundra. An avid hiker and photographer, he often uses his time in the mountains to work through various characters and plots. When he is not enjoying nature, Shea is a devoted father of two teenage sons and a serial entrepreneur.

Connect with Shea at SheaOliver.com

www.ingramcontent.com/pod-product-compliance
Ingram Content Group UK Ltd.
Pitfield, Milton Keynes, MK11 3LW, UK
UKHW020144250726
13967UKWH00002B/859